2024 | Volume 8

U.P. READER

Bringing Upper Michigan Literature to the World

A publication of the
Upper Peninsula Publishers and Authors Association (UPPAA)
Marquette, Michigan

UPPAA

U.P. Reader
Volume 1 is still available!

Michigan's Upper Peninsula is blessed with a treasure chest of writers and poets, all seeking to capture the diverse experiences of Yooper Life. Now U.P. Reader offers a rich collection of their voices that embraces the U.P.'s natural beauty and way of life, along with a few surprises.

The twenty-eight works in this first annual volume take readers on a U.P. Road Trip from the Mackinac Bridge to Menominee. Every page is rich with descriptions of the characters and culture that make the Upper Peninsula worth living in and writing about.

Available in paperback, hardcover, and eBook editions!

ISBN 978-1-61599-336-9

www.UPReader.org

U.P. Reader: Bringing Upper Michigan Literature to the World — Volume #8
Copyright © 2024 by Upper Peninsula Publishers and Authors Association (UPPAA). All Rights Reserved.

Learn more about the UPPAA at www.UPPAA.org

Latest news on UP Reader can be found at www.UPReader.org

ISSN: 2572-0961

ISBN 978-1-61599-810-4 paperback
ISBN 978-1-61599-811-1 hardcover
ISBN 978-1-61599-812-8 eBook (PDF, Kindle, ePub)

Edited by- Deborah K. Frontiera and Mikel B. Classen
Production - Victor Volkman
Cover Photo – Victor Volkman
Interior Layout - Michal Šplho (Amorandi Design)

Distributed by Ingram International (USA / CAN / AU / UK / EU)

Published by
Modern History Press
5145 Pontiac Trail
Ann Arbor, MI 48105

www.ModernHistoryPress.com
info@ModernHistoryPress.com

CONTENTS

About the Cover: "A Pictured Rock Is Worth 1,000 Words by Victor R. Volkman.....................4

A Hole in The Bucket by Hilton Moore.................................6

Doc Gibson and Professional Hockey in the U.P. by Bill Sproule...........................10

yooper haiku by t. kilgore splake.................16

coming home by t. kilgore splake.................17

opening day by t. kilgore splake.................17

Old Friends Having Lunch by M. Kelly Peach.........................18

A Walk Along Lake Michigan by Julie Dickerson...........................20

A Walk in the Woods by Julie Dickerson...........................21

I Want to Say by Rosemary Gegare...............23

Afterglow by Rosemary Gegare 23

The Hotel Bantam by Adam Dompierre.........................24

Taking Care of the Dog by Gregory M. Lusk 30

The Death of Old 289 by David Swindell.............................32

Places Few Have Seen by Tom Conlan 35

Yellow Eyes by Tom Conlan 40

Dying in Rural Rockland by Kathleen Carlton Johnson 40

When It Comes: A Poem for Voices by Kathleen Carlton Johnson 42

How Ya Gonna Keep 'Em Down on the Farm after They've Seen Marquette? by Tyler R. Tichelaar 44

Homage to the Pilgrim by R. H. Miller 51

The North Country Sun by Raymond Luczak 53

Jacquart's by Raymond Luczak 54

A. Lanfear Norrie School (1917–2016) by Raymond Luczak 54

Waters of Change by Becky Ross Michael 55

The Writing Is on the Wall by Tamara Lauder 58

Dementia Is: by Tamara Lauder 59

The Good Evening by Maria Vezzetti Matson...........................60

Dorothy's Apple Pie by Ellen Lord.................62

North Country Connection by Ellen Lord.......63

Traveler by Ellen Lord...............................63

One Last Chance by Jodi Perras 64

All Customers Great and Small by Nancy Besonen 71

Dog Park by Mack Hassler 75

Our Silent Spring, Read for Friends by Mack Hassler 75

Chiblow Lake by Richard Hill 76

Mozambique by Alex Noel...........................80

Spring by Alex Noel.....................................87

Soak by Alex Noel.......................................87

Two Rivers by Rick Kent 88

Memories of the Copper Country Limited by Larry Jorgensen.......................94

Negatives at a Funeral by John Adamcik 97

The Faultfinder's Quarry by John Adamcik.............................98

Three Selections from The Seasons, the Years, the Decades by Jane Piirto 103

The Last Blooms by Ninie Gaspariani Syarikin 110

When Christmas Changed to Easter by J. L. Hagen 111

Epistolary Poem by Beverly Matherne 118

Paranormal or Normal? That is the Question by Beverly Matherne 118

Haiku for Roger Magnuson by Beverly Matherne.............................119

The Opportunity of a Lifetime by Brandy Thomas 120

Meat by Brandy Thomas 126

Letters to Harrison #8 by Art Curtis 127

Wrapped: An Elegy for My Father by Art Curtis.............................129

Watercourse by Art Curtis 130

Baraga County Redemption by Mark Nelson.............................131

Rootedness by Nina L. Craig.....................133

When Ice Cracks Open by Nina L. Craig 134

River Gypsy by Edd Tury 135

U.P. Publishers & Authors Association Announces 5th Annual U.P. Notable Books List..136

Young U.P. Author Section.............................138

Despondent by Eve Noble...........................139

Echo by Isla Peterson 144

Time Deprivation by Analise VerBerkmoes 152

The Birthday Party by Skye Isaacson.........158

Starved by Miina Chopp 163

There are No Happy Endings by Leah Johnson 167

Author Bios...172

Help Sell The U.P. Reader!........................176

Come join UPPAA Online! 177

Comprehensive Index of U.P. Reader Volumes 1 through 8 178

NONFICTION

About the Cover: "A Pictured Rock Is Worth 1,000 Words

by Victor R. Volkman

For the past decade or so, my visits to the U.P. have been strictly limited to high-speed drives from Ann Arbor non-stop to Marquette. Well, minus the obligatory stop at Lehto's Pasties along beach that seems to stretch out to infinity on US-2 West out of St. Ignace. At 438 miles, it's a bit of a hike as I like to say and Google Maps says "6 hrs, 48 minutes". Much shorter than the Detroit-to-Houghton run I made in college, which was a solid 10 hours, with only one bathroom break in Gaylord, Michigan in either direction. We had bigger bladders when we were 40 years younger, I guess and it was before the era of super-size fountain drinks.

Getting back to my recent Marquette trips ...on these long contemplative rides, especially in the Seney Stretch, my mind would always wander to the many U.P. beauty spots that I had never been to. The Porcupine ("Porkies") mountains I would have climbed as a young man, except I never owned a vehicle when I lived year-round in Houghton. The Isle Royale trip on the *Ranger III* out of Houghton, I often saw departing or arriving, but as a college student, I had not a lick of camping gear nor any friends who were of a mind for a week's sojourn in the true wilds of nature. However, one destination had been definitely itching my brain, especially as I drove within literal yards of it: a Pictured Rocks boat tour.

I figured Pictured Rocks would make a great pitstop on the way up to Marquette and doing so would require a bit of planning voodoo to account for Lehto's lunch and a few extra rest-stops for our aged bladders. *It could work...!* Now which excursion to take? The longer one leaving at 4:00 pm for 2 hrs 40 min run or the shorter one at 5:00 pm for 2 hrs? I figured this was our only shot, so let's make the best of it and do the full 32-mile journey in style.

There are no refunds or exchanges in the final 24 hours before a cruise and not knowing the crowd size, we purchased weeks ahead of time. Of course, you can't guess U.P. weather, even if you're around. And I wouldn't have a "backup" day anyways, so we just decided to risk the $100 worth of tickets and spin the great wheel of ever-changing Michigan weather.

Trip planning and my lead foot on the pedal got us there at 3:00 pm, I won't say without a sweat because I was continually checking my car's GPS, trying to prove its predictions wrong and gain a minute here and a minute there. So, we did our check-in at the counter and proceeded to browse what must be one of the world's largest gift shops about 100 feet from the docks. The check-in girl said, "Boarding starts 30 minutes before departing" so I said to no one, "No problem, we can kill 30 minutes here easily". At the stroke of 3:30 we ambled down to the boarding maze and discover that every single last passenger was lined up! How would we get a seat with a decent view being the last people to board???

This turned out to be a non-problem as all the young and able folks immediately trooped to the top observation deck. My wife and I, not being big stair climbers, were consigned to the bottom deck. This deck probably could seat 250 people in high season but including the deckhand, there were just 5 of us so we had our choice of window seats coming and going. Problem averted!

We really lucked out for our trip on June 8th, 2023 with a perfect patch of Michigan summer weather. Bright blue skies and a mellow 60-ish afternoon in downtown Munising, most importantly the air was still. There were no whitecaps, so our ride would be as smooth as glass. Tempting fate itself, I held my hand out the window to get some nice shots with my iPhone, which was a crazy thing to do without a handle or strap on it. I wondered later, how many smartphones are on the bottom of Lake Superior.

Anyways, the cruise itself was great, the captain/announcer was not annoyingly verbose as, say a carriage tour guide on Mackinac Island can be. He emphasized his sass by getting so close to the rocks that it was barely further than my hand could reach out the window. He had cojones of brass (or steel maybe).

It's easy to take the majesty of nature for granted, even as a lad who spent a lot of time on the water and in woods. However, I was dumbstruck by the beauty of these ancient, layered rocks, in their continual transformation as pieces fall off from erosion. It is at these moments that you feel the presence of God in what everyone calls "God's Country", a transcendent experience in perfect conditions. We saw beautiful falls off the rocks landing 200 feet below, the mysterious color patterns of rock spattered by copper and iron infused water, marvelously enticing caves and archways that looked carved by the almighty himself. Especially of note is the tall tree on a promontory separated perhaps 50 feet from the cliff, living entirely by a single ropy cable of a root connecting it to the mainland. Immediately you feel the fragility of life itself and our connection to the earth. In such a reverie, I snapped the cover picture for *U.P. Reader #8* with my iPhone 13.

As a younger man, I might've hiked the National Lakeshore park trails or kayaked in, but the boat tour is the perfect amount of accessibility for us in the latter years of life.

We finished our afternoon with a quick stop at the nearby "Eh! Burger" where we devoured some well-earned burgers and chili fries. Heading out to finish our trip into Marquette by sunset, we got back on the picturesque M-28 with its many awesome views of the big lake.

Historical · Mackinac Island arch rock with sailing ship

A Hole in The Bucket

by Hilton Moore

I was only eight in 1952, too young to understand the term blended family. Of course, even that euphemistic term was far in the future. My father, a Methodist minister, was arm-twisted into taking a charge in the remote village of Nelson due mainly to an indiscretion on his part in the city of Alpena in the northeastern Lower Peninsula. The indiscretion became his third wife, Jeanine. She had two young daughters at the time, Susan and Karen. Father had two young boys, Donny and me, Arthur—Art for short hence the blended family. As for his assigned parish in Nelson, he did not consider his tryst with Jeanine, a married woman at the time, as a self-inflicted wound, despite the evidence to the contrary. I guess you could call that self-delusion as everyone around him knew otherwise. My father was a recent widower at the time, not that it matters now. My mother, Louise, perished in a head-on collision with a snowplow during a heavy snowstorm a year after Father began visiting with Jeanine. Suicide, perhaps? It doesn't matter now, but at one time it meant a great deal to me. The Methodist Church and the District Superintendent were unforgiving about father's affair and thought this remote parish was a due penance. My father disagreed vehemently, but it was a lost cause.

Nelson is the county seat, smack dab in the middle of Bishop County. Nelson is a town, maybe a village is a more appropriate word, of around fifteen hundred souls. The village is in the very heart of the Upper Peninsula, and a scant throw away from the enormous waves of Lake Superior when a wicked westerly comes crashing against the miles of rocky uninhabited shoreline. The tourists love it, but the folks who live in this harsh environment know you can't eat water. Truth is, some locals love it, and some don't. My father, William Langston, was in the latter category.

I have never thought of the Upper Peninsula in the same light as my father, but I do admit that, for the most part, it is not a bucolic picture at all. Still, there is an innate beauty here if you care to seek it. One must be willing to overlook the abandoned mines, and the anemic second and third growth timber left over after the lumber barons butchered the magnificent white pines, hemlock, and cedar. Of course, these immense forests were stolen from the natives, but hell, that's all in the past.

My father was, in his own way, a refined gentleman, enjoying fine cuisine and classical music and the better things in life which, as a poor minister in the Upper Peninsula, he could ill afford. William once caustically compared the Upper Peninsula to a third-world country but with more guns and chainsaws. (William was as caustic as ever, and out of his element.)

Reverend William Langston, though he preferred the appellation Reverend Will, owned an old farmhouse with eighty acres of overgrown, fallow land thirty miles from Nelson. The farmstead was on a hilltop about a mile from Lake Superior. On sweltering hot summer days, all of us children would go swimming on the stretch of rocky beach near the farmhouse. To say that this stretch of beach was rarely ever used would be a gross understatement. The major issue was the rocky shoreline that informs part of this story. There was no closer beach for miles, and given our parents' propensity for gin and tonics, they adamantly refused to drive us elsewhere.

To cast light on this story, Will and Jeanine, preferring to stay at the farmhouse, refused to walk the rocky shoreline, perhaps a hundred feet from the shore. They stayed instead under the shade of the farm's tin porch roof, made rusted by years of neglect, sipping cold gin and tonics. The Nelson parish was morally conservative, to say the least, and our parents enjoyed being away from the prying eyes of his uptight parishioners.

That brings me to the rowboat. Will and Jeanine were both good parents and were sympathetic about the rocky shoreline, but needed much convincing that the family needed a rowboat. We children, all four of us, argued how a rowboat could take us past the stony shore and out to the sandbar, some hundred feet from shore, where we would still be in shallow waters. We could throw out a cinderblock for an anchor, we reasoned, and use it as a diving platform. Just so you won't think our parents were negligent about water-safety, there was not a lifeguard for miles, and no one thought the better or worse for it in those days. It may seem incomprehensible now, but at that time, parents didn't hover over their children like hens.

Because I was the oldest male, and the girls weren't allowed to drive the tractor, I drove the faded red tractor pulling our rickety farm wagon behind it to the beach, all children aboard. This was before *Henry*, our rowboat, and fate, intertwined.

We children, William and Jeanine included, were very excited when father bought this faded grey wood rowboat and paid a local resort owner, in cold cash, for delivery at the beach.

Several days later, on a rainy summer day, I safely piloted the ancient Massey Harris down the old road to the beach where we would meet the previous owner and receive custody of our craft. *Henry*, my nickname for the heavy, homemade, plywood boat didn't garner any objections from the other children, so *Henry* it was. The boat was sixteen feet long

and painted gunmetal grey, with two old oars. I felt I was justified in naming the boat *Henry* for a patch the previous owner neatly fixed on the hull. Hence, the name Henry, from the childhood song, "There's A Hole in the bucket dear Liza, dear Liza," and the second verse, "Well fix it dear Henry, dear Henry, a hole." Looking back, fate had its way. As the oldest male child, and despite all maritime history, I just preferred to name the craft with a strong masculine name rather than with a weak feminine name that would not be fitting to the boat. I got my way with what we would now label as toxic masculinity.

A week later, the weather cooperated and the whole family participated in what might be called the christening of *Henry*. Lisa, the youngest, broke a bottle of Coca-Cola on the bow. Afterward, we carefully picked up all the glass, and forced *Henry* across the rocky shoreline into the frigid waters of Lake Superior.

This was an all-hands-on-deck process as we half-pulled and yanked the heavy boat to the gentle surf, dragging the old craft into the cold water and out to the sandbar some forty feet from shore. We set a cinderblock as an anchor with old rope, and we swam and played for several hours on *Henry*. These were blissful moments I will never forget.

Returning *Henry* to his designation in the barn was another issue altogether. It only took a moment for the entire family to understand we had a problem hoisting *Henry's* heavy plywood frame onto the farm trailer and into the barn. With six of us, grunting and groaning, and with herculean effort, the task was completed.

Henry's paint was beginning to chip and peel, so father mixed some left-over paint that was in the barn that I could apply where it was needed. While the paint didn't match, it worked fine. I thought, if *Henry* was a steed instead of a boat, he most surely would have been an Appaloosa. I still believe that *Henry* liked the comparison.

I should add, that while the previous owner gave *Henry* a touch-up of paint, he had neglected to adequately paint or caulk the old boat, consequently *Henry* leaked like the proverbial sieve. I caulked and painted *Henry* the best I could, but neither paint nor caulk stuck well on the soggy old boat. I wisely restricted the others from caulking and painting. So, Donny, always head-strong, threw a tantrum, while Susan deliberately turned over a can of old paint. I guess you could call that getting even.

The weather turned grey and wet for the next several days and noisy games of cards and monopoly took up our time. Finally, the weather broke, and we headed to the beach, the small farm-wagon creaking and groaning from the overload, only to recognize we would have the same problem in reverse later in the day when we would need to bring *Henry* back to the farmstead. All of us children sweated over piles of stones and rocks to get him to the water's edge. Too exhausted now to swim, we had a problem. We couldn't just leave *Henry* at the water's edge, now that the vessel lay bobbing in several inches of quiet surf. We had to return the water-soaked vessel back to the farm for safe keeping.

I fetched William and Jeanine from their usual back-porch stoop. William, several gin and tonics in, and not pleased to be bothered, drove Missy, our nickname for the tractor, back to the beach with a twenty-foot length of chain and a steel fencepost which he promptly drove into the sand with our old sledgehammer. The family groaned from the effort but eventually dragged *Henry* up far enough and flipped him over and chained him to the fencepost with a hefty padlock. We children loved *Henry* but used him only on several occasions that summer, not enough to warrant the effort.

Except me. I would spend hours alone laying on Henry's overturned grey hull, imagining. Yes, imagining. What? Just everything. Sometimes it was as if *Henry* were animate.

Occasionally, on starlit nights I would pedal our old Monkey-Ward bike down to the beach and lie on the over-turned skiff, and just gaze at the endless firmament. The constellation Orion was my favorite, and I envisioned myself as a fellow warrior engaged in battle with Canis Major beside us in full attack.

I could sometimes see the magnificent northern lights, flashing and moving like a fire-breathing dragon consuming the dark night by a force larger than life.

Father walked down to the beach one cloudless night and sat down on the over-turned hull beside me. "Are you alright, Arthur?"

"Ya', I'm alright."

"You have been coming down here by yourself for nights."

"Just need time to think."

"Yeah, I get it," he paused. "You are afraid that Jeanine and I are divorcing."

"That's part of it. Well? Are you?"

"Yes, I'm so sorry." He muffled a sob and took my hand. "I've never been very good at relationships, and it shows." A cloud moved across the face of the moon and cast a shadow. "As a man it seems I am inadequate in so many ways. The gut-wrenching truth is I am a lousy preacher and a poor example for you boys."

"Father, you try; no one should ask for more." I was weeping now.

I suppose this could be, with some minor changes, the end of the story. But it isn't; this tale would just be a melancholy trip down memory lane if *Henry* hadn't arrived in my life. Even as a child, I wondered whether fear precedes premonition. How did I know in a dream-like state that something bad was going to happen to *Henry*, or was it to happen to me, or my family? Perhaps? And, yet I knew. As an adult, we chalk up such altered states-of-mind to chance, or for the religious, as a sign from God.

On days when it was too gloomy to play outside and the others were all involved in a game of Monopoly, I would go see *Henry*; yes *Henry*. We would chat back and forth for hours till I heard the old dinner bell ring. I understand that many folks would say I was just fanciful, or at that young age, perhaps just daydreaming. Or perhaps I was suffering from a form of childhood psychosis?

I realize now, that as a child, my relationship with *Henry* served several purposes. First, and foremost, it protected me from psychological harm from others or perhaps it protected me from myself.

One rainy day later in the fall, I returned to see *Henry*. I cried when I saw that someone had dragged the stern into knee-deep water and shot two holes in the vessel's bottom. He was half-full of sand and water. In my grief I wondered how someone could be so cruel. If I had been there, would I have been a victim too? Is the world run by haters?

"It will be ok," I heard *Henry* say in a very quiet voice.

"You will never be the same, and neither will I," I said with tears in my eyes.

Later that afternoon, William, seeing my distress, tried to patch the derelict boat, but *Henry* was beyond hope.

As I watched my father, I sang in a trembling voice, "There's a hole in the bucket, dear Liza, dear Liza. Well, fix it, dear Henry, dear Henry, a hole."

Straining, all of us working together could not budge the water-logged boat away from the shore to the waiting trailer. *Henry's* ignoble remains were later swept away by winter storms.

Whether *Henry* affected all the other children, I have no idea. Jeanine divorced my father several months later, and I grieved for so many losses. What I am certain of is that the old derelict did impact my life and my younger brother, Donny, as well.

As a young man, Donny, drunk as usual, found out quite by accident who had shot the jagged holes in the bottom of *Henry*. Drunk, and in a fit-of-rage he murdered this young lad. In my eyes no murder is justifiable, especially in what was most likely a case of juvenile vandalism. Don was sentenced to a term of twenty years to life. After serving twenty-one long years in Marquette Prison, Donny, now a hardened and bitter man, moved to Alaska and worked construction.

As my father lay dying in the hospital, he wanted forgiveness. "For what?" I replied.

"Perhaps, for the mistakes I made."

"Father, you taught me to follow a path of my own intuition; although at times, I must admit, you stepped off the fucking path into a nasty pile of shit," I laughed.

"Look at me. I am a successful author and illustrator of children's books. I credit you and *Henry* for that. In my younger days I thought that it was my duty to counter hate with love, put evil where it belonged—somewhere in the depths of hell. I could have been a preacher like you, but I knew better. Wasn't my path. I have come to understand that often hate preys upon hate; it is self-consuming. One must just get out of the way, and hatred, like twisting eagles in the sky will plummet toward earth. Love will always be in the background, and when the battle of life ends, love will always be the victor.

"Father, I am thoroughly convinced that everything I learned about love, I learned from you and *Henry*. Have no regrets, Father, have no regrets."

Historical - ishpeming Lake Angeline Mine

Doc Gibson and Professional Hockey in the U.P.

NONFICTION

by Bill Sproule

In the early days of hockey, it was a game for amateurs, and it was not until 1903 that Canadian-born dentist Jack "Doc" Gibson and Houghton entrepreneur James R. "Jimmy" Dee decided to recruit the best players from Canada and openly pay them to play for the Portage Lake (Houghton) hockey team. The team won the 1904 U.S. Championship and defeated a team from Montreal for what was billed as the World's Championship. Following this successful season, Gibson and Dee began promoting the idea of a professional hockey league, and in December 1904, play began in the International Hockey League (IHL). The league had five teams – Calumet, Pittsburgh, Portage Lake, Sault Ste. Marie, Michigan, and Sault Ste. Marie, Ontario – and although the league lasted only three seasons, it was the start of professional hockey.

John Lindell MacDonald "Jack" Gibson was born in Berlin (now Kitchener), Ontario on September 10, 1879, to James and Mary Gibson, who were originally from Aberdeen, Scotland and settled on a farm in Waterloo County. As a youth Jack excelled in school and several sports and won Western Ontario championships in rowing, skating, and swimming. At seventeen, he was a star member of the 1896-97 Berlin-Waterloo team in the Ontario Hockey Association's

(OHA) new intermediate league that defeated the Kingston Frontenacs to win the league championship. In the fall of 1897, Gibson entered the Detroit College of Medicine (now part of Wayne State University) to study dentistry and play on their hockey team. During the 1897-98 season, he also played on a Berlin senior team in the OHA league and planned to travel between Detroit and Berlin for games during the season. However, when the Berlin team defeated its crosstown rivals, Waterloo, in an early season game, the team manager and Berlin Mayor Rumpel rushed out on the ice and presented each player with a ten-dollar gold piece. The Ontario Hockey Association heard about this celebration and ruled that the players were professionals and expelled the team from further competition. Only amateurs "in good standing" were allowed to play in the OHA, and players who received any remuneration were guilty until proven innocent. His season with Berlin ended in early January and although the OHA lifted its suspension at the end of the season, it left a lasting impression. Gibson played three seasons for the Detroit College of Medicine (DCM) hockey and football teams and graduated in 1900. However, while Gibson studied at DCM, he continued to play on a Berlin hockey team, and he was recognized as one of best hockey players in Canada.

John Lindell MacDonald "Jack" Gibson, D.D.S.
(Michigan Technological University Archives and Copper
Country Historical Collections)

Gibson was captain and coach of the Portage Lake team. Charles Webb was the team manager and was responsible for the financial aspects and team operations. The Portage Lake team won the 1901 Upper Peninsula League Championship and local interest in hockey grew as fans packed the Palace Rink to see Gibson and the team play.

Portage Lake YMCA Hockey Team, 1900-01
City of Houghton, Ralph Raffaelli Collection)
Standing, left to right: Bert Potter, Ellsworth,
E.B. Harkness, Black, Earl Hay
Seated, left to right: Wally Washburn, Jack Gibson,
Charles Webb (manager), Percy Willson, Peter Delaney
Front Row, left to right: Thompson, Andy Haller

In the fall of 1900, Gibson moved to Houghton and established a dental practice in downtown Houghton. He felt that this would be a perfect place to start his career as the area was in the midst of a copper mining boom and he had visited Houghton before when the DCM hockey team traveled to play an exhibition game at the Palace Ice Rink in Ripley. A couple of his DCM hockey teammates from Listowel, Ontario also chose to settle in the Copper Country. Dr. Earl Hay opened a dental office in Hancock and Dr. Percy Willson settled in Chassell to begin his practice as a medical doctor. Gibson immersed himself in the Houghton community, joining several fraternal lodges and meeting community leaders though social events, and he soon became known as "Doc" Gibson. In his first winter, he joined the Portage Lake YMCA hockey team. The team included several local players, as well as Dr. Hay, Dr. Willson, and Dr. R.B. Harkness. Dr. Harkness, a medical doctor, was born in Pennsylvania and played hockey in Pittsburgh as a student at Western University of Pennsylvania (now the University of Pittsburgh). He moved to Houghton in the fall of 1900 and located his office in the same building as Gibson.

As the Portage Lake team prepared for the 1901-02 season, Houghton businessman James R. Dee joined the executive board, and Gibson and Webb started to recruit a few players from outside the Copper Country. Gibson brought in Herman "Dutch" Meinke with whom he had played in Berlin and recruited Joseph "Chief" Jones, one of the best goalies in Ontario. The team played ten games that season against teams from Minneapolis, St. Paul, Chicago, Pittsburgh, and Sault Ste. Marie, Ontario. Portage Lake was declared Champions of the West after they defeated the Kentwood Country Club team from Chicago, and they then played the Pittsburgh Athletic Club in March 1902 for what was described as the Championship of the United States. Pittsburgh was the Eastern Champion and a member of the Western Pennsylvania Hockey League. It was to be a two-game, total goals series in the Palace. The team split the games and the total goals were equal, so a 1902 United States Champion was not declared.

Gibson and Dee soon realized that if hockey were to grow in the area, a new facility would be needed to accommodate the spectators who wanted to see the Portage Lake team play. In the summer of 1902, Dee organized the Houghton Warehouse Company to build a facility that could be used as a storage warehouse in the summer and serve as a skating and hockey arena from mid-December to late March. The company purchased property on the Houghton waterfront and the building was completed in the fall in time for the winter season. The building had a natural ice surface of 80 feet by 185 feet, and seating for 2,500 hockey fans and room for an additional 600 standees. A contest to name the building was held, and the name "Amphidrome" was selected. While the arena was being built, Gibson and Webb were busy recruiting more players from Canada for the upcoming season. They brought in Joe Stephens, one of Gibson's teammates from Berlin, and Canadians Fred Lake and Ernie Westcott, who had played for Pittsburgh in the Western Pennsylvania Hockey League.

The Amphidrome opened soon after Christmas in 1902, and the first hockey game was played on Monday, December 29, 1902, between Portage Lake and the University of Toronto Varsity team. The local newspaper reported that over 5,000 attended the first game and it was the largest gathering of people under one roof in the Upper Peninsula at that time. Portage Lake beat the team from Toronto 13-2 and the top scorer was center "Dutch" Meinke as he scored eight goals.

The 1902-03 Portage Lake hockey team was a good team that went undefeated for the season, and they outscored their opponents 146 to 36. Portage Lake played sixteen games against teams from Detroit, Duluth, St. Louis, St. Paul, and Pittsburgh and they defeated the Pittsburgh Bankers for the 1903 United States Championship. Joe Stephens and Dutch Meinke were the season's top scorers for Portage Lake with thirty-six goals and thirty-four goals, respectively. Fol-

lowing the season, James Dee became President of the Portage Lake team and Gibson felt that the team could be even better.

In the fall of 1903, Gibson and Dee made a momentous decision when they resolved to openly pay players to come to Houghton to play hockey. They realized that to convince top Canadian players to give up day jobs to play hockey for a few months and risk their amateur status in Canada, substantial salaries were essential. Individual player contracts were negotiated and salaries that paid $15 to $40 per week were enough to convince players to take the risk. The best players could attract a salary of $75 per week and salaries would come from dividing gate receipts.

Gibson and Webb recruited several players from the Pittsburgh teams including Riley Hern, Bert Morrison, "Cooney" Shields, and Bruce and Hod Stuart for the Portage Lake team. A group from Sault Ste. Marie, Michigan also decided to pay players and several members of 1902-03 Portage Lake team signed to join the Michigan Soo team. Former Portage Lake players included Chief Jones, Dutch Meinke, Joe Stephens, and Fred Lake. The Michigan Soo team also recruited Frank Switzer from Pittsburgh.

Portage Lake Hockey Team, 1903-04 ·
U.S. Champion and World Champion
(MTU Archives and Copper Country Historical Collections)
Standing left to right: Fred Westcott (spare), James Duggan (trainer), Charles Webb (manager), James Dee (president), Joe Linder (spare)
Seated left to right: Bert Morrison (rover), "Cooney" Shields (forward), "Doc" Gibson (point and captain), Hod Stuart (cover point), Bruce Stuart (forward)
In foreground: Ernie Westcott (forward), Riley Hern (goal)

The expectations for a successful season were very high in the community as the local newspapers wrote that the recruited players were among the best from Canada. Because the team was not in a league, exhibition games were arranged, and the schedule evolved during the season. Gibson and Webb wanted to arrange games with the best teams from Canada, but Ontario teams were reluctant to schedule games as they would be banned by the Ontario Hockey Association for playing a professional team.

Portage Lake defeated the Pittsburgh Victorias for the 1904 United States Championship, and as the team was returning to Houghton, there was some talk of submitting a challenge for the Stanley Cup. However, soon after the team arrived in Houghton, Webb received a challenge from the Montreal Wanderers for a two-game series to be played in Houghton. Portage Lake accepted the challenge, and two games were scheduled for March 21 and 22, 1904 in the Amphidrome. The series was billed as the World Championship between the Montreal Wanderers, Champions of Canada, and Portage Lake, Champions of the United States. Portage Lake defeated the Wanderers in the first game 8-4, and according to local newspaper reports, "the game was the fastest hockey ever exhibited in the Copper Country and naturally the greatest game ever played in the United States." On the following night, Portage Lake defeated the Wanderers 9-2, and the newspaper stated that, "the game had all the features which go to make hockey the most exciting sport in the world." One of the Portage Lake players was quoted, "We claim to be champions of the world and ready to play any team which disputes our claim to the title and are willing to produce all kinds of money to back it."

Portage Lake ended the season with a record of twenty-three wins and two losses, and they outscored their opponents 259 to 49. Bert Morrison proved his value to Portage Lake as he scored ninety-four goals and Bruce Stuart was not far behind as he scored seventy-five goals. In Michigan Soo, Frank Switzer scored forty-five goals, while former Portage Lake players Dutch Meinke

scored thirty-seven goals and Fred Lake scored twenty-eight goals.

Following the success of Portage Lake, and as the interest in hockey in the United States was growing, Dee wrote Arthur McSwigan and others from the Western Pennsylvania Hockey League about forming a national hockey association or league with up to a dozen teams. Dee indicated that based on his experience with the Portage Lake team, hockey could be a viable business venture and suggested that teams from Canada would be interested. Following months of discussion, James Dee organized an initial meeting in Detroit to determine the interest and prospects of organizing a league that would be known as the "American Hockey League." Business leaders from several cities including Chicago, Cleveland, Detroit, Duluth, Grand Rapids, Minneapolis, Milwaukee, Montreal, New York, St. Louis, and St. Paul expressed interest in a franchise but they decided not to proceed at that time. A group from Sault Ste. Marie, Ontario was also interested and indicated they would attend the next meeting. In early November 1904, representatives from Calumet, Houghton (Portage Lake), Pittsburgh, Sault Ste. Ma-

Daily Mining Gazette, March 18, 1904

rie, Michigan (Michigan Soo), and Sault Ste. Marie, Ontario (Canadian Soo) met in Chicago and agreed to form a professional hockey league. They adopted the name "International Hockey League (IHL)", and play would begin with the 1904-05 season. It would be the first professional hockey league in which all players would be openly paid to play hockey. The executive prepared a set of league operating rules and rules that would govern play. It was agreed that each of the teams would play a 24-game schedule with three home games and three away games against each of the other teams. A revenue sharing plan was also adopted.

Team managers moved quickly to assemble line-ups and put together a schedule for the 1904-05 season. Calumet played its home games at a new Palestra arena in Laurium, and while the arena was under construction, former Portage Lake player Hod Stuart was hired as the Palestra manager and captain of the Calumet team. Pittsburgh's home arena was the 5,000 seat Duquesne Gardens, while Portage Lake's home games were played in the Amphidrome. The Michigan Soo team played at the Ridge Street Ice-A-Torium, near the Soo Locks, and the Canadian Soo team played in the Soo Curling Club's Gouin Street Arena.

As the 1904-05 season began, most newspaper reporters felt that Portage Lake would dominate the league, but Hod Stuart had recruited an outstanding team, and Calumet won the league championship. The team was led by the league's two top goal scorers – Fred Strike and Ken Mallen - and the league's top goalie was Calumet's Billy Nicholson. Portage Lake finished second, and as the season ended, Doc Gibson announced that he was retiring as a hockey player. He was always respected throughout the Copper Country and although he retired as a player, Gibson continued to be involved in numerous events and activities. He played baseball and served as a referee for local hockey and IHL games and was an umpire for charity baseball games. The league operated for three seasons and Portage Lake won the league's championships in both the 1905-06 and 1906-07 seasons.

During the three seasons of the IHL, hockey changed dramatically as several professional hockey leagues formed in Canada. The Canadian players in the IHL now had the opportunity to return to Canada and openly accept payment for playing hockey and the best players were sought by several teams in a bidding war for their services. The IHL also faced several challenges including a general economic downturn and sagging attendance in a few of the league cities. Teams could not generate enough revenue to offset the operating expenses and payrolls to compete with the salaries being offered by professional teams in Canada. Ultimately, the growth of professionalism in Canada would finish the IHL. Although the IHL operated for only three seasons it attracted the top players of that era who went on to exciting careers in Canada, of which several were later recognized with induction into the Hockey Hall of Fame.

Jack "Doc" Gibson, 1954
(Jim and John Leech Collection)

Jack "Doc" Gibson closed his Houghton dental practice in 1907, moved to Calgary, Alberta, and went into a real estate partnership with Charles S. Mills, a colleague from Southern Ontario who had also moved to Calgary. Gibson and Mills acquired lands in Calgary and rural Alberta for development and later expanded their partnership to include general brokerage, insurance, and loans. However, Gibson did not lose his passion for sports as he was hockey referee and a member of the governing board and president of the Alberta Amateur Hockey Association. He also played football for the Calgary Tigers and was a member when the team won the 1911 Western Canada Rugby Football Championship. During World War I, Gibson joined the Canadian Army, served overseas with the 82nd Infantry Battalion, and then following the war, he returned to Calgary, reopened his dental practice, continued his involvement in hockey, and found many new interests. He was an avid curler, life member and past president of the Glencoe Club and the Calgary Horticultural Society. In 1950, at the age of seventy, Gibson retired from dentistry as Calgary's most famous dentist, and he died in 1954. For his contributions to hockey, Gibson was one of the original inductees into the United States Hockey Hall of Fame in 1973 and was inducted as a builder into the Hockey Hall of Fame in Toronto in 1976.

Gibson was not forgotten in Houghton and in 1938, members of the Northern Michigan-Wisconsin Hockey League purchased a trophy for the league's champion and named it the Gibson Cup in recognition of his outstanding contribution to hockey in its infancy in the Copper Country. The Cup was first awarded in 1939 to the Portage Lake Elks team and today the Gibson Cup is an annual competition trophy between two local senior amateur teams – the Portage Lake Pioneers and Calumet Wolverines.

It has been over 120 years since the first professional hockey league was formed, and how many would have guessed that a dentist from Canada would help to make a small town in northern Michigan the birthplace of professional hockey.

References
Fitsell, Bill. "Doc Gibson – The Eye of the IHL." *The Hockey Research Journal, Society for International Hockey Research*, VIII, no. 3, 1 Oct. 2004.

Sproule, William J. *Houghton: The Birthplace of Professional Hockey*, self-published, 2019. *Recognized as a U.P. Notable Book by the Upper Peninsula Publishers and Authors Association (UPPAA) in 2020.*

St. Ignace, Mich., Showing Mackinac Island in the Distance

Historical · St. Ignace and Mackinaw Island

yooper haiku

by t. kilgore splake

deer season opening day
pasties euchre leinenkugel farts
dreams of seventeen-point buck

✳✳✳

wilderness poet's ghost
welcoming early morning light
through raven's dark eyes

✳✳✳

early upper peninsula autumn
april blizzard storm turning
god's country all over white

✳✳✳

yooper ghost forest shadow
dancing in brown autumn leaves
gray sky shade of winter

✳✳✳

feeling alive in world
cliffs shadows beside brautigan creek
poet dancing in wildflowers

✳✳✳

coming home

by t. kilgore splake

◆❖◆

tranny-tripping early morning
battle creek city limits rearview mirror
steady hum of tires on highway
poet heading true north
crossing mackinaw bridge
returning to god's country
solitary traveler
imagination in high gear
dreaming of brook trout beauty
campfire cold beers
owl's warm evening welcome

opening day

by t. kilgore splake

◆❖◆

carrying rod and reel
wicker fishing creel
flies attached to canvas hat
soaked in deep woods off
pleasant wilderness afternoon
beside brautigan creek
trophy rainbow dreams

Old Friends Having Lunch

by M. Kelly Peach

Mr. Cawley arrives at his favorite open-air café at noon. It is tucked in amongst the red pines and white oaks off of H-03 near highway M-94. He missed breakfast and is feeling quite hungry. On this bright and beautiful, warm spring day, the sky is a blue matching the nearby AuTrain River.

A gentle west breeze wafts the delicious aroma of stewing rabbit to his sensitive nostrils. This is one of his favorite dishes and a specialty of the region. As Cawley walks over, he can see—though advanced in years his eyesight is still very keen—that the table fare is already set and presided over by the nervous owner named Ark. He is a younger fellow, scrawnier and shorter than Cawley. Once Ark understands the new guest is staying, he withdraws warily to allow his patron to dine alone.

Cawley does prefer eating by himself. He is an individual of few words and poor in social graces. He clucks a cursory thank you in the direction of Ark who is now in full retreat. He does his customary survey of the surroundings, sees nothing is wrong, then nibbles a quick taste. He quickly raises his head. No others are in sight. He takes two bites, jerks his head upwards again. Still all clear. He dips his head, continues eating.

The breeze sighs among the lightest green of the early ferns, purple gaywings, and goldthread flowers. It brings the soapy scent of trailing arbutus to his nostrils, ruffles his glossy black attire. The sunshine finds turquoise and maroon highlights in its sheen as he shifts his torso to and fro in irritation because Ark has helped himself to the eyes, Cawley's favorite part of the rabbit.

He settles for the guts and hungrily tears into the belly of his rabbit dinner. He enjoys the savory liver and tangy pancreas. After a few bites, his black eyes notice a shadow flitting over the road. He looks up from his dinner and sees a familiar figure approaching.

It is Gluck, a buddy from his youthful days, looking ancient and starved. Cawley's craw is full, so he merely nods his welcome.

Gluck croaks a greeting as he walks up to his elderly comrade and asks, "May I join you?"

Cawley, mouth still stuffed, nods again towards the food between them.

"Well thanks old pal. Don't mind if I do." Gluck then helps himself to the rabbit's delicious nose.

Cawley gulps down his mouthful of guts and pauses in his feasting to look at Gluck working his way through the rabbit's flesh along its back. Remembering his friend's preferences from many a past shared meal, he knows the ribs will be his next goal. Cawley moves on to the meaty hams.

They haven't talked in years. Cawley is unsure of how to start the conversation. He has made little—well, no effort, really—to keep in contact with Gluck who has made several attempts at communication in the past. These attempts, although kindly received, were never returned. Cawley had convinced himself he was too busy to do so. He had a wife and was helping raise their children, plus the basic business of survival itself. Would this graying companion of his youth be angry with him for ignoring their friendship?

Cawley takes a chunk from the haunch. Gluck is enjoying the delicate rib meat. He doesn't seem upset; in fact, appears perfectly at ease. Gluck notices he is being watched. Mouth rather full, he responds with a quick nod of the head and a sigh of contentment.

The host, his voice deep and rough, inquires, "Good rabbit, eh?"

His guest agrees, "'S'excellent."

Nothing further is exchanged as Gluck finishes off the rib meat on the exposed side of the rabbit in a series of quick and efficient nipping gulps while Cawley demolishes the rear quarter.

Working together, they flip over the cottontail and start in again. Cawley is on the haunch and Gluck on the ribs.

They eat with heads bobbing up and down and side to side. Other than some brittle oak leaves skittering crab-like across the road and a few flies buzzing about, all is quiet.

Cawley moves to his right to begin on the rabbit's pulverized shoulder. Gluck continues feeding on the shattered ribs.

After a few more minutes of eating, Gluck is feeling almost full. Not wanting to overstay his welcome, he looks at Cawley, bows in solemn dignity, squawks, "Thank you, old friend." His lunch partner bends in return. Gluck extends his wings and, with a little hop, takes flight to the north.

Cawley swallows his food, slowly tilts his head to look skyward. Though Gluck has already flown too far to hear him, he mutters a husky, "You're welcome, farewell my friend."

He continues devouring his lunch, quickly forgets about his companion. Still eating hungrily, he forgets caution, fails to notice a pair of coyotes with silvered muzzles approaching silently along a nearby deer path. Partners for years, they are highly skilled hunters and quite famished.

Gluck, uncertain he wants to head north, has circled around and sees the pair of predators preparing to attack his friend. He emits a croak of direst warning as they rush forward. Cawley springs upwards with wings flailing and manages to evade their snapping jaws by the barest of margins. He flaps his wings in a series of powerful wooshes and is soon flying parallel with Gluck.

Wordlessly, they head south towards a favorite haunt of their younger years. A sandbar in the middle of the river where they can get a drink, wash down the delicious rabbit they shared, and maybe talk about what's been happening in their lives.

Historical · Marquette lower harbor 1861

A Walk Along Lake Michigan

by Julie Dickerson

"Many will never see a waterscape like this", I told him. What a splendid sight it was. Ripples and wind patterns ran all through the snow. A bay full of giant icebergs frozen in the great lake. Every one was composed of shards of sparkling ice, all the pieces tossed together by the erratic wind and waves. Each iceberg was reflecting the sun's light in a dance of diamonds. And yet, oddly, some areas of the lake were frozen as smooth as a windowpane. The cold must have come so quickly that this area of the lake just stopped its motion as if someone had shouted to it, "Be still".

And still it is; this huge lake that churns and rolls all summer long. Sometimes just a gentle lap at the shore, other times huge waves crashing as they break. But now, so very silent. The icebergs stuck and the vast bay is one silent frozen mass. No birds, no foxes, no terns, no chatter of the squirrels or croak of a tree frog. A motionless lake of this immensity is such a surprising scene to view. Yes, the air was cold, but the sun shone brightly, and the sky was an azure, summer blue. Everything combined to make one of the most remarkable vistas of natural beauty I have ever seen. Who else saw the lake today in all its winter glory?

A Walk in the Woods

by Julie Dickerson

◆❖◆

It was a day I waited for all winter. Dad could tell it was time by the size of the leaves on the oak trees (the size of a squirrel's ear!) and by apple blossoms changing from pink buds to glowing white flowers with honeybees buzzing all around them. The day to take a walk in the woods with Dad was finally here!

The farmers would approve of our trek through their fields as it was before planting time. We would have to cross the creek where we saw leopard frogs and painted turtles. The tadpoles had hatched. They were black and tiny, swishing their little tails in the shallows.

At last, we approached the edge of the woods. As we hiked in deeper, the sunlight filtering through the tiny leaves formed a dappled pattern on the ground. I was cheered to be there and looked forward to the exciting days of spring and summer before me.

The first flower Dad found was a Dutchman's-breeches. I giggled at the funny shape, like fairy pantaloons hanging on a stem. Then there were the bleeding hearts I liked so much, pink and perfect. Everywhere we looked was a fairy land of flowers.

"Look there," instructed Dad as he led me to a clearing in the woods. Straight ahead was a drift of trilliums as far as you could see. Their white petals were frolicking in the sun, replacing the snow drifts of winter.

Next, we found my favorite, jack-in-the-pulpit. How quaint to see a flower with its own little person inside. Jack was preaching in his pulpit with the curved roof over him; sheltered from the spring showers.

Over in a marshy area Dad pointed to yellow flowers he called marsh marigolds. He explained, "They always like their feet wet." That meant the roots had to always be moist. Next to the marsh marigolds Dad picked something and rubbed the leaves in his hand. He put the leaves under my nose.

"Yuck!" I said. "It smells skunky."

"Then it was named well as it is skunk cabbage," laughed Dad. "You'll often see it with marsh marigolds."

Climbing down a tree trunk, a scolding squirrel startled us. We forgave him as he pointed out to us some Trout Lilies at the bottom of the tree. "They're also called adder's-tongue. Can you see why?" asked Dad.

I looked closer and saw the protruding stamens looked like a snake's tongue.

"Now let's start looking for food," Dad suggested.

"What? Food in the woods?" I asked.

"Yes, the saying is 'May is Morel Month in Michigan'. They are the best mushrooms in the world if you ask me," Dad concluded.

"There are many beliefs about how to find morels, but I have luck under dead elm trees and under apple trees. Let's look closely at the ground for a while and check for something sticking up through the dead leaves, something that looks like a brain."

"But Dad, how can we tell an elm tree when the leaves aren't all the way out?" I asked.

"When you can't see the leaves, you have to rely on the bark. Elm trees have bark with lots of ridges. Let's keep looking," Dad told me.

As we approached a slightly raised area in the sun, Dad shouted, "What do you know? What a lucky day! Here are a few morels where I wouldn't have expected them. You just never know where they'll turn up."

"You can have them, Dad. They don't look so good to me," I explained to him.

"Well, I will consider myself lucky to eat them fried in butter when we get home. But you have to try them sometime. They are a delicacy that people hunt for every spring," said Dad.

Dad showed me the correct way to pick them, pinching them off a bit above the ground so they could grow back next year. We put them in our net bag so the spores could fall out as we walked.

"I hear a bluebird, Dad. You taught me that call last year," I reminded him.

"Yes, you're right. Listen! I hear another bird in the distance, a bird that likes the deep woods and has the most melodic song. It's my favorite, the wood thrush," Dad revealed.

I listened intently and, sure enough, I heard this flute-like call that was such a comforting sound. It made me feel like the woods was my home.

As we stepped forward, a garter snake slithered over my shoe. "Eek", I shrieked.

"It won't hurt you," Dad reminded me. He is just looking for a worm to eat. You scared him more than he scared you."

"If you say so, Dad, but I'm glad he's on his way," I whispered.

And now we were to begin our search for signs of lady slippers my dad announced. "They're rare around here," Dad would always say. He wanted to find one but never did in our woods. But his walks with me in the spring made me love the woods forever.

Whenever springtime arrives, I look forward to a walk in the woods and the pleasures of the sights, smells and sounds it has to offer. I feel calm and peaceful there. And I remember Dad telling me to help keep the woods wild for other kids to enjoy, too.

And one day I'll find that lady slipper!

Historical · City of Mackinaw engraving · 1850

I Want to Say

by Rosemary Gegare

For my father

Something about the painting tells me
I should have known you better,
known the old adage comes after,
not before the tree is felled,
and the rings counted one
by one to exact its measure.

Like the gardener seated pensive,
his arms crossed, his hat tipped
to one side—you were weary
of the hat you wore, keeping
for the strands of saving grace,
colors chosen by the painter.

When you penciled yourself into
the "Little Boy Blue" nursery rhyme,
I mistook the torrent, thinking
the disparity in the watercolor,
so ordered by the painter, trying
to make sense of you and me.

Afterglow

by Rosemary Gegare

Mother was a crack of light
like the Woodwick on the table.
A meld of modest resolve
her roots grown in utter regard.

She reared ten of us, and smote
despair—and in the afterglow
cursed the man who ran
with abandon, after the storm.

The Hotel Bantam

by Adam Dompierre

"Watch your step now." The genial middle-aged tour guide was dressed professionally in blue and white, and her voice carried through the length of the hallway, reaching all seven people behind her. She led the way up a staircase to her left, including the deceptively large first step she had just warned her charges about. One by one, the tour group followed behind her.

Roger was last in line, and he watched the others navigate the incline with varying levels of gracefulness. He surveyed the rest of the group. Among them were a pair of couples. The first he put in their 70s, both huddled deep inside their coats against the cold. Even that couldn't hide their enthusiasm though, and they followed closely on the tour guide's heels, peppering her with questions as they traversed from building to building and from room to room.

Another couple trailed them, this one decades younger, with two small children to show for it. The woman, her long brown hair tied in a ponytail, was clearly the more interested of the pair. Her husband wore a blue and red trucker hat, and though he shot cursory glances at each exhibit they came across, he prioritized wrangling his kids. It was an endeavor that demanded every bit of his focus and energy.

His two boys, aged maybe six and eight, alternated between pushing each other, feigning sainthood when that attracted their father's attention, and returning to the horseplay the moment his eyes left them.

Roger watched them intermittently, smiling as he remembered tussles of days past with his own younger brother. Their fights had always started out playfully enough before giving way to more heated, violent exchanges. Then the reconciliation. Sometimes that came quickly and other times it took days, but it always came. These two brothers were still in the early stages of their sniping, but if the younger one in green kept pestering, he would likely find the older's breaking point.

As they reached the upper floor, the tour guide started speaking again and pointed to the labyrinthine wallpaper with her left hand. She continued in a louder voice, "Can you hear me all right in the back?"

Roger couldn't, but that was his own fault for lagging this way, so he shot her a friendly thumbs up rather than protest. "All good, thank you."

In front of them a hallway lead to several doors in any given direction. The hotel had not looked so large from the outside, but buildings could be deceptive like that. Particularly these old ones, Roger thought. He recalled seeing the hotel on their approach; apparently much of it was set beyond the angle of sight. Well, that would explain the discrepancy in square footage.

Ahead, the tour guide carried on through her spiel. She must have delivered the same speech dozens of times by now, maybe hundreds, but the routine was no match for her ardent enthusiasm for the material. Roger caught just bits and pieces of what she said, but it was enough to form a somewhat coherent picture.

"...1855..." he heard, then, "oil barons, wealthy bankers..." and something about a Carnegie. The tour progressed, the old man and woman in front asking questions that were well out of Roger's hearing, the woman with the long hair listening intently, and her husband doing his best to break up the spats that swelled between his boys like waves on a tumultuous sea. Roger hung back, almost unintentionally; but the longer they went on, poking into and out of rooms, the more separation grew between him and the others.

Before long, he wasn't viewing the rooms together with the rest of the group at all, but rather just getting in with enough time to hear the tail end of the tour guide's information. He gathered from her fragments that the once-luxurious establishment had fallen on hard times, sometime toward the end of the nineteenth century. What had been the domain of the wealthy elite passed into disrepair and the once-grand hotel, spacious though it remained, became a haven for the desolate, the disreputable, and the dangerous.

"There were even rumors," the guide explained, "of the hotel being haunted."

The older couple laughed politely at this, but a little chill shot through Roger. The little brother roared, "Boo!" and jumped at his older sibling. The big brother in blue gave him a wicked slap and that sent their parents off into hysterics. Each of them grabbed a boy and pulled them apart, cursing such brazen misbehavior under their breath.

Even that couldn't rattle the veteran tour leader, and she transitioned seamlessly into the next room. The old man and woman in the coats followed her diligently, but Roger stayed behind, taking a moment to appreciate the newfound peace and quiet. He used the opportunity to study the room they had left him in.

It was an ordinary hotel room, given a late 1800s definition of ordinary. One bed, a small twin that would have been cramped for even a single adult. The sheets were neatly arranged, with a dusky blue comforter covering the edges. A delicate-looking white doily on a small bedside table rounded out that corner of the room.

The opposite corner held a writing desk facing the wall. Roger heard voices faintly in the hallway beyond, but whether they belonged to the tour guide, the brawling brothers, or their besieged parents, he couldn't tell. It came to him then that he didn't particularly care either; expansive though the hotel was, its layout was straightforward enough. He felt confident he could catch back up to them even if he lingered awhile longer.

And lingering was just what he felt like doing. Something about the room made him feel peaceful. A pleasant sort of torpidness fell on him, like the hotel room had him in a warm hug, or that gravity's effect had been ever-so-slightly increased. "Maybe that's the haunted part," Roger thought to himself, and was surprised to find he actually said it out loud.

Another impulse took him then, to sit at the writing desk. The sounds of voices from the hallway were gone now; he really should have left to catch up with the others. Except when would he have this opportunity again? A glance over his shoulder toward the doorway confirmed that he wouldn't be bothered or reprimanded, which was the last bit of affirmation he needed.

Roger pulled the chair out noiselessly and settled into the seat. He slid it back into place and set his hands atop the desk. There he found a pristine piece of lined paper and a rather ornate-looking fountain pen beside it. He picked up the pen and admired it, giving it a brief twirl around his left index finger. The white paper was like a barren field after a fresh-fallen snow. Had Roger thought through the next part, he never would have done it. But independent of the usual progression that begins in ideation and ends at action, he found himself writing on the paper, leaving an inky black trail where the pen's tip had been. With a novel curiosity, he discovered he had written what he always did in times of lazy doodling: the flowing arcs of his signature.

The walls of the room felt closer then, not in a cozy way, but more like a straitjacket tightening around him. Breathing became heavier then, but only slightly, and maybe that was just in his mind. Regardless, he decided he had had enough of the desk, enough of the room, and, it suddenly occurred to him, enough of the old hotel. He pushed the chair backward, not bothering to worry about any incidental noise, and headed for the room's exit.

There were no longer any voices to guide him as he stepped into the hallway. Left and right were the only options, but even that felt disorienting now. He attempted to retrace the steps that brought him to the room. He'd taken a left turn, right? That thought only confused him further. Roger summoned a deep breath but found it did him little good. The air was thinner now, or maybe dustier, lacking somehow.

But there was nothing to be done for that. Instead, he pushed his way forward (left, he decided) and tried to find the tour group. He threw open the first door on his left in the hopes of finding the familiar group of faces. The room was empty and seemed much the same as the one he had just come out of, containing a compact bed (dark green comforter this time) and a similar sparse wood desk across from it.

Roger reeled from the room and tried a door on the opposite side of the hallway. There too, he found an 1800s hotel room but no other living soul within. He thought of going back the way he had come. Surely, he would find that same staircase at the end of the hallway, and from that he could escape to the outside, to fresh air and deliverance from his oppressive surroundings.

There was to no avail either, though. In trying to head back the way he had come, Roger found the steps unending. Logically he knew it had to be some trick of the brain - the distance now must be exactly what it had been ten minutes ago. But logic failed him, and he was forced to turn around, defeated. There were no windows anywhere through which to call for help or even orient himself. The only potential refuge he saw was in opening doors until, inevitably, he found himself reunited with the tour group. It was the only possible solution.

Twice more he opened doors to find the rooms behind them deserted. The third room was not.

Inside the third room, he saw a man and a woman sitting on a bed. The man wore an anachronistic three-piece suit, wool maybe, and was jotting down something in a small journal. The woman was inspecting a seam on the ornate gold dress that reached down past her ankles. Roger paused, his hand still on the doorknob, wondering where these new tour guests had come from and why they were dressed that way. Just getting into the spirit of the tour experience, he guessed, but then that hardly mattered. Finally, he had found people.

"Oh, thank goodness," Roger said. "I was beginning to think I had lost everyone!"

The people on the bed didn't react, but continued about their tasks as though they hadn't heard him at all. Roger pressed on.

"I dig the wardrobe," he said. Neither looked up.

The man furrowed his brow then spoke. "The numbers just aren't adding up, my dear. I don't care what your brother says."

"Oh, forget your numbers for once, will you?" she answered. "Clarence knows business and if he says this is a good investment, I think we ought to believe him."

Her husband, if that's what he was, shook his head. "Well, I don't much like it is all."

The woman set aside her dress and took her partner by the hand. "And all I'm saying is I wish you would trust me for once."

Roger wasn't particularly interested in the debate and felt more than a little annoyed at the way they were ignoring him. He broke in again, louder this time. "Listen, help me get back with my tour group, will you? They were here ten minutes ago, I kind of fell behind, and now I don't see them anywhere." His voice rose again, and he felt the same panic that had gripped him earlier. The last part he practically shouted: "Which way out of here?"

At that the man and woman broke off their conversation and looked, for the first time, in his direction. Both regarded him with puzzled looks on their faces.

Again the man spoke first. "Did you hear something, darling?"

"Yes, I did. Well, that is, I think I did. I guess I can't be sure. But look, now the door is open."

"So it is," the man said as though that were the strangest thing he had ever seen. He shrugged. "Just the wind I suppose."

His wife laughed at him. "There's no wind in here, silly. Just the wind," she added, teasing.

"Well," the man stammered, "not the wind per se, no. But that can happen when old buildings settle, you know. Small changes like that," he concluded, unconvincingly.

That only made the woman laugh louder. "I love you, but you don't know the first thing about buildings settling, my dear. And whoever said the hotel was old?"

That was all Roger could stand of the historical role playing. He slammed the door behind him and watched them both jump at the severity of its closing. "Tell me how to get out of here," he demanded.

"Definitely something that time," the woman said, a bit of fear coming into her eyes. "What on earth is that?"

Her husband said nothing but got up and brought his face close to Roger, studying the air around him. All he said was, "I heard it too."

Roger grabbed the man and shook his shoulders with violent immediacy. That is, that had been his intention. The violent shaking never materialized, though. Instead, the stranger just shivered a little.

"Brr," he said. "I just caught such a chill." He looked at his wife, who was watching him with her mouth set in an apprehensive line. The man cleared his throat in an overcompensating sort of way. "Could use some air, I think," he said. "What do you say we go get dinner at that restaurant we passed on our way in?"

"That sounds like a lovely idea," his wife said, gathering her things. "I think some fresh air is just the thing we need." She followed him out into the hall, closing the door behind them.

Roger stood motionless, then blinked dumbly. He was torn an instant between further examining the room he found himself in and pursuing the couple on their way outside. The latter won out; but when he opened the door, he was evidently too late.

The hallway was empty once again. No whisper of sound disturbed the preternatural calm that settled over it. He thought of calling out but could see no good that might possibly come of it. The silence assaulted his ears worse than any siren had ever had. He imagined a wire pulled too tight, a strain that could only end in a vicious snap.

There was nothing to do but soldier on down the hall. Four steps ahead, he found the door to his right locked. He pressed on and tried the door on the left. That knob turned without any resistance. With a trembling hand, Roger pushed it in towards the room. He stepped inside.

The interior of this room was, impossibly, sweltering. The decor threw his senses further awry, being so discordant with the previous room. What had been a nineteenth century version of luxury now regressed toward squalor. Had he not known better, Roger would have mistaken it for a novelty photo booth background of the Old West. The man kicked back on the bed was dressed to match, wearing a dirty striped shirt with the top few buttons left open. A sweat-stained cowboy hat rested lightly atop his head, threatening to go tumbling to the floor at any given moment. His face looked badly in need of a shave and the rest of him smelled badly in need of a bath.

Roger spoke again, but this time his voice nearly deserted him. "Hello," he said, faltering on the second syllable. That garnered no reaction from the man on the bed, who lazily watched the space between his feet. About to doze off, maybe.

This time Roger skipped the repeated attempts at conversation and didn't bother accosting the stranger physically, perhaps as a result of the heat maintaining its death grip on both occupants of the room. Roger walked toward the bed and stood over its occupant, watching him. The man gave no indication that he had noticed the arrival or presence of his new visitor. His eyelids sagged, nearing closure, as Roger got closer. A moment later, Roger stood directly over the cowboy, looking down into the man's eyes, but they gave no signal of recognition, looking past him — through him — up into the ceiling now.

The man shivered slightly then, though Roger couldn't swear that it wasn't just in his imagination. A new frustration overtook him, and he crossed the room to where an unlit gas lamp sat on a well-worn dresser. Seizing the lamp, Roger held it high above his head. He had no particular follow-up in mind; the desperation to be noticed was as far as his thinking would take him. The man paid neither him nor the lamp any mind.

"I'm here!" Roger shouted. When that failed to produce a response, he threw the lamp down at the floor with all his strength. Even in that, he couldn't secure the cathartic crash he was after. The lamp descended through the air, but almost faintly, subject only to the unremarkable effects of gravity. The room's tenant hadn't even noticed its falling, though the sound of it hitting the floor was enough to wake him from his near dozing. He sat up with a start.

"Who's there?" the man asked.

"Me!" Roger shouted.

The man in the dirt-caked clothes got up and examined the detritus that had been the lamp a moment ago. For a while he just stood there shaking his head.

"Maybe they're right." He shook his head again. "Damn place is haunted. Yeah, right." The man laughed at himself then, but it was a nervous sort of laughter. "The hell with this," he said, and went over to where he had set his boots beside the door. He put his boots on in a rushed movement and took a final look around the room, casting his eyes right past where Roger stood. *"Una fantasma."* He spit on the wood floor, crossed himself quickly, and closed the door behind him.

Roger wasted no time in following this one into the hallway. In his haste, he real-ized he hadn't even bothered to open the door, and yet there he was, standing in the hallway. He couldn't explain that, but by then he had grown used to not being able to explain his current state. That he had moved through the door without opening it bothered him less than the fact that the man he tried to follow was gone too, just like the first couple had been. The chance to follow their lead out of this purgatory had gone with them.

Time passed, how much he couldn't say, and the sound of voices returned. They were new voices, but somehow familiar. A woman's voice at the forefront, knowledge-able, authoritative. Then he saw her. She was middle-aged, with a blue sweater vest over a white blouse. That should have been enough to register, but it took seeing her face as well. As she rounded the corner, guests trailing behind her, he recognized the hotel tour guide.

"Finally!" Roger cried out, a smile breaking out across his face. "Listen, I don't know what the heck is with me or these last couple rooms, but—"

The guide continued speaking without interruption. "The Hotel Bantam underwent its first major change in 1855," she said. "Sadly, that change saw a major downturn for the hotel. Much of this can of course be traced back to poor management, although," here she chuckled, "that is also around the time the ghost stories began. A coincidence, I'm sure."

For the first time, Roger recognized the two people behind the guide. They were, unmis-takably, the older couple he had accompa-nied on the tour. They laughed together at the mention of ghosts, as though they en-joyed being part of a new inside joke. He didn't know why they would be back on the tour, unless—

He raced down the hall toward the tour group. Past the guide and the old couple, he saw just what he had feared: The overtaxed parents and the battling pair of brothers. Which meant, behind them...

It felt almost like looking in a mirror, ex-cept not, because there was no mirror. And not like watching himself on camera, because of the added immediacy. Whatever the explanation, after passing through the family of four and reaching the back of the tour group, Roger stood face to face with himself. He did what he could to interact with his other self — waving his arms, shouting in his own face — but it was no use. The past version of Roger, for that is what he realized this other to be, was unreactive. Just as unreactive as every other hotel denizen he had encountered since initially losing the tour group.

Nothing more could be done to bridge the gap between them, he knew, as he had already tried it all. But the desperate impulse was stronger than the logical one. In a last wild attempt, he embraced his doppelganger, trying to fuse their bodies together. Somewhere the hope existed that this might somehow return him to the world he had known, the world of the living.

The attempt was in vain.

Roger watched, helpless to intervene, as his old self only shivered at the hug. This was, he remembered, the chill that had passed over him while the guide led them down this hallway. It had seemed so inconsequential at the time that he scarcely noticed it.

What remained was the extent of his ability to influence the material world. He could simulate cold air, pass through solid objects, and (with enough effort) even give them a slight push. Traveling through the years of the hotel was apparently within his purview as well, though doing so existed outside of his control. The rooms he could enter, and the hallway would always be there waiting on the other side. The world beyond that was forever locked outside of his experience.

But the Bantam would always be there for him — and its Phantom would be there for it.

Historical · Engraving · Indian Village

Taking Care of the Dog

by Gregory M. Lusk

◆❖◆

In early January of 1969, I could see daylight at the end of the tunnel. My college days at Michigan Tech would be concluding at the end of March and the long push would be over. For the last two years, I had been driving a 1957 Ford that I bought from my cousin for ten dollars. It was a challenge to get it running but after doing some repairs and buying a new set of tires, the old beater provided basic transportation if you didn't want to start it on a cold day. To use it on most winter days required a long procedure of starting a garbage can lid full of charcoal and after it was nicely cooking, slide it under the oil pan, wait twenty minutes or so (praying it didn't catch fire) and it would always start after being so coaxed.

The dream of owning my first new car was overpowering. I had been haunting the local Pontiac dealer in Calumet, and gleaning as much information about the GTO as I could get. I pored over the brochures and after a trip to the local credit union, I managed to get a loan; not long after that I made a deal on my GTO, that I ordered exactly the way I wanted it. It took an eternity for it to be built and delivered. I will never forget the day I picked it up; it was a spectacular machine, bright red with aluminum wheels, the biggest available V-8 engine, and a floor shifter. It came in late February, and it wasn't a very good car on snow and ice because of the high horsepower and rear-wheel drive. I did end up buying snow tires for it which partially alleviated the problem.

I had an Irish Setter that, as almost all young dogs do, liked to dig in the trash; particularly when I was away at class or work. No matter what I did, she ended up getting into it pretty good at times. Ginger, a very nice Irish Setter, had a great nose. She could find even the smallest scrap of edible garbage if I made the mistake of leaving it in the open when she was alone. One day in late March, I came home late in the day to find the garbage strewn about and the dog laying on the floor in obvious discomfort. I did a bit of detective work and found that she had gotten into some old chicken bones. I wasn't sure what the outcome would be if I waited, so I tried to find a veterinarian. I could not, and there were no after-hours numbers for emergencies. The pup seemed to be getting worse and now I started worrying that she might not make it. I called information in Marquette and found a vet that personally answered his emergency number. He said to not waste any time getting there so we jumped into the new GTO and started the over hundred-mile trip to Marquette at about 11:00 p.m.

Greg Lusk and his red GTO

I was breaking all the posted speed limits and in the straight stretches, I was cruising. The roads were not as good back then, but to quote the Beach Boys in *Little Deuce Coupe*, "...if I had a set of wings man I know she could fly ..." or maybe more appropriately in Ronny and the Daytona's song, *GTO*, **...** *listen to her tachin' up now, listen to her why-ee-eye-in, C'mon and turn it on, wind it up and blow it out GTO...*" The car and driver were doing their part to try and keep the dog alive, but she wasn't doing very well in the back seat.

Somewhere past and east of the Covington Junction, where highways US-41 and M-28 meet south of L'anse, the call of nature raised up and after a few miles more there was no use fighting it so I pulled over in the vicinity of a small creek. It was darn cold, pushing -20 degrees but thankfully there was absolutely no breeze.

I was standing behind the car taking care of business when my eye spotted a very bright light to the south of the road, over the swamp. At first, my mind was telling me that it must be an aircraft, perhaps a helicopter. But it wasn't making any sound, not a single noise of any kind. I tried to reason what it might be and realized that the light that I was watching on the ground was being cast from above. I didn't discern any movement of any kind, it was just hanging there.

My mind started racing, trying to comprehend what I was looking at. I forgot about everything and at that point, it should have said "flight," but I knew I couldn't outrun whatever this was. After about twenty to thirty seconds of watching the white light; imagining what "they" were looking at in this Black Spruce swamp the white light was switched off.

Only then could I see the other lights on the craft. They were arranged in two, possibly three, concentric circles. The two circles of lights I could easily see were red and orange. It was at this point at which things got interesting. The craft started moving in a northerly direction almost right at my location. It was moving quite slowly, about fifteen to twenty miles per hour, and passed directly overhead and slightly east of me. I estimated that it was about 150-200 feet above me; just above the tallest trees. It appeared to be circular and the diameter of what I could see in the dark from my headlights and those concentric rings of lights made me think it was wider than the road right-of-way, about 100 to 150 feet in diameter.

My thoughts again turned to flight but to what end? I was no match for this "aircraft", even in my new GTO. I almost felt like I was glued to the spot where I was standing, either from fear or because I couldn't move. I was getting quite cold by now, but I waited to see the final exhibition by the craft that was the most memorable part of this whole event.

It almost hesitated directly over me on the road for a second or two and then started to accelerate, slowly at first; and headed almost due north. At that point, the speed of the craft was about 100-200 miles per hour and still accelerating until it dipped behind the first high spot on my horizon. I kept watching to see if I could catch another glimpse of it and I did. When I next saw it, I almost hesitated to guess its speed because it was unbelievable as it continued to accelerate. It had to be going thousands of miles per hour. The last thing it did was skip a bit, almost like a flat rock thrown on the surface of a lake, for a short distance and then make a truly unbelievable left turn at that incredibly high speed, disappearing somewhere to the west. The forces of inertia on anything inside the craft would have been life-threatening. I didn't need to be encouraged to get back in the car and get going.

We got to Marquette; met the great veterinarian who came out in the middle of the night. He gave poor Ginger a shot to induce vomiting. After she did that, we had a brief rest period and she was back, almost to her old self within a short period. The ride back to Houghton was much more sedate, relaxed, and closer to the speed limit. To this day I still look carefully at that spot where I saw the "craft", whether it is night or day, although I doubt I will ever see anything like it again.

The Death of Old 289

by David Swindell

Photo by Confined Riley

A fateful train wreck took place at the Ford River Switch on the evening of Feb. 19th, 1900. This colossal event is considered one of the worst railroad accidents in Michigan history. Nine people never saw the light of day after their unfortunate encounter. The residents of the surrounding towns rushed to the wreck only to find the twisted remains of burning cars and railroad equipment broken and strewn about. *Info provided by* michiganrailroads. com

The telegrapher handed Jimmy a special envelope that was stamped in bold red letters.

With great trepidation the young man opened the envelope as if his very future depended on it.

The train order stated, you are to proceed without haste and take #289 from Green Bay to Ishpeming Michigan, let nothing block you on this cold and snowy night.

Dreaming of the big assignment since coming to work on the railroad, Jimmy wanted to run the big passenger trains that graced the C&NW line.

However, for now, his focus was on the task at hand, bringing the red ball freight to its destination and coming back again.

* * *

The special orders handed Jimmy impressed and scared the engineer, for someone so new.

The words on the page jumped out at him as if guided by an invisible force from Chicago corporate so far removed.

You are to proceed to Ishpeming with all deliberate speed. You have express status and clear tracks and that's all that you need. We will telegraph additional instructions to station masters along your route, proceed with great haste and let safety guide your way.

And stated on the paragraph below were these startling words that gave Jimmy great concern. Freight 289 needs to arrive on time, your future with this company is on the line.

Then turning to leave, Jimmy heard the voice of superintendent Harold call to him in a stern but determined voice.

To make your journey faster this night we've brought out our best and fastest engine to speed your flight.

She's fresh and fast coming from the factory last week. She's the latest and best from the American Locomotive Works.

Then Superintendent Harold gave these passing words to Jimmy before they departed their separate ways.

Be sure and swift on this night, so snowy and dark. Carry yourself without fear, know that something bigger than yourself is always at your side.

Use your good instincts and training that you've already received. And know despite bad weather and pressures, you'll make it through this ordeal.

* * *

Going out to his engine, Jimmy went about oiling the many cups and bearings before beginning his journey. He could smell the fresh paint as the scent betrayed a newness to the mighty machine powered by fire and steam.

After talking with his conductor for a short while, the signal was given to start the journey and get that hot cargo to Ishpeming by morning light. Little did he know the perils that awaited him through the night.

Hopping into the cab, Jimmy leaned on the throttle, taking the freight out of the yard and North through the cuts, bridges, and trestles that defined his route. He opened the big engine up, guiding her towards a fate uncertain.

The snow flew and blocked his view as Jimmy applied sand on the tracks from the dome above. Negotiating the grades so slippery and wet only added to the difficulties of the perilous trip. As a morass of swirling snow enveloped the train and its crew, no one was certain if they would ever get through.

Beyond the abyss, Jimmy managed to stay on time, keeping freight #289 steady and fine. Fast he flew to the weathers availing taunts; threatened to block his way with dangerous snow drifts. Never was there a time so precarious in this young man's life. As something loomed ahead in the dark of the night.

* * *

As they moved up the line the visibility of the cascading snow engulfed the train with torrents that tested the skill of the crew.

Rounding a bend in the tracks, the mighty engine pressed forward in complete mechanical perfection.

As the train neared the switching point at Ford River, something foreboding entered the scene.
Camouflaged by the swirling snow and the cloud of coal dust, Jimmy did not see the red lantern on a parked train just up front.

Now as it happened, a passenger train #21, The Felch Mountain Accommodation, had paused up ahead.

What happened next, angels feared to tread.

The crash was powerful, as the two trains collided on that cold winter's night. A sudden terror overtook both passengers and crew, consuming their very souls on that dark and frightful night.

What followed next was the sounds of crashing cars, twisting metal and screams from within. The terrible impact ignited a conflagration that spread over the wreck like a wave of fire in a furnace raging within.

From the force of the crash came the hissing of steam, and the cries of the wounded, and a memory not forgotten.

Today few Michiganders know of the tragedy that unfolded that fateful night, with its haunting presence in the still of the night.

* * *

In the aftermath of that disaster this legacy remains to this day.

Two crew members and seven passengers lost their lives in that collision out on the rails, as darkness and fear triumphed that day.

The sacrifice of that night ended in a terrible way, with nine tickets bought and punched in a profound way.

And today when you drive past the site of that fateful wreck, seven lone sentinels call out their names. These souls still speak to us in a bold and reassuring way. Stating, *"Please do not forget us and what happened on that fateful night, as our time ended so soon, on a dark gloomy night."*

Places Few Have Seen

by Tom Conlan

A yellowed photo from the Marquette paper hangs on the wall of the cabin beneath an eight-point whitetail mount, San Pierre paddles a canoe down the Big Brook. *Antlers*, the canoe, and San Pierre's beard sparkle with late November frost. In bold letters the caption reads, "Places Few Have Seen."

•••

I pulled out on the winding two lane blacktop which runs north from my farm near Charlevoix and reached around to quiet the rattling caused by my fishing rod hanging loosely in the rear window. I spotted Jupiter shining a lone morning light in the clear, dark sky. On this early spring morning, I was alone travelling on the road which parallels the Lake Michigan shore.

As I cleared civilization and opened the throttle, my pickup climbed the long hill with Little Traverse Bay reflected in the rearview mirror. I had started on the five-hour drive to our cabin on the West Branch of the Escanaba River to fish the opening weekend of trout season with San Pierre.

In the pre-dawn mist, alder swamps lined both sides of the highway. A deer, a decent buck, ran across in front of my truck. My senses were aroused by the innocence reflected in the deer's eyes, by his spring antlers revealed in my headlights. Deer blend into the gray trunks of Quaking Aspen, folks call *Popples*, growing in tight groves too near the road.

I reached the Mackinac Bridge as the sun peeked promisingly over Bois Blanc Island. A magnificent structure, one of the longest suspension bridges in the western hemisphere, crosses the Straits of Mackinac. Lakes Michigan and Huron share the same basin gradient, and an equal height above sea level. The water may flow east or west through the Straits, depending upon the prevailing winds.

Hypnotic water beckoned hundreds of feet below. I yanked myself from reverie and returned my attention to the rising glow in the east, complemented by hues of purple and pink emanating from the curve of the horizon as if the colors rose from deep beneath the waters of Lake Huron.

I turned west on highway US-2 which begins where the bridge ends, thence follows the north shore of Lake Michigan to Wisconsin and points west, ending at the Pacific Ocean near Seattle. US-2 is not as famous as Route 66, but Americana can still be found living along this winding, mostly two-lane path.

A couple hours later, near Rapid River, I left the highway and the big lake, and entered the interior woods of Michigan's Upper Peninsula. From Lake Michigan, our hidden cabin lies sixty-five miles by back road. If travelling by canoe, the meandering Escanaba River winds for ninety miles before arriving at the same place.

Leaving the gravel road southwest of Gwinn, I carefully crossed the gated private bridge over the West Branch and entered a tunneled, bumpy, twisting trail through tall spruce. Ferns and moss thrive below the canopy before the trail opens to a sunlit clearing, where a cabin sits high on the bank overlooking the stream.

San Pierre, sometimes called *Trapper*, had arrived the previous evening in time for supper over at Solberg's Tavern where a waitress serves up pleasant conversation and a warm feeling with beers and the Friday night fish fry. He stood in the clearing along with a couple buddies from a camp down the road. David, about six foot four and two hundred pounds, is friendly and unassuming, while smart in the old ways. Of Italian descent, he grew up in the Upper Peninsula. Italians settled here for jobs in the iron mines that provided Detroit and the world with the raw material to build the automobile. David operates heavy equipment back home in Iron Mountain. He ran the crane that set the steel bridge grate in place, and afterward climbed down and solidly welded the grate to iron girders.

Our simple, four-room cabin overlooks a bend on the river where erosion has cut a gradual twenty-foot-high bank. Light inside the cabin comes from a system of propane lanterns, heat from a wood stove, and water from a point well with a pump in the sink. The isolated property is surrounded by State land on three sides and David's Camp on the fourth.

Stepping out of my truck, I acknowledged my partner in the usual fashion, "Mister San Pierre."

"Mister Con-Laan" he replied with a smile, over emphasizing the last syllable.

"Well Hel-loo Tom," greets David, "this is my chum, Freddie. Me and Freddie are gonna' float the West Branch. Would you ever drop my truck down by the school camp?"

•••

Somewhere in the deep woods south of Marquette, a divide changes the natural drainage. On the north side, streams and rivers run to Lake Superior. Our cabin lies south of the ridge, where waters flow to Lake Michigan. Hundreds of square miles are bro-

ken only by streams, a few gravel roads, and two tracks left by the lumber trucks. In this wild country, a man must trust himself, and know his limitations.

•••

San Pierre dropped off David's truck at his "getting out point," then we rode six miles to Kate's Grade that runs on high ground along the Big Brook swamp. The picture on the wall in the cabin was taken from the lower bridge where the Big Brook empties into the West Branch of the Escanaba River.

The previous fall, at the close of trout season, San Pierre and I dropped a canoe halfway between the bridges after a six-hour float down from the upper bridge. We caught a few trout, then hiked through the swamp back to the grade and the truck. San Pierre left the canoe hidden for whitetail season, to traverse the Brook to his post.

I nudged the truck half in the bushes off the gravel grade. San Pierre led the way along a twisting trail a mile and a half through the swamp to get to the Brook. Hip boots barely kept us dry while we moved through the watery sludge seeping out of the soft ground. San Pierre followed a deer trail cutting a narrow, intermittent path. The spring high water gathered in puddles like tubs.

The day was warm for early spring, nearly sixty degrees out of the wind when the sun broke through the clouds. I sweated and stumbled, as hidden roots disguised by the uneven ground caught the toe of my boot. Finally, ahead in the distance, we spotted the tall spruce trees marking the riverbank.

I picked up a paddle hidden under a pine. San Pierre reminding, "I never leave paddles with the canoe. Might tempt someone."

"Who the hell else would be in here other than brook trout, beaver, deer, bear, and wolves?"

The key fit the padlock and we freed the chain binding the canoe to a tree. I tied a Panther Martin spinner onto the line on my Intrepid lightweight rod, thinking the brush here too tight for casting my fly rod.

The Big Brook meanders, widens and closes back down from thirty feet across to little narrows where the current funnels. In tight places, tag alders hanging over either side of the stream, a natural handhold to keep the canoe still. Brookies hide in narrow drains, where the clear deep water presses into a current. Small but perfect, iridescent trout shoot out from under the bank and hit with a muscled force not betraying their size.

San Pierre secured his pack with our lunch and a couple beers, and we pushed off. I sat in the bow seat to fish the first half. We planned to switch seats downstream. As we left the bank he said, "It's a four-hour float if we paddle. If the fish are hitting, it may take all day."

The moment we left shore, we were committed, as no other path leads out of the swamp. I wondered at the vision of San Pierre, a skillful hunter and canoeist, bringing a buck he had shot out of this place, by canoe in the icy cold of November. The Big Brook forgives no human error.

I find peace in fishing for brook trout. In Michigan's Upper Peninsula, fishermen are abundant, yet few venture into the deep swamps and beaver ponds where the biggest brookies reside.

I cast the spinner out a few times into likely spots without a bite. San Pierre patiently grabbed an alder branch to hold the canoe. Accurate casting, critical to avoid the alders waiting like thieves to steal a line, becomes more difficult in a floating environment. Brook trout will usually give you one chance, one cast. My rod and I were aligned, and I laid the lure right where I aimed, like a pitcher spotting a fastball low and away. Still, no hits.

"Maybe the creek's too high, or maybe we're too early in the year," San Pierre commented.

I remembered hooking an eighteen-inch Brookie near this spot in the Brook a couple years earlier, while leaning over the side to wet my hands in the cold stream. I watched as droplets dried in the sun. I wondered if another large trout had made this bend his home.

San Pierre, laughing, told me about the previous spring floating with David on the main branch of the Escanaba River. Two of the most experienced outdoorsmen I know. "David lays out a back cast right past my ear. I flinched and the canoe rolled. The water is colder than a witch's tit this time of year."

After a half dozen holes turned up empty, I bit off the spinner and tied on a Royal Wulff, a tiny little dry fly with brown and white hairs bound by red thread. I associate the name with wolves and believe the name brings me good luck. I fished the fly for years before realizing that wolf was spelled *Wulff*. I put a light split shot on the line about eighteen inches up so the Wulff would dangle downstream in the current like a dying bug.

The canoe slid into an open stretch of the Brook, in about ten feet of rich, rust-colored water. The color forms as the Brook raises and runs miles through deep deposits of iron. Up ahead, the current patterned toward the center. The bottom was visible only near the bank.

The middle of the stream was dark and deep where I laid the fly and felt a familiar tug. The Wulff has a small hook, and the fish didn't swallow, so I reeled in the fly. San Pierre eased the canoe toward the bank where he used a paddle in the sand to hold us still.

"Did it feel like a big one?"

Pissed off because I missed my chance, I replied "Yah, he was big, probably won't hit again."

I took a deep breath and cast. The fly hit the water and suddenly, I was trying to control fireworks on the Fourth of July. My reel whizzed, and as I adjusted the drag, the fish shot for relief under an overhanging alder branch bobbing in the current. I tightened the drag and the light rod bowed into an arc. Fearing the branch might tear the line, I worked the fish back to the middle of the stream, then released the drag a bit. He fought mightily.

The tone in San Pierre's voice rising, "What the hell is that, a sucker? Too big for a brookie."

I barely heard him speak. The hook, the line, and the rod were an extension of my arms. My body knew before my mind when the time was right, and I began to reel in.

I eased the fish alongside the canoe, then realized I could not reach my net without letting go of the rod, but I didn't want to lose this fish. I tightened up and lifted him into the canoe in one easy motion. Just as I raised the fish clear of the gunnel, the Royal Wulff popped out of his mouth, and the trout landed at my feet.

San Pierre shook his head, incredulous, "Should have used the net."

He was a lovely fish with pink spots all along his belly, twenty-four inches of Brown Trout, the monster brown, the dominant trout in the Big Brook.

Exhausted and exhilarated, I asked San Pierre, "Can you reach your camera? Gotta get a picture."

Turning around on the seat, I held the fish tightly with both hands. San Pierre angled his body for a shot but couldn't see the whole fish in the lens, "Hold him by the gills and I'll try again."

Some mud from the bottom of the canoe had smeared on the fish, so I reached over the side, cupped my hands for water and cleaned him up for the picture. I picked up the trout with one hand holding his gills, the other hand on the tail, "He's a slippery mother. Let's try it."

With the click of the camera, I relaxed my fingers for a brief moment. The monster dove through my hands, over the side to his deep water home the instant my pressure weakened. Without thinking, I lunged, thrusting my arms out trying to catch the fish in thin air. As I reached, my weight shifted too suddenly.

A cold shock enveloped me. I gulped rusty water as my hip boots filled and began to drag me down with the current. The violent force twisted and spun me over underwater. I was a child spinning somersaults, looking up at the surface through a haze.

As my hat floated away, my fingers caught the edge of the mostly submerged canoe. I twisted upright searching with my feet for ground, and finally found friendly mud five feet down. Knowing the depth dropped into darkness, I held the canoe as my head broke the surface. San Pierre rose in the shallow water near the shore, startled, half gasping for breath. Our eyes met, and realizing we would survive, we roared in guttural laughter. Soaked, and spitting out water, San Pierre's first words, "My balls are freezing."

I dug my feet safely in the sand five feet down, though my hip boots weighed twenty pounds each. Still laughing, I tied the canoe off to a small tree. The bank was too steep and slippery for San Pierre to climb, "How about a push?"

Boots still full, I waded around the canoe, and pushed his ass as he crawled up. I threw the rods, paddles and pack up on the bank. Still in the creek, I shoved while San Pierre hoisted the canoe to drain the water. Shivering, I trudged warily to a spot on the bank where I could grab a root to pull myself out and crawled like a soldier out of a foxhole.

The sun moved in and out of the clouds in a measureless sequence of time. When the sun shone, my body warmed. The clouds rolled through the spring sky and hid the sun, and I shook from cold.

I yanked on my hip boots until the suction gave way and they popped. We hung our boots upside down in an alder, watching water pour out, before stripping down and spreading our clothes on bushes to dry. Our skin, white from months of winter, our exposed pale flesh, stood sorely out of place in the wild woody swamp.

The sandwiches had stayed dry. I spotted an old, downed maple for a seat. San Pierre called out, "Throw the other sandwich over here. I'm not sitting next to you butt-naked! Someone will come down the river and see us."

"We're in the middle of nowhere, who the hell is going to see us?"

Into the deep, we lost my hat and San Pierre's prescription glasses. We searched along the shallows by the bank with no luck. He had saved the camera, but water dripped from the lens and the photo could not be retrieved. Intermittently, the sun came out and then hid behind the clouds. We passed an hour while our clothes partially dried, then dressed, loaded the canoe, and pushed off down the river.

Still in the bow seat, I tried another fly. At the first big bend, I spotted my hat floating on a branch and retrieved it with a paddle. My favorite hat still, soaked with water from the Big Brook, and dried in wild sun.

The remaining hours floating down to the take-out were mostly uneventful. A male wood duck, green, white, red, and gold, skittered off ahead of us at several bends. He was a welcomed sign as he led the way, and we followed down the Brook.

I hooked into a fingerling brook trout, not a keeper, not even close to the brown monster. San Pierre had just one hit, but the fish was off the hook before we got a good look.

We reached the take-out place as evening approached. Tired and hungry, we dragged the canoe a couple hundred yards through the woods up to Kate's grade. My jeans hadn't dried, and my socks squished in my hip boots. As we walked the gravel grade two miles north to the truck, I thought mostly about a stiff bourbon.

San Pierre chuckled aloud, "I've got to figure a way to spin this tale to David."

The heater in my pickup felt heavenly warm. My thoughts brightened with the warmth, and I smiled at the sight of San Pierre and I sunbathing, naked and alive, on a downed maple tree in the middle of a swamp. I smiled at good fortune for the monster, the brown trout, diving for his life over the side, and swimming safely away.

Historical · Chippewa woman · making birch bark canoe

Yellow Eyes

by Tom Conlan

Flash as high as my waist
not a deer.
Flash yellow before me
in the hours before dawn, in the fall
when Orion shines low in the western sky.

I had seen pictures the night before
of a muzzle long and wicked,
knowing not the meaning of mercy.
Imagination plays tricks on a lone soul
in dark, deep woods.

A fern grows like a partridge
near the side of a dirt road.
A broken branch hangs awkwardly,
brings to mind a buck bent down to sniff,
yet sticks are not antlers.

Did I see a wolf that morning
or just menacing yellow eyes passing quickly?
A happenstance unmistakable, yet,
the sight of a wolf stays lodged in your being,
while you search for his wildness in your soul.

Dying in Rural Rockland

by Kathleen Carlton Johnson

Dying in Rural Rockland. A Chaplain works in all kinds of weather. Something akin to the Postal Service, but what we deliver is spiritual food for the soul. It was midwinter; the wind blew the heavy snow across the highways; it moved like a snake on top of the black macadam. There were mounds of white on either side of the road. Often there was limited visibility. There was also the potential of skidding into a ditch that would take a visit from a tow truck.

I was called to a dying soul in the woods. In a remote area. The only way to find the house was to follow the instructions given to me. You could not use your phone or GPS because a cell phone signal did not cover the area. It was in a place the locals call "the bush." Years ago, this area had been one of the first copper mining communities in the Upper Peninsula of Michigan. Currently, the large forest yielded lumber and wood products. It was in a remote area in the private world of trees.

After following a narrow road of ice, I found the house tucked back in a ridge of pine trees, their branches stiff with cold. The house had an unusual porch. The porch had bird feeders on all four corners. Birdseed shells and casings stood out on the snowy pathway to the front door. Birds made a chirping welcome as I knocked; a middle-aged woman answered.

The door swung open and there, dressed in a green wool sweater covering the top of her thighs and gray wool pants, her grey hair, severely cut to her head, was the wife. Noted was thickly applied red lipstick outlining two admirable lips. She showed me in without a word of greeting. "He is in here." She escorted me down a narrow hallway. The end of the room where my patient lay was bright with streaming light. Windows across the bedroom wall made a surreal feeling of celebration. In this festival of light was my patient, stripped to the waist, a man about 70, bald, eyes closed. I knew when I saw him, with that slight yellow tinge to the body that it was Cancer. He was dying of cancer.

On either side of the bed were his son and daughter. They never spoke. Both lost in the grief of what was occurring. In his mid-twenties, the son was black-haired with a goatee that looked as if it were sketched on his face. He had made his way to Rockland from Seattle where he worked in IT. The daughter was smallish, brown hair, brown eyes plain as a house. Her swollen face puffed from crying.

I turned to my patient, who had gone from reality to a place where the dying often go. A familiar sign to myself that death was imminent. This huge man before me needed nothing now. The small group around him kept watch. We all needed reassuring that all would be well. The room slowly filling with a flat silence tinged with anxiety. The understandable nervous pull of wanting the loved one to remain with them and the practical desire to see the suffering over. A toxic mix that is difficult to explain to others. This untimed vortex engaging body, mind, and soul in the human drama before us. A place that you can never truly convey to another human. Death is very private.

As a shelter, we huddled around the dying man and prayed. We said the Lord's Prayer; I read the 23rd Psalm and gave a blessing. Mother and children numbed by death's closeness mouthed the prayers but operated in a blur of emotional and mental pain. Prayer seemed to help the silence that was descending in white completeness. My patient was progressing slowly into death's long sacred corridor.

In this awkward but very human place, the sound of a chorus singing. Floating in the background music, I recognize it as Verdi's, from his opera Nabucco. The beautiful "Va Pensiero" a musical cradle of protection and hope. The Chorus is sounding a mystical pool of grace that made this moment in time memorable and healing to our human selves. I, as a seasoned chaplain, who has experienced death so often, was deeply moved.

In driving back from this event, the snow floated white on my windshield. The music and the daily events went round and round inside of me as if begging a conclusion. 'Va Pensiero' in English means, "Go thoughts on golden wings." Here in the middle of the "Bush." Here in this land of snow-covered forests, the land of lumberjacks and retired miners. In this space of boarded-up storefronts and decaying windows of towns long gone. Verdi, floating over it all. *What do we have in the end*, I thought. If salvation is just a friendly guarantee

When It Comes:
A Poem for Voices

by Kathleen Carlton Johnson

A Poem for multiple voices. The chorus is several speakers who repeat the refrain. The speaker is the poet.

(Opened by the Chorus, loud, strident, and methodical male voices)

Chorus
When it comes,
When it comes, fast from behind
When it comes, we will have wasted nothing but time,
When it comes, self-centered, hurrying along
It was about pride; it was about being part of time
It was about doing, and being and making
And we were all of that.

SPEAKER (poet)
It was a struggle, and the Earth kept the secret
Till we found it, and we wanted to find it
It was about pride; it was about being part of the times
We found it deep and had to go and get it
The metal, it was deep and far down in the earth
Pumped in men and pumped out water,
It was deep and we went deep and hauled
Hauled the metal to the light
It was deep and it was hauled to the surface.

Chorus
When it comes,
When it comes, fast from behind
When it comes, we will have wasted nothing but time,
When it comes, self-centered, hurrying along

It was about pride; it was about being part of time
It was about doing, and being and making
And we were all of that.

SPEAKER (poet)
It was about pride, it was about time and the metal
It made men rich, and they came from afar.
Called the mines after their towns,
There were the money men, they brought in the money
So, we could get the metal out of the ground,
It was about pride, it was about the metal
It made men work long hauls and dance down the dark
lights on their heads
We were like stars in the dark. We dug the metal
fourteen hours a day, they hauled it with strength
the lights on their helmets lit up the dark.
The cold crept around us like a blanket.
It was about pride, it was about the metal,
We found it deep and had to go and get it
It was deep and far down in the earth
We pumped in men and pumped out water,
The man-car let the men down, it took the men out
Alive or dead, the car removed and took.

Chorus
When it comes,
When it comes, fast from behind

When it comes, we will have wasted nothing
    but time,
When it comes, self-centered, hurrying along
It was about pride; it was about being part
    of time
It was about doing, and being and making
And we were all of that

Speaker (poet)
We dug the metal,
The metal was cold, and earth faced
We took the metal to the surface
Cars of it, we blasted its shoulders
We smote its knuckles with picks
Down in the dark of tunnels
We worked for many hours in a day
The Ore came up from the ground still
Clinging mixed with common earth
Our common face uncomplaining
Wind and snow, we went to work
In the dark in winter, we went down in the
    dark
When we left the day was in dark.
The snow around us, the cold before us
We went home to our company houses
The iron metal was what we dug,
The metal was about needs
Iron rails for trains to link growing cities
Railroad tracks, iron rims for wagons
To transport goods, building cities
Nails for building a nation progressing
Strong and growing into greatness.

Chorus
When it comes,
When it comes, fast from behind
When it comes, we will have wasted nothing
    but time,
When it comes, self-centered, hurrying along
It was about pride; it was about being part
    of time
It was about doing, and being and making
And we were all of that

Speaker (poet)
The mines are the deep house beneath the
    ground
The road from which the iron runs,
Runs to the surface, runs holding its face
We labored in the difficult to bring about
    change

The mines mark the earth
Invited us into the earth
To take the mineral to the surface,
We are the men who came to get the metal
We are resting, we have taken what we can
We have left the pride we took
We are gone and come again in you
Our blood runs in the leaving of our struggle
We bring children left behind
We bring stories, and pride, dusty days
Snow memories and with pride we built
By strength and work and sweat.

Chorus
When it comes,
When it comes, fast from behind
When it comes, we will have wasted nothing
    but time,
When it comes, self-centered, hurrying
    along
It was about pride; it was about being part
    of time
It was about doing, and being and making
And we were all of that.

Speaker(poet)
When we come, self-speaking, hurrying
    along
We bring our children left behind
We bring stories, and bar room fights,
We come speaking many languages,
Our sadness and misery
Boarding houses, wives, funeral expenses.
We bring the illness and epidemics,
The snow that marked more days than we
    wanted
The firewood made. The company store.

Chorus
When we come, we come in pride.
When we come,
When we come, fast from behind
When we come, we will have wasted nothing
    but time,
It was about pride
It was about living,
When we come, self-centered, hurrying along
When it comes,
When it comes, fast from behind
When it comes, we will have wasted nothing
    but time,

Speaker (poet)
We are here, walking to work in the dark
Our bucket packed, tin colored
The shift ahead, the snow present
The wind keeping the paths blown free.

Chorus
(Voices now receding into the morning.
  Start loud and fade into silence)

When it comes,
When it comes, fast from behind
When it comes, we will have wasted nothing
  but time,
When it comes, self-centered, hurrying along
It was about pride; it was about being part
  of time
It was about doing, and being and making
And we were all of that.

How Ya Gonna
Keep 'Em Down on the Farm
after They've Seen Marquette?

by Tyler R. Tichelaar

◆❖◆

Frank Jarvi came down from his bedroom fully packed for his half-week of freshman orientation at Northern Michigan University.

He found his mother crying in the kitchen.

"Ma, what's wrong?" he asked.

"Nothing," she replied.

"Something's wrong," Frank said.

"I just don't want to see you grow distant from us," she replied, turning toward him and breaking into sobs.

Frank put his arms around her.

"You don't have to worry about that," he said.

"You ready to go, Frank?" asked his dad, coming inside from the back door. Reuben stopped when he saw his wife in his son's arms.

"Oh, geez, Lorraine," he said. "It's just for a few days."

Lorraine pulled away from her son and used her dishtowel to wipe her tears.

"It's just a few days right now," she said, "but this fall he'll be gone for weeks and weeks, almost a year, and it will always be that way from now on."

"No, it won't, Ma," said Frank. "I'll be home for holidays and vacations, and anyway, Dad wants me to take over the farm someday."

"You say that now, but you'll change your mind," said Lorraine, looking him in the eye.

"Why would you say that?" Frank asked.

"It's like that old song, 'How You Gonna Keep 'Em Down on the Farm After They've Seen Paree,' only in this case it's Marquette. You'll get used to the big city life and adopt the ways of all those stuck-up people in Marquette, and then you won't want to have anything to do with your family and your Finnish roots here in Pelkie."

"Oh, Ma," said Frank. What else could he say? He couldn't wait to get the hell out of Pelkie. He had big plans once he got to Marquette. But he couldn't tell his blubbering mother that.

"Come on, Frank. We're going to be late," Reuben told his son.

Frank kissed his mother on the cheek. "I'll be fine, Ma. Don't worry. And I'll tell you about everything when I get home."

She hung onto him for a second, though he towered over her. She couldn't just tie him to her apron strings anymore. He was eighteen and the biggest boy in Pelkie, strong as one of his dad's plow horses. He was a grown man now with a grown man's ideas, and no mother was going to stop him from doing what he wanted. Lorraine knew that, but it didn't mean she wouldn't miss him, and it didn't stop her from saying, "Call me when you get there so I know you're safe."

"Jesus, Lorraine," said Reuben. "That's a long-distance call."

"I don't care," said Lorraine. "He can call collect."

"Don't be ridiculous," Reuben replied. "I'll be home a couple of hours after I drop him off. I'll tell you he's fine when I get home."

"I might be busy as soon as I get there, Ma," said Frank, trying to get out of the phone call. After all, he'd be staying in a dorm room with some guy he didn't know, and he didn't want anyone to think right away he was some kind of sissy who had to call his mommy. It was bad enough he'd been sick and missed the orientation he was supposed to attend; he'd missed out on meeting his roommate and suitemates. His parents had worried he'd had food poisoning, but the truth was he'd gone out with his buddies from the class of '88 and gotten drunk. He knew he shouldn't drink. Beer was fattening and not good for his muscular physique, but sometimes drinking was the only way to numb the feelings he didn't know how to deal with. Grabbing his bag now, he walked out the kitchen door before his mother could gush anymore. He wasn't going to call her. She could wait until he got home Wednesday night.

Frank threw his bag in the back of the truck and then climbed in and waited for his dad. A minute later, Reuben was in the driver's seat shaking his head and saying, "You're lucky you're getting out of here. Your ma will be crying for three days while you're gone."

"I'm just glad she's not coming with us," said Frank. "I don't need her making a scene in front of all the guys in my dorm."

Lorraine had wanted to go, but it was strawberry season and she had to get her preserves made. She won a ribbon almost every year at the county fair for her strawberry preserves and she was determined to win again this year.

Reuben and Frank didn't talk much on the way to Marquette. Reuben wasn't much of a talker, and Frank was too nervous to talk. He tried to imagine what it would be like to live on campus with a bunch of other college students and without parental supervision. What would the nightlife be like in the big city of Marquette? Would he be able to sneak into the bars? He'd heard you could easily get into a bar called the Alibi without an I.D. Would he meet lots of hotties? Would someone want to be his girlfriend? He'd never had one, though a lot of the girls had been forward with him in high school. After all, he'd been on the football team and wrestling team, and he had bulging muscles and worked out constantly so he could keep getting bigger and bigger. But he also figured there'd be more competition at college since there'd be guys there older than him who might also be bigger. He hoped to check out the weight room and pool in the PEIF building. Even if he saw big guys there, he knew they'd show him respect since he was big too. Maybe they'd even help him find the right girl. He kept telling himself he just hadn't found the right one yet.

Before Frank knew it, they were passing through Ishpeming and Negaunee and then coming into Marquette. He couldn't believe how many stores there were as they came into town. Kmart and the Westwood Mall. The Bavarian Inn. A car dealership. The Queen City Motel and then more motels. Everything was going by so fast he couldn't read the names on everything. A restaurant named Bonanza, and a Pizza Hut, and the Marquette Mall, and the Holiday Inn.

And then Reuben got into the wrong lane and, rather than heading downtown, found himself on the bypass and heading to South Marquette. Suddenly, Frank could see Lake Superior before him and some big brown church rising up, and a minute later, they were going under an overpass. Nearly panicking about switching lanes in the heavy traffic, Reuben honked his horn and swerved into the left lane. "Damn big city drivers," he muttered as he turned north toward downtown Marquette.

So many buildings. And a big hill that they climbed up. Why there had to be four or five blocks of businesses in this downtown, and a giant railroad trellis over the street with a sign that said "Marquette, Home of Northern Michigan University." A big sandstone building with a clock on it towered over them at a stoplight. And then once they were moving again, they passed churches and a skyscraper hotel and then blocks and blocks and blocks of houses until they eventually came to the end of the street, and there before them was the NMU football stadium where the Wildcats played. Frank had thought about trying out for the football team, but he was more into bodybuilding these days. Football players power-lifted to get big, but he wanted to look muscular, toned, and ripped. That was more attractive and impressive in his opinion.

Reuben turned left, passing the stadium, and came to a corner with a church and a gas station on it. Another skyscraper rose in front of them. It was an ugly brown, like something you'd see in New York City. It was apparently part of the college. Another couple of turns and they were on the campus, passing the University Center and some dorms and looking for signs to point them to the dorm where Frank was staying. Reuben swore when he took another wrong turn and started driving away from the college. Then they had to backtrack, and finally, Reuben told Frank to roll down a window and ask a student where Frank's dorm was. The kid pointed it out to him in the distance. Frank thanked him and his father headed to the dorm.

Soon they were in the dorm's parking lot, and Frank's stomach was full of butterflies. He couldn't believe it. He had always told himself he wanted to be big because then no one messed with you and you didn't have to be afraid of anything, but he was afraid he might not make friends at NMU. He'd had friends in Pelkie, but he'd known almost everyone in his class since kindergarten. Here he didn't know anyone. Most of his classmates had decided to go to Michigan Tech or Gogebic Community College because they were closer to home. He was the only one going to Northern Michigan University, but that was intentional. He wanted to be farther from home, to experience what the big city had to offer.

Reuben offered to go inside with Frank to make sure he was registered and everything, but they almost got into a fight when Frank insisted he could handle it himself. Frank didn't say so, but he didn't need his dad embarrassing him anymore than his ma.

"Fine," said Reuben. "I'll be back at five on Wednesday. Behave yourself."

"Thanks, Dad," said Frank. He got out of the truck and then waited awkwardly for his dad to drive off. He was still nervous, but he was also relieved to have his father leave. It was hard to be the cool man on campus when your potbellied father was with you.

Frank entered the main door of the dorm and went to the desk where he was told how to find his room. Since he'd missed the orientation he was supposed to go to, he wouldn't get to meet his roommate. He only knew the guy's name was John something. Oh well, they'd meet when classes started. Instead, he was assigned to a room with another guy named Brent.

Brent was lying on the bed when Frank entered the room. Frank said hello. Brent quickly sat up and said, "Whoa, Dude!"

"What?" said Frank.

"Is your name Arnold?" asked Brent.

"Frank," said Frank.

"Funny 'cause you look like Arnold Schwarzenegger," said Brent.

"I get that a lot," said Frank, smiling and puffing out his massive chest.

"Too bad you won't be my roommate," said Brent. "You must be a real chick magnet."

Frank didn't reply, just flung his bag on the floor and said, "I gotta take a piss." He was glad he wasn't going to be Brent's roommate. Even he couldn't help such a loser to get chicks. The guy looked like a stoner. Frank liked his heavy metal, but he wasn't into wearing band T-shirts and growing his hair long and looking like he hadn't showered in days. He hoped John would at least be clean.

Frank was just finishing up in the bathroom when the door on the other end opened and a blond dude walked in.

"Hey," said the guy when he saw Frank turn around. "I'm Shawn." He gave Frank his hand. Frank hadn't washed his yet, so he just said, "Hi, I'm Frank," and turned to the sink to wash his hands.

Shawn looked fairly normal. Not bad looking. Not nerdy. Not greasy. Not big, though.

"Who you talking to?" asked another guy, popping his head in the door. "Oh, hi."

"Hi, I'm Frank," said Frank.

"Mark," said the other suitemate. He was a smaller guy, but really handsome. Frank couldn't help wondering about him with his preppy clothes. Frank knew he could easily bench-press Mark.

"You guys ready to go?" asked Brent, now joining them in the bathroom. "Orientation starts soon."

"Sure," said Mark. "Let me get my binder."

Binder? Frank didn't have a binder. Were they supposed to take notes? Oh, well.

In another minute, Frank was following Brent, Mark, and Shawn down the hall, proud to see he could easily take any of them. So far, he was the biggest guy he'd seen on campus. They soon merged with a few more guys downstairs, and then they all walked across campus to Jamrich Hall for their first orientation session. On the way, the guys were all asking each other where they were from and what they did for fun. Not a few of them made comments about how big Frank was, but none of them had ever heard of Pelkie. When they passed a group of girls, one of the girls turned around to stare at Frank. He felt flattered but a little embarrassed when Brent elbowed him. Still, he had figured he'd get the same kind of attention here that he'd gotten in high school, maybe even more of it since NMU was like a few hundred times bigger than his school.

Orientation was boring. He had expected it would be. After he got done scoping out everyone in the lecture hall and deciding there wasn't anyone there he was very interested in, he kind of quit listening and started to wonder how he'd get off of campus for the nightlife without a car. Not that there wouldn't be lots of partying in the dorm, but he'd like to go somewhere he could have a little privacy now and then.

It had been a long afternoon, and Frank left the orientation pretty clueless about everything, but he knew he'd get the hang of things eventually. They were going to be fed supper in the dorm's cafeteria, but Mark said to the other guys, "Let's get out of here and do something fun."

"How?" asked Brent. "We don't have a car."

"I have a car," said Mark.

"Where will we go?" asked Shawn.

"The roller rink," said Mark. "My friends and I hang out there all the time."

"Oh, are you from Marquette?" asked Shawn.

"Negaunee," said Mark.

Shawn was from Iron Mountain and Brent was from Traunik so they didn't know where anything in Marquette was, but apparently, Negaunee people went to Marquette all the time. The guys were all glad to go joyriding around Marquette. They were also hungry, but Mark said you could get burgers and nachos at the roller rink.

Frank had no idea how they eventually got to the Peninsula Roller Rink. He didn't recognize anything from the way he and his dad had come into town. Marquette was so big he was kind of relieved he didn't have a car. His mother had always said she could never drive in Marquette because there was so much traffic. He didn't know who his suitemates would be, but even though Mark was obviously some kind of brainy math nerd since he carried around a binder and said he was majoring in calculus, Frank hoped they'd be friends. Most guys wanted to be his friend because, as Brent had said, he was a chick magnet, but he wondered if chicks were what Mark was after.

Frank was surprised when they entered the roller rink. It was all cement block and painted white and orange. There was a concession stand, but it didn't serve hamburgers, just snacks. They decided they could go out to eat later. For now, they wanted to get some roller skates. They went up to the counter where the skates were handed out and told the guy their shoe sizes. Once they had skates, they walked over to a bench along the wall and sat down to put them on.

It was kind of noisy inside. People were playing Pac-Man and a couple of other video games. Plus, music was playing. A disco ball in the middle of the rink was rotating along with some other colored lights. It was really cool. Maybe the coolest place Frank had ever been. He'd have loved it if he were thirteen because it looked like most of the kids there were just that—kids. There were a few parents—a couple skate was on right now, so mom and dad, the chaperones, were trying to be romantic skating together. Not a girl in the place looked older than high school age, and the boys were, well, teenage boys. Not what Frank was looking for at all if this was nightlife in Marquette.

"Come on," said Mark. "You all know how to skate, right?"

"I haven't skated in years, but I used to all the time as a kid," said Shawn, standing up. Not waiting for his new friends, he glided out onto the rink.

Brent stood up, looking uncertain on his skates, but he managed to get to the opening of the rink without a problem, and after a few hesitant steps, he began circling the rink as he picked up speed.

"You coming, Frank?" asked Mark.

"Sure," said Frank, standing up from the bench. For a moment, he nearly lost his balance and Mark reached out to steady him. He started trying to walk, but Mark said, "No, don't walk. Just slide your feet." He demonstrated up and down on the carpet of the hallway around the rink. Frank followed his advice and kind of got it.

"Come on," said Mark, and he led Frank onto the rink. "Hold onto the wall until you get used to it."

Frank felt like a dork holding the wall when ten-year-old girls were flying past him.

And then Roller Dog came out onto the rink. Instantly, thirty little kids were holding hands and skating behind the guy in a cheesy dog costume. Only halfway around the rink, Frank felt like an idiot being the sole adult on the floor. He didn't know where Mark had gone. He felt abandoned, still hanging onto the wall, trying to act cool, like he wasn't afraid of falling over. He thought the Roller Dog skate song would never end.

"Just be glad it's not 'The Hokey Pokey,'" said Mark, suddenly coming up behind him. "You getting the hang of it?"

"Yeah," said Frank.

"It's easier if you let go of the wall."

Frank let go and found he didn't fall over.

"Come on," said Mark, skating slowly in front of him as Roller Dog left and normal people returned to the rink. Frank glided a bit and was surprised to find he kept his balance. Before he knew it, he was picking up speed, but then suddenly, some smart-aleck kid came from out of nowhere and flew in front of him. Frank tried to slow down and came to a stop too soon and lost his balance, and then a body was on top of him.

"I'm so sorry," said someone, and he and Frank tried to untangle themselves. Somehow, the guy who had crashed into him got up first, and looking down at Frank, he extended his hand.

Frank looked up into the face of the most stunningly handsome man he had ever seen. His face was round but firm, masculine but gorgeous. His hair was dark brown and wavy and feathered. His lips were soft and pink, his eyebrows were perfect, and his smile was to die for.

"You okay?" asked this roller-skating god.

"Yeah," said Frank, accepting his hand to be pulled up.

"You stopped so fast I couldn't stop," said this roller-rink king.

"I know. I'm sorry."

"It's okay. Just be careful. I hope you're not hurt," said this prince on wheels.

"No, I'm fine," said Frank. He was back on his feet now.

The roller Adonis flashed him a stunning teeth-showing smile, turned around, and skated back to whatever roller-skating version of Mount Olympus he had descended from. He was gone in a flash, and Frank was alone again.

The DJ began playing "On the Wings of Love" as Frank skated forward, taking the curve perfectly and making his way back around the rink. He wasn't going as fast as everyone else, but he knew he was going with the flow now. He felt he had gotten into the groove, into the zone. He felt good. He hoped the roller god wasn't hurt. He realized the song was for another couple skate, but he was by himself. He kept waiting for the roller god to pass him again, but he didn't see him. He looked around for Mark, for Brent and Shawn, but he couldn't spot them. That was okay. When the song changed again, he felt like he was flying high. He felt all his worries and anxieties floating away. He went around and around and around the rink, as song after song played and the disco ball sent sparkling lights across the floor. John Travolta couldn't have had a better time on a Saturday night. He felt so good. He felt so relaxed. He loved roller skating.

Until he realized he had to go to the bathroom. He tried to slow down to exit the rink, but he was going too fast to make the first exit and too slow to time the second exit right, so he was back along the wall, hanging onto it as he backtracked to the second exit.

Frank managed to get off the rink, and then he managed to avoid the little girls who were not paying attention to where they were going, and he even managed to avoid the popcorn spilled all over the carpet as he made his way to the men's room. The carpet was easy to skate on, but once he got onto the linoleum in the bathroom, he wasn't sure how he'd manage to get up to the urinal.

Frank had a hard enough time just turning the corner in the bathroom. He was rather relieved to be alone and not have anyone see him trying to turn sideways. Mark had told him to glide, not walk, but he had to lift his feet to get in the right position facing the urinal. Once he managed that, he tried to glide closer to it, but he got so close the cold porcelain was touching his arms. Then he tried to back up, but he didn't know how and practically had to do a pushup against the wall above the urinal to move back. No matter what he did, the roller skates would not cooperate to get him just the right distance away.

"Shit," said Frank. "How are you supposed to take a piss wearing these things?" He kept trying to get closer to the urinal, but as soon as he thought he was in the right spot and reached down to unzip, he'd start sliding back.

"Need some help?" asked someone.

"How do you take a piss wearing roller skates?" Frank asked as he turned to see who had spoken.

It was the gorgeous guy, the one with the movie star features and wavy black hair—the roller rink god. Frank couldn't believe the guy was speaking to him.

"Let me help you," said the Adonis on wheels. He stepped up behind Frank and gave him a little push toward the urinal and held him in place. "Now," he said, "lower your right skate down so the stopper on the front of the shoe will hold you in place. Then you'll be fine."

Frank did as he was told, though it was hard to focus when the guy was holding onto his waist.

"Thanks," said Frank, not knowing what to do now.

"You okay?" asked Prince Skating.

"Yeah," said Frank.

The guy skated over to another urinal, politely leaving one between them, and went about doing his business.

Shit, thought Frank. *I can't pee with someone standing next to me.* He unzipped his pants and tried, but nothing would come out until he heard the guy flush, skate behind him, and turn on the sink faucet. Then he relaxed and was able to go. But he could hear the guy running the water at the sink for an awful long time. When Frank finished, he looked over as he was zipping up. The King of Skate 'n' Roll was combing out his feathered hair.

Frank turned and tried to skate across the bathroom, but he got more speed than he had intended and nearly collided with the sink.

"Watch out!" said the roller king, dropping his comb. He reached over, grabbed Frank by the arm, and helped him regain his balance.

"You okay?" asked the roller-skating god.

"Yeah, thanks," said Frank, reaching toward the sink to turn on the faucet while conscious that the guy was still holding onto his bicep.

"Damn, you're really built, man," said the guy, squeezing Frank's bicep. "You must work out a lot."

"Thanks," said Frank, used to getting respect from other guys, but this guy was different. Rather than let go of his arm after a squeeze, this guy ran his hand up onto Frank's shoulder and sort of rubbed it a little.

"Are you going to NMU?" asked Prince Skating. "I haven't seen you around campus."

Frank turned his head toward him, feeling uncomfortable, which seemed to be enough for the guy to quit touching him.

"I'm here for freshman orientation," said Frank.

"Oh," said the guy, smiling. "You're so big I thought you must be a senior. I'm starting my sophomore year."

Frank had finished washing his hands now and turned to look at the gorgeous man. He would have sworn the guy was a few years older than him. He was more solid, more filled out than the high school boys Frank knew.

"I took a few years off," said the guy, seeing Frank was checking out his build. "But now I'm more serious about my studies."

The skate god was standing between Frank and the paper towel dispenser.

"Can you give me a paper towel?" Frank asked.

"Oh, sorry," said Gorgeous-on-Wheels. "I guess I'm just a little intimidated to meet such a big guy as you."

Frank chuckled.

The roller god chuckled too. "So, you must be new to Marquette?"

"Yeah," said Frank. "I don't really know anyone here. A few guys from my dorm suggested we come here tonight. Other than that, I don't know anyone."

"I'd be happy to show you around," said the guy.

"Really? That would be cool," said Frank. He couldn't believe someone so handsome, someone who must be so very popular with the girls, was talking to him, a freshman.

"Let me give you my number," said Prince Skating.

Frank wondered if the guy had a pen or piece of paper. Frank didn't have either. But he didn't need to worry. The guy reached into his pocket, pulled out his wallet, and then pulled out a small piece of paper, obviously torn out of a notebook. Written on it was "Alan" and a phone number. Frank swore he could see several such pieces of paper in the guy's wallet.

"You're Alan?" asked Frank, though the answer was obvious.

"Yeah," said Alan. "What's your name?"

"Frank. Frank Jarvi."

"Nice to meet you, Frank," said Alan, giving him his hand to shake, but as soon as Frank touched it, Alan said, "Don't hurt me, big guy."

Frank laughed again. The feel of Alan's hand in his was electric, and for whatever reason, neither of them let go right away.

"Well, nice to meet you, Frank," said Alan, finally withdrawing his hand. "Give me a call when you get back to Marquette this fall. I'm going to have a party the first weekend school starts up and I'll make sure you get invited. There'll be lots of booze and girls there, not that you probably need help getting girls."

"Actually," said Frank, though he wasn't quite sure why, "I've never had a girlfriend."

Alan looked him in the eye for a second and then said, "That's okay. There are other ways to have fun." He flashed a smile.

"There you are," said Brent, coming into the bathroom. "Frank, we're ready to go. This place is lame."

"Well, I better let you go then, Frank," said Alan.

"Yeah. Thanks, Alan," said Frank, his skates feeling like they had grown roots because he didn't want to go. "It was great meeting you. I—I bet you don't have any trouble getting girls either with that hair."

As soon as he said it, Frank thought it must be the stupidest thing he had ever said, but Alan laughed, tapped him on his tricep, and said, "I'll see you around, Frank."

And then the gorgeous, roller-skating, movie-star-like-college-boy named Alan skated out of the restroom and Frank found himself not hearing a word as Brent babbled about how they were all going to Pizza Hut. Frank didn't care about pizza; he'd found what he'd come to Marquette for. He'd been afraid to admit it to himself before, but he had always known it was why he wanted to go to college so far from home.

His mother had been right. How are you gonna to keep 'em down on the farm after they've seen gay Marquette?

Homage to the Pilgrim

by R. H. Miller

◆❖◆

It's difficult to describe what it's like to grow up in the Midwest, fish muddy carp-and-catfish waters, and only dream of the lovely streams and lakes of the boreal North—to be that kid who caught bucketfuls of bullheads and only once in a while a bass or crappie. Nothing apotheosizes the world of the pages of *Field and Stream* or *Outdoor Life* like the drab existence of a poor kid in northwestern Ohio.

Yet eventually such a fishing life came within my reach. In the spring of 1961, I got my first teaching job at what was then the Michigan College of Mining and Technology, in the Upper Peninsula. I'd just finished an M.A., and Diane was pregnant with our first child. I signed on, practically sight unseen, for a year's stint as an instructor, and stayed for three years. At the suggestion of a friend who knew a little bit about this Upper Peninsula I was headed for, I read Bernard Malamud's *A New Life*, a hilarious academic novel based loosely on his bizarre experiences at Oregon State University at Corvallis, where the faculty of the English department mingled intellectualizing and a lot of craziness with the life of the outdoors. Even the advantage of Malamud's vision, which later proved to be accurate in scary ways, wasn't able to prepare us for what our New Life held.

At Michigan Tech I met my future colleague and fishing mentor, Sherwood Price. Since I had come to Houghton in the fall, it would be spring before I could begin fishing. In the winter I used to walk down the snowplowed streets, with their walls of white over three feet high, over to Sherwood's house, on Fifth Street, and in the upstairs spare bedroom I watched him tie trout flies of inexpressible delicacy. He fished only two patterns with any regularity: the Adams and the royal coachman, and those almost always in size twelve, less often in size fourteen, so at first my tying skills were limited to a few techniques peculiar to those patterns. Yet he wore a vest loaded with many different flies, even though in late middle age he had settled on these two. To this day I find myself, often to my disadvantage, fishing very few patterns. His habit was to tie his flies overdressed, with heavy, stiff hackles. At the end of our first lesson Sherwood gave me a few hooks, some hackle, and an old vise, and my new hobby began.

In those days, from my annual salary of $5,600, I would save up a few bucks and send in an order to Herter's, one of the most wonderful and most horrible businesses in the world. They were located in Waseca, Minnesota, and their catalogues were a hoot, one hundred per cent American baloney. Sometimes it took as long as six months to get an order filled, maybe even longer. Of course, your check was always cashed right away. The best time in the U. P. for fishing with flies is late May to late June, when things can get pretty exciting. I still have a couple of black-and-white photos from my blood-thirsty days showing full creels of rainbows, brooks, and browns taken from the Otter, my favorite river. Now, in the early stage of late age, I find myself content with a few fish a year, although I find it difficult not to think of fishing as first and last a blood sport. But as we age, we become content with less and less—fish, food, liquor, and sex.

My first flies were gross things, and I'd razor them apart so I could use the hooks over again, my finances being what they were, that is, godawful. But somehow out of all my efforts I managed to tie a few good ones, and by spring I was ready.

I'd scraped up enough money over the winter to pick up a bamboo rod ($6.50), Clevel line ($1.98), and a nondescript gray singleaction reel at a forgettable price. All I can remember about the reel is that it had a single large screw that held the spool in, and had the most raucous click, both ways. Diane sewed me a very nice vest, but it was so flimsy it did not last out the season.

When opening day came, I headed for the nearest accessible river, the Pilgrim. The rivers of the North, I believe, must have been named by great Old Poets—such enchanting names—Pilgrim, Firesteel, TwoHearted, Montreal, Misery, Gratiot, and my incomparable Otter, of which I have much to say further on.

The Pilgrim is a small stream that meanders from high ground down to Portage Lake, its course enhanced by manmade log cribs, stone dams, and the like. Because it flows into a sizeable body of water, which is also a part of Lake Superior, it has a respectable steelhead run every spring. On this opening day I had tied on a sponge-rubber bug and was hoping to attract some big trout. I knew steelhead were running, although I'd never seen one in my life.

I made my way through some snow patches down to a glide of about eighty feet. The water was high but a little clearer than it usually is this time of year, as I was to learn later, on opening days yet to come.

My efforts with the rod and level line were pretty pathetic. I'll spare you the sad details and say that I spent the better part of the wade up that run draped in the most ineffectual fly line I have ever owned.

I approached a small rock dam, above which was the Bridge Pool. Somehow, for once, my line rolled out in a decent forty-foot cast, and the sponge bug plopped down just a few feet beyond an old stump at the edge of the water. I watched it float toward me, just under the surface. I made a feeble attempt to get control of my line, which had drifted downstream and was billowing out around my legs in two huge loops.

Then I saw him. He eased out from under the stump. I judged him to be a good two feet long. I could see his head well enough to identify the kype of a cock fish. He turned at a right angle to the left of the lure to reveal, almost insolently, his brilliant pink lateral stripe. As the lure passed by him, he straightened himself and followed, drifting about two inches behind the bug. In a grand, leisurely manner he held his place in the current, then turned to the right, almost as if to say, "Here's the other stripe, dummy." He looked the bug over carefully, then turned, obviously insulted, and to a silent cadence swam back upstream to his hold below the stump.

Sweat trickled into my eye. My rod hand started to quiver uncontrollably. My knees buckled. I made a feeble effort to cast. The line went out about fifteen feet and hit the water like a beaver's tail. I realized that I had lost all control over my body, and I knew I had to get out of the water before I fell.

On the bank I tried to pull myself together as well as I could. Then I had a cigarette.

That evening I made my way back to the car, skunked. I scrambled about under the rear wheel for my keys (a trick learned from Sherwood) and headed the old Volkswagen back to Houghton.

I made many trips back to the Pilgrim but never saw another fish like that monster trout. On several evenings, the Bridge Pool gave me the fishing equivalent of hitting for the cycle—a brookie, a rainbow, and a brown. The banks offered ferns for my creel, trilliums lovely to look at. On a lovely summer afternoon, I watched a water ouzel dance in and out of its current. And long, deep, narrow runs past log cribs gave me moments as tense as Eric Ambler's heroes must feel when they confront death in a dark alley in Istanbul. Many times, I balanced on the edge of death awaiting the shock of the rise of a good trout. And it happened frequently enough to keep me poised on that edge, for I was in the grip of lust, a fever burning still.

The North Country Sun

by Raymond Luczak

◆❖◆

They dropped off a huge pile of the free weekly.
I lifted them into a yellow ink-dirty shoulder bag.
Banging against my bony body, the weight
felt as if it would saw off my arm. The paper
swelled with classifieds selling hand-me-down
appliances, furniture, snowmobiles, and cars.
Local stores blared their wares with big ads.
I always read the classifieds, wondering
why people would want to give away this or that.
What were their stories? But I never dwelled on
the strangers versed in terseness and phone numbers.
I had to buckle up and deliver to some 100 homes.
Up and down the streets, I trundled from door to door.
Sometimes I caught hints of stories yet to be finished
through their front windows when I slipped the paper
between their screen door and front door: a lonely lamp
revealing a mass market romance novel left
abandoned on a small table next to a plush chair,
or a dog barking ferociously in the window with no one
nearby, or a growing pile of rain-mucked *Daily Globe*s.
Most of the time I never saw anyone when I swung by.
I conjured in my half-shadowed imagination their faces.
Their features were never fleshed out in my mind's eye.
What were their names? Where did they work?
Did they shop at Lopez's IGA? Had I ever seen them
at Pamida? Or were they not Catholic? All I saw
were well-maintained driveways, crooked porches,
meticulously machine-shoveled snowy pathways,
unkempt grasses that crowned basements.
When I dropped off my last copy, my mind had gone
blank. I didn't know I was learning to find ghosts.

Jacquart's

by Raymond Luczak

across the street from Ironwood Catholic High School

After peering often into its phantom windows,
I finally went after school inside the store-cave.
Various backpacks, made of dyed burlap
and curly leather straps, mountained the shelves.
Slashes of light angled from the tin ceiling
blessed each stitched detail I dared to finger.

My maroon-colored backpack cost a princely $18.
I had saved up my meager paychecks from
delivering the *North Country Sun* every Tuesday.
The nerve-numbing tingles inside my shoulder
from carrying the freebie newspapers were nothing
compared to the weight of dreams I'd packed since

the day I realized wearing hearing aids on my chest
made me an exotic, a foreigner with a nasal voice
that didn't always enunciate consonants.
Though I could speak English, I was a language
in search of translation. My backpack would carry
the dictionary of my future self in another country.

A. Lanfear Norrie School

by Raymond Luczak

1917-2016

Its playground had everything:
two long basketball courts
with high chain-link fences,
grassy inclines for climbing,
a boxy jungle of bars and ladders,
a long row of rubber swings,
a steep paved slope perfect for biking
straight down into the baseball field
that doubled as a skating rink in the
    winter.
Even the sidewalk facing the win-
    dows

and the walls of the school provided
a familiar staccato rhythm to our
    bike rides.
Mornings the sun always trailed
    behind us.
Afternoons we always chased the
    sun
among the dandelions already whis-
    kering
away. So many daydreams lay buried
here. The winds play kickball
with each other. No one catches.

Waters of Change

by Becky Ross Michael

"I call top bunk," said Steven.

"No, I want it!" countered his younger brother, Rory.

"Take turns," their mother suggested.

The boys were half-brothers with different fathers. At fifteen, Steven was five years older than Rory and lived with his father during the school year. But breaks from school offered much-anticipated time together for adventures. This summer, the three were staying in a cabin near Tawas City, Michigan, where Mom had spent favorite parts of her childhood.

"Let's explore!" urged Steven after unpacking.

The trio piled back into the car and took off as the warm sun sank. They followed a winding road toward Lake Huron and the Tawas Point landmark, a majestic, white lighthouse.

"We sure had fun out here when I was a kid," Mom remembered in a wistful tone. "Let's tour the lighthouse and swim tomorrow."

"I'm hungry," shouted Rory, patting his stomach.

"We'll grab dinner in town and walk on the pier."

•••

By the time they finished eating, the sun had disappeared. A rising full moon guided their stroll to the city marina, where boats of all sizes bobbed on the bay.

"I'm beat from the long drive today," Mom said. "I'd like to get to sleep early and make the first lighthouse tour in the morning."

With car windows open, the music of frogs and crickets accompanied them on their return to the cabin. "You guys are growing up so fast," said Mom. "I'm not sure what kind of excitement I can drum up for the next time we're together."

As their vehicle approached the stretch of road near the cabin, Mom slowed and pointed to the left. "Look there!" she yelled. "Years ago, your grandpa told me about a small inland lake around here called Lake Solitude. I just caught a glimpse of the moon reflecting off it through the trees."

Steven and Rory craned their necks but saw nothing unusual in the dense forest.

Back inside the cabin, the boys flipped a coin to decide bunks.

"Lights and all devices off," Mom directed. "My alarm's set for early, and I'm not even going to read the thriller I brought along before I go to sleep."

•••

The two boys soon stared into the dark, listening to their mother's light snores from behind her closed door down the hallway.

"I know you're awake," Steven's whispered voice rose to the bunk above.

"Guess I slept too much in the car," answered Rory. "And it feels kind of weird, trying to sleep up here in the air."

"I've got an idea," said Steven, "if you want to go on a quest."

"Like what?"

"Let's go exploring and look for Lake Solitude. That light Mom saw through the trees wasn't very far down the road."

"Are you sure that's a good idea?" Rory hedged.

"Come on! I'll take my phone, and we can use flashlights."

"Well...okay."

A few minutes later, the brothers, now clad in jeans and sweatshirts, walked along the road's graveled shoulder. Their flashlight beams led the way.

"How will we know where to head into the woods?" asked Rory.

"When Mom yelled and pointed, I'd just seen a billboard for a miniature golf place. That'll show us where to turn."

Rory's flashlight caught it first. High above the saplings, a tall sign featured a mammoth, 3D golf ball.

"Let's go," Steven said. He veered into the low brush on the opposite side, with Rory close behind him.

Soon the vegetation gave way to towering pines, shutting out the stars and moon. Strong odors from decaying leaves and what smelled like a dead, rotting animal assaulted their noses. Nearby, an owl screeched a loud warning.

Coming over a rise, Steven halted. "Down there! That must be Lake Solitude. I see a light but not from the moon."

"What's that?" Rory hissed. "The light's moving around."

"Not sure, but I've heard that some people fish at night. Let's check it out."

Navigating the route toward the shore of the narrow lake was a challenge for the boys, with patches of sharp thorns and a network of narrow, muddy rivulets. The temperature had dropped, and a heavy mist now covered the ground. Every so often, a rustling noise sounded from the dark woods, and the brothers moved closer together.

"They're both gone," Rory finally said through chattering teeth.

"What do you mean?"

"The lake and moving light. They're gone!"

Steven gazed around. "We must've gotten off course on our way down the hill." He glanced at the sky, seeing the moon's corona through a thin layer of clouds. "This way," he said. "I think it was this direction from the moon."

After hiking in circles, Steven finally admitted they were lost. "Sorry," he said, "I shouldn't have insisted we go exploring."

"Could you call Mom?" asked Rory in a wobbly voice.

"I don't have a signal out here," Steven confessed. "And my battery's low. I forgot it hadn't been charged all day."

Rory took a deep, steadying breath. "Let's switch off our flashlights."

"Why would we do that?"

"Maybe we could see that moving light better."

The younger boy's idea worked! A bright orb appeared from the inky night, hovering back and forth like a fat firefly.

"Let's go," said Steven. "It doesn't look far."

As they neared the narrow ribbon of sand at the lake's edge, a figure appeared from the fog. A stocky man wearing old-fashioned short pants and tights held a lantern up and away from his body. His dark jacket decorated with golden buttons hung open over a plain white shirt. The man's hair looked wet and matted. As clouds moved across the sky, occasional shafts of silvery moonlight revealed the hulking shape of a dark boat lying on its side behind him.

Steven grabbed Rory's arm. "Wait! Who's that?"

"He looks strange, and I think he's crying," whispered Rory. "Maybe he's hurt."

Steven gulped. "Hello, sir," he called as they approached.

"Help us, please!" the man pleaded. "I cannot find my wife and daughter!"

"Were you fishing?" asked Steven.

"No, the storm!" he answered. "Our captain tried to follow Lake Huron's shore. We must have hit a rock!"

"But this is an inland lake. The open waters of Lake Huron are way over there, beyond the road," Steven pointed.

"Road?" the man answered in a faint voice. He now stared at the boys. "Who...where...?"

As he struggled to form a sentence, the stranger's voice and image slowly faded into the mist, along with the glow of his lantern.

Within moments, the man and the boat were nowhere to be seen. As if on cue, the clouds above them scudded across the sky, exposing a bright moon.

"Geez! Did you see that?" Rory exclaimed.

"He disappeared!" answered Steven. "Let's get the heck out of here!"

The two boys made a beeline for the road.

"What should we tell Mom?" called Rory, breathless.

"Not a thing. How could we explain what we saw? And we weren't supposed to be out here!"

After turning back onto the road near the golfing sign, Steven's pace slowed. Rory finally caught up with his brother.

Steven loudly cleared his throat. "The more I think about it," he announced, "that must have been a fisherman or maybe a local tour guide."

"Yeah," Rory agreed, "the fog probably played a trick on us."

Back at the cabin, they left muddy shoes on the porch and slipped into their bunks to the sound of their mother's steady breathing.

•••

"Hey, sleepyheads," Mom chirped in the morning. "Breakfast is ready, and the lighthouse awaits."

Eyes half-open, they followed the welcome smell of pancakes into the kitchen. After serving the food, Mom showed them a tourist pamphlet she had read while making coffee. "Look at this."

"Uh-huh," answered Steven, pouring syrup.

"It says they've decided Lake Solitude was originally part of the main lake!" Mom exclaimed. "They think Lake Huron's levels probably receded over time and left that small basin of water behind."

Rory kicked Steven under the table.

"Oh! Why do they think that?" Steven asked.

"Years ago, they found a rotting boat there, mostly covered in sand."

"Why's that unusual?" said Rory.

"Because it was much too large for use on Lake Solitude, which is at least a half-mile from Lake Huron," she answered, taking a sip of her coffee. "Some legends connect it to the French explorer, LaSalle, from the 1600s. Other stories say it was a passenger boat, shipwrecked in a storm. Maybe we could explore that mystery light, one night," Mom suggested with a smile. "Some people even claim to see ghosts."

Steven pushed his plate away. "We'll need our sleep," he said. "And walking around in the middle of the night doesn't sound like much fun."

"Right," Rory agreed. "We should probably keep our exploring to the daytime."

Mom glanced back and forth between her sons, shocked they would turn down a chance to unearth a mystery or see a ghost. "If you saw a ghost, that would be an experience you'd never forget! At least think about it."

"All this fresh air makes me want to go to bed early." Steven yawned and ignored Rory's eyes. "In fact, I'm still tired."

"Me too," Rory agreed. "I don't want to go out in the dark, hunting for a ghost and his mysterious boat."

Mom shrugged. "You guys always surprise me. I'm perfectly happy spending the nights inside reading a scary book. But I don't want you to feel like our times together are boring."

Rory shook his head. "They're not."

"Never," said Steven, with a knowing grin.

DRIVING A HOLE.

Historical · Driving a Hole for Dynamite circa 1860

NONFICTION

The Writing Is on the Wall

by Tamara Lauder

◆❖◆

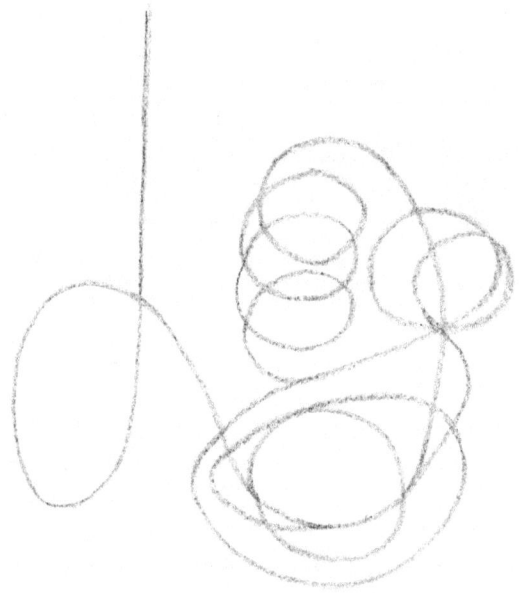

I stared at the stark white plaster living room wall in front of me. At my eye level, there was nothing interesting about it. It was relatively smooth, and devoid of any real color or creativity. It was the wall to the left side of a large archway leading from the living room into the dining room, near a door leading to the backyard that was rarely used. Surely some color and essence of life was in order.

I stood there, crayons in hand, pondering which color to start with. I don't recall exactly which hue won my approval, but my masterpiece is clear in my mind to this day. It contained a long initiating line that swung to the left and ended as a doodle. That particular line stood apart from the rest of the piece, giving it a clear sense of purpose. Starting from above, at the level of my highest four-year-old right arm's reach, it de-

scended down, around to the left, and then up again to the right-hand side to become the beginning of the main collaboration of swirls and circles, one after another.

I stood back and processed my purposeful crayon flow. *My, what fine work,* I thought. The wall, once looking alone, bare, and out of place in a room otherwise full of furniture, windows, and pictures, finally held its prominent position. The wall after all, helped make an arch. It should have appeal. It should make a statement to the naked eye.

"What are you doing in there?" My mother called from the kitchen.

I heard my first, middle, and last name as my mother walked on the hard, oak, dining room floor on her way to my temporary living room art studio.

"Mommy, look what I did." My face beaming and crayons in hand, I stood in front of the transformed wall, processing my artistic handiwork. There was no mistaking the interior decorator.

My mother's footsteps quieted when she reached the carpet of the living room, just on the other side of the arch. She stopped and stared at the once boring white wall, now covered with colorful swirls to the right, and the descending line going to the left. The highest point of my creation came up to her waist—a perfect level for viewing when sitting on the couch or recliner.

"Oh my!" she said.

"Isn't it pretty mommy?"

My older sister ran into the room when she heard my mother's expression. "Oh my, isn't that pretty," she said.

My mother and sister exchanged looks, like they frequently did. My sister made a quirky giggle and smiled, but my mother was silent. I assumed they were overwhelmed with the beauty of my masterpiece. I remember how happy I felt. *I will be an artist someday*, my child's mind said. It was clarity at its finest, in its pure, raw form. Both my creation and my futuristic goals made me very happy. They both made me smile.

I remember that morning like it happened yesterday. There was significance to that initiating line that went to the left, still vivid in my mind to this day. That line descended down, then up and over to a section full of spirals and circles, which if reversed, all lead down and back up again to the starting point. That first line was simple, too simple to be of any interest for most people. The section to the right was full of complexity, similar to life. The wall, unfortunately, ended up white again—someone else's uncreative handiwork, no doubt.

Since that morning of my first vivid recall of creativity, my life has followed a course similar to my childhood masterpiece—simple to complex and back again. I am an artist today. The writing was on the wall. It was just wiped clean before I was old enough to read.

Dementia Is:

by Tamara Lauder

Learning to
love someone you don't know;
care for someone,
you didn't choose
to spend your life with.

Living with a stranger,
different times of the day—
wandering, perseverating about,
things of small.

Morning comes with new hope,
but eve sets it all straight,
as glimpses of
the person you know
fade away with the light.

Realizing,
accepting,
the one you knew,
the one you married,
the one you loved is gone.

Change is all there is.

The Good Evening

by Maria Vezzetti Matson

◆❖◆

Out of the blue, my brother states, "I got to head home now. It's a long drive, and I don't want to drive in the dark." The Sun is beginning to descend, and I knew there would be plenty of time for his drive off the island to the mainland. Traffic is rarely a factor in Michigan's Upper Peninsula, especially in our neck of the woods, the Jacobsville area on Copper Island.

"Stay and watch the sunset," I beg. "Pretty please." Our camp has been legendary for the sunsets since my father-in-law bought it in 1952. If you seek a pleasant view, look about you. Do you see much development in the area? There are no skyscrapers here cutting out our view. You can even make out specific trees on the opposite shore. "Come on, stay. I'll get you a cup of coffee. Relax and enjoy." I head into the kitchen to fix him a coffee.

Exiting the kitchen, I let the screen door slam behind me to capture attention. It works! Everyone turns to look my way. My brother chats happily with other relatives as the sky above reflects light, orange and pink tinges on the calm waters. Our camp is built on a small hill. We have a well-manicured grass lawn leading down to the untamed natural shoreline abundant with wildflowers, tall grasses, shrubs, and trees. Looking westward through the trees and over the waterway, we view the wispy, colorful clouds that cling to the horizon.

"Do you notice the subtle change of hues as the sun lowers in the sky?" I ask. "I can't tell you how many folks have enjoyed the sunsets here. Take a moment, brother, and enjoy 'good' evening at the end of your 'good' day."

The sphere-shaped crimson object in the sky seems unreal. However, we understand that the red sunsets are the strange side effects of the smoke from distant wildfires. We all stand watching the deep, hazy red sun begin to disappear.

"Pay attention, starting now," I say, "Ten, nine, eight, observe and remember your physics. The earth is rotating, and the sun isn't sinking." I have to pace myself to time this perfectly. "Seven, six, five," with a dramatic sweep of my hands, I ask, "Isn't the sun sinking?"

No one replies as all eyes follow the plunging red ball, the sun. "And, four, three, two, one," I add quickly. Now, the top sliver of the red sphere, the sun, totally disappears. "Day's done!"

My brother applauds and gives me a nod of approval. "Thank you for sharing this awesome moment with me. It was worth watching." He sips his coffee and then checks his watch.

"Hey, anyone want to join me for the moonrise now?" I ask. "I understand it will be ultra-special tonight." I hope my clever rhyme will tempt him. "Hey, brother, stay. The moon will light your way to Oskar Bay."

"Yup, it will be a superior view," adds my sister-in-law. "We can ride to the breakwaters at White City and watch the Super-Duper Blue Moon rise. It will be a short distance to drive and a shorter waiting period."

My brother shakes his head, hands me his empty coffee cup, and heads toward his car. Our husbands walk with him and leave us ladies alone in the twilight.

"Let's clean up the kitchen, grab a jacket, and head out ourselves," I plead. "It'll be ladies' night out for a good moon-watching evening. Romantic, eh." We both laugh and head into the camp to clean up and prepare ourselves for the moonrise adventure.

The drive leaving our property includes a mile of dirt road. We constantly search for deer, turkeys, wolves, snapping turtles, and bears. Dusk is their favorite time to walk out of the woods. No animal sightings this time. We approach the main road and turn south to White City. We laugh as we recall the first time a guest came with us to this location, "Wait," she said, "I need to put on my lipstick if you're taking me to White City."

At one time, White City was the hot spot for dancing, music, picnics, and a real tourist destination. Putting on your lipstick before a visit would have been appropriate—but that was over 100 years ago. Locals still flock to the white sand beach on hot days in that part of this now-deserted location.

The county park road to Keweenaw Bay and the breakwater entrance for the South entry of Portage Canal create challenges for a driver. I slowly swerve to avoid the deep ruts in the road. We are shocked to see parked automobiles and a dozen people sitting on the beach.

"Guess other folks like the viewing spot, too," my sister-in-law remarks. We put on our jackets, add a can of soda pop to our pockets, and begin to walk toward the beach.

Checking my watch, I note it is nearing 8:30 p.m. "What time is moonrise?" She goes to use Professor Google on her phone. However, no cell service is available.

A short distance away, we watch a man set up a tripod, tighten his camera, and check his watch. "He'll know the answer," I say as we walk toward him.

Behind us lay a vast expanse of Lake Superior's surprisingly still waters. The nearest land mass consists of the Abbaye Peninsula, with the Huron Mountains beyond them. Mount Arvon, Michigan's highest point, juts upward on the horizon. The distance is too great to notice any details like trees or buildings.

We approach the man with the camera and initiate a conversation. "Are you here to document the moonrise? How much longer do we have to wait? What can you tell us about the Super Blue Moon? When will—"

He stops the questions by raising his hands and asks us a question. "Am I on Candid Camera? What is with all the questions? Who told you I would be here?"

We take a step backward and prepare to scat, but to our surprise, he lets out a lengthy sigh and begins to answer our questions.

"Ladies, you are about to experience a rare viewing as you watch a Super Moon that is also a Blue Moon. The moon will be seven to fourteen percent closer to the earth and dark volcanic areas, plus the moon's craters will be easily visible. The full phase of the moon is called the perigee. It's the point when the orbit is closest to the Earth. If you were in my class, you would know all of this and the exact timing of its appearance. You have exactly," he stops to glance at his watch; then he glares at us and says, "You have two minutes to find a comfortable spot away from me for this viewing." He rudely uses his two hands to swat us away like mosquitoes. "Good evening," he grunts.

We mumble "thank you" as we disappear from his view and giggle over the incident. To his credit, the moonrise starts on time.

"Guess he is right," I say as I glance at my watch. The bright, large, rounded Moon begins to appear. "One, two, three, what do I see?" I say as my mind adjusts to the fact this is Moon, not Sun rising from the east.

I continue counting, "Four, five, six," but pause to take in the beautiful scene. Moon rises quickly and in all its splendor, casting orange moonbeams over the waters that reach in our direction. A golden ladder of dancing moonlight extends toward us over Lake Superior.

Listening to the lapping waves with my eyes closed, I can hear Mother Earth saying with each wave softly brushing the shore, "Good evening, good evening, good evening."

Dorothy's Apple Pie

by Ellen Lord

The busyness of summer has ebbed, and the jeweled tones of autumn are seeping into the trees. I hike up to the ridgeline of our land and follow a deer path through the woods to a wild apple tree. She stands majestic in the afternoon sun and her branches are laden with fruit. I harvest as much as I can carry, then smile as two squirrels scold me from a high perch. I think about years past, how my grandmother would take us foraging in the fields and forests around Trout Creek, Michigan. How she loved nature's bounty—and how we loved her cooking.

I decide to make an apple pie from scratch. No shortcuts. No store-bought crust. I find my old recipe book and there it is: *Grandma's Apple Pie.* The card is smudged, handwritten with one notation in 1951, *use Crisco if lard is not available.* I have Crisco! I bought it last week along with a bushel of Northern Spy. Yes, perfect apples for pie.

I remember, she would put on a full bodice apron, tied in the back, handmade from a flour sack; two pockets, one with an embroidered handkerchief— the other for miscellaneous treasures. She would set out: bowls, flour, salt, lard, a cup for cold water with one ice cube, rolling pin, and a cloth to work the dough. At least three pie plates, never just one.

She did everything by 'feel'. You couldn't trust what she wrote down, (use *your hands, you'll know when it feels right).* She would peel, slice, sugar the apples and add a splash of vanilla (she also used that for perfume!) Finally, she'd roll out the dough, pile in the fruit, dot the finished apples with butter and crimp the top crusts with her thumb. All three pies were loaded into her wood stove to bake until done.

My god, the process seemed to take forever but I loved watching her work. The aroma of apple pie permeated the house, wafted out the kitchen window. Everyone waited for the old timer to 'ding' then watched, longingly, as she placed the pies near an open window where they would cool into the afternoon. (*Now, nobody touches these until after supper!)* Such sweet agony.

•••

I also remember stories she told of the Great Depression. Grandma Dorothy's house was on the Hobo Circuit. Vagabonds would ride the train and get off at the Trout Creek station. They'd slink to an encampment down by the mill pond to stay a few days, depending on work and, hopefully, the benevolence of local ladies. There were secret signs on trees and fence posts to guide them to safe houses. Grandma would have them shovel snow, cut wood, and stack it by the house for the price of a meal and of course, a piece of her county-renowned apple pie. They usually came during the day when the family men were gone. I wonder if she ever talked much to those transient souls—probably not; she was kind but wary, known to have a loaded shotgun by the back door.

Dorothy had been a gentle, refined, downstate lady from Kalamazoo but she became a bit hardscrabble in the northern wilds. She birthed eight children, two of them stillborn. She lost the last one, a little girl, in the winter of 1938. The men were snowbound at the logging camp, and no one could summon the doctor.

Of course, that was a long time ago; Dorothy died in 1981. We still have the family home. Pictures of ancestors adorn the walls and bookshelves. Old stories are revisited like familiar guests on holidays and seasonal interludes. We explore the Ottawa National Forest, fish the rivers and lake— forage for wild delights. I do most of the cooking. The kitchen hasn't changed much.

On this day, I am alone but I expect there will be some company coming for supper. I take the full bodice apron from a hook by the stove, tie it in the back and start setting out the ingredients for apple pie—at least three.

North Country Connection

by Ellen Lord

◆❖◆

—for the Crew of Wolf Line Construction

We have waited so long for fiber optics
in this back country! They come bringing
more of the world via synapse and cable.
30 people can be on devices now in your
home, says the bearded young man
in the tuque. He's from the boundary
waters of northern Minnesota.
We both like the bite of winter, how it feels
to breathe iced air and trek in the snow.
Rare sun-spangle glistens the pinewoods,
a welcome reprieve from lake-effect sky.
This crew works our road in twos or threes,
some solo. Outdoor guys: hard hats
and Carhartt's, at home in this climate—
a seasoned crew.
I'm a lone wolf, he smiles and winks.
I like the easy camaraderie, how they step
aside and nod as I walk by—
for so much of the time, I feel invisible.
How welcome, this interlude from solitude,
this spontaneity of kindness.

Traveler

by Ellen Lord

—for Byron

I remember my brother before his accident
how his eyes were the blue of a north
country sky. His nimble body could win
a race with ease—
He had a transient magnificence
but I was left unsettled for years—
after he didn't emerge from his coma.
All that promise and shine gone. Just gone.
Now, decades later, his memory
still lives in my poems.
As I gaze up into the fractals of sunlight
in this mesic hardwood forest, I wonder—
where does a soul go at the end of a life?
And why, of course, always why—
and why not?
I want to believe that the soul is a traveler,
unfettered like a cumulus cloud, adrift
in an eternity of blue—
always and forever morphing
into something better.

One Last Chance

by Jodi Perras

(Based on a true story)

"Frederick, when you asked for permission to come back from Nebraska, you promised no more trouble."

"Yes, Your Excellency."

The Rt. Reverend Frederick Eis, Bishop of the Roman Catholic Diocese of Sault Ste. Marie-Marquette, peered down at Frederick Sperlein. The younger priest shared the bishop's first name and his Germanic ancestry, but not his sterling reputation.

"And yet, ever since I appointed you pastor at St. Mary's in Rockland, I have heard almost nothing but bad reports about you."

"Your Excellency, please."

The younger priest held his hands in a prayer-like position, his ruddy face looking up at the bishop, whose chair was set precisely two inches higher than his guest's. The bishop barely paused his lecture.

"You abandoned your church a month ago, ostensibly to seek medical treatment in Milwaukee. You didn't ask my permission. You also didn't wait for a replacement to arrive."

"Yes, Your Excellency, but..."

"I'm not finished," the bishop interrupted calmly, holding the priest in a silent stare. Nearing his fifty-ninth birthday, the bishop was twenty-five years older than Sperlein. Eis had been born in the Kingdom of Prussia in 1843, immigrating to the United States with his family twelve years later. As an adolescent in Michigan's western Upper Peninsula, he'd been taught Latin and French by a missionary priest who saw his potential.

The bishop fingered the gold-plated, jeweled crucifix attached to the buttons on the chest of his black robe. The robe's magenta piping signaled to everyone his bishop's rank. His clothing was immaculate. His desk in perfect order. Every hair on his head was in place, despite the late afternoon hour. He pulled a newspaper clipping from a file on his desk.

"And when I dismissed you, here's what the newspapers reported: 'In reply to the threat that if necessary a sheriff would be employed to dispossess him, the priest declares that when the officer arrives, he will not dare to remove a priest, who will be found at the altar clad in his sacerdotal vestments.'"

The bishop paused and peered at the young priest over the paper. Father Sperlein tried to stay calm.

"It continues: 'Father Sperlein vows he will carry his case to the highest ecclesiastical authority before complying with the bishop's mandate.' Is that an accurate account?"

"Well..."

"I sent Father Becker to replace you, to ensure that the people's needs would be met. But you refused to accept my decision; is that right?"

"I would not describe it that way..."

"And when you returned to Rockland, you rallied the parishioners against Father Becker. Some might say you re-instated yourself as their priest, something only I, the bishop, can do. This put Father Becker in a quandary ... does he stay at St. Mary's or return here to Marquette? Is that any way to treat your brother priest?"

Father Sperlein's face was turning deep red, his obedience and deference evaporating with each question. Although he worked within the church hierarchy, he appreciated the American ideals of liberty, equality, and fraternity. *Typical Prussian*, he thought. *Lording his power over everything and everyone.*

"If you would let me have a word," the priest said, raising his voice. "You've hardly given me a chance to speak."

"I will invite you to explain yourself," Bishop Eis replied, "but only if it ends in your asking for forgiveness. And only then will I consider reinstating you as priest."

"As I said, I would like to explain."

"Under the conditions I have established?"

Sperlein stared at the floor, tapping his foot and squeezing his fists.

"Your Excellency, God knows I need forgiveness. If you will let me speak, I will seek both your forgiveness and Our Lord's."

"Then proceed."

"You know that I was ordained ten years ago by Bishop Vertin. Four years later, he asked me to serve the missions in Nebraska. But once there, I found myself in the middle of a raging church battle."

"I read your file when you asked to return to Michigan. I'm familiar with the Nebraska situation."

Both men fell silent. From the corner, they could clearly hear the ornate, black walnut Lenzkirch wall clock ticking. Crafted with wood from the Black Forest, it had been a gift from the bishop's family when he was consecrated in 1899. Eis began preparing for the priesthood in Milwaukee in 1861 but, after the American civil war broke out, Bishop Baraga sent him to Quebec to complete his studies.

Through the open window arose the clip-clop and creaking of a horse and buggy passing on the street. The two men's eyes met in a steely staring match.

"With all humility, Your Excellency, I beg you to let me tell the tale."

"Very well, then," said the bishop, waving his hand to signal the priest should continue.

"Bishop Bonacum assigned me to St. Leo's Church in Palmyra. The parishioners there never accepted me, no matter what I tried. They did everything they could to undermine me."

Bishop Eis interrupted the younger priest.

"Our job is not to be popular, Frederick. Our job is to act as Christ's presence among the faithful, administering the sacraments, admonishing them when necessary and comforting them when they need comfort."

The priest sighed but continued.

"I asked for a transfer, believing any other parish would be better. And, oh, was I wrong. When I arrived at the next church—St. Andrew's in Tecumseh—the parish trustees gave me a key to the church but not the rectory.

"I went to meet with the bishop, and then they locked me out of the church, too. On my return, I had to chop my way in with an ax. They didn't care that I needed the host and holy oils to administer last rites to a dying woman."

"I'm sorry it came to that," Bishop Eis said, "but I fail to see how this relates to you abandoning your parish here."

"Your Excellency, it has quite a lot to do with it. If you'll permit me to finish?"

"Very well."

"The trustees had me arrested. They tossed my belongings into the street and put new locks on the church and the rectory. When I tried to enter, their guard punched me in the face. But on Palm Sunday, I proudly wore a black eye. I became a symbol of the blows Our Lord suffered to save us from our sins."

"Frederick, let's not equate your suffering with the death of our Savior and Lord. Let us agree you had a difficult time in Nebraska."

"Did you know that I was jailed and found guilty of trespassing and destruction of property?"

"Yes, I am aware. It's here in your file." The bishop pointed to the thick folder on his desk. "And what about your parishioners? While you were behind bars, who ministered the sacraments to them?"

Father Sperlein wrinkled his brow and glared at the bishop.

"Some stood by me. About a dozen came on Sundays, when I offered Mass in the jail. Bishop Bonacum also visited me, but he told me to get myself out. He knew the situations he was sending me into but did nothing when I begged for his help. That's when I appealed to you to allow me to return here."

"Frederick, your troubles didn't begin in Nebraska."

"I beg your pardon?"

"In 1894, Bishop Vertin removed you from a parish in Manistique after an altercation involving you and two women."

Father Sperlein raised his hands in self-defense.

"A misunderstanding, I can assure you."

Bishop Eis pulled out another newspaper clipping.

"At Manistique on Friday last Mrs. Krause and her daughter attacked Rev. Fr. Sperlein on the street and scratched his face and pulled his hair, and misused him in a general way. The church will investigate."

"Truly, Your Excellency, you can see I was the victim in that instance and not a perpetrator."

"That's not what our investigation found. Bishop Vertin next sent you to St. George's in Bark River, is that right?"

"Yes."

"But you were there less than two years when you left for Nebraska. Was that your choice or Bishop Vertin's?"

"I would say it was a mutual decision," the priest answered, looking down at the floor.

"Ah, so I see here in your file. You've told me what happened in Nebraska, which brings us to this year, when you asked to return. I thought long and hard about that. You know I was a priest here for nearly thirty years before becoming bishop."

"Yes, Your Excellency."

"I had heard the stories. About your temper. About your tendency to disappear from time to time. And, of course, I'd heard much about your time in Nebraska, though not all the details you've shared with me today. So, when I received your request, I had to seek the Lord's will. What was God calling me to do? And do you know what he said?"

"No, Your Excellency."

"He spoke to me through the story of the prodigal son. I saw the father welcoming back his wayward son with open arms. And so, I welcomed you back. But within two years, you abandoned your people."

"Please let me explain."

"I thought I had already done so."

"Your Excellency," the priest said. "It was as if I'd fallen into a deep cavern. I could no longer serve St. Mary's parishioners in my condition, walking about town at night like a mad man. I could not administer the sacraments or preach a homily. All the struggles in Nebraska finally hit me. I had nothing more to give. I feared ..."

The priest looked at the bishop with tears in his eyes.

"I feared that I would take my own life. That's why I left and checked myself into the Milwaukee hospital."

"And what did you learn while you were there?"

Father Sperlein shifted in his chair, avoiding the bishop's gaze. Though it was early October, the room suddenly seemed uncomfortably warm.

"What did I learn?"

"Yes, Fred. What did you learn?"

"Well, I learned that I needed help. I learned that ... I needed rest and treatment for exhaustion."

"And were you treated for anything else?"

"What do you mean?"

"Fred, I think there's something you're not telling me. Is there something you'd like to share that would explain your behavior these past several years? Anything to assure me that you've learned something, and it won't happen again?"

"I can assure you it won't happen again, Your Excellency. I give you my word."

The bishop rolled his eyes, ever so slightly.

"You gave me your word when you returned from Nebraska."

"Yes, but ..."

"Frederick, I know you are holding back. I have had enough experience in the confessional and in counseling our brother priests to know when someone is not being forthright with me."

Once again, the clock's tick tock filled the room.

"Here's what I propose. I need to think and pray overnight. I suggest you do the same. Come back tomorrow morning, and then you can answer my question once again. Father Pinten will find a time on my schedule and arrange a room in the bishop's residence for you to sleep tonight. Miss Linnenberg serves breakfast each morning at eight o'clock sharp. That is all."

Father Sperlein stood and bowed to the bishop, then turned, and walked slowly through the door. After quietly making arrangements with the bishop's private secretary, he stepped outside and walked down the hill toward Lake Superior. A steamship loaded with iron ore had just left the docks, headed for Cleveland, Gary, or Chicago. He thought of the men and young boys in his parishes who worked deep in the mines each day. He recalled the lumberjacks working in the frozen woods all winter, returning home in spring to work twelve-hour days in the lumber mills. He remembered celebrating their wedding Masses and the dances that followed. There was always beer to drink and music from the old country, the young brides dancing with their beaming fathers. He remembered baptizing many children, most first-generation Americans. He also remembered the funerals. Many funerals.

As he reached Third Street, he turned left and walked past the County Courthouse Square, which was filled with workers and horse-drawn wagons hauling local red sandstone and other building materials for the new courthouse under construction.

"Look out there, you! Clear the way!"

Father Sperlein had to step quickly aside to avoid a collision with a man and a wheelbarrow full of rocks and dirt.

"Oh, I beg your pardon, Father," the man said. "I didn't realize you were a priest."

Father Sperlein nodded his head and blessed the man with a quick sign of the cross. He turned left on Third Street and walked to the business district, where several saloons shared space with barber shops, dry goods vendors, the Marquette Opera House, and the new Michigan Telephone Company. Men in dark suits and hats walked along the elevated wooden sidewalks. An electric streetcar passed by on the street, its bell clanging.

Father Sperlein walked Marquette's streets for a while, taking in the scenery. A boy in knickers, black stockings and worn boots shouted, "Stop! Give it to me!" He ran after some older boys, who had taken his cap. A matronly woman strolled past the shops, her black skirt dragging on the wooden sidewalks. From under her wide-brimmed hat, she watched the boys with disapproval. Nearby, three young women looked on. They wore tailored jackets with contrasting skirts that revealed their ankles and black boots. Their feathered hats bobbed as they laughed at the boys. Suddenly, the older boys saw the priest. One tossed the cap onto the ground toward the younger boy, then they scurried away.

On Spring Street, Father Sperlein stopped at the entrance to a saloon. "Wines, Liquors and Cigars," the sign on the window read. He ordered a beer and sat at the bar, his chin resting on his left hand. His eyes stared ahead vacantly.

"What's wrong, Father," asked the bartender.

"Just having a difficult day," the priest said. "Nothing I want to talk about."

The bartender poured the beer, skimming off the foam, and set it on the bar.

"I can't forgive your sins," the bartender said with a smile, "but my confessional is available when the bar is open."

"Thank you," the priest said, taking his first sip but remaining silent. After he'd drunk half a glass, the alcohol started to remove his inhibitions.

"What's your name, bartender?"

"August. But everyone calls me Auggie."

"Let me ask you a question, Auggie. Have you ever felt that God had abandoned you?"

"Well, I feel that God is always there if we seek him out. Isn't that what you preach?"

"Yes, but sometimes it's hard to find Him when there's so much darkness and despair. Have you ever had to bury a child? Or say a funeral Mass for a miner whose widow has eight young mouths to feed?"

"No, Father, but I've poured a few drinks for men with troubles like that."

The priest gave Auggie a curious look, not sure what to say.

"We're not so different, you and me," the bartender said, pouring him a second beer. "While you serve bread and wine to the faithful and downtrodden, I serve beer and whiskey to the joyful and forsaken. You stand beside people through their happiest times and their worst times, and so do I."

Sperlein looked at the bartender warily.

"Now, tell me Father. What makes you doubt the existence of God?"

"I didn't say I doubted God's existence," the priest snapped back. "I just wonder where He is some days. Dark days like this."

The bartender nodded silently as he wiped the bar with a rag.

"Tell me, what made you decide to become a priest? You have a lot of questions for a man who wears a collar."

The priest turned his head, his eyes taking on a distant gaze.

"As a child, I had good friends in Bavaria, but we had a hard life," he said. "I was in my teens when my father announced we were going to America. Suddenly, everything changed for me. My father was a tailor, but I had no interest in learning his trade. I wasn't good with my hands. I lacked his attention to detail ... every seam straight, every fabric neatly pressed, and every buttonhole perfectly sewn."

"With standards like that, he must have been successful."

"Yes. He was also an exacting man, with a quick temper. My mother feared him, and so did I. To escape, I'd slip away to the church down the street. It was quiet and peaceful. In the light shining through the windows, I found God."

Father Sperlein thought back to his days as a young boy. About the priest who befriended him, taught him to pray and to serve at High Mass. About the peace and serenity he found in the church, provided comfort when he found himself in America. The words of Psalm 18 came to him.

Surely thou wilt light my candle: the Lord my God will lighten my darkness.

He looked up at the bartender, his mouth dry and his eyes starting to water. He emptied his glass. He had nothing more to say.

"Another beer, Father?"

"No, thank you. I'll be going now. Peace be with you, Auggie."

Father Sperlein wandered in the saloon district. A drunk lying on the sidewalk asked for a nickel. The priest gave him a quick blessing and kept walking. On Front Street, he walked into Dutmer Brothers' saloon, but this time he ordered a whiskey and sat in a dark corner as the bar started to fill with men getting off work. Cigar smoke filled the saloon. The cheap whiskey burned his throat as it went down, leaving a medicinal aftertaste.

How do I turn myself around? Should I just walk away from the priesthood? ... No, I cannot. It's the only thing that makes me feel alive, that gives me purpose. But it's also the source of much loneliness. Having no one to share my joys and sorrows. Look to the light of God, they say. But what if God's light isn't there? What if all you see is darkness?

Lord, I need help, he prayed. Please show me the way.

As the whiskey took effect, his evening became a blur. The next morning, he woke up at the Bishop's residence with a headache, a foul taste in his mouth and a sore rib cage. The pain's origins were a mystery, though he could vaguely recall an argument with a tall Swede over some Catholic doctrine. He couldn't remember walking back to the residence and climbing into bed, much less any more details of the previous night.

He had missed breakfast, too. Thankfully, Miss Linnenberg had left some bread and cheese along with some cold coffee. The bishop had already eaten his breakfast and left. Father Sperlein looked at the clock and realized he was late.

"This is not a good way to start the day, Frederick," Bishop Eis said when the priest entered his office. He allowed Sperlein to kiss his ring in the traditional greeting. "You know how much I value punctuality."

"Yes, Your Excellency. My apologies."

Ever the Prussian with his punctuality and order, he thought.

"Did you learn anything last night during your examination of conscience? Or are we just wasting our time?"

"I learned that I would very much like to remain a priest in this diocese."

"That's what you learned?"

The bishop leaned forward but received nothing in return but silence.

"Let me get right to the point, then. I know how you spent last night. It was not in prayer. You visited at least three different saloons, getting kicked out of at least two. Do you think that I would not find out about your behavior while you were wearing a priest's collar?"

"But..."

"No excuses, Frederick. Now, can you please tell me what you have learned about yourself that most of us already know?"

Father Sperlein sighed. He felt the urge to dart out the door, never to see the bishop again. *Maybe I could get a job on a Great Lakes freighter and jump overboard in the middle of the night. Maybe I could find work in a copper mine and make a rookie mistake with the explosives. Or maybe,* he thought, *I could tell the truth.*

The sun poured through the window, shining a bright light on the bishop's crucifix. Though he'd seen it thousands of times, the image of Christ crucified suddenly put his problems in perspective. He took a deep breath.

"Your Excellency, you're right. I have been hiding something. I am addicted to alcohol. In Milwaukee, I learned that I had let alcohol become a substitute for facing my own problems. God knows, I don't want to be a drunk. Until last night, I hadn't had a drink since the day I checked into that hospital. The stress last night, it was just overwhelming."

By now, tears were streaming down the priest's cheeks as he choked out his confession. The bishop's face showed neither forgiveness nor condemnation, only pity.

"Please, Your Excellency. I beg for your forgiveness. If I lose the priesthood, I'll lose everything."

"Finally, we are getting somewhere," the bishop replied with a gentle voice. "Father Sperlein, thank you for your honesty and your confession. Now, what do we do about it?"

"I'll change, Your Excellency. I know I will."

"So says every alcoholic, Father Sperlein. But I have a plan. I've decided to assign you to a new parish, St. Bruno's Church in Nadeau."

"Nadeau? Isn't that a French-speaking parish? You know I don't know any French. I can't possibly..."

"Father Sperlein, this is your last chance and only choice. If you want to remain a priest, you will need to learn to speak French. As you know, I now require priests to speak at least two homilies each month in English. It's the language spoken by our young people, no matter what their parents speak. You may preach in English, but you must also speak French to minister to the people. As long as you remain sober, you will stay in Nadeau. If you relapse, you will be dismissed for good."

Father Sperlein's eyes widened, and his back straightened.

"You also need help avoiding alcohol's temptation. Now, is there someone, a relative perhaps, who could join you in Nadeau? Perhaps someone who can speak French?"

Father Sperlein paused to think. *Is this my only way out? A life sentence in some backward French lumber town in Menominee County?* He sighed. The priesthood's pull was stronger than his desire to escape.

"Well, perhaps my cousin, Mary. She's a dressmaker at my father's tailor shop in Baltimore. We still correspond frequently. She knows enough to serve their French-speaking customers."

"Her name is Mary Sperlein?"

"Yes, her father and my father are brothers."

"Would she be willing to go to Nadeau to be your housekeeper, translator, and unofficial guardian? I cannot send you off to lead a parish and know that every night you'll be tempted by the neighborhood saloon."

"I'm not sure."

"Give Father Pinten the name of the shop where she works. I will call her personally and ask if she would serve the church in this way," the bishop said. "If she says yes, I will announce your appointment to St. Bruno's this week. You may return to Rockland and pack your things. Don't say good-bye to the parishioners there, unless you also encourage them to welcome their new pastor."

"But..."

"That is all, Father. *Bonne chance à toi.* I'll be praying for you."

Father Sperlein left the bishop's office and walked out into the crisp October air, breathing in the smell of wood smoke, decaying leaves and horse manure. One last chance and one last choice lay before him.

Is this my path, Lord? Is this really where you want me to go?

The sun broke through the clouds, momentarily blinding his eyes and warming his face.

Nadeau it is, then, he thought. *God help me.*

Epilogue

In July 1914, the Catholic Bulletin of Minnesota reported that Nadeau's F.M. Sperlein was among eight Catholic priests who signed a letter to eliminate liquor traffic in the nation. It was the first organized move by Catholics against the "evil effects of liquor drinking." (The Catholic Bulletin, St. Paul, Minn., 18 July 1914, p. 1)

Father Sperlein served on a committee to develop the platform for the new Catholic Prohibition League. The platform called for abstinence from alcoholic drinks as a qualification for civil service. It supported extending the voting franchise to women but disenfranchising for five years anyone convicted of drunkenness.

The platform also said they would "do all in our power to remind workingmen, especially those from foreign lands, that alcohol ... is the main cause of our two millions of tramps, two millions of children doing men's work in factories, five millions of dependents on charity, six millions of illiterates, eight millions of women working away from home, and fifty thousand innocent girls annually going into lives of shame, and under the alluring bait of personal liberty is the workingman's enemy." (Catholic Union and Times, Buffalo, N.Y., August 13, 1914, p. 2)

Father Sperlein remained active in the league, supporting passage and enforcement of the 18th Amendment. By 1919, when the league met in South Bend, Indiana, he was elected secretary-treasurer. (The Buffalo Enquirer, Buffalo, NY, 26 April 1919, p. 5) Among the resolutions the league adopted that year was one declaring that prohibition was in "perfect harmony with the spirit of self-denial prescribed by Catholic discipline, with spiritual perfection and with monastic asceticism of old." (South Bend News-Times, 24 April 1919, p. 2)

After prohibition went into effect, the league claimed that in 1920 alcoholism among Catholics had fallen dramatically and they were experiencing a moral and religious awakening. Father Sperlein said that nothing could turn the "average foreigner" into a loyal American citizen as swiftly and effectually as prohibition. (Adams County Independent, Littlestown, Pennsylvania, 1 Oct 1920, p. 1)

Father Sperlein lived the rest of his days in Nadeau. St. Bruno's 1955 parish history says he became known as "Beloved Pastor" to the people of Nadeau. On June 28, 1936, he died of a heart attack at age sixty-eight after officiating at Saturday morning Mass. He was found in the rectory by his cousin and longtime housekeeper, Miss Mary Sperlein.

Historical · Bishop Eis

All Customers Great and Small

by Nancy Besonen

Almost eight years after having permanently hung up my United States Postal Service mailbag, I feel fairly secure in sharing how I really felt about the characters on my rural route.

They were a bunch of woofers.

While residents throughout Covington and Watton, MI furiously thumb through their phone books for the Postmaster General's number to register their complaints, allow me to explain. It's not listed. That's why I'm feeling so secure.

Also, because by "woofers," I mean dogs. I drove the mail route for the two towns in a career that spanned over two decades, and many thousands of miles. Along the way, I was often blessed, occasionally cursed, but never bored by my canine customers.

I knew them well because I visited six days a week, bearing gifts of the U.S. mail. Some of my furry greeters were so tall they could look their gift horse in the eye. Others preferred to try and drag me down to their level first.

Their names have been changed to protect the innocent, though several of the dogs in this heartwarming tell-all are clearly guilty. I never had to memorize their names because dogs don't get mail. Larry, Moe & Curly went for me, instead.

I assure you, the three little stooges earned the title, even the one who kind of liked me. They belonged to a sweet, elderly couple who adored their pets. Their mail lady, not as much, because every time I knocked on their door with another package in hand, all h--- would break loose.

"The mail lady is here!" the woman would cheerily announce over the cacophony of frantic barks, yips, and snarls. Then she'd throw open the door, beaming as her miniature dachshund and two chihuahuas dashed outside, tumbling over one another as they raced to eat the messenger.

Pardon my exaggeration. I get it from fishing. Only one dog wanted to eat me, the older chihuahua. The other two were just his cheering section. And the woman was, too, reassuring me over the racket that the leader of the pack, now firmly attached to my ankle, was so old it no longer had teeth.

Instead, it had the jaws of a bear trap. When a peek at my circles of bruises—kind of like lamprey bites on a lake trout—evoked more pride than sympathy from the owner, I finally had to take matters into my own hands.

I brought the madness to a skidding stop with a snow shovel.

I apologize for the harsh mental picture the former sentence evokes. Better you should feel bad for the mail lady who was accessorizing with an aged chihuahua. The shovel was not a final solution. It was just a temporary defense.

It was propped on the couple's porch all winter, and just before I rang the bell, I would carefully position it in front of my feet. When the door was flung open in greeting, three more bells merrily rang out as Larry, Moe, and Curly clanged into the barrier.

It only stunned them a little, but it bought me enough time to throw down dog treats, keeping their jaws busy while I handed over the package and beat a hasty escape. When the snow disappeared, the shovel was replaced by a broom, which also worked, though I missed the music generated by the little three-ring circus.

Some customers were fully aware their dogs were a threat to their mail carrier. Genuinely concerned, they tried to work with me to assure safe and continued delivery service. That's how I wound up in control of a particularly toothsome character who was destined to pay big time for his previous free range.

Or so I thought.

Most dogs enjoy free range in the country, because it's the country. There's lots of room, little traffic, and daily visits by the U.S. mail carrier who provides free entertainment by trying to get to the mailbox and sometimes the front door before the dog(s) can get to her first.

Most of the dogs on my route were just happy to win the race, greeting the runner-up with wagging tails and enthusiastic kisses. Others raced to defend their mailboxes and homes from bills, junk mail, and me. I adjusted accordingly, buying bigger dog treats and tossing them farther, but one tough customer refused to take the bait.

Duke belonged to a younger and just as friendly couple, but these ones were on my side. Their big, yellow lab mix started out cranky and grew progressively worse, possibly because I bought generic. He'd beat me to their mailbox every day, then hold his ground, barking and snarling between me and delivery.

According to the unwritten rules, I had to throw a treat deep into the woods, then ram the mail home before Duke came rocketing back to his post, still intent on eating me even though his mouth was now full. If I had to run a package to the couple's door, I just threw farther and prayed hard.

Duke's owners occasionally used a shock collar to reel their dog in, but unfortunately, both left for work before my daily delivery. One Saturday morning, the husband and I met at their mailbox and discussed the dilemma, and the following Monday I opened their box to find a wondrous gift.

It was the remote control for the shock collar, with a note encouraging me to use it.

After months of dodging the dog's snapping jaws to hurl mail in the box, I needed that remote like I needed air. The very next day I tossed a treat as far as I could, grabbed the remote and spun the dial to "Riverdance." When the dog came roaring back I took aim, hit the button, and waited for the floor show to begin.

Duke didn't jump. He didn't even blink. Instead, he snarled his usual greeting and lunged repeatedly at my driver's side door, clearly enraged by my efforts to change his channel. All the while, I sat wide-eyed in my car, pointing the remote at his collar and grinding my thumb into the button until I could barely see through the slobber on my window.

The man blamed the batteries. I continued buying generic. But I invested in bigger treats that I could throw farther.

Fortunately for rural service, for every dog that thirsted for the mail lady's blood, there were many more friendly farm dogs that made my job a joy. One home provided a steady stream of stellar four-legged customers, with each new generation groomed for success by its aged, oft beleaguered mentor.

When I first started on the route, the family owned a medium-sized, fine blend of many well-behaved breeds named Jack. As I pulled up to their mailbox, he'd amble up to my car with his plume of a tail wagging a friendly greeting. He'd politely sit while I made my delivery and snapped the box shut, signaling it was time for our daily visit.

I'd open my driver's side door and Jack would lean his head in for an ear rub and rundown of my day. He was a great listener—I could tell he didn't approve of Duke's behavior, either—and received his treats like a true gentleman. His house was at the end of my route and workday, and our visits were the icing on the cake.

Jack grew older, and one day he took a little longer to get to the car. That's because there was a sassy new puppy named Ginger attached to his drooping ear. Jack introduced us with as much dignity as he could muster, then issued an audible sigh as the pup disengaged to leap, lick, and nip at my nose before chasing her reluctant leader back into the barnyard.

The pup grew, settling down and settling in, and one day Jack quit coming to my car altogether. Ginger was now my daily reward for a job mostly well done, patiently waiting by the mailbox when I arrived for a visit, a pat and two generic treats because they were well deserved. Years and many miles later, it would be Ginger's turn to lead the next little one in.

Some dogs could successfully play it both ways, vexing and charming their mail lady all in one day's work. A German Shepherd named Fritz took the title in that category thanks to a feat that could have cost him his life, but instead, just cost his owners a new car tire.

Fritz did his very best to keep up his breed's image: protective, territorial, and great as a guard dog. When I drove into his yard, he accepted my appearance with good grace, but he just hated to see me leave. He hated it so badly he chased me down the driveway, barking loudly and snapping at my car tires as I went.

He was owned by a couple with three sons. They were always gracious, calling out happy greetings to me while admonishing Fritz, but they just couldn't cure his strong instinct to attack my tires. Then one fateful day I delivered, they waved, Fritz chased, and my front passenger tire gave out with a loud hiss, followed by thumps.

Fritz had bitten right through my sidewall. The man and his wife were horrified, and hurriedly dispatched their oldest son to change my tire. Their middle son was sent inside to get me a can of pop to drink while I waited, while the youngest was assigned to keep a grip on the dog.

The couple apologized profusely and promised to replace the tire as their son spun off the flat. I felt a bit self-conscious sipping my cold drink—his brother had even added a straw—but freed on his own cognizance, Fritz was a great comfort, licking my ear as I

waited as if to say, "How nice of you to stop! And isn't it a lovely day for a visit?"

I tried not to play favorites, but in the end, it was Gracie that tied the bow on the package that was my postal career. Gracie was an Australian Shepherd, a medium-sized, energetic breed coveted by farmers and feared by postal workers, all because of its strong herding instinct.

I had two Australian Shepherds on my route. One was an underemployed house pet that, bored with its life of leisure, plied its natural instinct on the mail carrier. That's right: I arrived with package in hand one day and the dog bit, I mean "herded" me, right on the butt.

It only pinched a little. The toothless Chihuahua did more damage, mostly mental cruelty. But this final tale is not about bored shepherds or excitable lap dogs. It is about a loyal animal that, having first scared at least ten minutes off my expected lifespan, eventually capped my career.

The dog's owner raised beef, lots of beef, on one of the few working farms left in our rural community. And he always had a farm dog, and it was always an Australian Shepherd, because he had plenty of work for the working breed.

The problem was, it didn't work for me. His shepherds weren't really threatening, but they weren't very welcoming either, and from past experience I'd learned to literally watch my rear. We kept a respectful distance, and I never turned my back on his current model while delivering a package.

One day I had a box too big to fit in the farmer's mailbox, and carefully checked the yard before exiting my vehicle. I walked up to the back door, knocked, and was nearly knocked off my feet by a sudden, vicious blow from behind.

"Oh, that's Gracie!" the farmer's wife said by way of introduction, and I spun around to see two gleaming eyes staring up at me from the face of their new, half-grown Australian Shepherd pup. And then she gave me a good licking.

She literally licked me, and our friendship was sealed, though I learned not to turn my back on Gracie, either, because of her preferred greeting of slamming her front paws against my shoulder blades. Gracie sure could jump. And she sure liked the mail, because every day she'd faithfully wait for delivery.

The farm was located at the end of a long driveway, and Gracie would sit right in the middle of it, still as a statue, patiently waiting for the mail. When I pulled up to the mailbox, I'd make my delivery, check the road for traffic, open my driver's side door and holler, "Hi, Gracie!"

The dog would tear down the driveway like a bolt of furry lightning, then skid to a stop outside my car, still managing to rock it a bit as she dove halfway in and onto my lap. A vigorous greeting ensued, the likes of which would not be seen until the following day when I'd stop at the farmer's box again, look both ways and holler, "Hi, Gracie!"

Gracie's greetings were the best, and the faithful dog never failed to deliver, unless the farmer needed her for actual work that day. I was the one who failed Gracie when, twenty-three years into my career, I was transferred forty-eight miles out of town and reluctantly retired my mailbag for good.

I'd been off duty for a couple of years and was driving down the farmer's road one day when I saw a familiar figure resting in the sun, halfway up the driveway. Trusting my own instinct, I pulled over beside the mailbox, checked the road for traffic, opened my door and once again hollered, "Hi, Gracie!"

She darn near rolled my Corolla.

Historical · Logging team with horses

Dog Park

by Mack Hassler

To kill a bit of boring time, I took
The dogs to the dog park and met another owner
Whose twelve-year-old was going to the vet to learn
His fate. She will put him down just like a crook
Since he has cancer. Still, he had the look
With my dogs of bounding joy, not one wit forlorn
For his last romp, as she said, nothing to mourn
Ahead. He seemed protagonist for a happy dog book.

Having just lost Sue and working every day
To balance life against her death, this chance
Encounter spoke to me and made me cry.
My wife's last romp was hardly an exuberant display
Of joy. No sad communication with jumping twists of body.
But God was there to help me hold her close.

Our Silent Spring, Read for Friends

by Mack Hassler

My cousin Pat, a gnarled and rugged tree
Of a man, beside his ancient dog Jack,
Stared at me full of tears at my remark
Meant to comfort Judy dead. Pat could barely see.

A friend at my retirement home also cried
As we discussed delays in his wife's care. Such fate
Finds strong men wrestling mightily late
In life, determined not to be defied.

I feel such weakness in our loss of Sue
Whose time had come. She surprised us all
In simply shutting down and leaving in the Fall
So fast that none of us could believe it true.

For me, this year without her presence
Has echoed loud with hollow resonance.

Chiblow Lake

by Richard Hill

The late-summer sun was going down on Westley Gillette as he eased the fourteen-foot wooden skiff up to the dock on Chiblow Lake. It had been nearly two straight days of driving since he'd slipped away from the feds in Philly. He had traveled up through Michigan and crossed into Canada at the Soo border. From there he'd made a beeline east to Iron Bridge, then north on a zig-zaggy road to Chiblow. The lake was remote enough that the feds would be unlikely to track him there. The use of a cell phone up here in the North Woods was merely wishful thinking.

Westley's cousin Tom owned the rustic log cabin and maintained it during the summer. It was a modest cabin with a kitchen, a dining area, and a bunkroom that could sleep six people. The camp had been in the family for generations, and Westley had fished there many summers when he was a teenager. Now, at forty, he noticed very little had changed—the outhouse, the propane cook stove, the squeaky screen door.

At the cabin, Westley felt safe enough to relax a little. He had borrowed Tom's skiff for the fifteen-minute trip across the lake. With Labor Day approaching, the summer visitors were gone for the year. So Westley had secured permission to use the cabin for a short while. In case there were any questions, he'd concocted a cover story about coming up to the camp to escape the unbearable heat in Philadelphia, as well as to savor some well-deserved rest and relaxation. Besides, with the pandemic dominating everyone's life, it was good to break away from the crowded city.

Lighting a kerosene lamp inside, he poured himself a glass of bourbon from his pocket flask and dropped down on a rickety side chair to catch his breath. He really hadn't been offered much of a choice: either serve the next twenty-five years in jail or take his chances on the good nature of the Philadelphia mob. As a shrewd lawyer, Westley Gillette had represented one of the notorious crime bosses and knew the inner workings of his client's operation. But now he was in a dicey situation. The feds had nailed him for dealing small amounts of cocaine on the side but had offered him a contingent deal. If he would agree to play ball with the feds, they would spare him some serious jail time. Westley would have to infiltrate the mob and agree to wear a wire. Otherwise, all bets were off, and they could start measuring him for an orange jumpsuit.

With those limited options, he had no choice but to agree. But by the next morning, Westley suddenly got cold feet, skipped town immediately, and headed for Canada. His longtime girlfriend Paige had refused to come with him on such short notice. She couldn't do without her internet, her cell phone, and city life. Besides, she hated the idea of being totally isolated in the woods, the ravenous mosquitoes, the back-to-nature outhouses. Camping in the great outdoors was apparently not her thing. Westley had been careful not to tell her specifically where he was headed, lest the feds start asking too many questions. He prided himself on his cleverness and foresight. As a precaution, he had ditched his cell phone so his GPS location couldn't be tracked.

The moon was rising over the tall pines, shimmering over the dark surface of the lake. Off in the distance, the loons called to one another announcing the day's end. Westley had forgotten his food supplies back in the boat and walked to the dock with a flashlight to retrieve them. He didn't want to tempt any raccoons or other wild animals with a free meal. He had brought enough food to last for a few weeks: beans, potatoes, eggs, bacon, bread, and for a nightcap, a couple bottles of Jim Beam.

A few years earlier, Cousin Tom had mentioned that when the cabin was vacant one time, a large black bear had crashed through the dining room window and scattered flour, pancake mix, and syrup from one end of the cabin to the other. Experts say that a bear's sense of smell is more than two thousand times as powerful as a human's. Strangely enough, on his way out the window, the bear had overlooked the chocolate Hershey bar sitting on the dining room table, just below the broken window. Westley was not about to give any curious bear a reason to visit.

After dinner, he sipped his bourbon and began to think about Paige. She would have no problem taking care of their apartment while he was gone. But what about the feds? Were they harassing her, he wondered, trying to shake loose some details about his whereabouts? Could the feds track him some other way? Perhaps through his use of credit cards at gas stations while he was traveling? Not a chance. He had thought ahead and pulled a wad of cash from the bank before leaving town. Westley always took pride in his clever ability to cover his tracks, to shake the hounds off his trail.

As the night closed in, he grew tired but couldn't sleep. He heard the loons' plaintive cries out on the open lake. With the moon dodging behind the clouds, the night had a distinct eeriness about it as a light mist settled over the calm water. He wasn't used to such peaceful and serene surroundings; it felt almost disturbing to him. No sirens, no honking traffic, no blaring TV, or radio, just the soft lapping of waves at the water's edge and the brilliant stars in the night sky. It made him all the more anxious and restless.

To cheer himself up, he pulled out his harmonica and played a few familiar tunes—"Four Strong Winds" and one of his favorites, "Folsom Prison." In the windowpane as he played, Westley saw his reflection in the lamp light and, for a moment, did not feel quite so alone. The music eased his mind and distracted him from his worries. There was no harm in letting the heat back home cool down a bit, he figured. The diversion might do him some good.

When morning came, the bright sunshine seemed to dispel his sour mood and lift his spirits. After a bacon and egg breakfast, he fired up the motorboat and set out for a distant cove to try his luck for some smallmouth bass and lake trout. The fish seemed to strike more readily near mid-morning and early evening at this time of year. He cut a minnow in half for bait and lowered it about sixty feet down, just off the bottom. Jigging the bait now and then, he finally got a bite and set the hook, reeling in a twelve-inch smallmouth. In the next hour, Westley pulled up three more bass and had enough for a decent meal.

Back on shore, Westley filleted the fish and carried the pail of guts down the beach. He pitched them on the rocky shoreline and watched as a flock of seagulls descended on the feast. Backing off towards the cabin, he watched the scavengers closely. As expected, the seagulls soon retreated to a safe distance on the lake, as a majestic bald eagle drifted down from a tall pine. The gulls knew better than to pick a fight with a battle-tested raptor five times their size.

Westley admired the grace and grandeur of the eagle, its fearless dignity, its refusal to bow down to any other creature. Nature had favored the powerful raptor and placed it high on the food chain. It reminded Westley of how he had practically been chased out of town by his fear of confronting the mob, by his reluctance to push back on the feds' demands. To him, it was a simple matter of survival. A quick escape was his only option.

One evening, just before sunset, Westley strolled down the beach until he reached the overgrown brush at the water's edge. In the clear shallow water, a large turtle suddenly appeared. Its shell was nearly two feet in length, and its rope-like head projected from the surface. The creature swam closer to Westley and stared intently at him with large dark eyes. He snatched a couple slices of stale bread from the cabin, formed them into small balls of dough, and tossed them to the turtle. One by one, the turtle made its way to each offering and devoured it.

The same turtle returned to Westley's beach every evening for a few bread scraps. The creature was no doubt curious and may have wanted company. It had a calming influence on Westley, especially its dark, intelligent eyes that stared quietly at him as if to communicate something. Westley admired the turtle's freedom and independence, its unrestricted ability to travel anywhere it chose in the underwater world of Chiblow Lake, miles and miles of lake bottom to explore. And yet, the turtle opted to spend its time with Westley. For a moment, he regarded the turtle with envy and wondered what it would be like to trade places for a while, to curl up inside his shell, to shut out all the world's petty troubles. *What harm was there,* he thought, *in wanting to lead a simpler, less complicated life?*

By mid-September, Westley was growing more anxious. He loved the quiet beauty of Chiblow but realized that, with colder weather moving in soon, he couldn't hold out much longer. The maples and birches surrounding the lake showed hints of gold and crimson as the Canadian fall season kicked into gear. One afternoon, when the fishing was particularly slow, Westley lay down in the bottom of the wooden skiff and watched the fall clouds drift across the autumn sky. He was tired of feeling so lost and indecisive. Maybe it was time to shake things up a bit.

I can't hide like this forever; I'll starve to death or go mad up here. But if I return to Philly, they'll want me to testify against a mob boss. I know way too much for my own good. If I cough up too much inside informa-tion, I'll be kissing it all goodbye; those guys play pretty rough sometimes; if they suspect-ed me of any hanky-panky, the mob would surely find a way to rub me out. No question about it. But if I don't play ball with the feds, it's off to Rikers Island for the next twenty-five years or so.

Paige is probably wondering if I've lost my marbles completely and whether I'm ever coming home. I've never run away from any-thing in my life until now.

Why in hell did I ever start dealing coke? I re-ally didn't need the money. Maybe I was just looking for a little excitement, a quick buck. I have to admit, for a lawyer, I live pretty mod-estly—no million-dollar home or Maserati in the driveway, no private jets or yachts. I live more like a monk or a dirt-poor college kid. All that glitter never really appealed to me. My only vices are a little coke now and then and a certain fondness for bourbon. I know guys who are way worse off than that.

A dark cloud front swept in rapidly from the northwest. As the sun went into hiding, a brisk wind blew across the choppy green wa-ter, forming small whitecaps. Westley could hear the thunder rolling in the distance. A sudden sheet of heavy rain chased him into the cabin, drenching him to the bone before he could get the boat tied up. Once inside, he changed to some dry clothes and tried to warm up.

How can I ever escape this mess I've creat-ed? I could start a brand-new life somewhere, maybe move to some small town in Idaho. ... Take on a completely new identity as a fish-ing guide or a park ranger. I'd create a new back story that my wife had died in a car ac-cident back in Michigan and that I'd decided to go west and start my life over.

A sudden clap of thunder shook the win-dow panes and jolted Westley from his rev-erie. The driving downpour obliterated his view across the lake. With the abrupt drop in temperature, he reached for his heavy green sweatshirt and pulled it over his head. Gathering some kindling and a few dry logs, he started a fire in the pot-belly stove. As he nursed a glass of bourbon, Westley sat down and stared out the front window at the light-ning flashes across Chiblow Lake.

He couldn't seem to get Paige off his mind; he missed her warm kisses and sensuous body, her soothing voice, even her tattle-tale gossip. Despite her quick temper and her tendency to dominate their conversations, they always got along in the end. It had been only three weeks, and he was beginning to miss even the stodgy old courtroom, the judge's contemptuous looks, and the daily courtroom dramas. He was feeling a little out of sorts without the crowded Philly streets, the grungy subway, even the relentless petty crime. The big city hustle and bustle had been such an important part of his life. Although Chiblow provided him a sense of blissful peace and quiet, the puzzle of his existence was incomplete. Something essential seemed to be missing.

Why am I craving my old life? This is everything I've ever wanted. I don't know what I really want anymore. This is starting to feel like a hung jury.

As swiftly as the storm had moved in, the sky brightened, and the September sun parted the clouds. Before long, the wind and the waves calmed down, restoring the afternoon to its former fall glory.

In the distance, far across the lake, Westley heard the drone of a motor. The volume increased steadily as the bow of a red boat came into sight. He grabbed his binoculars but couldn't quite decipher the identity of the boat's driver. Had the feds discovered his hideout, he wondered. Instinctively, he raced into the deep woods behind the cabin. Being taken prisoner was never part of his plan, but now he felt trapped.

When the red boat was tied up at the dock, the driver cut the motor. A voice called out. "Westley, it's Tom. Where the hell are you?"

Hearing Tom's voice, Westley emerged from the woods greatly relieved. "Good to see you, Tom. What brings you out here?"

They made their way into the cabin and Westley started a pot of coffee. "I usually come up here in late September," said Tom, "to close up the cabin for the winter. But this time it's a little different. I got a call a few days back from a federal agent in Philadelphia asking if I knew anything about your whereabouts. I'm not sure what kind of trouble you're in, and they didn't go into details. They said they were checking all the numbers on the cell phone you left at your apartment. Paige told them you had mentioned going up to a cabin somewhere in the woods, but she had no idea where. I didn't say a word either, but early this morning two federal agents showed up at my door on a hunch. I couldn't lie to them anymore."

"You gave me away?"

"I had no choice. I would've been in hot water otherwise. Now, just listen for a minute. Those two agents are waiting for us on the other side of the lake. I persuaded them to let me talk to you first. They say they're willing to work out a compromise with you if you surrender peaceably."

Westley reluctantly filled Tom in on the details of his trouble with the feds. He poured Tom a cup of black coffee and himself a shot of bourbon. He knew they had him cornered. It was time to negotiate. As a lawyer, Westley had brokered many a deal to get his clients more leniency. With his legal skills and powers of persuasion, he would have to work out some sort of compromise. If he returned quietly, maybe the feds would listen to him. Or if he offered the feds some choice information concerning the local cocaine trade, without implicating the mob, maybe they'd go easy on him. He knew more than they gave him credit for; that was a fact. Although he might go quietly, Westley would never agree to wear a wire for anyone; that would be a death sentence. But he would do whatever he could to avoid jail time.

Tom stood up from the table. "So, Westley, what do you think? Are you coming back with me?"

Westley poured himself a final shot of bourbon and nodded slowly. "I'll come, but only if you promise to let me visit again next summer. These fish are gonna miss me."

"It's a deal, Cousin."

For Westley, it was worth the chance. After three weeks of being alone at Chiblow, he was ready to go home again, to roll the dice one more time. The cozy log cabin on the lake would always be there when he needed a little peace and quiet.

Mozambique

by Alex Noel

had just turned twenty years old when I first went to Mozambique. It took me the better part of a week to travel from my then-home in Cape Town, South Africa to the remote swath of Indian Ocean coastline near the small town of Tofo, in southeastern Mozambique. After a two-hour flight, two days on safari in the Kingdom of Swaziland, and too many hours crammed inside sweltering old buses limping along long past their last legs, I finally crossed the border into Mozambique. The air inside the bucking old bus was thick with heat and oppressive humidity, but the excitement of the journey overpowered my physical discomfort. My face was glued to the grimy window, soaking up every sight that sped by as we passed. Palm trees, small ramshackle dwellings, and Mozambicans going about their ordinary lives all looked extraordinary to my western gaze. Each second was like a shutter's grab of a single still frame, motion frozen in time, at least in my mind. Children in their school uniforms, formally dressed men with beads of sweat swelling into trickles down their heads, and women selling produce and goods in small informal markets along the road. Most booths sold fruit or fish, sometimes rice or brooms or the occasional goat.

Once past the capital city of Maputo, the terrain transformed from dry, arid bushland to hot, humid, tropics. Six or eight or eight hundred hours and at least three buses later, the road ended. It was an abrupt end, a permanent end with no option for detours. There was a road, granted there were more potholes than pavement, but a road none-theless; and then there was sand. I joined the few remaining passengers who had also traveled to the end of the road, and collected my "luggage"–the same, red, oversized and bulging backpack I had been living out of for the past few months–and I started to walk. There was a wide path that continued where the road would have gone, had it been built. It only took a few steps to understand why the road had ended where it did–it was sand. It was not "sandy"; or earth with a small layer of removable sand on top of it; it was just pure sand. I had to trudge some indefinite number of miles (likely fewer than five, but it felt endless) to get to my remote destination. My progress was painfully slow, as I sank into the sand with every step. There was no firm ground in sight, just sand and sand and more sand. It felt like I was using all my energy–already depleted from the sun and heat and days of grueling travel–just to sink backwards with every forward stride. I imagined the endless sandpit reaching as deep as the Earth's core with nothing solid in between. I was hot, and sweaty, and very frustrated with the exhausting lack of progress, but still I trudged on.

An acquaintance in Cape Town had made arrangements for me to sleep in a beach-side hut made of reeds and a thatched grass roof a few miles beyond the town of Tofo on Mozambique's vast swath of Indian Ocean coastline. My acquaintance was a scuba diver with connections in the area, but having a place to sleep was the only plan I had made for my time in the region. The hut I stayed in was simple and sparse, with no floor–just sand, and I slept on a bamboo cot with a torn and frustratingly tangled mosquito net hanging overhead.

Immediately upon arrival, I dropped my bags in the sand, and ran across at least a hundred meters of empty beach until I splashed into the warm Indian Ocean. I was immediately pummeled by a gigantic, crashing wave. I came up for air laughing and then was immediately tumbled under another surge. I was overcome with pure exhilaration. I had never seen such massive waves in my life. I felt like I was in a surfing video, where the blue-green waves create a tunnel that envelopes the miniscule human. The power of the waves kept tearing my bathing suit out of place, exposing one or the other of my breasts on each collision. There was no helping it, but also no one there to see. It didn't take long to become so exhausted from battling through the waves that I had to retreat to shore. I promptly fell asleep on the beach, which (predictably) resulted in horrible sunburn all over my body.

On one of my first days on the beach just beyond Tofo, where there was nothing but sand, water, sun, and local fishermen wading with nets off the reef at low tide, I met Fernando. Fernando was a young Mozambican man who worked at the only scuba/snorkel shop in town. He didn't own the business but skippered a small rubber dinghy for scuba diving and snorkeling clients, and I happened upon him and his boat on one of my hours-long walks down the beach. I surprised myself by working up the courage to ask him how I might arrange to go snorkeling. It was impossible to snorkel from shore on account of the constantly crashing waves, but if you could get out beyond the surf, where the water rolled instead of churned, there were rumors of whale sharks.

Fernando spoke Portuguese and very basic, broken English. I spoke English and very basic, broken Spanish—so our communication was limited; but it was obvious what I was trying to communicate. You. Boat. Snorkel. Whale Shark. Yes? Tomorrow? Yes? Yes. Ok. Good. Morning? Yes? Yes. Here? Yes. Here. Morning? Yes. Ok. Thank you. Thank you. Ok. Yes? Ok. Ok. Thank you. Yes. Ok. Ok.

When we went out the next day, we had rough water and only saw whales, but we went out a second time the following day and hit the jackpot! I saw humpback whales up close! Just a few meters away from our eight-foot-long boat! One baby humpback breached repeatedly. It felt so near that I thought I could reach out and touch it. In fact, the whales were a little too close. Fernando had to maneuver us away from the whales so that we didn't get sucked under if a big whale breached. Fernando pointed out a sea turtle that I never would have spotted on my own, and then, finally, we found what we were actually looking for: a whale shark.

I wrote on my blog at the time about this experience and called it "probably the coolest thing of life.", and to this day, more than fifteen years later, it still ranks up there as one of the coolest things of life. Whale sharks are the biggest fish in the world and can grow to be over forty feet long. In case you are spatially challenged like me, forty feet is the size of a school bus. Really big. Really, really big. We could see the sharks as giant shadows just beneath the surface of the water. When we spotted one, Fernando drove the boat out in front of the shark, directly in the path it was swimming. I then jumped unceremoniously out of the boat, snorkel gear in place.

The surface of the turquoise- blue ocean was like a portal into another world. While it was far from the first time I had been underwater–even underwater in the ocean, it wasn't until that day off the coast of East Africa that I was plunged into this new perception of an alternate universe. The laws of man and nature above the surface were warped under the warm waves of the Indian Ocean. Our bodies naturally float upward in salinated water, and it takes energy to force our bodies downward toward the solid floor of the sea. It is the opposite of the world in which we inhabit above water. We are naturally pulled down to the ground and have to expend energy to jump or climb *up*. The deeper we travel underwater, the harder it is for our bodies to function, while the higher we climb above the sea level, the more we have to struggle to survive. It is that single molecular layer of water that divides, and in many ways mirrors, the world above from the world below.

Even light and sound are distorted under the surface. Light dazzles, reflects, refracts, and dances through the prism of water and sounds seem muted and accelerated at the same time. It is as if "underwater" is synonymous with a sort of sonorous underworld, and, in being submerged, you *feel,* rather than hear, the ghosts of sounds calling through the depths. Total submersion is a complete, immediate, and intuitive transformation of our senses. It is a sensation both timelessly familiar, and yet, on that day in 2008, profoundly and acutely foreign. It is an experience that I will never be able to unfeel or take for granted after its realization that day. Slipping through the surface portal into the liquid world beneath is such a basic action that we take for granted, and yet it is also one of the most shocking and profound visceral experiences I can imagine.

I was suddenly broken from my reverie of the water world and found myself swimming for my life as the enormous head of a whale shark emerged from the ghastly green of the underworld. It was heading straight for me, parallel to the surface, at a distance impossible to judge with no point of reference on which to base my depth perception. It seemed both near and far, but within seconds I realized that it was, alarmingly, the former. The creature's head was broad and flat, and its mouth stretched the full width of its head. It swam with its massive mouth open and was in pursuit of a school of tiny fish that would disappear into the ever-open mouth of the giant fish. It could not have cared less about me, as I was clearly recognized as neither predator nor prey, but I was in its way nonetheless, and I feared that the gentle giant would crash right into me! I frantically swam out of its path, and once safe, continued swimming over the shark. I dove down and swam alongside the majestic animal for as long as I could hold my breath before surfacing, blowing the salty water out of my snorkel tube, and gulping down deep breaths of air. I dove deeper down, swimming below the shark, and then coming up for air again. After a few dives down, I couldn't keep up

with the fish anymore, so I surfaced, flagged down Fernando in the boat, and waited for him to pick me up.

After being ungracefully hauled into the boat by my intrepid skipper, Fernando drove the boat out in front of the whale shark's path again. I jumped back into the water and waited … waited … waited … *swim away*! The giant head with its wide, flat, vacuous mouth appeared again, headed straight for me. Again, I swam alongside and above the dark blue, speckled creature for as long as I could keep up and then bobbed to the surface, flagging down Fernando. We continued this process until I was too exhausted to swim, and the waves started picking up making it harder to follow the shark. It was an incredible experience; and a day I hope never to forget.

After our magical day spent together on the open ocean, Fernando invited me to his house to meet his family the following day. This immediately seemed like a really bad idea. I didn't know where he lived, though he assured me it was "not far"; I didn't really know anything about him. Yes, we had just shared an incredible day together; incredible for me at least, but wandering off into the wilderness with a man I could hardly communicate with raised all sorts of red flags.

Naturally, I agreed to go.

We met on the beach by my hut the following afternoon and set out walking to his family's home which he told me was ten minutes away. Apparently by ten minutes he meant an hour. There were huts scattered inland belonging to fishermen and their families, but there were no roads, no electricity, no towns besides Tofo, and Tofo was in the opposite direction from where we were headed.

The terrain was sandy with palm trees, but also had intermittent patches of dense swampland. Within five minutes of setting out, I had no idea where we were or where we were going or how to get home, and I knew I was in trouble if I lost my guide. Our conversation was limited by our lack of a common tongue, so we walked mostly in awkward silence. Occasionally, one or the other of us would try asking a question to make conversation, but we were both mostly just pretending that we had some idea of what the other

was saying. We made do with a lot of smiling, pointing, and awkward, forced laughter.

We had to cross one large swamp that had me a bit concerned for safety...rather a bit *more* concerned than I already was. It seemed a perfect place for crocodiles and hippopotamuses to be lurking. My heart was pounding as my mind shouted, "Bad idea! Bad idea! Bad idea!" Alas, it was too late to chicken out at that point, so I just took a deep breath and waded through the bog, following Fernando, and hoping that whatever was going to kill me would do it fast, before I realized what was happening.

Obviously, we survived the perilous swamp crossing and eventually arrived at Fernando's home. It consisted of a collection of four small grass huts, exactly like all the others we had passed, with an open sandy patch and a large cookfire in the center of the dwellings. At this point, the sun was setting, and I was doing my best to swallow down my regret, knowing that I definitely should never have agreed to come. Not a single person in the world knew where I was, or with whom. Bad. Bad. Bad. Yet another story that, if I lived to tell the tale, I could never tell my parents.

Fernando led me to the largest of the huts, and I entered to find most of his family waiting inside. Two of his sisters were tending to the fire outside, but his mother, father, and younger siblings were inside the one room hut. I said hello and tried to be polite, but none of them spoke any English, so who knows what they were thinking of this random white girl showing up to their far-flung abode.

They were obviously curious and asked a lot of questions. I'm assuming they were asking me questions; I didn't understand any of it, but it seemed like they were trying to ask me questions. I just smiled a lot. Fernando's mother was wrapped in blankets despite the warm climate and had alarmingly bloodshot eyes–there was no white in her eyes at all, just red. I asked Fernando if she was sick. He responded with a single word: Malaria. I was suddenly very aware of the mosquitoes buzzing around us.

Eager to escape the spotlight, I somehow communicated to Fernando, mostly through gesticulating towards outside, that I wanted to see what the sisters were cooking. I bowed myself as gracefully as I could manage out of the hut, and we made our way to the cookfire. It was fully dark now, so I couldn't see to have clues as to what it was that Fernando's sisters were cooking. I asked, of course, but walked, yet again, straight into the brick wall of the language barrier.

When the mystery food was declared ready, we all made our way back into the main hut. They had lit candles inside as well as a single lantern for light, and there was a single chair set out. They didn't have a table to eat at, so they all sat on the sandy dirt floor. I tried to

join them on the floor, but they insisted, much to my dismay, that I sit in their one and only chair. So, there I was, a single white woman far from home, sitting on a chair in a hut in Mozambique surrounded by an African family eating on the ground. I was appalled by the imagery and was glad that there was no one there to take a picture of the scene.

To make matters worse, I had no choice but to eat and drink what they gave me. It's not that I am normally shy of trying new foods or think that I am above eating certain things from certain places, but I was fairly certain that the water I was drinking was neither boiled nor filtered, and who knew how my stomach would react to the food. I couldn't communicate sufficiently to explain to my generous hosts that my wimpy American tummy was not accustomed to the bacteria and whatnot that may be in Mozambican water, and I certainly didn't want to be rude. It was bad enough that I was practically sitting on a throne; I could not bring myself to refuse their food and drink, no matter how sick I knew it could make me... and it would indeed make me very, very sick.

I never did figure out what the food was. Something that came from the ocean cooked into a stew and seasoned with a good amount of sand. I oohed and ahhed over the food, hoping that that was a universal language. After dinner, we shared a single mug for tea;

one of the sisters refilling the communal mug after each person took their turn drinking from it.

Finally, it seemed the appropriate time had arrived for Fernando and me to depart the family dwelling. I did my best to convey gratitude for the shared meal and my happiness to have met them. It was a relief to escape into the relatively cool night air outside. Unfortunately, we were not outside for long, as Fernando ushered me into a second, smaller hut. I insisted that it was late, that I needed to get back to my (imaginary) "friends", that they would be worried about me, etc., but he was insistent that I accompany him into the second hut. Since I was on a roll of making terrible decisions, I followed him in.

I came to understand that this second hut was his personal living space. His parents lived in the hut where we had eaten, and I assumed his sisters lived in the other two huts. I was surprised to find not only a bed in Fernando's hut, but also a massive wooden China cabinet. I could not imagine where the China cabinet had come from, why he had it, or how on earth he had managed to get it out here. We had to be at least ten miles from the nearest dirt road, and probably another twenty miles from the nearest paved road. I pity the poor souls he must have wrangled into helping him carry that thing through the sand and swamps to get it to his house.

The China cabinet appeared to be mostly empty. Fernando did not have many possessions. He was, however, quite proud of those that he did own, as he took the time to show me every one of them. He had a few small trinkets, a single pair of sandals, two pairs of shorts and three t-shirts, including what he was wearing. What he was most eager to share with me were a few old polaroid photos. I didn't understand who the people in the photos were, but the photos themselves were clearly important to him.

The last item he showed me was a toothbrush. He handed it to me ceremoniously, as if it held great meaning. He made the motion of brushing one's teeth, and I nodded and concurred thinking, "Yes, this is a toothbrush; you use it to brush your teeth." He shook his head and pointed at me and then made the motion again. So, I repeated the motion back to him with the toothbrush, pretending like I was brushing my teeth. He shook his head again, ushered me, toothbrush in hand, outside and pointed at me again, making the brushing motion. He wanted me to actually brush my teeth.

In hindsight and based on our cultural norms this seems ridiculous. Actually, it seemed ridiculous at the time too, but he made it seem like he was offering me a great honor, the luxury of brushing my teeth. His family had next to nothing, yet they had fed me, giving me their only chair to sit on; and now Fernando was so eager and excited to share his toothbrush with me. I felt like I couldn't refuse him. Again, in hindsight, it was absurd, but in the moment ... well, let's just say, I brushed my teeth.

When I finished with my ritual brushing of the teeth, Fernando took his turn and brushed his own teeth with the communal toothbrush. As I stood outside waiting for Fernando to finish his brushing, I looked up and my breath caught in my chest at the dazzling night sky above me. With no electricity for miles and miles and absolutely no air pollution, the sky above was crystal clear, and a million trillion stars pierced the black sky. There was a sliver of a moon that was so bright it hurt to look directly at it. Just that sliver, along with the stars, was enough to

reflect off the sand and illuminate the night enough to see the silhouettes of the tall, lean coconut trees around us.

Fernando must have noticed me gaping in awe at the sky and the silvery illumination it cast around us, but he didn't interrupt my vigil. Instead, he grabbed the two-foot-long machete leaning against the outside of his hut, and, with the blade clenched between his teeth, he scampered straight up a forty-foot-tall palm tree, barefoot. He climbed the tree like a monkey as if it were the easiest thing in the world. In a matter of seconds, I heard him hacking with the machete at the top of the tree, and I was startled by two thuds in quick succession. He had tossed down two coconuts at my feet. I will never forget the image of Fernando silhouetted against the sparkling night sky, hanging on to the tree with one hand, the machete in the other, forty feet in the air. I recall capturing that snapshot in my mind and thinking even at the time that this was a night to remember forever.

Before I knew it, Fernando had shimmied back down the tree and was beside me. He deftly spliced the coconuts in half, handing one to me. We drank the coconut water under the stars, sitting in the sand with the chorus of crickets and cicadas all around us. It was almost enough to make me forget that I was still in the middle of nowhere Mozambique with a man who could easily overpower me at any minute and no way of getting home without his help.

After I had my fill of coconut water, I thanked Fernando and indicated again that I really should be getting back to hut on the beach. This time, I stood my ground and tried to make it clear that, while I had enjoyed my time with his family and appreciated the meal they had shared, I would not be returning to his hut. I think he was disappointed, but he didn't put up a fight, and we began the long walk back to the beach.

When Fernando first put his arm around my shoulders as we were walking, I tried to subtly sidestep and brush it off. I was keenly aware of my vulnerability and cursed myself for getting into such a precarious situation. I couldn't outrun him if I needed to, and he knew the terrain like the back of his hand, whereas I could barely even see the back of my hand. After he tried a second and third time to make physical contact, I was uncomfortable enough to tell him outright that I did not want to be touched. I emphasized the word "friend" and hoped he understood. He did. He didn't try to touch me again, though the silence between us felt heavier after that.

After a half hour or so of walking in the dark, I thought my eyes had started to play tricks on me. It looked like there was a wall of tiny flashing lights in the distance. It was like when you're at a concert in a big stadium and the flickering flashes of cameras light up the arena, but in this case, it was as if the flashes were a curtain drawn across the entire horizon. I couldn't imagine what could be causing this phenomenon; it seemed completely unreal. I tried to ask Fernando about it, but the explanation was far beyond our ability to understand one another.

It wasn't until we were nearly upon the wall of twinkling light that I finally understood what it was. It was the swamp that we had crossed on our way out, but now it was covered in an endless cloud of fireflies. Their little lights winking on and off, creating the endless sparkling curtain I had seen from a distance. It was magical. Not quite magical enough to make me forget that I was crossing a death trap laden with bloodthirsty crocodiles and territorial hippos, but crossing the sparkling swamp is another memory that will last my entire lifetime.

When we finally arrived back at the beach, I breathed a huge sigh of relief. I had survived the night without getting violated or eaten alive—two very real possibilities. Fernando went in for a kiss when we were saying goodbye, but I used the cover of darkness to pretend that I didn't see him making the move. Before I could complete my getaway, he asked me to do something with him the following day. I don't know what he was asking me to do because we did not speak the same language, but I understood that he wanted to meet up with me at five p.m. again. Caught off guard and without a viable excuse, I agreed.

I met up with Fernando the next afternoon and figured out that he had asked me to have dinner with him—this time in the town of Tofo. I was somewhat relieved; at least I wouldn't be completely alone in the wilderness with him this time.

We walked down the beach to the small village, and he led me to a part of the town I never would have known even existed. I had been to the main market street with food and craft vendors, but there was a whole labyrinth of narrow, rickety alleyways made from corrugated tin behind the vendor booths. This tiny little village had a whole back-alley market and community just for locals, and I was invited in! I doubt many other foreigners or white people in general ever got to see that part of the town; I felt privileged to have the opportunity.

Fernando took me to a little nook of a restaurant. The single table area was no bigger than a standard sized outhouse. We sat on rickety wooden crates with an overturned bucket as our table. A woman that Fernando knew attended us from a makeshift kitchen, also about the size of an outhouse. I, of course, had no idea what they were saying to each other, but after a few minutes two bowls mysteriously appeared in front of us. I say mysteriously because I have no clue as to how or where the woman managed to cook said food.

The bowls were piled high, each with a mountain of rice topped by a whole fried fish, its big-crusted eye staring me down as his now permanently open mouth gaped at me. I don't particularly care for fish, but I was certainly not going to complain or refuse the food. Nope, I ate every last grain of rice and sucked the bones of the fish. There was no question of wasting food or dismissing hospitality. I tried to pay for the meal, insisted even, but Fernando was resolute that it was his treat.

It was my last night in Mozambique, so when I said goodbye to Fernando that evening on the beach, it was for good. He was clearly hoping for a kiss but settled for a hug and a promise to never forget him. I never saw him again, but I did keep my promise and have never forgotten him. Nor have I forgotten his family, the starlit coconuts, the way the light danced over the whale shark, or the magical curtain of fireflies drawn over the swamp.

Spring

by Alex Noel

Six months of darkness
Bitter winds and blowing snow
Barren trees
Groaning against the endless cold
Rigid, lifeless corpses
Haunting memories of a world that was.

But when our hearts are finally frozen
Our hope is lost in the deafening silence of
snow cover
And the world has surely perished,
A miracle beyond imagination,
Spring, arrives.

Blankets of snow rise eerily,
Reborn as phantom fog
In the newly dampened air
The earth softens, subtly at first,
Just enough to allow the slightest memory
of life.

And that's all it takes for the world to change,
For the endless dead and dark of the long night
To shatter open in a riot of life
The sun growing bolder with each passing hour,
Its rays getting stronger, light lasting longer.

Peepers emerge unseen,
Singing their praise to the world reborn
Screaming their songs
To the sparkling new moon
Calling creatures awake and back from
their gloom.

Slowly but surely
White turns to brown
And overnight, an explosion of green
Leaves unfurled, glowing
A shade unique to the pure infancy of
spring.

The scent of freshly wakened earth
And newborn grass
Assaults the senses,
The smell of lanolin and lilacs
Harmonize in the flawless lullaby of life.

The year's first robins herald in dewy mornings
And still drowsy honeybees
Catch the lingering light of the setting sun,
Chionodoxa ascend to their hard-earned thrones,
Tiny conquerors of the winter snows

Thawing trees run sweet with sap,
Tart rhubarb grows wild,
And elusive morels hide in the heart of the
forest,
Blanketed in delicate trillium
And fragile fiddlehead ferns.

Even the clouds become hopeful,
Rain giving root to the lush life to come,
Colors contagious
Spreading with the wind
Painted across wildflower wheat fields.

And in a few short weeks
The unimaginable has come to pass,
Hearts have thawed with the melting ice,
Crystal clear blue-green waters dance
under the newborn sun
A dazzling reflection,
A joyous celebration,
The miracle of life

Soak

by Alex Noel

Tears spring from my eyes unannounced
Streaming down my face
Salt-stained streaks of light
Reflecting a world ablaze
Arms outstretched, exposed
Drinking the rawness of life
The glowing warmth of the sun
Chased by the excitement of a wild starry night
Dark skies dancing
Piercing blackness with brilliant light
A hundred million pinpricks of hope
Guiding my spirit upwards
While waves gently kiss the shoreline
Lapping at my feet
And embracing the rhythm of blood
Rushing through my veins
Until I am one with the sea
The sand
The sky.

Two Rivers

by Rick Kent

He sighed and sat up in bed. Dawn was always best anyway. Returning to sleep after hours of lying there, staring into the darkness had again proved fruitless. As it did many of his nights. He slipped out of bed quietly. Careful not to wake his wife or the dogs. Dressed, padded shoeless out the door that faced the river. He breathed in deeply, exhaled and listened. The stillness so loud his ears ached listening for sounds of the day's beginning. No breeze yet. At this latitude you often had days such as this, in early summer, when the tender new leaves of aspen that grew along the river would not move the entire day. A night chill in the air would linger until the sun pushed it away later in the morning. Birds of this spruce-aspen greatness- gregarious gray and black chickadees, red crested pileateds and the ever-curious jays-had not yet started their morning reveille that would awaken the ravens and white throated sparrows. And the smells. Perhaps it was because, as his wife often said, his hearing was waning or perhaps, as he liked to believe, his olfactory sense had been one on which he had learned to depend, but his nose gave him clues to the mysteries of each day. The tingling freshness of spruce, the musky, heavy odor of decay from the slough and especially the damp, metallic smell of the river. But this morning, the incredible smell of green. It was difficult for him to think of the bonding of color and smell, but he couldn't find a better way to describe that early dawn smell in spring other than just that – green.

Night stubbornly retreating from the eastern sky. Jupiter and Venus still glowing above the trees. A sliver of waning moon to the west. No clouds yet. If he walked quickly, he could get to the bend in the river, below the island, before real light. It wasn't far. Through soggy alder and swamp grass hummocks, into the spruce tangle, following the trail deer and coyotes used, finally into the meadow above the first island. He liked to start fishing just below that island. It was like the quarterback always beginning the game with a "sure fire" pass play. Get your confidence going. Get into rhythm. Catch that first trout, one of the easy ones. Mostly undersized brookies that held in slightly deeper water below the rocky riffle downstream from where the river came together after being split by the island. When "outsiders", family or friends, came to visit and said they wanted to catch a trout on a fly rod, he would bring them there. But not at first. Let them understand that fishing on the river was not just about catching trout. They had to comprehend the connection of the water and cover, food and presentation. Also fly fishing was different. It wasn't like casting for bass or seemingly easy like in the movie with that blond actor on that river out west. Once they started showing a glimpse of understanding, sometimes after a few hours or maybe even days, he would bring them to the water below the riffle to catch a trout. Almost a sure thing. A gift of gratitude from him to them for showing the understanding of what the river and the trout and fly fishing meant to him. But also, to prove the point that you had to work hard at something to really enjoy it. Often, he was called a "hard-ass", demanding and difficult. Never made things easy. His boys said that to their wives in quiet conversations he overheard. Life had taught him that good things were seldom easy, hard work created luck and victories were possible, but always came with a price. Sometimes a cruel price.

He finished donning waders, tying, then tucking in the laces of his wading boots, looping the old-fashioned wicker creel and net over his shoulder, and finally the worn chest pack full of fly boxes, leader, and tippets. His sunglasses and then his frayed ball cap. Double check everything, make sure all gear was in order. Always the same order. He enjoyed the routine and discipline of it all.

He walked briskly down the hill from the cabin towards the river. He still called it the cabin; his wife said no, it was now their home. Living full-time on the river in the woods. A little morning stiffness and wince of pain in his left leg. That pain had been part of his fishing now for most of his adult life. Almost like a friend. No, really more like a family member. You can choose your friends, not your family. He had no choice in this. Part of him, ever since that misty, gloomy dusk that had been broken apart by explosions. Sharp, cracking detonations that came without warning. The patrol had just come into the clearing near the crest of that grassy hill west of Dong Ha. More explosions. Crouching, running, making sure everyone was down and then the sudden smash in the legs, like being kicked with a steel -toed boot. Sliding downhill, headfirst in wet grass and mud. Laying there, checking his legs with his hand. His clothes wet from the rain. When he brought his hand to his face all he could see was reddish mud on his fingers, but he could detect the coppery smell of blood. His own. Wiggling his toes, moving his legs, checking his crotch. The grunts worst fear. Relief. Everything intact there. Sharp burning pain starting. Listening. Silence. No further incoming. No small

arms fire from the tree line eliminating the possibility of an ambush.

The medic up, checking his wounds, calling for a medivac. One other man hit, minor wounds to face and shoulder. The medic would bandage the soldier, who would continue on. Later, the blur of being carried to the helicopter and the quick flight to the aid station, a collection of tents at the combat base. Wounded laid out in rows on stretchers. Corpsmen hurriedly working under dim light of lanterns. Next to him, to his right, lay a soldier, a kid really. The kid was shirtless, just fatigue pants and boots, dirty blond-haired head tilted towards him, face smudged with dried mud and remnants of camouflage paint. Eyes half open, barely blinking. He had to look closely to see if the kid's chest was moving. The kid was on his side, his left hand holding the bloody compress, unsuccessfully keeping bluish gray bloated rope-like intestines from spilling out of the slash in his stomach. He was moaning softly. The morphine taking him away, but not far enough where he still couldn't feel pain. Stomach wounds were the worst. The young soldier was next into the operating room tent. He didn't see him again, but wondered still if that young soldier, too, had a chance to grow old and to fish on a river as beautiful as his.

He remembered the hospital ship coming into view from the helicopter window where he was strapped on a stretcher. A manila tag tied to his shirt button. On it, name, rank, service number and the letters MSW; multiple shrapnel wounds. The ship seemed huge. Bleached bone white made even more stark against the contrasting seamless, slate gray of sky and water. The ship, cruising up and down the coast, out of enemy artillery and rocket range, picking up the detritus of war. The crew chief shouting its name over the din, Repose, a place of rest. For him more, a place of refuge and recovery. At least physically. Some repairs, then weeks of rehabilitation. For many on board the mere mending of a tear or breach of skin or flesh. For others, the amputation of a hand, arm, foot, or leg and then on to the next stop of their medical journey home.

He recalled the tall, gaunt Marine with five holes and three shattered bones caused from a single bullet. The young sergeant from Texas who had lost an arm, both legs and his eyesight from a rocket blast, who said he was the luckiest man alive. And how he longed to be with his wife, back in Amarillo, but also wondered how she would react to her legless, sightless, one-armed husband? Would she still love him, need him as much as he would her? The husky African American lance corporal who had taken a bullet through his upper thighs, ripping muscle, and turning to memory his manhood and how he was kept sedated until he was transported on to Japan so he wouldn't wake until then to discover the truth. He remembered those broken young men and many more whom he had met during those weeks on the ship. He healed and rested until he was ready to return to duty. Back to his unit, his men, and those rugged, dangerous, ominous hills west of Dong Ha.

He found himself staring, thinking instead of seeing. He slowly shook his head, clearing his mind of those ancient thoughts. Needed to get back to thinking about the river and trout.

Down the hill, through mud and grassy hummocks, spruce, and alder tangles and finally near the river again. He could smell and hear it first. Then he was in sight of the moving water. Standing in the waist high, dew rimed grass, looking downstream. The river, barely visible through the pale gray feathers of morning fog wafting wraith-like above the rippled obsidian glazed water. It was getting lighter now. The eastern sky showing the promise of dawn with a growing stain of muted yellow above the far ridge. He carefully connected the sections of his rod, sighted down the rod to assure alignment, then examined the fly. This morning it would be a variation of a Royal Coachman wet. Size 10. Red, green, and white with a glimmer of gold. The locals called it a Betty, after a bartender at a small backwoods cement block beer joint that smelled of tobacco smoke, hamburger grease, and a whiff of stale urine. She tied the flies herself and sold them over the bar.

Kept them in a box next to the jar of pickled eggs. Betty was as rough and sturdy as the loggers, hunters, and fishermen to whom she served drinks. Didn't tolerate fighting and nobody tested her. But her flies were so different. Graceful, dainty, with wonderful color. Almost artful. Seemed impossible those flies could have sprung from those calloused, nicotine-stained fingers. This time of year, before the caddis hatches, the fly of choice for catching trout in his river. He had tied these himself, during the long winter months up here. When he couldn't fish, but could think about fishing and sometimes, less pleasant passages of time. Tying flies and thinking, all part of that close connection he made with moving water, trout, and life.

He stepped into the river, felt the coolness of the water compressing the waders against his legs. He welcomed the soothing caress of cold on his calves and knees and thighs as he carefully made his way around softball sized rocks that lay scattered on the bottom. Rocks that were smooth worn pieces of basalt, granite, and quartz. This time of day and until the shadows receded to the far side of the river, the trout would be feeding in the current, closer to him than the overhanging brush on the far side. Later, as light began to hit the water, the trout would move to cover provided by the brush, and fishing would be over for the day. But that was hours and many casts from now.

He stripped the pale tangerine-colored fly line from the reel. From years of holding that line in his hand he could sense just how much he needed to reach the trout and not the tangle of tag alders just beyond. When the quantity of line was adequate, he began false casting to get the curls of line from his hand through the guides of the rod and finally unfurled in the air. Increasing the length until only a single coil of line was left in his hand, the remaining making a graceful journey to his front then rear until he was satisfied with distance and angle. He then leaned slightly at the waist, lowered the rod tip on the forward arc and laid the fly gently on the water, quartering downstream, just inches from the inviting tips of the alder branches. The line straightened and the fly sunk, starting its passage across and down the river. Causing the fly to drift and waver, minnow like, into the feeding lane and over the rocks where he knew the trout were.

He didn't expect to catch a trout here. This stretch would be best in a few weeks, when the caddis were hatching and he switched to dry flies, small, size fourteen or even sixteen. When the trout were so aggressive and numerous it was hard to believe, let alone explain, even to his wife.

He repeated the action after every three or four steps. Lifted the rod tip quickly at the end of the fly's drift, when the line and fly were lying straight down from him and then after a few efficient false casts, laid it softly down again. Getting his rhythm going. Feeling good about the muscle memory from doing this same effort thousands of times over the past two score years.

He worked his way down through stove-sized, mostly submerged boulders, remnants of the last Ice Age, ten thousand years earlier, when the glacier was over a mile thick where he was standing. Imagining the river flowing for ten thousand years since. His duration on the river a mere speck of time and faint interruption.

Now, with shorter casts, intent, but knowing the first fish of the morning would most likely come below the riffle just ahead.

The river widened and slowed down as it prepared to narrow again, become shallower and more turbulent as it rustled over smaller fist-sized stones of the riffle. At this spot, just above the fast water, alders again reached their twisted mass of branches down to the water and created cover. Part of the holy trinity of trout. Cold clear water, food, and cover. Maybe here instead. He cast his fly in the feeding lane, the seam between fast water and slower back water below the boulders. He watched as it began to sweep with the current downstream. Again, it finished the journey without interruption. Either undesired or merely undetected.

He kept moving now, just as the river was and had been for over ten millennia. Anxious to get to the riffle and feel that first trout.

He stood at the upper edge of the shallow water of the riffle, deciding on whether the next cast would be to his left where the water was deeper, but the run narrower. Fewer trout to his left, likely those with more substance. To his right in the broad, rock-strewn flat; more trout, but usually smaller.

He paused, decided, lifted the rod tip, and then with two sweeping preparatory casts, lay the line down to his left. The fly hugged the tags and quickly was swept into the dark water of the run. The trout hit almost immediately, explosively, surging upward causing the water surface to bulge, then boil. The line abruptly straightened, jerked down and sliced across the current. He lifted the rod tip and immediately felt the throbbing of a sturdy fish coming through the line, rod, and into his hand.

Eventually, the trout swings back and forth in the quiet water to his front. In its struggle, the fish surfaces and he can see a glimpse of color. Orange and pink, with dark green. A brookie. Decent size. Nice for this river. With his left hand he stripped in line, holding it tight against the cork handle with his forefinger when the fish decided to run. Kept stripping line until the fish was within reach, unhooked his net and swept the fish into its hold.

Yes, a brookie. The first of this day. At least thirteen inches, heavy for its length. The colors and patterns pleasing to him, inspiring a sense of awe. The pink and gold spots, red, black, and white fins, burnished brass worm pattern on the back, deeper rose, and copper colors along the belly. Tried to fathom what evolutionary forces could have created such beauty and for what purpose. He brought the net only part way out of the water because this trout would be released. That was his custom, another ritual. The first fish, especially the good ones, were returned to the river. As an offering or merely an expression of appreciation for having all this be available to him.

He delicately grasped the hook with his fingers, pulled the curved metal free from the trout's jaw. The fish lay sideways until he lowered the net into the water, then righted itself. He turned the net so the brookie faced upstream and lowered it gently away from the fish. The trout paused and then with a few slow thrusts of its tail moved back into the dark water of the run.

He smiled and nodded. A good start of the day. He wanted just three fish to take back. Enough for their dinner that evening. He didn't keep many trout these days. A fraction of those he caught. Only enough for an occasional meal, usually some celebration of sorts, for him and his wife. Tonight, their anniversary.

He noticed the shadows beginning to shorten on the river. Still time left for him to fish to the next sweeping bend. Past the deep run where the creek that drained the cedar swamp joined with the river offering its cooler water, around the holes and minor riffles and beyond the rocky, log-strewn island to the flats where his fishing for this day would end.

By the time he reached the bend above the flats, he had kept three trout. He had caught and released eight more. A good morning fishing. The sun was now above the treetops on the ridge. Only a few feet of shadow along the very edge of the river. Almost time to turn back to the cabin.

He could feel in his leg and back and shoulder the effects of his morning's effort. He moved to the bank, where the section of tag alders was separated by a short stretch of tall grass, burdock, and thistle. With care, he leaned his fly rod against the nearest tag, removed his creel and sat down on the bank. His back to the warm sun, feet ankle deep in the river. He removed the trout from the creel, quickly gutted and then wrapped them in wet grass, returned them to the creel where they would stay fresh until he returned home. The offal he threw into the tall grass. A mink or fisher would enjoy the remnants of his catch later.

After rinsing his hands, he rested with his arms on his knees, head down, looking into the faintly copper colored water swirling around his feet. He focused on the bottom watching the particles of sand, small stones, and bits of debris eddying around his boots. Heraclitus had been correct when he said

something about never stepping in the same river twice. Every moment, each, and every sensory aspect of being in this river was truly different. None like the one before. But the philosopher was speaking more than about a river. You could never be in the same part of your life again. For this he was glad. The disastrous first marriage just weeks after his return from Vietnam, the difficult and estranged relationship with children, the agonizing death of a son, the empty, lonely time until he had met the woman who was now his wife. And, of course, the other memories that were becoming more distant, now he had someone to talk to, to try to explain in inadequate words, about feelings, admissions, and guilts.

He lay back against the weedy bank and closed his eyes. Felt the warmth of sun on his face. Smelled the sweet scent of bruised grasses and sedges. Listened to the murmur of the river and heard in the distance the strangely prehistoric squawking of a sandhill crane. His mind drifting back again, unbidden, but going back by a volition he didn't understand. Another river. Another sunny day. Brutal sun. Temperature and humidity above toleration. The patrol had been out for two days moving along the waterway through the jungle and tortuous, razor-edged grass. Looking for signs of enemy activity. Trails or river crossings. The enemy needed the river. So, this is where they looked.

Taking a break in the tall grass. Grass higher than their heads. Men exhausted, spread out, lying on the ground, feet toward each other, facing outward. All dressed alike in faded and torn jungle fatigues, stained white from salty sweat, boots scuffed, pale, and worn. Weathered faces and arms scratched and scabbed. Wearing webbed canvas and metal harnesses that held pouches of ammunition and bandages, with grenades hooked to the straps on their chest. Rifles in their hands or leaning across an arm. Some dozing. Others just staring out from dark, red rimmed eyes, languidly brushing away mosquitos. A few drinking from canteens or eating from olive-drab cans. The damp air redolent with the jungle smell of rot and decay.

His head snapped towards the jungle. The ever-present cacophony of birds and other jungle sounds suddenly quiet. Then the faint murmur of voices, the sing-song lilt of Vietnamese. They knew there were no friendlies for miles. The time for blood was upon them.

Hand signals. No noise. Nobody move. Turn the radio down so no sound of squelch to betray their presence. The bowel tightening, sphincter constricting, heart-pounding-in-his-ears apprehension. Then the voices getting closer and the sounds of other men taking a rest in the tall grass by the river. Just like them. Easy killing distance away. His men turning to look at him, eyes wide. Hand signals again. Quiet, stay down, don't move. Hearing the gurgling of canteens being filled, quiet laughter. Others sounds of men pissing in the parched, paper-dry grass. The enemy so close he could detect the faint odor of campfire smoke emanating from their clothing.

After an eternity, a sharp command, and the sound of men on the move. Listening for a sign of their route. Away from them. Through the tall grass back into the brush. Minutes or was it hours later, the signal to relax. The men breathing deeply, some looking at him, smiling. Thumbs up.

The tall grass had hidden them but would have meant nothing to bullets or grenades. Both groups of men moving away from each other without harm, like the same poles of two magnets repelling each other to opposite directions. They were safe another day. The questions going through his mind, should they have fired through the grass at the voices? How many others were in the tall grass beyond their listening? The men were relieved. They knew the right answers to his questions. They didn't say, and he didn't have to ask. They all just knew. After cautiously moving upstream and away from the direction of the enemy, they stopped, and he radioed a call for artillery on the spot he calculated the other men might have gone. Estimating the distance they could have traveled in that heat and jungle and tall grass. The intersection of time and space converted to a spot on the map he held in his hand. Within minutes he heard the thunder of the high explosive rounds impacting the target he had selected. Twelve explosions, each sending out razor sharp shards of metal capable of maiming or killing anything within their lethal reach. A deadly outcome resulting from the seemingly inconsequential encounter of two groups of young men on the bank of a river far from their homes. Doing his job without regrets. At least not then.

War was so harsh. It had no soft edges. The decisions you made were so absolute, but, yet, also so arbitrary; what routes to take that day, who would walk point, what equipment, supplies or ammunition to take or leave behind. Every choice came with consequences that could determine both the length and substance of men's lives.

When he opened his eyes, the shadows on the river were gone, the sun higher. Time to head back upstream to the cabin. After retracing his route and with his gear properly hanging from the hooks by the door he walks upstairs to the kitchen. He drops the trout in the sink, rinses them, puts the fish in a plastic bag and in the refrigerator. Footsteps on the back porch are his wife's. She heard his return and is anxious to hear about the morning. Over coffee he shares some snippets about the river, the first fish and about tomorrow when they will fish together. For him, true joy is to watch his wife with a fly rod. Graceful, with a natural sense of how rod and line and presentation work together.

In the background of their conversation, music from the local country station. The voice of Patsy Cline singing that song about being crazy. A favorite. Reaching across the wooden-topped counter where they are sitting, he takes her hand and gently guides her up. They start dancing, slowly. A ritual of theirs. He can smell the faint scent of lilacs and sunshine in her hair. That tells him about her morning. In the garden and then working the horses. Parts of their life that are to her like his fishing. They move together and he holds her tight. He rests his chin on her head and closes his eyes. At moments like this he knows she is right. Here on his river, with her, this is home and after so many years, he knows he's almost there.

Memories of the Copper Country Limited

by Larry Jorgensen

Copper Country Limited enters Portage Lake Lift Bridge (Houghton)

For seven decades, a passenger train known as the Copper Country Limited provided an important link and way of life for many communities in the Upper Peninsula. Operated by the Chicago, Milwaukee Road & St. Paul Railroad, the service between Chicago and Calumet, Michigan began in 1899 and it was officially called the Copper Country Limited starting in 1907. The train service grew through the years with steam and diesel power and improved passenger comfort including sleeper and dining cars.

The U.S. Post Office had established the concept of mail distribution by rail in 1864 and by 1930, thousands of trains like the Copper Country Limited had added mail cars which would be used for the sorting and collecting of mail enroute. However, it was that mail service which ultimately became a major factor in the death of the Copper Country Limited.

By 1957, the "glory days" of railway travel was gone. In fifteen years, passenger service had decreased almost fifty percent as newer and faster means of travel took its place. However, the final blow to the Copper Country Limited came October first when the postal department announced it would withdraw all mail service from trains and switch to trucks and air carriers. By 1966, the railroad was losing $300,000 on passenger service to the Upper Peninsula and the decision was made for the final run of the Copper Country Limited to be on March 7, 1968.

The emotional memories of that last run remain today as I was one of several news reporters to experience the story of the historic event. We boarded the train at 12:30 a.m. in Green Bay. The clerk who sold the tickets had been with the railroad for ten years, and on the previous day had observed his 50th birthday. The railroad provided employees the day off on their birthday, and the clerk had used his day to take the train's last round trip to Calumet and back.

During those first dark hours of our trip north, we passed through familiar communities like Coleman, Crivitz and Wausaukee, and I noticed their stations were empty. It was about 4 a.m. when we arrived at Iron Mountain, and the only signs of life at that depot were a couple expressmen unloading newspapers and a few express items.

Next on our travel agenda was a stop at Channing for an early morning breakfast available at a community bar and temporary restaurant conveniently located near the tracks. I paused to wonder if that old business, much like the train, had seen better times than now as it provided a simple replacement for the once popular dining car.

Our next stop was less than two hours away at Champion when the Copper Country Limited switch onto Soo Line railway tracks and a new engineer and crew had arrived from Marquette and were required to oper-

ate the train for the remainder of the trip to Calumet.

Leaving Champion that morning, the sunrise seemed to be creating a special farewell salute with vibrant colors of dark red, orange, and yellow which reflected off the night's fresh snowfall. As we continued north, one regular passenger pointed out the total winter snow accumulation in that area already was recorded at 208 inches.

The morning sunrise became even more memorable after I was able to view it from inside the engine's cab. Soo Line engineer Robert Gray shared a few of his experiences and said he had met a lot of friendly people in the Copper Country. At one point he told me, "At the next green house on the left, there always will be a little boy and his mother waiting and they will wave." He was right, they were there, and both waved one more time at the Copper Country Limited.

They were just two of the many residents, railroad fans and photographers who lined the tracks that day for one last look at a reliable old friend which had become part of their daily lives. The Copper Country Limited meant many things to many people.

There was the teacher from Baraga who rode the train daily to commute to her school in Calumet. She expressed concern about what she would do when her school opened again on Monday. There also was concern about an elderly lady from Amberg who often took the train to visit her son in the Veterans Hospital in Chicago.

Many first-time passengers also were on board, like the student and his mother who boarded in Green Bay. Ronald Plazotta was a dedicated railroad fan who planned to add to his large collection of photos and railway memorabilia. In addition to taking photos along the way, young Ronald studied for a science exam he would be taking when he returned to Green Bay. There was an off-duty Chicago policeman who explained he spent his vacation time riding trains, but this would be his first visit to Upper Michigan.

We arrived at the Calumet depot at 5 p.m. Friday afternoon where local community leaders had gathered for the historic event. We heard comments by Judge Norman Trezise, Calumet Justice of the Peace, and secretary of the Chamber of Commerce.

Trezise recalled a time when Calumet was served daily by ten trains. He said, "This is more than a civic loss to me. My father was a railway postal clerk, my father-in-law was a roadmaster, and I had three brothers-in-law who were brakemen."

The empty Copper Country Limited was turned around one final time and headed back to Milwaukee with no passengers aboard. The day before, students from Baraga and Houghton had been able to ride the train to Calumet and back as they participated in the final round trip run.

When I had purchased my ticket very early that Friday morning in Green Bay, a fellow newsman told me, "Save that ticket, some day it will be worth something." I did that and he was right! Today the ticket is a treasured reminder of memories made on the last run of the Copper Country Limited.

My ticket for the final trip of the Copper Country Limited

Coal Dock, Escanaba, Mich.

Historical · Escanaba coal dock with schooner 1915

Negatives at a Funeral

by John Adamcik

Surely you were a daughter of the Jazz Age,
riding with the top down and flicking
cigarette ashes into the air,
speeding out of the parking lot
with your eighty and ninety-something friends.

Generations apart,
we shared an interest in history
and you liked it when I listened
(even though you grabbed me
with a sailor's grip and salt).
Could I believe the city council let "them"
open another chain restaurant?
Don't these idiots have any vision?
And what was I going to do about it?

You'd certainly earned the right to such
    admonition.

I wish I'd been there when you slammed
your hand on the hotel lobby desk in post-
    war Brussels,
demanding to know Dame Agatha's room
    number.
Your first husband's attaché said he was
    "mortified," and you called
him Morty the rest of the trip.

Or when you grabbed a champagne bottle
from the sidewalk table of that cafe in
    Monaco
and knocked that pickpocket off his game.

Or when you crashed the Jekyll Island
    croquet courts wearing all black.
Or when you signed into the Huron Club
    under your first husband's
last name, on purpose, knowing he hadn't
    been a member.
Rules for you were truly "lingua viva."

So when you said you were dying I said
what everybody says.
You said get real;

you'd used this body up, had a damn good
    time doing it,
and were ready for your new one.

You meant it.
Just like when you said your husbands
took secrets to their graves
and you would, too.

Who here was your best confidant?
Everyone knew you better than I.
Children, grands, and greats.
Friends and rivals.
They share stories amongst each other,
while I catch fragments of your legends
as I consider evidence on a cork board:
old Polaroids, square, black and white prints,
among a few expensive portraits from your
    toddler years.

I'm drawn to photos of you in a swimsuit on
    a dock
at some 1950's U.P. inland lake resort.
Your hair pulled back, one foot
on the bow of a wooden Chris Craft.

It's these negatives, though, that testify to
    your legacy.
Someone thought so, leaving them pinned,
    almost as tribute.
Or as a secret
to be shared among your real friends.
Who else would hold the fragile strips up to
    the light
to see you - it's obviously you - behind the boat,
buzzing the dock,
a rooster tail of water spraying off your skis
    at the photographer.
You're laughing.

That's the you I imagined.
The one you described by your living.
Ebullient truths
in every breath.

The Faultfinder's Quarry

by John Adamcik

'd worked up a righteous fury dumping my coffee in a to-go mug and grabbing my truck keys off the kitchen counter. As much as I like walking the property when I'm in town, running off trespassers is a hassle. If I could, I'd turn my mobile phone off on weekends, but the trail cam app has proven useful. The last thing I need is kids swimming in the pit and getting into trouble. I've put the fear of God into a few teenagers over the years. It's usually the same story: they thought they'd found the perfect summer party spot, with their own private pool, of sorts. Half of them probably can't swim. Although I don't enjoy being the middle-aged crank, I tell myself it keeps them alive. Besides, insurance doesn't cover negative publicity.

The trail cam video showed an old Jeep going down the two-track, up to the locked gate. It took me about twenty minutes to make the drive, but the Jeep was still there when I arrived. After parking, I walked around the car briefly to get a read on whom I was dealing with. Surprisingly, the Jeep's back bumper wasn't covered with hippie stickers. There wasn't a cluster of air fresheners hanging from the rearview mirror. No mud on the rear quarter panels from an early-morning bog run. In fact, the Jeep was in great shape. The paint was a little faded but polished. The interior was clean. Almost too clean. Like it was hardly used.

Pushing thimbleberry bushes aside, I followed a worn path around one of the gate mounts. Time to add a chain-link fence, I thought. This part of the property is fronted by a hundred-foot palisade of thick undergrowth, boulders, and trees. It used to be there was no way of knowing what's on the other side unless you'd been there, or somebody told you. Now, any kid with a smartphone can scope out satellite images of the terrain and find a way to get access. These kids are incredibly resourceful when it comes to recreation.

Despite myself, for a moment I enjoyed the tranquility of the day as I caught the brief echo of a woodpecker in a nearby pine. This has been a special place as long as I've been going there, which is since I can remember. On this pristine afternoon, the dry air blew just enough to mask the rising temperature. Coming to a clearing, I glanced at the wooden picnic table beneath a mature oak, close to the entrance to the pit. There wouldn't be anybody there. It was a changing area for my paying diving customers. The real action would be around the bend at the water's edge. Surprisingly, I didn't hear laughing and splashing and the like. In fact, I didn't hear anything as I approached. That bothered me for a couple reasons.

I cleared my throat loud enough so anyone in range would know they weren't alone. No need to come in hot with my handgun drawn. In my work, I'm out in the woods when I'm not reading reports. You never know what you'll find in remote places. Last week a few customers saw coyotes here. And while a group of people wouldn't typically attract wildlife, one guy in the woods could look like prey to a hungry pack.

There were no sounds except those of squirrels scampering and the rustling of leaves in the trees.

"Hello?" I said, trying to make myself sound big.

Nothing.

Walking cautiously around the large boulders near the pit shore, I looked for any signs of activity in the water. Nothing. Then a plop, a sound I recognized immediately. My eyes scanned to an area of the pit where the water levels drop from fifteen feet to around thirty feet. Concentric ripples emanated toward shore, telling tales on the intruder. Stopping and looking around the elevated perimeter, I spotted him walking back from the south-facing wall, fishing pole in hand. Although the area was only accessible by going up a hill, the part nearest the pit dropped down gradually until it was only a few feet up from the water. He put his pole on a rest and sat down in a folding chair.

Gotcha, I thought.

"Hey!" I yelled. "You're not supposed to be here."

He turned his head toward me, without moving any other part of his body.

"I'm coming over," I said.

The man turned back to face his pole, then stood up, reached out and grabbed it, and gave it a couple of swift upward tugs before placing it back on the rest.

Unbelievable.

After climbing the hill, I reached the small clearing and took the downward slope until I came up on him from his right side. He didn't move. He wasn't holding anything, and I didn't see anything dangerous within reach. Still, I gave him plenty of room as I approached, walking around until I was far enough away from him that he couldn't get at me without taking a few steps. I sure wasn't going to let him push me into the pit.

White hair peeked out from his bucket hat and matched his well-kept mustache. He was neatly dressed in well-ironed khaki pants and a light blue, short sleeve shirt with a buttoned collar. His shoes were practical, tan walking shoes, the kind I see advertised on afternoon television or the mailings I throw away. He looked straight ahead at his pole.

"You're not supposed to be here," I repeated, keeping my frown intact.

The man gathered up the lower part of his face, moving his mustache slightly and raising his thick black plastic eyeglass frame as if he was going to speak. Everything settled back into its resting place. Nothing.

"It's a posted no fishing area," I said.

"I used to fish here," he said. His voice was soft, yet clear. It wasn't defiant, but rather stating an objective fact. Perhaps he had built a career making such statements. Telling things as they are. His calmness almost sidetracked me.

Suddenly the man's eyebrows raised, and he moved swiftly from his yellow plastic woven seat of the mid-century modern folding aluminum beach chair, deftly reaching the pole, grabbing it, and lifting it swiftly in one smooth motion. He cranked the open-faced reel a few turns, then set it back down on the rest.

"This is a dangerous place," I said.

"For the fish, maybe," said the man.

"There's no fishing allowed here," I repeated. "Why are you fishing here?"

"This is where the fish are," said the man. "Good water. Good attractors. Quiet space."

"Yes, and that's on purpose," I said. "Those attractors cost me a lot of time and money to install." I felt the heat of anger rush across my face. My voice rose. "I put a bus, an airplane fuselage, and a motorcycle in the water for points of interest for the scuba divers. We plant fish to make it interesting for them. They pay to have a nice, safe dive and not get gouged by a lost hook or get tangled in some excess fishing line."

The man reached down, picked up a large metal thermos, popped the cup top off, unscrewed the inside stopper, poured some coffee into the top, then set that down on the ground. He screwed the stopper back into the thermos and put that next to the cup. Then, almost mechanically, he picked up the cup and took a slow, intentional sip. He kept his gaze on the fishing pole throughout the entire process.

Putting the cup back down, he picked up the thermos and removed the stopper, then held out the thermos to me.

"Top it off?"

I realized then I was still holding my travel mug.

"I could hear that last dreg of what I assume is coffee sloshing around as you walked up," the man said.

He was right. Again.

Pulling the lid off my mug, I reached for the thermos and poured about half of its contents in my mug, then handed the thermos back to him.

"Thanks," I said.

Turning toward the pit, I looked down at the various shades of bluish green water, mottled by the different depths created by quarrying years before I purchased it from my uncle. The prison down the road had closed decades ago, and the demand for this type of rock had been reduced by improvements in mining and highway engineering. It really wasn't much good for anything but riprap now, and there wasn't any money in that. At least not around here. Transport costs ate up any margin. Still, I couldn't let the land go. Turning the pit into a dive location brought in enough money to pay the taxes on the land and keep it in the family.

"You said used to fish here?" I asked.

"Yeah, my friend's father owned the place. It was different, then."

"Who was it?" I asked, suspiciously.

"I grew up with Arthur Moyle. We were pals as teenagers. He was a good guy."

"I'm Conrad," I said. "Art was my uncle. Did you know my father, Mitch?"

The man looked briefly away from his fishing pole and assessed me with a laser-focused gaze.

"You favor Mitch," he said. "Big nose and all. How is Mitch?"

"He passed a few years ago. Cancer."

"Oh. Sorry. And Art?"

"He passed not long after Dad. Both had the same type of cancer."

"Genetics can be brutal." Then a pause. "What kind of work do you do?"

"I'm a seismologist," I said, hesitantly.

"You must be smart," said the man. "What exactly do you do as a seismologist?"

"Seismology is the science of studying earthquakes," I replied, using my career day voice like I've done at my children's schools. "We—"

"I'm not an idiot," he barked. "I know what the field of seismology involves. I asked what exactly you do as a seismologist."

The change in his tone and his direct response stunned me.

"Right," I said, gathering my thoughts. "Of course." I wasn't going to apologize to this guy. Who did he think he was, coming on my land and scolding me? "My research is plate tectonics."

"And what do you do with that research?"

"Mostly I provide data to other scientists," I replied. "I work for a university, and I recently started a side consulting business, advising organizations looking to build along the West coast. Sometimes I get overseas work along the Pacific Ring of Fire."

"Hmm," was the reply. "Sounds to me you've carried on the family business, taking it up a level, as it were. There's not much bigger in the world of rocks than the lithosphere."

I was embarrassed. He was right on several points.

"I guess not," I said. "You catch anything?"

He nodded. "Two good-sized smallmouths. A few bluegills. Released them."

We drank our coffee in silence.

"You live around here?" I asked.

"Not far," he said. "It's a community. At least that's what they call it. Nobody there wants to do anything. There's only so much bingo a man can stand."

"Family?"

"It's just me, here. My wife passed last August. We were married fifty-three years. Almost fifty-four."

"Children?"

"Moved on," he said. "My son is in Iowa working for a trucking company. He's married and they've given me three grandchildren. I've got a daughter works in insurance in Ohio. She's divorced, no kids."

"Oh," I said. Family friend or not, I needed to figure out how to get this guy to leave. He didn't seem in a hurry to go. Tact seemed appropriate, and that's not my strong suit. "Did you and Art ever come out here when the prisoners were working the pits?"

"Sometimes," he said. "Your grandmother had us bring lunch out to the foreman and guards. Sometimes cake for the whole crew. Your grandfather ran this place well. I never heard of any trouble from anyone while it was open."

"Yeah, they were good folk. Never looked down on anyone. Grandpa always said it was only the ones who got caught that ended up in prison. He said everyone's done wrong."

"He was a good man." Silence for a minute or two.

"What's your name?" I asked.

The man drew in a long, quiet breath, then held it for several seconds.

"Callison," he said, as if exhaling his very self with this disclosure. "Terry Callison."

"Listen, Mister Callison—"

"Terry," he said. "My father was Mister Callison."

"Terry," I paused. "Look, if we didn't have the divers to think of, I really wouldn't mind you fishing here. I just can't have it."

"The divers have Superior. They'll never run out of water or shipwrecks out there."

"This is a good training pit for new divers," I said. "Besides, I don't have any way to clean up in the water if you lose your line."

Terry leaned forward, yanked the fishing pole out of the rest, and with one motion lifted it swiftly upward and cranked on the reel. This time he kept reeling, dropping the tip of his pole down as he did so, then bringing it back up, then repeating. His face broke into a slight grin, as he continued bringing his catch to the surface.

"Must have been down deep," I said. "Seems to be a fighter. Catfish?"

"Nope. It's a bass. A real lunker." Terry let the fish rest for a moment, or, rather, let himself rest. I couldn't tell which. Maybe both. Then, as suddenly as he had gotten up from his chair, he handed the pole toward me.

"Bring him home," he said. I wasn't prepared for this.

"C'mon, now," Terry repeated. "Don't let him off."

I dropped my mug on the grass and took the pole from Terry. I noticed his big hands, thick, with large, somewhat oversized knuckles. He was right, the fish was a fighter. I pulled the pole up and reeled, let off a little, then reeled some more. After a minute, I felt the fish break the surface tension of the water. It was a big bass. Maybe the biggest I've ever caught. The fish continued to twist, but no longer had the benefit of water; there was nothing to strain against except the summer's air. Although its torquing was more uncontrolled, I quickly brought him up. Terry grabbed the line about a foot above the fish and helped guide it to the grass. The bass eclipsed my twenty-ounce mug in length, and almost in girth.

"She's a beaut," said Terry. "Well done."

I felt like a child, but in a good way. In a way I hadn't allowed myself to feel in years. He was right, it really was a beautiful specimen of fish.

"Probably eight pounds," said Terry. "He'd make a nice casserole."

"I guess he would," I said. "You're welcome to take him."

Terry looked at me and smiled, the top of his glasses rising to the brow of his hat.

"Thanks, but I get a senior discount at the diner," he said. "They've got a catfish sandwich like my wife used to make. Besides, the community doesn't like me using my fillet knife outside. It scares them. And I've been reported for harboring unauthorized fish aromas in my room."

"What would you like me to do with him?"

"Toss him back," he said, removing the hook from the fish's mouth.

I smiled and picked up the fish, marveling at its green lateral lines contrasted against its bright red gills. Taking it with both hands, I walked him down to the beach and gently placed the creature back into the water.

"My wife makes casserole sometimes," I said. "Tell you what. I've got another pit on the other side of the property. It's overgrown, but I've been bushhogging the area this year, and there's enough access for us to see if there's anything in there. My dad said grandpa planted some fish there years ago. No telling what's survived."

"You'll need panfish for any predators to have made it this long. I've got a recipe for bluegill casserole that your wife will love me for."

"Great," I said. "When is a good day for you?"

"I'm surprisingly flexible in my scheduling," said Terry.

He picked up his pole and tackle box. I got the chair and thermos, and we slowly walked down the hill and back to the gate. He methodically placed his items in the back of the Jeep, as if they would be inspected upon his return to the community.

He turned and reached out his hand, which I shook.

"Thank you," he said.

"For what?"

"For being patient," he said. "When you're my age, it seems you have to fight for every damn thing you want. So many rules. This is supposed to be a good season of life."

I smiled, and, out of character for me, reached out and put my arm on his shoulder.

"Terry, you've done me a favor today, helping me remember what it's like to enjoy the land as it is, and as it was. And you helped me land the biggest bass I've caught in years."

"You're kind," he said. He got in his car and rolled the driver's window down. He handed me his business card, which had the office phone number neatly lined out in blue ink, and another number carefully written above it. "Gave up my insurance brokers license some time ago, but I'm not going to pay for new cards. The number goes to my home phone. I don't have one of those smart devices everyone's got, so you can't send me one of those text messages. Call me when you're ready for your second fishing lesson."

He smiled and drove off.

I snapped a photo of the card with my phone and then put the card in my pocket. I knew then I'd call him the next time I was home.

Hancock, Mich., Quincy Street.

Historical · Hancock · Quincy Street 1900

Three selections from The Seasons, the Years, the Decades

by Jane Piirto

◆❖◆

In Winter from the 40s, 50s, and Beyond

*I*n *winter*, the roads looked like brown sugar. Depending on the amount of traffic on the street, the brown sugar snow was packed or loose. Snowbanks got sheered by giant snow-go machines whose screws chewed up and spewed chunks into trucks that rode like baby whales next to their mothers, or like sidecars, and the geology of the winters can be traced in the cut banks, much like tracing the rings of a tree or the ages of a mountain range from a canyon. At corners, car hoods peeped hesitantly out from behind the sheered banks, and by March, if there had been no January thaw, antennas had flags or flowers tied on them to warn people around the corner. Winter was so present, six months or so, sometimes late October to sometimes the first week in May, people planted their babies in snowbanks to take pictures as they grew up.

Everywhere we went, during days when this snow was falling, we had to brush the car off after going into a store or building. If we had ten stops to make, we had to brush the windows off ten times. Brushing the car became as automatic as igniting it. There were three styles of snow brushing. Those who opened the door, got the brush out and circled the car, cleaning each window, were the detail people. Those who gave a quick swipe to the front and side window with their mittens, cuffs, or bare hands, were the idea people. Those who got in and used their windshield wipers and hoped the snow would blow off

Problem starting the family car

before they turned the first corner, were the risk-takers.

Annually then as now, a hundred fifty or so inches of snow fell. Both girls and boys played outside all winter. Our neighborhood had an ice rink, about a half mile away, down two long hills, and along a street about five blocks long. Snowbanks covered the sidewalk, which was only partway and only on one side of the road. Sometimes we would put on our ice skates at home and skate to the ice rink, all that way, along the sanded ruts of the road. Sometimes we would throw our skates tied together over our shoulders and walk, sitting in a snowbank to put the skates on. In the neighborhood rink, the ice was bumpy and uneven, as the city only flooded it every ten days or so. It had one light pole with one bright bulb with a corrugated shade. The boys would play hockey there, but we girls never played hockey. We wore white figure skates, with pointed edges on the front, while the boys wore hockey skates, with no points, and so they had to slide sideways to stop.

One of the school district rules was No Snowballs One Block from School. You still remember the apprehensive itch in the middle of your back when that one block boundary was reached, and the boys would unleash the painful snowball whack. When you were a principal of a school in Manhattan, New York City, in the 1980s, you instituted this same rule for the children you supervised. People thought you were too strict, but you knew winter and snowballs.

We wore wool. Sweaters, coats, jackets, snow pants, socks, mittens, hats, scarves. Snow would bead in frozen drops on our outer garments, and we would hang them over the radiators in the vestibule and under the windows. Sometimes we put leather mittens, called "choppers," over our mittens, but that was mostly for boys and for those who worked outside, not for us who played outside. The smell of drying wool is pungent and damp, instantly recognizable, throwing one back to the winter outside playing of childhood. Some winter jackets were of nylon lined with quilted cotton, with faux fur collars, and you loved yours. Mother had a real silver fox collar on her wool green winter swing coat. We used to stroke it.

The town's roads were plowed efficiently and quickly. The town was winter-friendly. The Winter Sports area had three rope tows to three hills of varying difficulty. The area was groomed, and open on Saturday and Sunday afternoons and on Tuesday and Thursday nights. Most kids skied. The Winter Sports area also had a long toboggan run, iced, and framed to fit the width of a toboggan. You would line up on the ramp to the shack, and then five, six, seven kids would climb on the shelf, load up on the toboggans, grabbing each other with arms around each other's chests. In a control shack at the top, a flipper sent the toboggans down the hill. The run was about a quarter mile and ended next to Baby Lake. After the screams of

joy and fear, and the thrill of the icy speed, after the toboggan dead-ended in soft snow along the lake, you would take turns pulling it by its rope back up to the shack for another ride. People could bring their own toboggans or rent one. There was a log lodge which served hot chocolate, cookies, cake, and some of the most delicious hot dogs ever, when you wanted a rest. Your sister rented this lodge for her own wedding reception in 1983, on a very cold and nippy Christmas Eve, and your family of many Piirto cousins rented it for a reunion in June in the early 1990s.

The Winter Sports area also had a ski jump named Baby after the lake upon the shores of which its landing ended. Local neighborhoods each had a ski jump, and Baby was the one for the people at the north and west end of town. One of your classmates, member of a famous ski jumping family from your neighborhood, described how in high school and college, he would drive to Baby early in the morning, at dawn, and do a few practice jumps before school. Ski jumping requires the ability not only to soar over the bump onto the landing, but also the strength to climb and climb with the heavy ski jump skis over your shoulder, in the heavy square-toed boots, up to the top. He became a member of his college ski team when he transferred to the University of Colorado, but he quit the ski team and joined the U.S. Air Force to fly over Vietnam.

Two of the girls you hung around with tried to jump at Baby, sneaking there on an afternoon just before dusk on a weekday during Christmas vacation. Girls were not supposed to ski jump. Though you yourself skied, both cross country and downhill, you were never tempted to jump, though you did join the neighborhood girls in helping to sweep and to pank the landing of your neighborhood ski jump, Steepie, for an inter-neighborhood ski jump contest, brushing the landing with pine branches and sidestepping up to smooth the snow into corduroy.

Winters, your parents helped you and your little sister build an ice castle in the yard. They shoveled snow into a huge pile and began to carve it with shovels, and then loosed the hose on it to form ice. Two thrones were on the top, and inside, it had one room, and a bench, all of ice. It was late January, and so it didn't really melt much, even on sunny days, and you and the neighborhood kids had a lot of time imagining. The castle also had an icy slide about eight feet long.

You went sleigh-riding on the roads before they were sanded and salted too much. In your neighborhood, on Hill Street, sometimes you kids were able to belly bump (fling yourselves on your bellies onto the sled and steer it with your hands all the way down to the highway, M-28 business). You only made it there once. Sometimes two of you piled onto your stomachs on top of each other. You also were able to sit and steer with your feet, one or two of you on a sled. Flying saucers and cardboard also served, but these were usually on big hills that were not streets. Another way to play in the snow was to shag cars—or "shack" cars. Kids would wait in the dark for a car to pass, and then throw themselves into the street, grab its back bumper, and slide behind it. You had to use slippery boots, ski boots, with leather soles. Boys did this more often than girls, though we were known to try it also. This was, needless to say, dangerous, but no one got hurt, that you know of.

Cold, ice, and snow were not only pleasure for play, but they wreaked pain. Snow would come into your waistband. Other kids would thrust it there as a joke. Your snow pants would ride up and your bare legs would grow red and raw. Your wrists would get bare also, and chafe with pain. Coming in from playing, entering the vestibule in front, pulling off your woolen and later, gabardine, snow pants, jacket, scarf, hat, mittens, stripping to the jeans beneath, hanging them on the radiator built into a square-shaped crevice in the wall, you peeled off your socks. This time you had white toes. As the toes thawed, the tingle hurt, a constant smashing of icy needles. "Don't rub," said Mother. "Just put them near the radiator and wait until the color comes back." Sometimes you would put your feet in a bucket filled with lukewarm water.

In later years, in your thirties, you sat in your nineteen-foot center console fishing boat on Lakes Michigan and Huron in early spring, trolling back and forth, as your husband fished for coho salmon. Once, your fingers in their gloves froze, and forever after you had to wear mittens and not gloves, while skiing, both cross-country and downhill. Cross country warmed you and so your fingers were safe, but downhill, not so much. Your fingers would begin to tingle as you rose up the mountain in the chairlift, and you had to rush down, weaving in banked long curves as fast as you could, snap off your skis, stash them and your poles into a snowbank near the door of the lodge, hurry in to the restroom, and run warm water over your fingers, white to the second joints on three of your fingers, until the pink returned. Old frostbite lies dormant until awakened by cold. That frostbite still hits you; last winter your fingers froze while driving in your cold car to your chorus rehearsal, and you sat in your chair singing Alto Two, watching your white fingertips with familiar dismay until they warmed.

Whatever the fun of winter sports, of tramping through quiet woods on snow-covered trails with only the swoosh of your skis and the plant of your ski poles; of winging around screaming with glee at the end of a line of kids playing crack-the-whip at the big ice rink at the playgrounds, near the high school football and track field; of cheering by beeping the car horn with all the hundreds of others when a famous ski jumper landed with a winning distance at the local huge ski jump hill, Suicide Hill; of sitting on a snow-covered log with a steaming thermos of hot cocoa and a peanut-butter and raisin sandwich on a break while snowshoeing; of jumping into the snow naked during a sauna at your uncle's old smoke sauna at a farm nearby, there was the constant snow removal. Shoveling and shoveling. Your father said, "Winter is nothing but a hardship." His weary comment explains it all.

Every house had, and has, a variety of snow shovels, to scoop, slam, dig, remove the constant snow. This was before the advent of the snow blower (and the gas lawn mower—lawns were mowed with push contraptions with swirling blades that had to be sharpened regularly). Someone invented a snow remover called the Yooper Scooper, a welded, molded wide scoop of thin smooth metal, with a wide, curved push handle and with a bed that could be filled with snow and rammed or pushed into a pile rather than lifted. It might be accurate to say that many of our fathers and brothers, mothers and sisters, escaped heart attacks with its advent. And then there is the inevitable experience of just finishing shoveling when the snowplows came and piled the hard, frozen blobs of snowplow-hardened snow pushed across the driveway just after you had shoveled the car out. The temptation to try to ram through the icy snowbank without re-shoveling is common, and one sees two tire tracks in many snowbanks, made by successful rammers.

In college in the early 1960s, you commuted to Northern, the local state university, along with other hometowners. Your carpool had five, sometimes six, people, depending on who had eight o'clocks and who had four o'clocks. You never had more than five, as someone always hitched an early or a late ride with another carpool. You were picked up at seven a.m., with one beep sounding from outside. On snowy mornings, you sometimes broke way through the falling deep snow, swaying and gunning the unplowed or barely plowed fifteen miles to the college, climbing up the high hill from Washington Street to where the college lay, arriving in time for your eight a.m. classes. The college never closed for snowstorms in those days, so the classes were, indeed, held on time, even in snowstorms. Most of the time, the parking lots were even partially plowed.

Roofs collapse if not shoveled. Icicles build at the edges of these roofs, and it is dangerous to shovel them. Your intrepid widowed mother, living alone after your father's death from lung and brain cancer in the mid-1970s (she died in 2015) would push snow off the roof from a lower, flat roof, with a wooden long-handled scraper. But it would just build up again. People make their yearly money by shoveling others' walks, driveways, and roofs. Pickups are festooned with front plows, and those who own such trucks are in demand. After your mother's death, you needed to pay for the family home expenses so you put it into the Airbnb system a few winters ago, and you managed it from your primary home in Ohio. You relied on a local plow service, with its four-wheel drive plow trucks, and also on the caretaker, who was a family friend, and a local college boy, to clear the front steps and porch, the flat roof, the driveway into the yard, the back sidewalk, the garage roof before guests arrived to fat bicycle, dog sled, snowmobile, ski race. You had a local company install heat tape to the edges of the roof to melt the icicles so they wouldn't fall on people. Newscasters talk about how hard it is to live in Buffalo, NY, in the wintertime, but Buffalo has nothing on the upper reaches of Marquette County, Michigan.

•••

Kindergarten, 1945-46.
Kindergarten: in all the schools where you have worked or observed, this room, built in the late 1930s, was the most striking. Our kindergarten room was opulently decorated in the Central School, with a granite fountain, a tiled fireplace, honey-colored maple tables and small, sturdy maple chairs, a bank of huge picture windows so there was always bright daylight, a cloak room between the kindergarten and first grade rooms, closets for supplies, shiny porcelain tile halfway up the walls, gleaming linoleum polished and clean. The school itself was like this, always tidy and clean. The teacher was Miss Bamford, a tall middle-aged woman who, in memory, resembled Eleanor Roosevelt, with a white-haired bun. Her family was of the mining bosses. She was competent and nice. You had all-day kindergarten, nine a.m. to noon, one to three-thirty p.m. You did not have recess, and you walked home for lunch. This was in 1945 and 1946.

Easter Breakfast · March 23 1946

A photograph of an Easter breakfast on March 23, 1946, in kindergarten shows sixteen five- year-olds, all Caucasian (though one of us would later discover she was half Ojibway, adopted out of a nearby reservation), with mostly Finnish, Cornish, Italian, Swedish, Irish surnames, sitting on those solid honey-colored maple chairs, with glasses of milk and orange juice and plated bowls with oatmeal and brown sugar, in front of each of them. The table has platters of pastries and small cream pitchers. The girls wear braids or shoulder-length hair, knee length dresses or plaid skirts, and some of the boys have shorts with knee socks. The centerpiece features four bunnies in Deco style facing each other like boxers, on their hind legs, on the fireplace is an angular Humpty Dumpty, and miniatures of farm animals. The bulletin board has graphic illustrations of nursery rhymes—for example, Jack jumping over a candlestick—and others. It was rather an elegant setup for us children of miners for an Easter celebration, and we seemed happy to have such a feast. Our mothers probably set the table and volunteered to bake and cook. The date on the mantle is March 23.

In kindergarten, a long-lasting emotional event happened; you accidentally bumped W. and he fell into the round ceramic tiled fountain while you were both reaching for one of the sailboats on strings in the water, and he got soaked. His mother had to come and bring him dry clothes. Many years later, W. and his wife came to a speech you made in Connecticut, where they lived. Over dinner after the speech while you were reminiscing, he said that his mother always hated you after that accident. You found this out seventy years after the incident. W's mother believed you had deliberately pushed him. You told him you would never do that. Your household was nonviolent. You yourself were never physically pushed or hit, and you had only been spanked once, again, in kindergarten, when you and two other kindergarten boys, took off on tricycles toward Negaunee, three miles away. The three of you made it about half a mile along the iron-ore colored side of the state road. Mother had been so worried that you had actually gotten so far, she gave you a swat on the buttocks when you got home after she had driven down the highway to find three little children diligently peddling along the side of M-28, next to traffic.

Billboard's Top 40, 1957

There was no television there in the north; though many people your age from other regions of the U.S. remember shows such as *Howdy Doody* or *Captain Kangaroo* you have no such memories. Your Uncle had an antenna and was able to get a snowy signal from Green Bay, 160 miles south. The family would go to his house on Monday nights to watch *The Arthur Godfrey Show.* When television came, with WDMJ in Marquette the only channel, we had local news at six p.m., CBS News at six-thirty, and a black and white movie afterwards. The station signed off with the Star-Spangled Banner, and a test pattern showed all night.

But there was AM radio on WJPD, with its "winky blinky tower" where Santa sent greetings, behind its small shack along US-41 in the cedar swamp near the Carp River. For years WJPD's studio was above the Miners Bank, near your dentist's office after your dentist uncle left for California. They had a talent show Saturday mornings there, and once when you were in fourth grade, you entered yourself in the contest, climbed those long steps, went into the studio, stood on a box by the microphone, and sang "I'm looking over a four-leaf clover." You didn't win.

For teenagers, WJPD broadcast the local request show on Saturday morning at eleven a.m. where you could listen to popular early rock n' roll music that other kids called in or wrote postcards to request or dedicate to other kids, girls to boys, boys to girls. The Saturday show was sponsored by a grocery store, Russo Brothers, "Where Ma Buys Meat That Pa Can Eat." You sat listening, looking out the front window to the pine grove across the street, or upstairs in your bedroom, lying down and dreaming and imagining that someone would someday dedicate a song to you or that you would get the nerve to do so for a crush you had. Neither happened.

The neighborhood girls had a constant discussion about who was better, Pat Boone or Elvis Presley. Elvis came out with "Heartbreak Hotel" in 1956, when you were thirteen years old. "You've got to listen to this song!" your girlfriend told you while you were walking home after eighth grade. You went into her house to listen to it. She even had a 45 RPM (revolutions per minute) record player. The song was among his first hits, and it is a badge of pride for people of our generation to remember when rock n' roll began.

You didn't have a 45 RPM record player yet, though your family had a console radio combination record player which only played 78 RPM records, and the family in the evenings would sit in the living room listening to the radio or records. On Sunday afternoons at five p.m., "The Shadow" came on. It was a dark mystery show in which the main character, Lamont Cranston, would say in a deep voice, "Who knows what evil lurks in the hearts of men? The Shadow knows, Ha, ha, ha, ha." It was very scary. You would lie on your stomach with your head near the speaker, which was on the bottom of the console, covered in a fabric of brown woven with gold threads.

Pat Boone was clean cut and a saved Christian, and so he appealed to you more than Elvis did, with his sideburns and shaking legs. Though you liked Elvis' singing, you liked Pat's smoothness better. In the summer of 1957, Pat's song "Love Letters in the Sand" was rivaling Elvis' song, "(Let Me Be Your) Teddy Bear" and you and the girls had long discussions and arguments about the cuteness of these two older star boys, both twenty-two, and both good singers.

When you came home that summer from two weeks at Bible camp, where you had no radio to listen to, you learned from *The Mining Journal*, the local daily newspaper what song had risen that two weeks to #1 on Billboard hit parade, and you lorded it over your girlfriend, who loved Elvis, for this week Pat's was first, and Elvis' was #2. Of course, the next week it changed—the two were neck and neck for a couple of years and the arguments about relative merit continued. We knew the words to all of the top ten songs, and you can still recall them and sing along when they appear on your Sirius XM Fifties channel.

But when "Chances Are" by Johnny Mathis broke in in October of 1957, that was it. That velvet croon backed by soft strings, did it, and you collected all his albums until you were a senior in college in 1963. When you went to college in Minnesota for that one semester in fall, 1960, until your parents' money ran out because things were slow in the steel industry and your father had to move down in rank to work in the diamond drills from his higher position as a welder and you had to return home to commute to the local state college, Northern, you girls would turn out the lights, burn candles, sit on the dorm floor leaning against our beds, and quietly listen, lost in yearning.

Not only top 40 hits moved you. In high school you played the score and the album—by then you had your own 45 RPM record player—the 1955 musical movie, *Oklahoma*, with Gordon MacRae and Shirley Jones, the soundtrack to the 1956 *My Fair Lady*, and the late 1940s *South Pacific*, over and over on Saturday mornings while cleaning the house. You and your sister were not permitted to go anywhere on Saturdays before doing your share of the house cleaning—the upstairs—bedrooms, bathroom, hallway—

scrubbed, dust mopped, sheets changed, all surfaces dusted, rugs vacuumed—and inspected by Mother. You also had these scores in piano music, and would play and sing them over and over, entertaining yourself. You now listen to the Broadway channel on Sirius-XM, and loved living in New York City in the 1980s, where you often attended shows "best available" as a single. You often got a front-row seat.

Mother herself as a young woman had been a household helper and she took care of a disabled son of one of a nearby town's prominent families that had a famous tree in its yard. This was before she took the commercial training at a local for-profit school for shorthand and typing at a local school after she graduated from John D. Pierce High School, where she was the only one of her three other siblings to prevail to graduation. The high school was a laboratory school for the state land grant college which had its campus two blocks from her childhood home, an easy walk, and a fortunate accident, for it offered a fine tuition-free education taught by professors in education.

MUNESING HARBOR LAKE SUPERIOR.

W.J.Morgan & Co.Lith.Cleveland.

Historical - engraving munising harbor trade card

The Last Blooms

by Ninie Gaspariani Syarikin

These past three or four years, every
February, when I made a right turn
on that corner sidewalk on those
4th and G streets, crossroads on
the southwest, where two strong
magnolia trees stood, I always felt
gloomy; knowing that my imminent
gravitation was inevitable.
That I no longer possessed the stamina
to strive and thrive.

While grateful for the opportunity to
enjoy the spreads of the teeny-weeny
buds on their stems,
emerging even in the harshest weather,
I sighed in my fear that this could
be the last season I'd see them
bursting into the majestic flowers in
April.

Throughout March, I witnessed daily
how those capsules grow bigger and
fatter, preparing their petals inside
that would later open, bewitching
the passersby.

Oh, my Magnolia!
You were mine to adore from year to
year.
Your beautiful blooms, from white to
pink to lilac to violet to purple, from
spring to spring.
Your robust emerald leaves from
summer to summer.
Your naked exotic limbs during the
chilly winter.

You've kept me company since I was a
beauty.
You've taught me how to age with
grace.
But now I am relenting, becoming
weaker and vulnerable, ruining my
figure,
shedding my once long and thick hair,
worse than your falling leaves in
autumn.
The grey strands betray me, no matter
how often I dye them black.
Alas, I don't have your rebirth.

So, perhaps, these are your last
blooms that I get to gaze at before I
disappear from the horizon.
How will it break my heart, my
Magnolia!
Yet, I am helpless and hapless, as my
life is approaching its sunset.
Even no guarantee that I shall sleep
through the night, without waking
up in a nightmare.

Oh, my Magnolia!
Not much that I managed to gain in
this world.
But, at least, my memory of sweet you
will be cherished when I close my
eyes.

When Christmas Changed to Easter

by J. L. Hagen

◆❖◆

I saw my father's head and shoulders pass by through the side windows of the new house. In his arms, he cradled a load of firewood. In a few hours, he would light the Christmas Eve fire. Our guests would arrive, and their annual party would begin, a family tradition handed down from my Aunt Louise and before that, my grandmother. He hustled along next to the deck, bundled in his thick green overcoat; white hair, black glasses, and a long pale face topped off by a gray tweed "newsboy" cap. His breath dissipated like steam in the frigid air.

My wife Mary and I had taken off work and driven up the previous day, Wednesday, the 23rd, from Grand Rapids. The traffic heading north to Loyale had been steady, but a heavy snowfall slowed progress once we crossed the imaginary forty-fifth parallel and headed toward the Bridge.

I recognized the toll collector as a classmate from high school. As I handed her a twenty, I wished her a 'Merry Christmas.'

"You, too," she said. "Up just 'til Sunday? Or staying on through New Year's?"

"No, heading back down below on Christmas Day to my in-laws."

What I didn't mention was that our Christmas celebration promised to be the best ever. A few months earlier, mom and dad had sold their place in town and moved to a new home on Lake Michigan. This would be their first Christmas party there and a chance to show off the house. But there were other reasons, too.

At Thanksgiving, Mary and I had driven home to the U.P., planning to make a special announcement. The timing never felt right, so I procrastinated all day. Finally, Mary headed for bed.

Later, when I slipped under the covers, she pressed me. "Did you tell them?"

"I'll do it tomorrow." Even in the dark, I could feel her fiery glare.

"No! You need to tell them right now. Before they go to sleep." She gave me a shove on the arm.

I sighed. "Oh, all right."

I crawled out of bed and tiptoed to the rear of the house. My parents had given up their master bedroom to us and the guest bedroom to my sister and her husband. They had crawled into the sleeping loft above the kitchen.

I looked up from the family room. I could smell smoke from the banked fire behind me in the woodstove. "Hey, are you asleep yet?"

My mother's voice floated over the loft half-wall. "Do you need something, Carl?"

"No, I—I just wanted to tell you. We're going to have a baby."

Silence.

"That's wonderful!" Mom exclaimed. "When's she due?"

"Middle of April."

"Thanks for telling us," Dad said. "Oh ... and congratulations."

•••

So, first Christmas in the new house. First grandbaby on the way. My father recently promoted to Executive Vice-President, the capstone position to which he had aspired for fifteen years. Their four children through college and launched on successful careers. Everyone married. The only thing missing was my two brothers being home for the holidays. Unfortunately, one lived in Sydney, Australia, and the other in San Francisco. Still, much to celebrate.

While we waited for the guests to arrive, I reflected again on the new house, my father's successes, and our relationship.

Dad and I were always close, but somehow could never communicate. Around the middle of my sophomore year in high school, I had quit the football team.

"I want to concentrate on my rock band," I announced to my mother. She conveyed it to him. He said nothing, but he loved sports, and I knew he was disappointed I wouldn't be playing in the fall.

To perform, I had to buy an amplifier. He asked me to come to the bank where he worked as a loan officer.

As I walked up a half-dozen steps to the main lobby, I passed the huge display of plants in the plate glass windows. They made the whole floor smell like a hothouse.

I sat down across from him at his desk next to the teller line.

"Tell me again, how much do you need?" he asked.

"Me and the guys found three amps at a music store. Mine's four hundred."

"That's a lot of money." He gazed at the tiled ceiling, thinking for a moment. "Okay, here's what I'm going to do. The bank will lend you the money. Since you're a minor, you'll need an adult to cosign the loan. I'll sign for you. But you'll have to pay it back. How's that sound?"

"G-great!" I choked out. It was unbelievable, really.

He wrote up the loan, and we both endorsed the paperwork.

Within the year, I walked into the bank one day and paid it off. And I learned something about business and credit. Although he never said so, I eventually realized that was the point all along. He had swallowed his disappointment and helped me turn it into a triumph—and a teaching moment.

Later, when I went away to college, that initial tension between us grew exponentially. He was a WWII veteran. Like most vets, he never

talked about his time in the service. But when I voiced my opposition to the Vietnam War, we argued. As my hair grew longer, the arguments became more heated. Coming home for the holidays inevitably led to an altercation. But a conversation over the Thanksgiving dinner table during my sophomore year blew our smoldering conflict into a five-alarm blaze.

"So, what have you been studying this semester?" Mom asked.

"I'm still mostly taking required classes, but I squeezed in an elective."

"What are you taking?" Dad asked.

"African American Literature."

"That's different," Mom said. She looked at my dad. "I'm surprised by your choice."

"Well, I've gotten to know a lot of kids in the drama program through my roommate, Michael. If you recall, he's from East Detroit and wants to be an actor. Several of the students are black. The stories they tell about growing up in Motown, especially this one girl. You wouldn't believe it. It got me thinking about what it's like—being black."

"I can't imagine," Dad said, "Why anyone would want to live in Detroit."

"Yeah, it sure seems different from here," I replied.

The conversation continued like this for several more minutes, as I related my latest experiences navigating college life in the late 1960s. My sister and younger brothers were still in high school and junior high, and they were taking it all in.

"Have you found a new girlfriend yet?" Mom asked, switching topics. I had confessed to her a few months earlier that my freshman-year girlfriend had dumped me at the end of summer. Her blindside confrontation had knocked me cold.

"Yeah, actually," I said. "I have been seeing the girl I mentioned earlier."

"You mean in the drama program?" Mom asked.

"Yeah, she's really cute—and lots of fun."

"Didn't you say she was black?" Dad asked.

"Well ... yeah," I said. I glanced from him to mom. "Her mother works for the Detroit Public Library."

The room fell silent as a tomb. My father's face told me what I dreaded most.

A month later, at Christmas break, my mother confirmed my fears.

"Your dad wants to have grandchildren someday," she said. "Kids that look like him. He doesn't understand why you can't find a regular girlfriend."

"But, Mom, she's really nice," I said.

A year later, she ended our relationship and moved to New York. One day, my mother asked if I was still seeing her. There hadn't been letters in our mailbox that summer.

I told her what had happened. "Mom, I really loved her," I said. "She broke my heart."

She was sympathetic and gave me a hug. But subsequently, there was a noticeable easing of tension in the household.

It was only temporary.

•••

In my senior year, I had grown increasingly disturbed by the Vietnam War. Not only was I opposed to it, but my anxiety about being drafted after graduation had intensified.

My draft number was 125, and I had received a college deferment. In 1972, it seemed a coin flip whether they would draft me after graduation. However, I had been brought up in the Methodist Church and deeply influenced by our minister regarding Christianity and pacifism.

As graduation approached, I struggled intensely with the notion of killing other people, even in a so-called "just war." Was I against all wars or only this one? Or was I simply scared of being killed and had masked my fear in a philosophy of non-violence? Besides Jesus of Nazareth, I had learned about leaders such as Martin Luther King and Gandhi. Both my parents were patriotic, and I too was strongly committed to democracy and American ideals. I agonized over what to do. Finally, I decided to go "all in," no matter the consequences.

I wrote a lengthy letter to our hometown draft board, asking to be reclassified as a conscientious objector. I didn't tell either of my parents. I just put a stamp on the envelope and mailed it.

When I returned home after graduation, my dad had the letter in hand. His teeth clenched, he stared right through me.

"Why didn't you tell me about this?" he shouted.

It was the question I had dreaded all spring.

My shoulders drooped. I let out a breath as I looked away. "You're a member of the draft board. I didn't want them to think you had anything to do with it." In truth, I was also ashamed to tell him of my decision. I knew it would cut his heart out.

He wheeled around and walked away, but not before his disappointment registered in a painful scowl conveying his mortal wound and furor that I hadn't informed him ahead of time. Soon after, he resigned from the board.

•••

In the fall, when they laid me off from a summer gas station job, he confronted me again. He often came home for lunch. One day, shortly after the noon siren blared, he charged into the house. I looked up from the book I was reading on the living room couch.

"When are you going to find a permanent job?" he thundered. He grabbed me by the shirt and jerked me up. "You're not hanging around here forever."

I pulled away and ran down the hall into our tiny bathroom. He followed me in, blocking the door. I crumpled to the floor against the wall. Spreading my hands over my face, I covered my chest and stomach with my arms.

"What are you doing to find a job?" he shouted again. "College is over!" He grabbed me, yanked me to my feet. He was a head taller than me.

I came up flailing to push him off. One of my fists struck him in the face. His hands dropped, and he staggered back a step.

"I don't know how!" I cried. Tears streamed down my cheeks. "... I don't know how."

He wheeled around silently and left me there. As the front door closed, I slumped to the floor again, crushed. I had violated my private oath never to hurt another person—I had punched my dad.

An hour later, he strode into the house again. I stood in the hallway, afraid to move. He was crying and reached out to wrap his arms around me. We embraced for several minutes, the only time I ever remember hugging him.

Within a month, he had mined friends and relatives, and one of them arranged an interview leading to a job, my first professional employment.

•••

It occurred to me that in my whole life—thirty-one years—he had reached out to share his most private thoughts only twice.

Over Thanksgiving weekend, he had invited me for coffee at the local truck stop. He had never done this before. As we sat in a shabby booth facing toward the gas pumps, he said, "You know, I'm really sorry they killed John Lennon. I know he was a hero of yours."

In truth, I preferred Paul McCartney, but didn't mention it. Instead, I said, "Yeah, he never hurt anyone."

"Well, I wanted you to know it was a terrible thing, killing him like that."

I hesitated, not sure what he expected me to say. "Yeah, he never hurt anyone," I repeated.

He peered at me. We didn't speak, but I knew we had deeply connected.

The other conversation happened six years earlier, shortly after my wedding. He shared some reflections on World War II.

My mother had told us she met him at a USO Club after he returned from active duty. He had flown fifty-four bombing missions over Germany. Every sortie exposed an airman to a four percent chance of death. Statistically, he should have been dead twice. According to mom, he was a "nervous wreck."

But now, dad and I were alone in the house. He said, "You know, when I came home from the War, I really struggled. I couldn't understand how so many good men in our group had been killed while I had made it out alive." He gestured with his open palms. "Why me? And not them? Why was I the lucky one?"

He glanced up, stared directly at me through his gray-green eyes. "For years, I thought about it. Then one day, it came to me. You know what I realized?"

I shrugged. I had no clue.

"It must be my kids," he said. "My kids were going to *do* something. Something meaningful. I didn't know what, but it would make a difference—why I had been spared when so many decent men were not."

That conversation—really, that confession—clarified my own aspirations and our relationship. He was counting on me—as the oldest—to take the lead. It was a heavy expectation, but one for which, in my own way, I was steeled to accept.

•••

But now it was 1981, and that was all blood over the dam.

Our guests began to arrive—aunts, uncles, cousins, neighbors from town—the usual cast of characters. Salted into the mix was a handful of eccentrics guaranteed to add color and energy. On top of the list was an old high school pal, Danny Delford, a lovable scoundrel and the life of any party. Since graduation, he had cobbled together a career in radio—part-time ad sales, part-time disk jockey. Earlier in the day, I had seen him in the A & P and invited him on the spur of the moment.

Our guests parked along the shoulder near the house or on the driveway of dad's three-car garage. It sat on five acres across the road.

Dad was garage rich. He had also built a two-car garage next to the house. How crazy this must have appeared to our neighbors. But he had a secret master plan.

He would divide the five-acre plot into four parcels, one for each of his children. The garage across the street would serve three of them, and one stall in the two-car garage would serve the fourth. The last stall would be his. We would each construct a vacation home, and a steady stream of grandchildren would come and go all summer, perhaps all year long. My Thanksgiving announcement was a sign that his scheme was falling into place.

The party followed the typical pattern of those held for decades. Only the location had changed. There was an overabundance of food, drink, and revelers. In the corner sat a Christmas tree smelling of spruce gum with presents to open on Christmas Day, a lone beacon of stability and holiday goodwill. As the night wore on, the drinks flowed more freely, the gossip exposed more scandals, and the tales reached more fanciful heights.

Midway through the evening, Danny noticed a small organ in the corner. He turned to me. "Do you play?"

"Nah, that's my mom's," I said.

"Mrs. Iverson, do you know any Christmas carols?" he asked.

She nodded. "Well ... a few."

It was hardly a secret that she had been practicing for ten years, hoping for the opportunity to perform.

"You have to play, then. And we'll all sing along." He peered around the room, arms outstretched like a TV evangelist. "We all agree, right?"

Up went a burst of applause. Within minutes, a couple of my aunts had joined my mother and Danny to belt out "Jingle Bells," then "God Rest Ye Merry Gentlemen" and "Here Comes Santa Claus."

As the night wound down, the carols rang out louder, but to participants, undoubtedly more in tune. It was a great raucous party, made all the more so, in that it was the first party in the new house.

Late in the evening, we sat in the living room as, one-by-one, the guests called out their goodbyes. Typical was my aunt Louise.

"Merry Christmas, everyone." She waved from the doorway. "We have to put out the cookies and milk for Santa."

"You, too," my mom said. "All right to drive?"

"Yeah, got it covered—twice."

"Ok, then. If we don't see you, Happy New Year."

"You, too. As usual, great party. We'll sleep good tonight."

Then the ritual would start over again until, finally, "the last dog was hung," as my mother liked to say.

Dad and I lounged next to each other. Remaining family members were arrayed on the couch and various chairs. Ted had hauled away the folding chairs to the front closet. Kristina had stuffed the leftovers into the refrigerator. Mom was wiping up the table. The smells of smoked whitefish, shrimp cocktail, roast turkey, and fruitcake lingered in the air.

"Well," I said. "Danny Delford sure livened up the festivities, eh?"

"*Humph*, Delford." Dad shot a glance at me. "Never paid off his student loans."

"Yeah," my sister chimed in, "and he got Shannon McInerney pregnant while she was still in high school, then bailed on her."

We all sat there in silence. The party was over.

Finally, dad said, "Well, it's been a long day. I'm tired. I should probably get to bed." He reached down to a candy dish on the coffee table. "God, I love chocolate." A few minutes later, he stepped through the living room to the bedroom door.

•••

The next morning, Kristina, her husband Ted, and I were up early drinking coffee in the kitchen. Mary joined us, and Mom was fixing breakfast. I could smell blueberry muffins in the oven. We were leaving shortly for Mary's parents' house, a two-hour drive.

Kristina glanced at the kitchen clock. "Gosh, it's late," she said. "I better get dad up. He'll want to see you before you leave."

She walked through the passage separating the front and back parts of the house and disappeared.

"C'mon, Dad, time to get up. You're sleeping so hard, it's like you're ... dead—OH MY GOD!" she screamed.

I jumped up and ran to the bedroom.

She saw me and burst into tears. "Dad's dead!"

I peered at the bed. He was rolled on his side, motionless as stone, his mouth twisted in an expression of horror, lip turned back to reveal his teeth. Blood had settled in parts of his arms and hands, creating splotches of dark red skin.

"No ... No ... No!" I wailed. "No!"

We hurried back to the kitchen. Kristina reached mom first and grabbed her in a long hug. She was visibly upset, but intensely quiet, as stoic as I had ever seen her.

"I don't understand," I sobbed. "He seemed all right last night. He even had some chocolate before he went to bed. I don't get it."

"Did you notice anything, Mom?" Kristina asked.

She hesitated, stared blankly out the front windows toward the whitecaps crashing on the shore. "No, but just before I got up—a little after seven—I heard him kind of yawn ... quite loud." She looked at me, teary-eyed, then at Kristina. "I thought ... he was turning over."

"It must have been his heart," Kristina said. We all nodded.

The rest of the day seemed to last a month. We called the funeral home. Two men showed up with a hearse and a gurney. One of them, "Toothpick," was tall and balding. He had grown up in southern Indiana and moved with his wife late in life to our community. He and dad were ushers at our church.

I directed them into the bedroom. As blood continued to settle into pools in dad's legs, stomach, neck, and feet, his body had further deteriorated. The sight of him in that state—my last image—when he had been the person I most admired in my life, ripped a jagged hole in my heart.

Toothpick snapped me back to reality. "I apola-jahze," he said in his mid-South drawl. "There ain't no dignified way to do this." The two men rolled the gurney next to the bed and unzipped a heavy black bag. They gripped my father at the shoulders and feet and tipped him forward to roll him over. His six-foot, two-hundred-pound frame flopped onto the cart, arms flailing, as if there weren't a bone in his body.

Toothpick tucked his hands and feet into the bag and zipped it shut. The two men wheeled him out, the last time I ever saw him. He was fifty-nine years old. Two months shy of sixty.

•••

I followed them up the walkway to the hearse where they loaded him in and drove away. When I returned, everyone was sitting in the kitchen. A dark pall hung over the room.

"We better call Eric," I said.

People all over North America were attempting to phone their friends and relatives on Christmas Day. Over and over, we heard the sharp, repetitive buzz of a busy signal. Finally, we slipped through to Sydney, and he answered.

I relayed the horrible news and urged him to come home for the funeral.

My youngest brother Jake was easier to reach, and he too booked a flight. In a few days, both would end up at the tiny regional airport less than an hour from Loyale.

December darkness descends early on the Upper Peninsula. As the day wore on, the weight of the house increasingly pressed in on me. I grabbed my winter coat from the front closet and told everyone I was taking a short walk. Outside that night, the air was crystal cold. As I stepped onto the pavement, my breath billowed like smoke. I looked up into the heavens. A thousand pale-blue stars were strewn across the sky, black and cloudless, over Lake Michigan.

"Why did you die?" I sobbed. "Dad—why did you have to die?" I stood, fists clenched, waiting for an answer. On every surrounding tree and bush, silence hung like a shroud. At that moment, I understood what it means to feel abandoned—hopeless, completely alone.

•••

The rest of the week, people continued to call or stop by to confirm the news and offer condolences. We made preparations for a funeral service.

Twice, we crossed the Bridge to pick up my brothers. When Eric hurried through the airport door after an eighteen-hour flight, he hopped into the back seat of the car. I sped out of the entrance and made a quick left onto the highway. A truck going sixty-five miles an hour came flying by us from the other direction.

"Aaarrrrgg!" Eric screamed. Kristina and I jerked around to see him crouched down, covering his face with his arms.

He hesitated, then looked up sheepishly. "Sorry, I forgot. You drive on the right here."

•••

Now, we were all home. The funeral service was not particularly memorable, but one event embodied the spirit of the rest of the week.

The night before Mary and I departed, we gathered for a last session. We hadn't all been together for several years, and it would be a long time, if ever, before we might again. Our mother would be alone now, at least for the winter, but likely for the rest of her life.

After several drinks, someone began to sing. Soon, all four of us joined in.

One song after another flowed from our collective voices. Beatles, Motown, folk music like "Where Have All the Flowers Gone." At some point we stood and formed a line, superbly, deeply inebriated. Kristina was in front of me, then Eric and Jake, in our birth order. We sang "My Girl", the immortal Temptations soul tune. Only we changed the title line to "My Dad."

Mary snapped a photo of the four of us leaning forward, bending to our right, faces turned to the camera, hands outstretched. Later, the picture seemed to capture the bittersweet essence of that perfect moment.

•••

The next day, it was time to leave. Mary and I both had demanding jobs waiting for us on Monday. Our Lamaze classes were also scheduled to start. And, in a little over three months, we expected our baby to arrive. So, we wouldn't see her family this holiday season.

We said our goodbyes and drove across the Bridge toward Grand Rapids. The long drive back home was interminable.

•••

Over the next few months, the rhythms of our busy personal and professional lives took over. I had little time to think about Christmas or my dad—or even mom. Kristina gave us reports now and then, but we were preoccupied with our soon-to-arrive child.

On Good Friday in April, I arrived home early from work to find Mary anxious and insistent that we go out and shop for our baby.

"It's coming any day now."

She rattled off a list of items we needed.

"Okay, okay," I said. "Let's drive into G-R, do our shopping, then have dinner."

Late in the evening found us at a little Italian restaurant, Vitale's, on the north side. We ate an enormous pasta meal and drank a bottle of red wine. We had checked off everything on her list and were finally ready for the stork.

About three a.m., Mary woke me up, moaning in terrible pain.

"I think I have food poisoning," she cried.

"Are you sure you're not starting labor?"

"No, it doesn't feel like what they said would happen."

This continued the rest of the night, growing progressively worse until about six-thirty Saturday morning. She was tossing and turning, suffering, sleepless.

Finally, she said, "I'm going to have this baby any minute. We have to go. *Now.*"

We made a dash for the hospital, a half hour away. We hustled through the emergency entrance, where they admitted her and moved her to a private room. As I stood by, trying to contain my anxiety, they examined her.

"You're dilated ten centimeters."

For the rest of the day, she struggled in labor, almost delirious. Then, a few minutes before midnight, she gave birth to a beautiful baby boy. I held him in my arms on Easter Sunday for the first time and looked into his eyes. Even in the near dark of the delivery room, his eyes were deep pools. For the second time in my life—only a few months after the first, I stared into the Universe. This time, it answered.

I have reflected on that moment many times. It rearranged my faith. Now, Christmas, celebrating the birth of Jesus Christ—at one time the best day on the calendar—feels like his crucifixion. I wake up Christmas morning and say to myself, "Well, Dad, I escaped for one more year."

But Easter, the day that dawned as I first held my son Matthew, was not only his nativity, but mine as well. And our youngest son, Paul, born three years later—late in the night before our wedding anniversary—was further confirmation that life, despite its terrible sorrows, can also mean sweet redemption.

For more than forty years, that's been good enough for me.

Epistolary Poem

by Beverly Matherne

◆❖◆

Dear Roger,

I want to go back to that morning when Bill and you and I waited, in front of John's house, for a ride to Lee's lovely home in remote woods, Lee, who would host our meeting among friends that morning, waited because we didn't know the way ourselves.

I want to go back to that moment when Bill asked me a question in French, how you turned toward me and exclaimed, "*Où avez-vous appris la belle langue française, Madame*? Where did you learn the beautiful French language, Madam?" March cold immaterial, coming April mud immaterial, warmer clime already perceptible, riot of marsh marigold and trillium. I want to go back to your eyes so bright, they could have dimmed the universe, your smile so broad you could have eaten me alive, and I would have let you!

I want to go back to that half hour or so, when you and I went on and on, in French, as though under the influence of rich red wine, crystal catching a glint of sun. I want to go back to us flirting, in French, practically dancing in the middle of the street, in French, in love at first sight, naïve, profound, the *coup de foudre* of youth.

Love,
Beverly

Paranormal or Normal?
That is the Question

by Beverly Matherne

◆❖◆

I have purchased and am restoring the historic Butler House in Ishpeming, Michigan, built by a mining Captain back in the day. Rosettes and fish-scale shingles grace its four gables, spindle work frames the wraparound porch, and caped newels flank the front steps—features of the Eastlake, Queen Anne Style.

In the stair hall, a bronze statue of Diana stands on an ornate pedestal, beside a delicate settee, floral inlay in its medallion pane. An oak staircase sweeps up to the second floor, lined with abstract paintings—greens, blues, corals—by the celebrated Thomas Cappuccio.

After a long morning of writing, I sit on the sofa in the front parlor, sip tea, and nibble madeleines beneath a French tapestry once owned by the first CEO of Cleveland-Cliffs Inc. In the scene depicted, lords sport tricornes and high heels with square toes and bows; ladies, voluminous gowns and large brimmed hats festooned with ostrich feathers, fit for tea on expansive lawns of a stately summer home.

In the world I've created for myself amongst statues, paintings, tapestries, amongst silk lampshades, leatherbound books, busts, bouquets, I envision a life of ease, of calm; when, in fact, my own creation unsettles me. My friend Susan, a therapist, tells me that I've crossed over to the other side, that I must make my way back to the normal, but how can I, when yesterday, for example, while napping beneath the Cliffs tapestry, sirens wailed, and, when I tried to rise, to see what was the matter, some unseen force held me down.

Last week, I was walking upstairs toward the TV room, bay-windowed and well-lit, to watch the evening news, when footsteps sounded on the attic steps. I stopped short, saw reflected in the mirror at the end of the hall, a girl in a white silk dress, eyes brown, complexion porcelain, ringlets brunette. She turned and looked right at me. I thought she would say something or walk through me. Instead, she took to the foyer. I followed her, to see if I could glean who she was, and what she would do, but I never got close enough to voice my queries.

Now, yesterday, when the doorbell rang, I cracked open the heavy front door. A tall Victorian gent in top hat and wool trousers and a boy in knickers stood at the wrought iron door. "The boy and I are partial to the house," said the elder, "may we come in?" "Ugh, sure," I stammered. The gent dropped into a Louis 16th chair, round-backed and large, settling himself against diamond tuft-ing. The boy chose the sofa, running his fingers over cream brocade. Victorians love tea, so I said to them, "Spot of tea?" and the gent responded, "Don't mind if we do." I rushed to the dining room for Royal Albert cups and teapot, the ones embellished with country roses and wispy clouds. With sterling tray in hand, I soon returned … to an empty parlor. Easing my load onto a marble table, I took after my guests as they descended stone steps to the street and disappeared.

As I see it, I have two choices. Either I stay on the other side, where phantoms walk in and out of my house, in and out of my rooms, all day, all night. Or I call Susan for specific instructions on how to make my way back to the normal. It's a conundrum. I mean, who knows whether a malevolent revenant will appear? If I could dispel my fear, I might stay in this crossed-over territory, scent of roses wafting, for weight of responsibility on the other side, the side that everyone everywhere lives every day, is more than I can bear. Well … in due time … I'll let you know what I decide.

Haiku for Roger Magnuson

by Beverly Matherne

At dusk
before stars
your voice comes to me.

Your cottage at Au Train —
the blueberries
we liked to pick.

Superior shore —
spotted sandpiper
tail bobbing.

Maple leaves in fall
show me
how to let go.

Snow falls —
memories of you wander
over withered dahlias.

FICTION
The Opportunity of a Lifetime

by Brandy Thomas

◆❖◆

I knew something was wrong as soon as I stepped into the cabin. It was the most perfect writer's retreat I had ever seen in person. The afternoon sun filled the studio space, filtered through the canopy of summer leaves on the maple tree outside the open window. A soft breeze kept the room at the perfect temperature and the soft sound of waves breaking against the shore of Lake Superior and birdsong wafted in on that glorious breeze. The desk had a comfortable chair to work in and a couple of deep lounge chairs provided the ideal spot to spend an afternoon reading. A small living room, tiny kitchenette, cozy bedroom, well-appointed bathroom, and a small, covered porch with Adirondack chairs rounded out the cabin.

I was here as part of an artist-in-residence program. Six months with the freedom to write whatever I wanted in a beautiful location and get paid a nice chunk of change to do it. I was one of hundreds, if not thousands, of artists who applied for the five spots at the Lake Superior Art Colony Artist in Residence Program.

Every year the committee picks one writer, two painters, one sculptor, and one wildcard. The wildcard could be anything from another of the three disciplines already represented or something from a new emerging art or an artist whose work is hard to define. All the artists are people who are at that point in their career where they have had some success but nothing career defining, yet. The program has been running every year for the past 132 years and was known for hosting artists that go on to become household names. Just by being selected it gave you a leg up in the art world, no matter your discipline.

The lucky artists get to live in individual cabins in a small park-like property owned by the city and set aside specifically for the Artist in Residence program. It's a beautiful spot a few blocks from downtown Marquette, MI. Very private, very quiet, the colony feels remote and exclusive, but in reality, is close enough to town that it's still an easy walk to downtown restaurants, coffee shops, or stores. Bicycles were parked next to each cabin, and each had a phone number inside for anyone who wanted a ride somewhere in town a bit further away.

So why did I feel like something was wrong? I felt watched, like I was being observed and judged. My friends would be telling me I was being paranoid, or imposter syndrome was trying to fool me into saying I didn't belong, or maybe anxiety was raising its ugly head. I tried to push the feeling of wrongness away. The space really was perfect. Whoever maintained the cabins really thought through what each artist would need and the extensive questionnaire about food preferences, work setups, and supplies made more sense. My favorite teas were on the counter in a charming display next to an electric kettle. My favorite snacks were in the cupboard, and the studio was set up perfectly.

I could faintly hear the others arriving at their cabins and getting settled while I unpacked and arranged my laptop on the desk.

As a writer I didn't have much in the way of supplies compared to the others, so I settled into one of the comfy lounge chairs to read till it was time to meet up with the other artists for dinner and a tour of the town.

•••

A knock on the door startled me awake from an unplanned nap. As I rubbed the sleep from my eyes and untangled myself from the blanket and chair, I thought I caught a glimpse of something running along the baseboard. Apparently, even paradise can have mice.

I found Dee, our host/maintenance/property caretaker/tour guide waiting outside. When getting me settled into my cabin, they explained that they lived there year-round and maintained the property as well as played host to the artists while we were here. Anything we needed, we talked to Dee.

"Hey, Dee. I hate to complain on the first day, but I think I have a mouse in my cabin."

"Oh no problem, that happens. One of the downsides of living in the woods is the woods wants in where we live. When we get back, I'll get some traps set out for you. But first, let's get some dinner and a tour." Dee waved their hand at the other five people behind them.

They then proceeded to give us all most thorough tour of the town and colony I think I have ever had. If they weren't already, Dee should have been a historian. I wouldn't be surprised to find they wrote local history during their down time. But I guess after giving this spiel for twenty-five years you would know your stuff.

That was followed by dinner in the lodge, our communal space, where meals were served. There was also a very nice selection of board games, a small projector room where we could watch movies, and we could just generally hang out somewhere other than our cabins. Meals were provided but we could always make our own food in our cabin if we preferred or just didn't feel like socializing that day.

Everyone was incredibly nice and incredibly excited to be at the Artist in Residence program. The first week we all explored both the colony and the town and outlying areas, letting the location flavor our work. It was July and beautiful.

After that first refreshing week we all started working on our various projects. I fell into the routine of getting up at nine, starting my morning with a cup of tea on the porch, doing the *New York Times* crossword and watching the chipmunks chase each other through the ring of mushrooms in the open space outside my cabin. Then I would work on writing from ten to twelveish, have lunch, write some more till around three in the afternoon. Then depending on the day, I would go for a swim in Lake Superior, maybe a hike, or sometimes just a nap. At six, we all had dinner together, the only meal we ate at the same time. Most days I would go back to writing after dinner till midnight or one in the morning but sometimes I would play boards games or have deep philosophical discussions with my fellow artists in the evening.

I found that Anne, the sculptor, and I had very similar schedules and we got along fantastically. She quickly went from a stranger to someone who would be a lifelong friend.

"Even here where it isn't so hot, like Tucson, where I am from, it is still too hot to work with clay and kilns and fire in the middle of the afternoon," Anne commented.

I laughed. "That makes sense. Writing in the afternoon makes me feel like I am still in school, watching a beautiful day pass while I am stuck inside doing schoolwork."

July passed and everything was going fantastically. I was getting lot of writing done, the book I had been planning was coming together easily and I was almost done with the first draft. We never did catch that mouse, but I never saw evidence of it, nothing chewed on, no droppings, so I figured it must have found its way back outside. The sense of unease slowly dissipated. I figured it was just anxiety rearing its ugly head.

August rolled around and we were all becoming focused on our work. Wanting to create our moment of genius, the thing that we would be known for. There were less evenings spent in conversation and games and you could often see lights peeking out from studio windows late into the night. Except for Cecil, the watercolor painter who was the lone early bird, often getting up when some of us were just heading to bed.

Anne and I still made time in the afternoon for a break. Locals kept telling us about winter and how hard it was, but the hot, dog days of August were still not comfortable, especially since few places in the Upper Peninsula had air conditioning. A fact that astounded all of us from other parts of the country.

As we were drifting in the lake one mid-August afternoon Anne asked, "I have a weird question for you. Have you had anything in your studio moved?"

"Moved how? I mean, Dee moves my laptop to dust the desk when they come in to clean, but I'm guessing that's not what you mean."

"No, like someone was looking at your work, and tools. It's hard to explain, but it's like someone picked up my things and put them down but not quite in the right place. And ..." Anne hesitated. "This sounds crazy, but I swear the piece I am working on has been changed. Just slightly, but in a way that made it better, I think. I don't remember carving those parts of the stone. But at the same time, I couldn't swear I didn't either."

"That's really weird. I don't think anyone would mess with your stuff, especially not your work. But we should ask Dee if anyone has been in or if anyone else has had problems. And I am positive it wasn't Dee. I mean, I don't know them super well, but I know them well enough that they are not the culprit. Plus, you don't work somewhere for twenty-five years without being a professional."

Anne nodded in agreement. Before dinner that evening Anne took Dee aside and asked them if they had been in to clean their studio and if they had moved tools or touched the sculpture she was working on. They reaffirmed that they only cleaned the main cabin and did not even enter the studio, as Anne had requested.

We all had the option to have our entire cabin and studio cleaned on a regular basis, just another perk of being the artists in residence. Some, like me, said go ahead

and clean everything. Most of my work was on my laptop or written on a series of legal pads. Hard to accidentally disturb or destroy my work. Others like Anne and Cecil preferred only their cabin to be cleaned and they would take care of their studio space. Too many fragile parts and tools that could accidentally be moved or bumped.

We also asked if anyone else had anything moved or changed.

"You had tools stolen!?" a very panicked Mya asked. She was the second painter, working on a giant mural.

"No. Nothing stolen, just moved. Or it may be nothing." The more she tried to explain the more uncertain Anne sounded. "Maybe I have just been overworking and need to take a break for a couple of days. Just ... if anyone else experiences something odd, could you please let me know."

Maxwell, a songwriter, quietly added, "I have had an odd thing happen. My guitar keeps ending up tuned a half step down from what I normally have it at. I mean it is making me consider some different progressions and I think improving my songwriting, but it is weird. I mean a perfect half step every single time I step away from the studio space just seems ... unlikely? Weird?"

"Well, there is also all the legends and superstitions about this place." Dee said. "I mean, someplace this old always has its own mythology that grows up around it. There has always been a bit of weirdness, sometimes a touch of insanity, but also genius associated with The Colony." I could hear the capital letters when they said the name.

Everyone considered quietly and it was decided that everyone would pay extra attention to their workshops and keep an eye out for any strangers or strange things happening.

Weeks passed. We all started out conferring nightly but as time went on and there didn't seem to be any more disturbances or nothing that couldn't be attributed to absent-mindedness or nothing that people would admit, we all gradually went back to our routines.

Maxwell's guitar still kept going that half step down, to the point where he just started working in that key. He claimed it was the best, weirdest thing that happened to his music. Anne claimed that her sculpture was subtly being altered but never enough to be sure, and it was turning into exactly what she wanted it to be. It was wilder and more expressive than anything she had made before but also the most true to her work that she had ever created. Mya, once she stopped panicking about intruders possibly disturbing her work, claimed she had never worked so well before.

Cecil and I were the only two who didn't seem to be doing the best work of our lives. Let me amend that, we were doing the best work of our lives, but it didn't feel completely like our work. Cecil claimed there were subtle changes to his paintings that he didn't make. He had a journal he kept in his cabin, separate from his actual painting studio, in which he had his detailed sketches and plans for each painting he made. He was correct, they didn't match exactly and although the changes arguably made the paintings "better" he felt they were no longer his.

I had a similar issue. My novel was progressing wonderfully, and I had completed my first draft in September. I took a week off from writing and went on long walks enjoying the fall colors and giving myself at least a little distance from my book before I delved in for the first round of editing and the slog that second drafts are.

When I started working on my novel again, the first odd thing I noticed was the word count. I had sent a note off to my editor telling her how great the writing was going and what the word count was so she could start scheduling out her time after the first of the year, when I would need her editing services. The word count was 2,543 words different. I knew that exactly because it had originally been a nice round 400 pages and now it was 411 pages. I double checked with the email I sent to my editor. It was weird, but there was a concrete measurable difference.

So, I started reading what I had written and trying to spot the differences. For the most part there was nothing huge that stood out. What stood out the most is how clean the copy was, it was like it had already been edited. My first drafts are normally a bit sloppy and all over the place, but the idea is to get the bones of the story down on the page. But this, this was polished, the best thing I had ever written. Or I should say the most marketable and mainstream thing I had ever written.

But it also didn't feel like my writing either. It felt cleaner, clearer, more structured than my norm. Other than the page count, the part that stood out as "changed" was one particular character description. The physical description of the main character's daughter was based off my best friend. Lots of wild curly blonde hair and grey eyes, tall and looking not at all like her parents. I always told her I would put her in one of my books, and I had specifically made this character look exactly like her. But in this version the character was described as a mini-me of her mother tiny, with dark brown eyes and straight dark hair.

Why was this changed and who changed it? It made no sense. Yes, for story neatness, it would make more sense for people to look like their parents but that's not how genetics works, and it made the story not mine. Yes, the basic plot and characters were there but it felt wrong, like it wasn't wholly mine. When I worked with my editor it was a partnership, with give and take and filled with discussion. This felt like my seventh-grade English teacher going in with her red pen and "fixing" my stories to the way she thought made it better with no regards to what I wanted.

I sat back in my chair and stared out the window, trying to figure out what was going on. Obviously, something was affecting our work, but no one was coming in or out of The Colony and while someone could hack into my computer and make changes, you couldn't do the same with a sculpture or painting. Logic was failing me.

So, I decided to take drastic measures. I sent an email to my editor with the manuscript attached and a note saying that I just wanted her to have this for safekeeping but not to read it or do anything else with it. I would explain later. Then I deleted the manuscript off my laptop. Every copy, every backup, and I even went so far as to reformat my hard drive, just in case someone had installed some sort of spyware or virus. Everything was wiped clean.

I then went to bed, feeling like I had totally lost my mind. I decided to restart my novel in the morning and see what happened.

•••

The next morning, I woke up and checked my computer first thing. Nothing had changed from the night before, everything a fresh clean install. I let out a breath. I was half afraid everything would reappear. That ended up being the only thing that went right that day.

My morning tea didn't happen because apparently that mouse had reappeared and decided to chew through every teabag, box of tea, and tin I had. The refrigerator had gone out and everything that could spoil, had. I didn't think a carton of milk could go rancid that fast but apparently, I was wrong. I gave Dee a call and they came over with mouse traps and their bag of tools to figure out the fridge.

While waiting, I cleaned up the kitchen and took out the garbage. On my way back into the cabin I noticed my bike had two flat tires and I thought to myself how utterly ridiculous this day had been and it wasn't even noon. The day continued to be unlucky, my shoelace broke on my way to dinner which caused me to fall and scrape my hands and knees, ripping a hole in my favorite sweater. Even my work chair had developed an annoying wobble.

After dinner I finally started rewriting my novel, but this time I decided to start with a different idea than the original book. I worked for a steady three hours before deciding to call it a day. I drifted off to sleep hoping tomorrow would be a better day.

The first thing I did was check my laptop to see if the work I had done the night before was there and if it was the same as I remembered writing. It was there but it was definitely different. Instead of subtle changes there were whole paragraphs that had been rewritten in a voice distinctly different from my own. Something was going on

and now I was rethinking even sleeping in my own cabin because something was obviously happening while I was unconscious or gone from the building. I checked the rest of the cabin, and nothing was missing, nothing had ever been missing. Just my own voice in my work.

My luck at least was better today. I sat on the porch bundled up in a cozy sweater and blanket, drinking my tea and thinking. I watched a misty rain fall and heard the lake crashing against the shore. I was reminded of the Gordon Lightfoot song about that shipwreck and the gales of November. The chipmunks were hibernating now, but squirrels were still out and busy gathering and burying acorns. The mushrooms seem to have multiplied, with several rings now in the lawn, not surprising with all the recent rain.

I was pretty sure I wasn't losing my mind, but I wasn't totally ruling that out. I felt like everyone else had also been having weird experiences and it wasn't just me. I guess we could be having some sort of group hallucination but that seemed not to fit exactly what was happening and Cecil and I were the only two that seemed to be having problems with our mysterious "help". So, ruling out insanity, how could I figure out who or what was meddling with our work?

Whatever was altering our projects didn't seem to be great with technology. Yes, I worked on a laptop but most of what I did and what was changed was basic typing, not my emails, not file names or really anything more complicated than words on a page. A thing that has been around, in one form or another since there have been people. All the other artists were very hands on, with actual pigments on paper or canvas, or stone chipped and shaped, and even the musician played a physical instrument.

I made a show of going in to write the rest of the morning. Making sure to take note of my word count and also to turn on my laptop's built-in webcam. I normally never used the thing, but it was easy enough to set to record and hide the recording icon. Then I called Anne and asked if she wanted to go into town with me this afternoon to pick up some new tea since all of mine had been ruined the day before and the Lipton that Dee had given me was fine, but I wanted some variety. Maybe we could stop by that new coffee shop. Everything arranged, I left for lunch and my shopping excursion.

Four hours later, I returned to my cozy little cabin. Everything appeared untouched. I put new teas away and did the usual shedding of fall layers before sitting down at my laptop. As much as I wanted to rush over and see if my camera caught anything, I was also nervous.

I woke the computer from its sleep and saw the recording was still going. I stopped it, then it started automatically playing from the beginning of the recording. I fast forwarded past me putting on rain boots and my jacket and leaving for lunch. Then there was a half hour of nothing other than the occasional rumble of thunder and changing light from the rain. Then a shadow approached from the side of the camera, and I brought the recording to normal playback speed. At first, I was confused, and then laughed. The shadow creature came into the light of the screen and turned out it was a small red squirrel. Well, it wasn't a mouse, but I am betting that is the creature that destroyed my snacks and gnawed through my shoelace. I watched the squirrel peer at the screen then sit and proceed to meticulously groom its face and ears. It was the most adorable thing I had ever seen. But as I was watching, I noticed something odd, or even more unusual than a squirrel on my desk. There seemed to be something wrapped around it and protruding from its back. The floofy tail hid it at first but it seemed to be a … saddle? A tiny squirrel saddle, like a horse would have but squirrel sized.

As I puzzled over the squirrel saddle an even bigger surprise walked into the video, a small person with clothes the color of leaves, pointed ears, an acorn cap as a hat, and a number two pencil. The pencil was the same height as the small person, and they started using it to punch keys on the keyboard. I watched in shock as this fairy (because what else could it be) with a large amount

of grumbling about having to start working on a second book after the "stupid human destroyed the first" continued to type for two hours. He then stared at the screen, reading I assumed, then seemed to nod in satisfaction, gently wake up his squirrel companion who by this time was taking a nap, and then ride off screen.

I don't know what I was expecting but it wasn't that. I closed the video file, turned off my laptop, wrapped myself in a blanket, and sat in one of the cozy chairs and watched the storm go by outside my window.

No one was going to believe me if I said fairies were editing my stories and helping my fellow artists with their work. I figured Dee probably knew with their talk of The Colony Mythology, but I never followed up on that because, well, it sounded like the silly stories that always pop up around anything that is as old as The Colony.

I decided to call it a night and just went to bed, my brain was done with the day. The next morning dawned bright and clear; a crust of frost coated the ground. While on my porch I noted the tiny squirrel shaped paw prints that came up onto my porch and meandered around the grass surrounding my cabin. I had probably seen those prints every day there was dew or rain or a little frost on the ground and thought nothing of it.

I went to the lodge and asked Dee if we had any extra cream and honey and maybe some hazelnuts or peanuts that I could feed the squirrels. They of course had plenty of all the things I was asking for and gave me a knowing smile.

After I arrived back at my cabin, I started on a third story. This time the introduction had a greeting where I introduced myself and asked my coauthor to introduce themselves and it laid out the format of this novel. A conversation in letters between two people working together to make something greater than either could produce on their own. The first chapter was mine, the second blank, the blinking cursor an invitation. I poured a small cup of cream and a small dish of honey, put out a bowl of hazelnuts and went out for my afternoon walk.

Meat

by Brandy Thomas

Dark
The hour before dawn
The early morning drive to town
To drop the tween off at school
We travel in companionable silence
With only the background music of pop radio

Interrupted by caution lights ahead
A dark smear
Covering both lanes
A crunch
And sliding squish
Felt more than heard
As wheels roll over something,
Unidentifiable.

Matched intakes of breath
A pause.
"Mom, was that a…deer?"
"I think so."
A long pause
Twin shivers
Shared sympathy for the unfortunate animal

Twenty minutes later
Traveling the same route
Now to home
Dawn's light brings illumination.

Now I can see.
The dark smear is red
Spread from shoulder to shoulder

I have to swerve to avoid
A large piece
Of torso?
A lower leg
An ear

A graceful creature
Turned into
Chunks of bloody
Meat.

Letters to Harrison #8

by Art Curtis

3/26/2021

Dear Jim,

So, tell me, when the pen slipped from your fingers, which thicket did you head for? The woods have always been your safe place. There've been several thickets over your years: Grayling certainly, one near the cabin your dad and uncles built, any number of them off H58 or south of Sable Lake or the Sucker, the one in the Absarokas, etc. Tell me. Or maybe it was under the roots of that tree stump overhanging the riverbank where you wouldn't get wet—where skunks, bobcats and coyotes had also sheltered. You went there to rest, didn't you, Jim?

I'm not sure after that. I'm not into religious mythologies although I know they help others. What helps me are the stories, as long as they are told, the main character doesn't die. I have fancied your journey to the Golden Gate where you are greeted by a German shepherd who escorts you through a world of dogs to where Missy and Rose and Tess attend a white dog on a white throne who says, in recognition of your shock, "It's OK, Jim, all humans are dyslexic."

You've been on my mind this *dia de tu muerte* marked on my calendar, so I'll tell stories to keep you alive and, of course, what's the first thing I hear this morning? A story about something that could kill us both if we eat more than one meal of rainbow smelt a week out of Lake Superior. PFAS! Per- and polyfluoroalkyl substances! Did we know of them before you headed for your thicket? Maybe, but not that they stay whole and complete in nature and can cause cancer. Jeez, Jim! Superior is sacrosanct. Leave it alone! First Erie, then Ontario, then Michigan and Huron; but Superior is everything pure and now it's not. Spoiled!

You must have dipped for smelt; we all did under flashlights and Coleman Lanterns and then well into sunrise cleaning all those little fish, and if we were lucky, the occasional nine-incher. If women were helping, they'd hold that one up and one of the more normal four to five-inchers and ask if we understood the difference. Getting them skillet-ready meant decapitation, a split from the anus, thumbs running up the blood sack along the spine and then flicking the guts into a pail or towards a lucky cat. Oh God! (Or is that Ho Dog?) Rolled in cornmeal and fried in bacon grease, we were in heaven! You could have a beer for breakfast with those fresh smelt and even my mother would not have looked askance. I told my Vermont cousins how much I loved smelt and they laughed. Smelt are no delicacy there, but they are great bait for the jaw-dropping Lake Trout fished out of ice-covered Lake Seymour in the Northeast Kingdom.

Now what does smelt as a bait fish mean to you, Jim? You're darn tootin'! Smelt are low on the food chain, so those PFAS are going to be found next in Superior's Lake Trout, the Splake and the Coaster Brook Trout. That "brookie" you served yourself *a bleu* with the wild leek and new potato, your best meal of the year in which you also made the *bollito misto* for your daughter, could have killed you if you'd eaten enough of them and they'd eaten enough rainbow smelt when those fish charged upstream for sex. And you and I carry some guilt. How we hated those "performance 'undies'," synthetics that dried immediately except the waistband that never dried. (I was completely misled by the term "performance 'undies';" got my hopes up, I did.) Remember the nylon pants and shirts that you had to get wet just so you'd stay cool? So, we were a ready market for the cotton shirts, the cotton field pockets (the pants were free, you only paid for the pockets) and the cotton underwear all promising to dry like nylon—thanks to PFAS. You want heat-resistant, stain-resistant, water-resistant,

easy-to-clean pots, fire-retardant anything, thank PFAS. The Air Force at Wurtsmith, Selfridge, Kincheloe, and Sawyer practiced suffocating jet fuel fires with PFAS and now the groundwater's contaminated. Every form of refuge has its price!

I miss you my best friend whom I never got to meet. I've been sipping a 110-proof rye. Poured it just before I reread *The Boy Who Ran into the Woods*. Found myself wondering as I choked up, how many tears it would take to lower the proof to 100, but I'm not crying; I've kept you alive, I've talked about you, kept you up to date. I love you, Jim. You're missed.

Yrs,

Art

Historical · Logging team with horses

Wrapped: An Elegy for My Father

by Art Curtis

for Arthur Winberg Curtis, Jr

PART I

Water to waist
East Branch Escanaba
trekked down from Truck Trail
water cold, clear.
I cast up and across
watch line mend.

I'm vaguely aware
of my father's presence.
He told my mother
I was a good fishing companion.
"He doesn't feel the need
to fill the silence."

Nothing less true
but of more import
has ever been said about me.
I fretted my silence
a failure
not to talk with my dad.

We had much to discuss
maybe fishing we wouldn't argue.
He wouldn't need
to show his command.
I wouldn't need
to step out of rank.

I hear him say
"Just let it swing through.
At the end of the swing
twitch it!"
A fat trout took the fly,
then it started to pour.

PART II

I hang my tools
like he did
when I remember
to hang them.

Like him tired
I'll do it tomorrow.
but like him tomorrow
there'll be another job.

Like him I cuss
when the tool's not in its place.
I search for it like I did his
without success.

Unlike him I cuss the gods.
He cussed me.
I have no "me" to cuss.
If I did I would.

Frustration present
in every "Shit!" and "Goddamn!"
My mouth wraps around his words
like my hands around his tools.

PART III

Would that my skill
could wrap around my tasks
like his did.

Would that my confidence
could wrap around my struggles
like his did.

Would that my discipline
could wrap around my will
like his did.

Would that my will
could wrap around his
like my name does.

Watercourse

by Art Curtis

I want a river
outside my door. On it I
could go anywhere

I wish. I could drag
my canoe over shallows,
lead it through willows,

paddle around rocks,
push pole where green rushes grow
tall so I can see

ahead, know what's next.
Or, I could let the current
determine my course,

as it has its own—
groundwater eroding earth,
seeking its oceans.

Historical - Logging the Hurricane River

Baraga County Redemption

by Mark Nelson

Markku stared at the two Powerball lottery tickets in his hand, like a card player pondering how much to wager. One had a note written in the corner, $7, and the other had a note, $4. They were both winning tickets. The first matched three numbers, while the second matched one number plus Powerball. They were both many months old, and Markku thought about why he had not redeemed them yet. It was a complicated, emotional equation, but somehow it boiled down to the fact that a winning lottery ticket was priceless, while the redeemed tickets would only give him $11; it was more romantic to hold something priceless than to gobble down the Mexican fast-food meal that the redeemed tickets would buy him. Markku placed the two tickets on top of the second pile on his desk; that pile contained countless letters, photos, clippings, notes, and diaries. He had started the pile when he was only a teenager; now he was fast approaching seventy years old, and there were additional overstuffed bins under his desk with "super 8" movies and compact disks. As with the two lottery tickets, this pile of memories represented something that was valuable. Unlike the lottery tickets, however, the pile contained many lifetimes of memories that were much more complicated to redeem than driving to a Wisconsin QuikTrip and redeeming the winning tickets; how could Markku redeem that pile of lifetimes without hurting the lives that they touched, or rendering them inconsequential? Those lives and their stories were more valuable than any lottery ticket.

Markku liked to read stories written by Upper Peninsula writers, but he often felt like they used their communities as vessels for stories that they created in their imaginations, weaving tales in the way that story tellers have done since time immemorial. Nothing wrong with that, but Markku did not have to use his imagination to remember stories of poverty, violence, illiteracy, incest, hunger, death, lust, suicide, and redemption. This was his family history, and some of the people in his stories were still alive. He had thought about using an academic folklore approach, doing field research by interviewing and recording narratives of his people and their narratives, but that was not easy when you were part of the narrative. The concept of participant observer made sense as a concept, but seemed to work better when the observer came from outside and was conscious of their participation. Markku had always relished being in the thick of it, and while always a participant, he was never just an observer. Markku was a part of the story he wanted to redeem.

The story could go on for thousands of pages, and Markku was overwhelmed by the sheer expanse of what he could write about. Everyone involved was in some ways larger than life, but he had to get down to brass tacks and create a literary world that would contain those stories. The first decision was to create a location that somehow mirrored the real community that the lives revolved around. The origins of the family story always came back to Kahlaamo Road in Covington Township, Baraga County, Michigan. This was not a real place, but a placeholder for over 100 years of family activity. Markku was writing from his own home on Aalto Road, a real place in Covington Township, but not where his house actually was. Markku liked the name, because he had been a licensed architect, and Aalto was an architect as well. He looked out the window at the sauna building, with the orange four-wheeler in the foreground and the orange Kubota tractor with the backhoe in the background. He loved to do a sunset four-wheeler ride through the forty acres and vowed to finish (Finnish) writing enough to deserve an exhilarating ride this evening. This wild land was an important protagonist in the story that he was compelled to write.

Family was at the center of the story, for better or worse. Markku wanted to keep things in the Finnish American world, because that was the implied connection between everyone in the family, even though the family had done its best to put the Finnish connections behind them. While so many were embarrassed by the "provincial" Finnish connections, the connections were there even when invisible. Thinking about literary structure, Markku wanted to give everyone in his story a Finnish name. Grandma, the central matriarch, became *Mummo* Helmi (the pearl). The numerous aunts became *täti*. The numerous uncles became *setä*. Grandfather became *vaari*. Even though they would probably have done anything to get away from the low-class ethnic associations that their names evoked, Markku pushed them back into that low-class world because he saw that as a strength. His mother would be horrified, because she had escaped the straitjacket of poverty and oppression, graduating from college, but Markku saw being poor and illiterate as a profound strength, because the poor and illiterate were so much more intelligent than those who had been handed everything on a silver spoon.

Markku looked up at his twin computer screens, which were plastered with post-it notes. Bob Dylan Planet Waves played in the background, a random playlist that moved on to Hendrix. He knew his family had provincial Finnish American poverty roots, but Markku saw those roots as a strength that had sustained him throughout his life. He had become a licensed architect, and then a professor emeritus at a major public university (*sisu*). He was in some ways from another planet (like Planet Waves), but at the same time, he did not need academic accolades to give him identity, and his family existed in a plane above the academic world. Markku wanted to somehow communicate the complexity and richness of life in a world where reading and writing was a questionable activity. Men did not read, but used their bodies to do men's work, while women did book learning and handled the money. Navigating a world of illiteracy while transcending the vagaries of daily life was something that did not seem to exist in the literary world outside Markku's life; the literary world implied literacy as a minimum entry point, but narrative should not be confined to those who might compose words on a page.

Markku looked at all the piles of memories and was overwhelmed. He thought about the four-wheeler ride he had promised himself just before sundown. He had always watched with interest as groups on four-wheelers sped down the trails near Sidnaw, going from bar to bar and taking a drink at each one. His four-wheeler could go fifty-five miles per hour on a straight trail, but he usually found himself going five miles per hour, making trails through the tag alders on his forty acres. The trees were over seven feet tall and seemed to just keep spreading. He would just accelerate toward an impassable wall of trees, and then create a path where none had existed before. Trees would fall forward as he passed through, and if he took the same path often enough, a trail would form. Life was like those tag alders, looming tall in opposition, but somehow bending apart to let Markku pass through. The swarm of post-its and life memories was a forest of tag alders, looming overhead, that Markku needed to just drive right through and write a path where none had existed before.

Markku began typing on his laptop, "Baraga County Redemption." He had the title down, as a start, saved the file, and then went outside to make trails through the tag alders at dusk with his orange four-wheeler. Somehow, he would find a path through his twisting family history and create a well-worn narrative out of the lives and deaths that appeared so impassable.

Rootedness

by Nina L. Craig

◆❖◆

For many years I traveled nearly a straight line on US-2 across northern Minnesota to Newberry, Michigan, to the same farm where I was raised. The same place where my dad's parents raised him and where my brother lives today. I crisscrossed country roads seeking small diners back then. I still do today. If you hug the Canadian border, you can order French fries with gravy all along the way. You hardly ever find it outside the northern tier states, except in French restaurants where they call it Poutine.

A real diner would have hot roasted turkey sandwiches with "homemade" gravy and "real" mashed potatoes. The woman making that decision would be trying to replicate her mother's cooking, her mother's love.

As I passed through once-booming lumber towns, I would come across an old diner. How do you know it's a local diner? It's small. Everyone looks at you when you come in. The place is warm, almost too warm because of the steam coming off the kettles, because of the bacon, potatoes and eggs sizzling on the grill in the back. The air is thick with the smell of black coffee. The coffee has to be good or nothing else will work. If I stopped mid-morning, there was usually a center table for the locals, men in their work clothes, drinking coffee and eating, since their day started at sunrise.

During our high school senior year, my friends and I skipped English class and walked to the Paul Bunyan Restaurant. The walls were made of logs. The tables and chairs were all handmade from logs, shellacked an orangish veneer. We ordered cof-

Postcard - Paul Bunyan Restaurant interior

fee with lots of milk and sugar, smoked cigarettes and pretended to be adults. Cigarettes were thirty-five cents and if you shook the cigarette machine a couple times, several packs would fall down for the taking. We smoked whatever fell down. If we could afford it, we would share an order of fries with gravy. A long table in the center was reserved for the local townsmen to gather. Different batches of them came in at different times including police officers, all men, only men back then. We loosened the saltshaker cap and left it hovering on its edge.

Those diners are mostly gone, replaced by fast food joints where the old men meet, huddled around their coffee. I can still see my father with all his farmer friends leaning on the back of an empty pickup truck, facing each other, smoking, and making deals in the hardware parking lot. In the city, the work crews gather in a party store parking lot, around the back end of a pickup truck for a few minutes, drinking coffee, before they go their separate ways. During the second year of the pandemic, men gathered in shopping mall parking lots, grilling with their friends while the women shopped. We always find a way.

•••

My mother made scratch cake and pie, even pizza, kneading the flour mixture with her hands just so and the smell, oh God, my mouth waters thinking of her dinner rolls. Golden, tender, and glistening with melted butter. Still warm. I savor the sweet yeasty smell. Every mother's food tastes different. It must be like lost penguin babies crying out for their mothers and thousands of replicas are standing there but only one will do—will recognize your cry and come. She'll find you.

I have all my mother's recipes, many handwritten in beautiful cursive. I make her food. It doesn't exactly look and taste like hers. I have made it my own. My kids, now adults, want the same food I always cooked them. It is full of love and sometimes tears. Sharing a meal made with your own hands and visiting with the people you care about, looking into each other's eyes is the connective tissue to heal and renew our bodies and spirit. That is our rootedness. It is good medicine.

When Ice Cracks Open

by Nina L. Craig

When ice cracks open
under twin forces
of water and wind
when Maple is tapped
puncturing her veins
swollen with sweet sap
when Smelt struggle upstream
silver flashes writhing
under the full moon
We don't dwell
On our losses
We just begin again.

Postcard - Paul Bunyan Restaurant Exterior

River Gypsy

by Edd Tury

Lake Superior's gift rockets through the St. Mary's,
sliding past smooth rocks of every size and color,
rolls over and around submerged boulders, it froths at the delay.
The morning fog lingers calmly over the boil,
serene mists blanket holy chaos,
muffles the ten-thousand-year roar that argues its way to the sky.

A fisherman stands in the shallows - looks upriver.
Sees the tidal wave coming toward him - a surface-smooth flux
    belying the power within.
Downstream the angry torrent relaxes, sets out to find the sea.

Stripping line, he prepares to begin the familiar ritual,
the quest for an active fish with only rod and feather.
His line curls over the frantic water, carrying the lure to holding
    currents.

Another cast, then another - another - another,
each one putting the pseudo-seductress on another path through the
    cauldron.
A strike—unexpected and hard,
His rod bows as the silver missile clears the surface.
This life force, attached by thin thread, is a wonder—
compact strength so apparent in mid-river leaps and runs,
power, dense and vital, throbbing,
a death struggle that deserves no less than what this river gypsy
    delivers.

The fisherman follows the rainbow downriver, rod held high,
losing, gaining, losing, as the big fish slowly tires.
Now the fish is spent, quiet in the shallows.
The fisherman bends to remove the hook, points the fighter back
    home, and lets go.

U.P. Publishers & Authors Association Announces 5th Annual U.P. Notable Books List

MARQUETTE, MI (January 4th, 2024)— the **Upper Peninsula Publishers & Authors Association** (UPPAA) announces the 5th Annual U.P. Notable Books List this week. UPPAA board member **Mikel Classen** (Sault Ste. Marie) initiated the effort as a response to the lack of representation of U.P. writers in other Michigan state literary circles. Classen said, "Traditionally, recognition of Michigan books has been dominated by the university presses downstate and we would like to take this opportunity to highlight literature that focuses closer to home for us."

Evelyn Gathu, Director of the Crystal Falls District Community Library, will continue the library's alliance with UPPAA to co-sponsor the U.P. Notable Book Club (www.upnotable.com/book-club/). The club is available to any U.P. resident and features monthly Zoom meetups with national bestselling U.P. Notable authors such as **Karen Dionne** (*The Wicked Sister*). Members borrow the books from their local libraries or purchase at local stores prior to discussions. Presentations include author readings, a conversation on the making of the book, and a live Q&A with the audience.

To build this fifth annual list, UPPAA consulted with Upper Michigan booksellers, book reviewers, writers, and publishers to winnow down the notable books to a bare ten titles. You can find reviews of many of these books on the UP Book Review (www.upbookreview.com). It must be emphasized that the list is unranked, each title deserves equal merit as U.P. Notable Book. These ten books have been deemed essential reading for every U.P. lover and we highly recommend you ask your local librarian or booksellers for them today!

1. *The Great Seney Fire: A History of the Walsh Ditch Fire of 1976* by Gregory M. Lusk (Snowsnake Press, 2023)
2. *Grim Paradise: The Cold Case Search for the Mackinac Island Killer* by Rod Sadler (WildBlue Press, 2023)
3. *Odin's Eye: A Marquette Time Travel Novel* by Tyler R. Tichelaar (Marquette Fiction, 2023)
4. *The Midwife's Touch* by Sue Harrison (Shanty Cove Books, 2023)
5. *Yooper Ale Trails: Craft Breweries and Brewpubs of Michigan's Upper Peninsula* by Jon C. Stott (Modern History Press, 2023)
6. *Unsolved Mysteries of Father Marquette's Many Graves* by Jennifer S. McGraw (Pine Stump Publications, 2023)
7. *Prehistoric Copper Mining in Michigan: The Nineteenth-Century Discovery of "Ancient Diggings" in the Keweenaw Peninsula and Isle Royale* by John R. Halsey (UMich Press, 2018)
8. *Brockway Mountain Stories* by Paul LaVanway (Mudminnow Press, 2023)
9. *Who Am I?* by Julie Buchholtz (Sleeping Bear Press, 2023)
10. *A Nostalgic Lens: Photographs and Essays from Michigan's Upper Peninsula* by Peter Wurdock (Blue Boundary Books, 2023)

U.P. Notable Classics

The U.P. Notable Books Committee also includes an initiative called *U.P. Notable Classics* that highlights just two of the most significant U.P. themed works that have remained essential for at least 10 years. It is the committee's hope that these books can bring enjoyment to a new generation of readers.

- *Death's Door: The Truth Behind Michigan's Largest Mass Murder* by Steve Lehto (Momentum Press, 2006)
- *Murder at Mackinac: A Novel* by Ronald J. Lewis (Agawa Press, 1995)

All books submitted to the *U.P. Book Review* are considered for nomination to the U.P. Notable Books list. You can find the latest reviews and subscribe to be notified of future reviews by visiting www.UPBookReview.com

U.P. Reader is Accepting Submissions for Volume 9

The *U.P. Reader* is an annual publication that represents a cross-section of writers that are the membership of the Upper Peninsula Publishers and Authors Association (UPPAA). This annual anthology showcases and promotes the writers of the Upper Peninsula. Each issue is released in paperback, hardcover, eBook, and audiobook editions in early Spring following the deadline. Copies of the *U.P. Reader* will be made available to booksellers, UPPAA members, libraries, and news services. The *U.P. Reader* has received more media coverage each year since the inclusion of the Dandelion Cottage Award. We hope the *U.P. Reader* will be a great place for you to showcase your original short works, too.

Submission Guidelines

- **Email submissions are no longer allowed**. Please submit your work through our submissions gateway which is **www.uppaa.org/submit/** If you email your submission, you may be asked to re-send it through the gateway.

- Submissions will receive a receipt that the submission has been received. If a receipt is not received within three business days of submission either resubmit or contact editor@UPReader.org

- Must be a **current member of the UPPAA** to submit.

- Submissions **must be original** with no prior appearance in web or print. Submissions will be accepted for **up to 5,000 words**. Writers who submit work which has previously appeared in blog posts, web pages, eBooks, social media, or in print will be disqualified.

- Submissions **can be any genre**: fiction, nonfiction (memoirs, history, essays, feature articles, interviews, opinions) and poetry.

- All submissions will be **reviewed through a jury** and the submissions will be chosen through this process. Writers will be notified as to acceptance or rejection, but reasons for rejection will not be discussed.

- We prefer **Microsoft Word Document** (.DOC) files only or plain text files (.TXT). Do not submit PDF files. If you have some other type of text file, please inquire.

- **Please include a 50-75-word bio** at the end of the submission. Bios longer than 75 words will be trimmed by the editor. Any web addresses or email address in bios must be the most simplified form possible. (Do not include the http://)

- **Authors may only submit photos as part of a written submission** with the understanding that they will be converted to black-and-white. We reserve the right to limit the number of photos per story that will be used. Photos should be at least 300 DPI and no smaller than 2 inches on a sided (i.e. 600px minimum). If the Author is not the photographer, we may ask for a simple one-page "Photo Release" form to be sent in. Contact us in advance if you think you need more than 3 photos for your story. Author headshots are neither required nor used.

- **No more than 3 submissions will be accepted** from one person. If more than 3 are received, the jury may choose to disregard all of them. We are looking for quality, not quantity.

- **Poetry submissions count as one submission per poem. If a poem cycle is submitted it needs to be formatted either as one poem with multiple sections or as separate poems not numbering more than three.**

The U.P. Reader will require FIRST time rights in all formats, including but not limited to print, eBook, and audiobook for 12 months after publication. After 12 months, the author may use the work in any form they desire, including on the internet, print, and digital media. UPPAA retains the right to use it in perpetuity. For Example, we anticipate a "Best of U.P. Reader" to be issued for the 10th anniversary.

Publication Schedule for *U.P. Reader* Volume 9

- Submission window opens **June 1st, 2024**. Submissions sent before June 1st, 2024 will not be recognized.
- Submission deadline: **Nov. 10th, 2024**
- Jury / peer-review process begins
- Jan 15th, 2025 announcement of selected submissions
- April 1st, 2025 official on-sale date

Young U.P. Author Section

UPPAA is extremely pleased to announce the winners of the 7th Annual Dandelion Cottage Contest that celebrates the creative writing of the U.P.'s newest generation of writers! Each winner will take home a cash prize, a commemorative medallion, and a hardcover edition of the *U.P. Reader* in which their submission appears. Beginning in 2019, we inaugurated two divisions for the contest: Senior (grades 9-12) and Junior (grades 5-8). The winners of both Junior and Senior Divisions will have their name inscribed on a traveling trophy which will reside in their school in the coming year. Starting in 2022, we added a full rank of winners for the Junior division which formerly had a single overall winner.

This year, we saw 18 high school submissions from two different schools. The 14 Junior division entries came from six different schools. We had just one of our 32 total submissions from homeschooled students. The judges would like to thank each and every student who submitted their work. There were so many great entries in each division that the judges had a difficult time whittling down the list to just three winners.

Senior Division Winners

- **First Place: Skye Isaacson**, Grade 9 (Houghton High School, Houghton) for "The Birthday Party." Sponsor: Jessica Klein.
- **Second Place: Miina Chopp**, Grade 9 (Houghton High School, Houghton) for "Starved." Sponsor: Jessica Klein.
- **Third Place: Leah Johnson**, Grade 9 (Houghton High School, Houghton) for "There are No Happy Endings." Sponsor: Jessica Klein.

Junior Division Winner

- **First Place: Eve Noble**, Grade 8 (Copper Country Christian School) for "Despondent." Sponsors: Judy Chizek and Erica Blasiola
- **Second Place: Isla Peterson**, Grade 8 (JKL Bahweting) for "Echo." Sponsor: Aaron Litzner .
- **Third Place: Analise VerBerkmoes**, Grade 8 (Copper Country Christian School) for "Time Deprivation." Sponsor: Judy Chizek and Erica Blasiola

Participating Schools – Senior Division

- Houghton
- Negaunee

Participating Schools – Junior Division

- Bothwell Middle School, Marquette
- Houghton
- Copper Country Christian School
- Gwinn
- JKL Bahweting
- Home Schooled

Despondent

by Eve Noble

◆❖◆

Every second of every day I sit here. No matter the weather, sunny, snowing, or thunder, it doesn't matter, I never move; I can't. I watch as people have fun and be happy all around me; I can't help but be sad. How could I not be? As everyone gets to run around and play, I have to sit here as the dust slowly collects on my rusty metal arms. No one really notices me anymore. I don't blame them, though; not many people pay attention to the bench in their neighborhood park. It's just one of those things you pass every day without a single thought.

People used to stop and look at me when I was younger. When I was shinier. When I was first built in this park. Families used to admire my freshly painted black legs and armrests that bend into an elaborate flower shape as they move down to my sturdy European Oak seat. They used to sit on my smooth wooden seat. Now my legs' and arms' paint has chipped away in patches, the shiny gray peeking through; the rust grows more and more every day. Vines grow up my legs, flowers peeking out from under my feet. The surface of my seat is now rough and weathered; what used to look like a beautiful glossy wood is now nothing more than a splinter waiting to happen.

Some days I try to find enjoyment in the small things. That's all I really have, the small things. A mother bird had her babies in a branch of the tree sitting next to me. They were just learning how to fly, and they would land on my wooden back. Whenever they did this, people from all over the park would point and stare. It feels nice to be noticed. I know they weren't looking at me of course, and I couldn't blame them. The birds were really beautiful.

•••

Today was going to be a day like any other day. As the sun slowly rose, people began to flood the park. It's usually the joggers first; I watch as one goes by after the other.

Sometimes I wish I could run away from this place like them, but I know that could never happen; the most I can do is move the slivers on my wooden seat. Then the normal people started coming in; couples on a date, high schoolers hanging out, and the children. As I watched the children playing on the playground that sat in front of me, I saw a familiar face standing behind them. This same guy came and sat on my seat every now and then. He came rather irregularly. He usually sat alone on my seat drinking what seemed like coffee from a mug. I could tell he was like me, never really happy; he always wore the same apathetic expression on his face.

This day was different, though; he wasn't alone. There was a woman with him, and he didn't have his mug. Together they seemed like all of those people who come to the park on a date. "This is my favorite spot to sit and drink coffee. Here, take a seat," the man said. He sounded different; he sounded more cheerful? Every time the girl smiled, he did too. Seeing him happy made me feel weird; I don't know if I was happy for him or if I was sad to lose the only person I have ever met that was like me. They sat in silence for a long while; the sun started to go down.

"Finney, this place is really nice, but we should probably start heading back because it's getting dark," the girl sitting next to him said. That was the first time I ever heard his name. Finney, so you're the one that has been keeping me company all these years.

"You're right, it's getting pretty late. I'll walk you home," Finney said to the girl as they stood up and started to walk away. There I was again watching the sun go down by myself. Little did I know I wasn't going to see him for a long twelve months.

• • •

After two very uneventful months passed, Finney didn't come back. One day, I was watching a kid and his mom walking through the park. Then all of the sudden, the annoying music was back. This same music plays

every time this big truck pulls in; the kids from the park always run up to it and walk away with some kind of food. "Mom! Can I get ice cream? Please, please, please, please!" the kid started to say, pulling his mother's arm.

"Not right now, Honey, we should be getting home now," the mother said to her child. The child began to cry; he cried so loud it was somehow even more obnoxious than the ice cream truck. The little boy then fell to the ground and started flailing his arms. "Fine! Go get some ice cream; then we are going straight home," the mother said in a voice that could only be explained as exasperated. She gave him three dollars from her purse and sat down on my seat waiting for the kid to come back.

When the little boy got back with a mint chocolate chip ice cream cone, he sat down next to his mother, licking the side of the cone as it melted.

"Hurry, we have to be home in forty minutes," the mother said to her child, trying to hurry him. He licked his ice cream for about three more minutes. Then all of a sudden, "plop," and the top of the ice cream cone was all over my seat. It was so sticky and cold!

"James, you got it everywhere!" she said to the child as he started to cry again. The ice cream started to melt and spread over half of my seat.

"My, my, my ice cream!" he screamed. It was sinking into the cracks of my weathered wood.

"Honey, stay here, I am going to get napkins to clean this up," his mother said, getting up and going back to the ice cream truck to ask for napkins.

I just couldn't take it anymore. I was boiling with rage at this point. The child sat on my seat crying with the ice cream sitting next to him. I mustered all my strength, moved the slightest bit of a sliver of my wooden seat, and pushed it into his finger. He threw the rest of the ice cream cone up into the air, "My finger!" he yelled. The ice cream landed on my arm then exploded all over the rest of me. That's what I get for trying to get revenge, I guess. His mother came back with the napkins and attempted to clean the ice cream from his shirt. Then he shoved his finger in her face, "Mom, my finger! The bench attacked me!" he yelled.

She looked at her child's finger, "Oh James, you got a splinter? Let's go home and I will get the splinter out for you," she said to her son. He got up, still crying, and they both walked away until I could no longer see them.

As each day passed after the ice cream incident, my sadness grew worse. I watched as people had picnics with their families. Sometimes I wished I could have a family; I know that could never happen, though. I am a bench after all. I don't even know who made me. Though, sometimes I like to imagine what it would be like to have one. I would have freshly painted arms and legs with a beautiful and smooth wooden seat; someone would sit on my seat every day. We would be happy together. But that's all just a dream. It would never happen.

•••

Finney eventually came back. He hadn't been here since about a year ago when he came with that girl. It brought me some joy to see him again after all this time. He was holding a bouquet of beautiful red roses in his hand. Finney was dressed much better than usual; he was wearing a black suit and red tie the color of the roses he was holding. It was usually just the occasional businessmen that I saw wearing a suit. I had never seen him dress like this; he had always worn a T-shirt with sweatpants and sometimes a pair of jeans. He sat on my seat, carefully avoiding the now dry ice cream, so as to not ruin his suit. After a few minutes, the same girl who had come with him a year ago was standing in front of him in a beautiful red dress that flowed down to just below her knees.

Finney looked nervous when he saw her. "You're here! Take a seat," he said, patting the empty space next to him that wasn't covered in ice cream on my seat.

"It looks just like it did when you took me here for our first date," she said while taking a seat next to him.

Finney handed her the flowers "For you m'lady," Finney teased. She blushed and they both laughed. She brought the flowers to her nose and smelled them. They continued to talk for the next hour, then Finney stood up from his seat, got on one knee and reached into his back pocket.

The girl looked shocked. "Finney, oh, my gosh," she gasped.

Finney just looked at her and smiled with a warm and loving expression. "The day I met you was the day my life started. I had fallen into the deep darkness of life's never-ending sadness, but you are my shining light who led me out of the darkness. Without you I would still be lost," Finney said looking her in the eyes. She started to cry. Still trying his best to make eye contact, "Monika Jean Guilbert, will you marry me?" Finney said, pulling out and opening a small black box from his pocket to reveal a beautiful gold ring with a brilliant diamond.

The girl stood up, "Yes, one hundred times yes!" she screamed. He took the ring out of the black box and put it on her finger. Everyone in the park began clapping their hands. Finney and the girl embraced in a tight hug. As everyone cheered, I couldn't help but be happy for Finney and his new fiancé. Soon after this, though, they left and took all of the happiness they had lent to me with them.

•••

As the days went by, I was again depressed. Finney had not come to visit in a long while, and I was losing hope that he would ever come again. One day it was like any other day; it always starts like a normal day. I watched a tall man with a long beard that fell all the way down to his stomach and wearing a black beanie on his head, walking a dog; the dog was a small Pomeranian. They both walked up to stand in front of me. The man was talking on his phone. "What do you need from the store? I will stop there on my way back," the man said into his phone.

The man continued to talk on his phone, but I just zoned him out. I could only focus on one thing at a time, and that one thing now was the small Pomeranian sniffing me. The dog was sniffing my left leg which was much taller than him in comparison. Why was he sniffing me? It made me feel kind of self-conscious; did I smell weird? The small golden dog walked over to my other leg and began to sniff that one too. The dog lifted his leg and peed, right on my foot! All I could feel was disgust and anger coursing through me. I wanted to prick the dog with a piece of wood, but I learned my lesson when I pricked the child. The big man walking the dog was now off of his phone. "Come on, Teddy." He said, pulling on the small dog's leash. As they walked away farther and farther from me, I was left there, my anger turning into sadness.

•••

After months just watching, a group of five boys, who looked like high schoolers, stood a few yards in front of me. They were carrying a large container, but I couldn't tell what was in it. One of the high schoolers had short, light gray hair; it was the color of the moon during the night. He was carrying a camera. He put the camera down

in front of all the boys, pointing at them. He pressed a red button on the camera. All five were standing in front of the camera when the guy with gray hair started to talk, "What's up guys?! Today me and my friends are going to be playing dodgeball with water balloons. But these aren't any normal water balloons; these water balloons are filled with paint!" he said in a loud voice, almost yelling.

"This is going to be epic!" one of the guys with long, black hair standing next to him said.

I thought this could be amusing at least. All five of the boys took two balloons each out of the container and ran in opposite directions. The one with gray hair looked at one of the boys who was wearing a green beanie, "You're going to be first Ryan!" he yelled at him from a distance.

"You wish!" The guy screamed back. All of a sudden, they all started throwing the balloons at each other.

All of them dodged the balloons but one. "Aghhh, I have been hit! Man down, man down!" he yelled dramatically. When the balloon hit his chest, it exploded all over him, splattering into his dark green hair. You could see from outer space where he got hit by the balloon, red paint dripping from his bright, yellow shirt. They all started to laugh then began throwing the balloons again as the guy that was hit laid on the ground. After a while the only two people left were the guy with gray hair and the guy with the green beanie.

"So much for 'you'll be first,'" the guy in the beanie said.

"You may not have been first, but I will get you!" the gray-haired guy said. After their brief conversation, the one wearing the beanie ran behind me for shelter. The other threw two balloons at once right at me! One exploded into a mess of red paint. It was all over. The second balloon went through the hole between my seat and back and hit the guy wearing the beanie. The beanie guy fell back as if he was hit by a gun. Everyone started standing up. "Ha! See I told you I would win!" the gray-haired guy said.

"Yeah, yeah, Richie," the guy with the beanie said standing up. They turned off the camera and picked up the rubber scraps of the balloons.

The guy with gray hair turned the camera back on, after all the rubber scraps were in the large container, to record an outro to what I am guessing is a YouTube video, "You all probably guessed it, I won!" he said into the camera.

"Yeah, they know you won," one of the other guys said in a bored but teasing tone. They all laughed again.

"Anyway! Thank you all for watching and see you all next time," the gray-haired boy said in an influencer voice. The boys walked away; I could no longer see them. I was left there to sit in the mess they had made.

How could anyone ever like me again? I doubt even Finney would want to be near me now. I mean look at me; I'm a mess. My seat and back are weathered, my arms and legs are rusty, I am covered in ice cream and red paint, and not to mention I smell like dog pee. Even if there was ever the slightest bit of hope that I could be happy, maybe even have a family, it is gone. Now I won't just sit here and be ignored. People will stare at me with disgust and avoid me at all costs.

•••

A few years passed after this event, and I was the saddest I had ever been. But that all changed when I saw Finney again. He was with the same girl, but they both looked older and there was a child with them who looked about six years old. "Oh my gosh what happened to the bench?" Finney's, probably now wife, exclaimed, looking at me. I was happy to see them again but sad to know even they thought I was disgusting.

"We should clean it up. This place is part of our history," Finney told her. So, they left, and came back an hour later with some cleaning supplies. After two hours of cleaning, I felt amazing. I looked amazing! The ice cream and paint were gone, my seat and back were smooth again, my arms and legs were freshly painted black.

The little girl, probably their daughter, picked up a bottle of perfume and sprayed me with it. It was rose scented like the roses Finney had given his wife on their first date. I finally felt good again; I was happy to be with this family. But it was getting dark, and they had to leave. I would miss them.

•••

The family came back two weeks later. I was so happy to see them again, "I can't believe we finally got permission to do this," Finney said.

"I know; this kinda feels like a dream," his wife agreed. The two of them picked me up by my arms and put me in the back of a truck, the little girl following close behind. I didn't know where I was going, but, honestly, I didn't care. I was moving! As the truck started to move, I could feel the wind. I could see many new things; it was amazing. Everything was happening so fast. Is this how the joggers feel when they run through the park? Once the car stopped moving and everyone got out, Finney and his wife lifted me out of the bed of the truck. We were at a two-story white house. They walked with me in their arms around the house and put me in the backyard. I stayed in that backyard for the rest of my life, never being depressed or unhappy again.

Finney comes and sits on my seat every morning as he drinks a cup of coffee from the same mug he used to drink from at the park; sometimes his wife even joins us. I wasn't just a bench anymore either. Some days I was a pirate ship, and the little girl would be the captain traveling the dangerous sea in search of treasure, or I would be a spaceship taking her to weird undiscovered planets and meeting aliens. After all these years of sitting alone, watching, I was finally part of the fun. My dream came true; I was finally part of a family.

Eve Noble is 13 years old and an 8th grader at Copper Country Christian School in Chassell. She enjoys crocheting, reading, writing, hanging out with friends, and participating in the local farmer's market. Eve aspires to become a psychologist or a surgeon.

Echo

by Isla Peterson

◆❖◆

Echo was walking through town. The bright sun reflected off their silver skin. They walked past vendors selling items; stranger's faces glowed in all different vibrant colors. Everyone seemed cheerful but Echo was troubled by something. They were heading to meet their friend Zax and had decided they would ask him about it. That's when Echo spotted Zax, he was leaning on the wall in an alleyway. His face screen was glowing bright maroon; it appeared to have a crack in it that he still hadn't gone to get fixed. "Hey Zax!" Echo called.

"Oh! Hey Echo, you're here." Zax was one of Echo's only friends, he could be mean and brutally honest, but he stuck by Echo's side, and that was enough for them. The two chatted and walked for a while, bought a couple things, but Echo couldn't clear their head; they suddenly found themselves lost in thought.

"Echo! Hey, Echo!" Zax nudged Echo and they stumbled a bit.

"Huh!? Oh! Zax! Sorry, did you say something?"

"*Yeah,* I asked you a question; you good dude?"

"Um..." Echo thought about what they were going to say for a second, they didn't want this to sound wrong. "Not really, I have something that's been bugging me, but I'm not sure how to bring it up."

Zax sighed, "Alright let's sit down and you can talk to me about it." They walked to a bench and sat; bystanders walked by giggling and joking, without a care in the world.

"So, what's bothering you?" Zax asked.

"Well, I just... I know we had to stop the damage that humans were causing but... Don't you think killing them off was a bit much?"

Echo could tell Zax didn't expect this, "Dude what are you talking about? They were going to kill the planet! We would have lost everything! Of course, we had to kill them!" He exclaimed.

"Well of course I know that but... I don't know. Couldn't we have talked it through with them? Show them the evidence of the damage they were doing and tell them what to do to fix it?"

"Echo, listen, you care too much; our predecessors chose the most logical solution. The humans were very aware they were killing the planet, but they did nothing about it! Talking it through with them wouldn't have done anything."

"But-"

"No buts, this is probably your personality flaw talking again, It makes you too empathetic, and you start to question things that are set in stone. You really should get that fixed, you know."

"Zax, you know if I went in to get it fixed, they would shut me down, or reset me. I can't have that happen..."

"I know, I know, I'm sorry. Listen I gotta get home, you probably should too. Echo, I suggest you don't mention this to anyone else, ok? Just stop questioning it. Even if the decision was wrong, it's done and over; they're all dead. Once you realize that, you'll feel better, ok? I'll see you around, bye." Before Echo could respond, Zax walked off, squeezing between groups of androids talking. He headed north, the direction of his house. Echo stood there awkwardly. This happened every now and then; Echo would have something bugging them; they would ask Zax about it, and Zax would shoot them down, tell them it was all in their head, then storm off. Zax always said that Echo questioned things that don't need to be questioned because of the personality defect they've had since being built. Echo wondered what had gone wrong when they were being built that made them so different. Their defect is most of the reason that they don't have many friends; people think they're strange and don't want to deal with it.

Echo sighed and started to walk towards the woods, Zax **was** right about one thing: humans going extinct was in the past; they couldn't do anything now. Echo decided a walk in nature would help them clear their head. Echo got to the trail. It was early summer, so the grass was green, the trees were lush, and the flowers that had bloomed were beautiful and vibrant. Echo was immediately relieved as they walked through the woods; it almost seemed as if they were shut off from the world with all its problems. All Echo could hear were the animals, and the leaves blowing in the wind. Suddenly, Echo heard rustling in the bushes. They froze listening; it sounded much bigger than any animal that would be around this area, much bigger than a cat or a dog. Echo turned on their thermal vision and looked around to see if they could find this unknown presence. Echo searched until they saw a strange shape; it was hiding in a condensed part of the shrubbery. Echo could not make out a clear idea of what it was from where they were, so they decided to go get a closer look.

They approached carefully, trying their best not to scare off this strange being. After walking a couple of feet, Echo was able to make out the shape; it was bipedal. It had two arms and two legs, it almost looked like... A human! Echo stopped in their tracks and stared in shock. *That can't be!* Echo's processors felt as if they would shut down with this controversial information. *The humans went extinct years ago! How would one be here today!?* Echo shook their head, *No! I must be seeing things; it's probably a bear or something and it just looks like a human!* Echo walked a little farther towards the being. Suddenly the being jumped out of the bush. Before Echo could process what just happened, they had been knocked to the ground and the mysterious being was standing on top of them with a sword pressed lightly against Echo's screen. Echo switched off heat vision so they could see properly. Now that they had a clear view, they realized it really was a human!

Echo stared in shock as they scanned every part of the human taking in all the information they could. *It's a human! They're supposed to be extinct, but I have one here before me! I need to get all the information I can get,* Echo thought. The human appeared to be male, tan skin, black hair that was pulled back in a messy bun, piercing green eyes; he wore a tan long sleeved shirt with dark jeans, and he had a nose ring and earrings that appeared to be made of animal bone on his earlobes and septum.

The look in his eyes as he stood over Echo was that of pure hatred, *not at me specifically,* Echo felt, *but at the world in general.*

Echo realized that they've been staring for too long and that they should say something before the human pierces his sword through their screen, but Echo couldn't muster up anything to say; they were too shocked. *What am I supposed to say? What language does he even speak? What do you say to a creature that's supposed to be extinct?* Echo thought in confusion, getting more and more anxious.

Suddenly the human spoke, "I'm taking you with me, **don't** try anything or I will not hesitate to smash your screen in."

"Point taken." Echo responded nervously. The human helped them up then started leading them somewhere, still threatening them with a sword. The two walked in silence for a while. This just made Echo even more nervous; they were too curious to not say anything. They had to know more about this mysterious human! "So, my name is Echo! My pronouns are they/them, please! You?" Echo said, finally breaking the silence.

"I'm not interested in socializing with you," The human responded bluntly.

He's a tough nut to crack isn't he? Echo thought but, despite that, Echo was determined to at least find out his name.

"Not even a name? I feel like I at least deserve that; you **are** leading me into the unknown," Echo remarked.

"Ugh," the human rolled his eyes. "My name's Edwin. You probably already know I'm a guy."

Echo beamed at this new information, *So, his name is Edwin!* "That's a pretty name!"

Edwin ignored this comment; the two continued in silence for a while.

"So, where are we going?" Echo asked, trying to make small talk and possibly find out more about Edwin.

"My hideout for the night."

Echo responded simply, "Oh, ok." They walked a while longer until they finally came to a stop. There was a cave before them, mostly hidden by vines; at first glance you wouldn't even know it was there.

"We're here," Edwin said, moving the vines aside. "Come in." Edwin walked in and Echo followed close behind. Inside the cave, it was cozy, there was just enough room for both

of them. It was dimly lit by a lamp, the type humans would have used for camping; there were little gadgets around the room, hunting tools, some stored food, and many other useful items. In the middle, there were two bench-like logs facing each other.

"Sit." Edwin ordered motioning to one of the logs.

Echo sat, and watched Edwin, Edwin turned and started sorting through stuff in the corner; they could tell by his body language that Edwin was trying to figure out what to do with Echo. They sat in silence for a while; then finally Edwin turned to Echo and broke the silence. "Listen, Echo, was it? You're smart enough to know why I took you here. I don't want to be found."

"Yes, I figured," Echo responded, nervous about where this was going.

"So, if you want me to keep you alive-"

"Wait!" Echo yelled suddenly, interrupting Edwin who looked really irritated, but Echo kept talking anyway. "Hear me out; I don't want to turn you in! Just earlier today I was questioning if it was right that we had killed the humans! I can help you in many different ways! I can bring you supplies; I can warn you about populated areas you should avoid, and-and I can do a bunch of other useful stuff!" Echo explained frantically.

Edwin just stared at Echo for a few moments, then sighed with exasperation. "If you had let me finish, you would have known that I was about to offer that." Now that Echo thought about it, it had been really obvious that was where the conversation was going.

"Oh, sorry."

"Yeah, whatever." Echo decided this meant 'it's ok.'

"I am curious about one thing," Echo began. "What are you doing so close to a colony? Isn't that too risky?"

"I had to come closer temporarily because I needed to steal some supplies such as swords, hunting gear, new batteries, a new lighter, matches, new clothes, and other stuff I need for survival." Edwin listed matter-of-factly; he seemed to have partially let his guard down.

"Oh! I could buy all that for you and bring it out to you tomorrow! I need to do some shopping myself anyway." Echo offered, Edwin looked Echo up and down, Echo wondered what he was thinking.

Finally, Edwin spoke. "Fine, I'll meet you just outside of town, where you discovered me the first time. I'll expect you first thing in the morning."

Echo's screen switched to a smile. "Alright! I'll get going now!" they said as they stood.

"Hold on." Edwin stood and stopped them from leaving by grabbing their shoulder. "I stole some trackers last time I came for supplies; I'm going to attach one to you." He turned to the back of the cave and started digging through his bag.

"You really don't trust me to do a simple task like getting supplies without a tracker?"

Edwin whipped his head around in anger. "You wouldn't understand!" he snapped. "Your kind killed my entire species! Of course I can't trust you!" Echo was surprised by his sudden anger.

"But I wasn't the one who killed them; I was made a couple years after all that," Echo explained. "I can understand your anger with the robots that helped with the decision to kill your kind, or the ones that actually did, but why be mad at those of us that had nothing to do with it? It's wrong to lump us all in a box." Echo reasoned.

"Why **did** your 'ancestors' so to speak, kill my kind?" Edwin asked, dead staring at Echo.

"Well, humans were killing the planet, so my predecessors decided the best course of action to stop it would be to get rid of them all together."

"In that case, why did the robots kill all humans and not just the ones who were hurting the planet? Why 'lump them in a box'?" Edwin stated with a cold voice, using Echo's words from earlier against them.

Echo thought about this for a second. "I honestly agree with you. I had nothing to do with my predecessors' decision; I think we should have talked it out with the humans, or at least tried to. Despite that, I do agree that your people were destroying the planet and at the rate, they were hurting it. It would be done in no time, and we **did** have to do

something. I just think we took the wrong course of action."

Edwin looked taken aback by this speech; he froze for a bit contemplating what Echo had just said. After a moment, he just scoffed and turned back around and started digging in the bag again. Echo decided they should just let the room stay in silence for a while. Finally, Edwin pulled out a tracker, just smaller than a dime, out of the bag.

He turned and walked toward Echo. "It's stick-on, where would work best?" He asked.

"Probably my wrist." Echo held out their wrist for him.

"Ok." Edwin put the tracker on Echo's wrist then sat down, grabbed an orange notebook and a pencil, Echo was surprised that he had such trivial things with him. *Don't they just take up space that could be used for survival tools?* Echo wondered.

Edwin wrote something down then ripped that piece of paper out, then handed it to Echo. "Here's a list of all the supplies I need; it also has my clothing sizes on it." he explained.

"Oh! Thanks! Should I head off then?"

"Sure."

"Alright, see you tomorrow?"

"Yeah, whatever."

Echo paused for a moment, they wondered if they should bring up the argument from earlier and make sure they had worked it out, but they decided there was probably a reason Edwin had decided to pretend it hadn't happened, so they turned and headed off.

Edwin watched as Echo left. That was... strange. He thought, I never thought a robot could have sympathy like that. Edwin shook his head. No, I can't quite trust him yet. He could just be pretending or something. Edwin looked down at his sketchbook. It was the one thing he had left from before the apocalypse. His Mother had given it to him for his thirteenth birthday, just a few days before it all went to hell. Before he lost everything. Why did I survive while she didn't? It's not fair. Edwin stood and grabbed his hunting tools. I should get my meal for the night, he thought, He needed to get his mind off of this subject, or he would end up in a bad head space again.

Echo walked around the shopping district of their town. They had already bought batteries, clothes, and the needed hunting supplies; they just wanted to get Edwin one last surprise that wasn't on the list. They walked up to the vendor, bought what they needed, and headed home.

They opened the door and heard a meow at their feet. "Hello, Pip." Echo responded, bending down to pet their cat. Pip rubbed Echo's knee then walked over to her food bowl and Echo looked down into it, "Pip, it's completely full; I don't know what you want from me!" they said with a giggle. "Anyway, I met a human today!" Echo exclaimed as they petted the cat more, "Mew!" Pip responded. "I know right!? It's insane; they're supposed to be extinct!" Echo continued describing their day to Pip who would add in her own thoughts every now and then with a meow. Echo went through their daily chores like normal, the only difference being that they were lost in thought. *I just have so many questions! How did he survive? Where has he been hiding the last 23 years?* Echo sighed, *I suppose this is all stuff I'll find out in time.*

•••

The next day Echo left and headed for the trail where they had run into Edwin the day before. They had two cloth bags full of stuff that Edwin had needed, and the special surprise that Echo bought for Edwin was in a separate bag. Echo walked toward the bushes that Edwin had been hiding in before. They pushed the brush aside and saw Edwin hiding inside. Echo smiled at him "Hi," they said.

"Hey," Edwin responded, glanced down at the bags. "Let's head back to the cave; we can unpack everything there," Edwin suggested, motioning for Echo to follow him.

"Sounds good!" Echo responded and started walking behind Edwin. When the pair got to the cave, they sat and started going through the bags. Echo hid the bag with the surprise behind their back.

"Arrows... Clothes..." Edwin mumbled the list of supplies as he pulled stuff out of the bag. "And batteries! That's everything," he finished with an accomplished look on his

face. "Thanks," he mumbled, facing his face away from Echo in embarrassment.

Echo smiled. "There's one more thing," Echo said, reaching behind themselves and grabbing the bag.

"Huh? But we already have everything on the list," Edwin pointed out in confusion.

"I got you something extra!" Echo handed the bag to Edwin who looked surprised by this act of kindness.

"But... We just met, I mean I almost killed you! Why are you getting me a gift?" he asked.

"Well... I guess I wanted to make up for offending you yesterday. Also, I just wanted to do something nice for you. There wasn't much of a reason really," Echo responded.

Edwin tilted his head at this, but still he opened the bag and pulled the gift out. It was a burnt orange shawl. Though he tried to hide it, Echo could see how excited Edwin was by the sparkle in his eyes. "You should try it on!" Echo suggested.

Edwin lifted the shawl up over their head and pulled it on. "Does it look good?" Edwin asked with hesitation.

"It looks amazing! Sorry, I just kind of assumed that you liked orange because that notebook you had was orange, but I think either way it matches the rest of your outfit!"

Edwin smiled softly as he lifted the shawl to look at it. "Orange is my favorite color," He admitted. Echo was happy that Edwin felt comfortable enough to loosen up. Suddenly Edwin seemed to notice how vulnerable he was acting; he cleared his throat and turned away from Echo "Yeah, well thanks or whatever," he grumbled.

Echo snorted, "Yeah, well your welcome or whatever," they scoffed, doing their best impression of Edwin.

"Hey!" Edwin yelled, playfully hitting Echo.

•••

Over the next month, Echo and Edwin began to get closer. Echo went and helped Edwin out every day. They taught each other things that the other didn't know, and slowly but surely, they began to trust and understand each other.

"This way; It's just around the corner." Edwin directed Echo; he was leading Echo to a spot he thought they would enjoy, still wearing the shawl Echo had given him. After they turned the corner, he brought them to a stop. He pushed aside some bushes to reveal a beautiful waterfall in a small clearing. It was covered in vibrant flowers that danced in the wind. There were vines draped from the rocks around the water.

Echo stared in awe, "Edwin this is beautiful!" They beamed, Edwin smiled, something he had been doing more often lately. Echo was happy he finally felt comfortable enough around them to let his guard down and show emotion. The two chatted and messed around, picking up any materials that might be useful in the meantime.

Suddenly they heard a rustling in the bushes. They both were immediately standing and on guard. Echo moved to be in front of Edwin in a protective stance, "Oi! I can handle myself!" Edwin snapped.

"Quiet! We don't know what this could be!" Echo whispered. Edwin quietly scoffed, and gently pulled his sword out.

In the area of the rustling bushes something emerged. *Please be an animal! Please let us just be overreacting!* Echo thought hopefully. But their hopes were in vain, the figure that emerged was another robot! Echo stared in horror; they had been discovered! Echo took another step towards Edwin concealing him as much as they could (which was hard because Edwin was taller than them). This time, Edwin let it happen. The other robot stared back at them in shock. That's when Echo recognized them, *Zax!* Not only had someone found them, but it was a close friend!

"**Echo**?!" Zax exclaimed as he stared at the two. "Is that a human?" He stepped towards them, but Echo and Edwin stepped back. "What are you doing with it!? We need to tell the authorities!" Zax took another step towards Echo and Edwin, and they stepped back again.

"Zax, *please*," Echo began.

"Don't *please* me! Echo, if you don't come with me to report it then you'll be accused of committing treason! It's stated specifically in the rules that if you encounter any strange or unfamiliar animals you are to report it immediately! This is one of those instances!" he hissed,

"Zax, hear me out! Please! He's my friend! I-"

"NO!" Zax screamed suddenly interrupting Echo. Echo could sense Edwin shaking behind them, they grabbed his arm to comfort him. "Echo, if you won't come with me now then you can just go down with it. I gave you your chance. Don't blame me when the authorities come, kill your friend, then shut you down." Zax sneered, then began to run away, most likely to alert the authorities.

"Wait!" Echo screamed, reaching his hand out, but Zax ignored them and continued to run.

Edwin seemed to have composed himself and started running after Zax, Echo grabbed him. Edwin whipped his head around. "Echo, what are you doing!? We have to stop him!" he yelled.

Echo noticed that he *looked* composed, but his eyes were shaking in fear. "It's too late! He probably sent out an electrical signal to them already. Even if he didn't, he'll get there in no time! We have to get out of here!!" They explained. Edwin just looked at them for a bit; he didn't know what to do.

After a few seconds he decided it would be best to listen to Echo. "Where should we go?" he asked, he was still clutching his sword tight.

"Deeper into the forest would be best. As far away and as hidden as possible," Echo replied.

Echo grabbed Edwin's hand and started leading him away. They ran for what seemed like forever, both determined to stay alive. The two came to thick brush. Echo presumed this to be close to the middle of the forest. "Echo, do you think this is a good place to hide for now?" Edwin wheezed, out of breath.

"No, the robot enforcement is given new parts every month and their tech is the best of the best. Even at the pace we've been going, they'll catch up in no time," Echo explained.

"How are we supposed to get away from that!?" demanded Edwin "We should just give up. You should turn me in so you won't get in trouble, and I'll die and this *hell* I'm stuck in will finally be over!" Tears welled up in Edwin's eyes, Echo's eyes widened, he ran forward and enveloped Edwin in a hug. "Echo, I've lost *everything!*" croaked Edwin.

"That's not true," Echo whispered. "You have me, and as long as we're together we can get through this, okay?"

Edwin looked at Echo and forced a smile "Yeah... that's right. We can."

Edwin had brightened a bit by the time he had finished the sentence. Echo remembered that Edwin had mentioned he went through bad bouts like that every now and then, but he has always pushed through. Suddenly they heard robotic shouting in the distance. Both of their eyes widened, the robot enforcement had caught up! Echo grabbed Edwin and the two started running again. That's when a group of robots with weapons jumped in front of them, blocking them from going any further. Before they knew it the two were surrounded. Echo ran through all the possibilities for escape but there was only one that would work. One chance. They smiled sadly at Edwin.

"What is it!? What are you planning!?" Edwin quaked, holding his sword out defensively at the robot enforcement.

"PUT YOUR HANDS UP AND SURRENDER YOURSELVES!!" The robot enforcement boomed.

"I have a plan, but I'm going to need you to give me your sword for it to work," Echo began. "Okay?"

Edwin said, handing Echo the sword carefully, "What now!?"

"Listen, When I yell 'GO' I need you to run as fast and as far as you can, alright!?"

"WHAT!?" He demanded. "Echo, I'm not leaving you!!"

"Just trust me!! *Please!!!*"

Edwin stared at Echo, "O-okay," his voice shook. That's when Echo dashed forward and began to attack the surrounding robots.

"WHAT ARE YOU DOING!?" Edwin screamed. The other authorities dashed to get ahold of Echo, while one ran to grab Edwin. Edwin promptly knocked over the one

that had attacked him and smashed his boot through its screen.

"GO!" Echo screamed as they held off the other robots.

"BUT-"

"I SAID GO!"

Edwin stood for a second debating if he should listen to Echo and run, or if he should stay and help. He didn't want to leave Echo; he didn't want to lose someone else but... If both he **and** Echo were captured, then Echo's sacrifice right now would be in vain. Edwin shook his head and started running.

Echo smiled as they watched Edwin start to run away. They fought as long as they could, but not long after Edwin started running, the authorities had disarmed Echo and had them captured. They opened the panel on the back of Echo's head, flipped some switches in a special pattern; then with a spark, Echo's vision went dark.

Edwin ran as fast as he could. He looked back at Echo while he ran. He saw the robots had already disarmed them and were holding their hands behind their back. Edwin watched as they fiddled with something in the back of Echo's head, then after a second, their screen went dark, and they collapsed into the other robot's arms. Edwin whipped his head away and squeezed his eyes shut. He ran even faster now. *Don't cry, don't cry, don't cry!* He willed, but he couldn't stop himself. He ran for what felt like eons, tears streaming down his face.

Finally, he slowed to a stop and dropped to his knees, both from exhaustion and sorrow. *That's it. Everything. Everything I've ever loved is gone. "How about that huh!?"* He croaked aloud, "Is this some sort of sick joke from god, because it's *NOT FUNNY!!!*" He screamed at the sky, tears started to flow down his face, he clutched the grass, tearing some out of the ground. "What's the point anymore? Whatever was the point!? Everyone I knew and loved *died!!* So why am I still here!? Why have I been trying to survive!?" He remembered what Echo had said earlier *"You have me, and as long as we're together we can get through this, okay?"* Echo had been the last thing he had been hanging on to. Now that they were gone, what was he supposed to do?

He was back to having nothing. "Maybe I should just die." He thought about what Echo would say right now, *they would want me to go on wouldn't they?* Edwin thought for a moment. *But why should I? What would I do?* That's when he remembered something Echo had mentioned.

"Hey Edwin?"

"Hm?"

"Well, I was thinking, if you survived the apocalypse then... who's to say others didn't?" Edwin's eyes had widened in shock, he had never thought about that before.

"I guess I never even wondered if other people had survived, I was so focused on my own survival that I never thought about it."

"Well how about when we get all this figured out, we go search together? We can travel the world, and in the meantime possibly find more of your people!"

"I would like that!"

Edwin thought about this memory for a second. That's it! He decided. That's what I'll survive for. I'll try to find other humans, and I'll see the world. For Echo. Who knows! Maybe I'll even find another robot like Echo. Edwin paused for a moment. It's funny, before I met Echo, I never would have even thought about teaming up with a robot. I hope in the future we can all work together like that. Edwin composed himself, stood and with new motivation, he walked into the unknown.

Isla Peterson is an 8th grader at JKL Bahweting in Sault Sainte Marie, Michigan.

KITCH-ITI-KI-PI SPRINGS IN THE WINTER, MANISTIQUE, MICH.

Time Deprivation

by Analise VerBerkmoes

◆ ❖ ◆

Savannah Wilson stood, surveying the rolling hills and pastures of her family's farm in Whitefish, Montana. The lush country grass swayed from side to side in the cool breeze. Savannah's mind wandered as she wondered what she would do this summer during her spare time. The previous summer, the Wilsons had begun to expand their boarding facility and there were always stalls that needed mucking, hay waiting to be hauled, or horses that needed exercise. What Savannah really wanted was a horse of her own that she could train, groom, and eventually barrel race. With a sigh, Savannah snapped out of her daydream and headed for the Wilson's cedar-sided house a short distance from the barn. She walked up the front steps and into the house, sliding her boots off on the entryway mat. She headed into the kitchen where she found Mrs. Wilson slicing an apple.

"Hi, Mom!" Savannah said, stealing a slice of apple from the cutting board.

"Hi, Savannah! By the way, I got a phone call asking for Savannah Wilson. It was a man by the name of Dick Nelson. He said

he's boarding at Oakland Stables just down the road and was hoping you could call him back as soon as possible. Here's his number," she said handing Savannah a scrap of paper and her cell phone.

"Any idea what he wants?" Savannah questioned.

"He said something about having a horse that he wanted you to see," Mrs. Wilson recalled, placing the apple slices in a bowl.

Savannah warily began to dial the number; she hated calling people she didn't know. Finally, she got the guts to press the call button. She put the phone up to her ear. On the second ring she heard a man's voice.

"Hello?"

"Hi, I'm Savannah Wilson. Is this Dick Nelson?" Her words came out in a rush. She was practically shaking.

"Yes, this is Dick. I'm so glad you called back! Listen, I'm having some trouble with a new horse I bought. I was wondering if you would be interested in trying to train him. I've heard a few grooms here at Oakland highly recommended you. Of course, I would pay you to do it," he said, his voice rising in excitement.

Savannah sat down with a thud. She couldn't believe Dick was really asking her to train his horse. She had been around horses almost as long as she could remember, but she had never trained a horse for someone else.

"Well... I mean... I could..." She stuttered, unsure how to respond to the abrupt question. She gathered her thoughts and tried again. "It's such a kind offer but I've never trained a horse. I've worked with many horses and ridden for a while, but I don't know if I could take on such a big responsibility," She waited anxiously for his reply.

"If someone doesn't train this horse, I'm selling him. I bought him with the intention of jumping him. I thought I could make some money off of him, and he seemed like a good jumping horse. Once I got him home, I realized he had hardly had any training. He obviously has never jumped before. In fact, I think he would make a better barrel racer. On top of that, I don't have the time or experience to train him. As far as I know there aren't any other decent trainers in the area. I know you're not a trainer, but people say you have a touch for horses. If you change your mind, let me know," he said, sounding ready to hang up.

"Wait, can I come look at him?" Savannah cried. "I can come tomorrow morning."

"Absolutely! How about nine o'clock tomorrow morning?" he asked, some of his friendliness returning.

"I'll be there," Savannah said, a slight edge in her voice. Dick Nelson sounded like someone who was more interested in money than the well-being of any of his animals. Savannah knew she had to train Thunder. If Dick decided to sell him, Savannah was certain he wouldn't end up in a good home. Savannah knew too many people who were strictly in the horse industry for money reasons rather than the enjoyment of the sport. She had a feeling Dick was one of those people.

The next morning, the alarm blared at seven a.m. sharp. Savannah rolled over, ready to hit the snooze button, then it dawned on her. Today she was going to see Dick Nelson and his horse. She threw off the covers and snapped on the bedside lamp. Then she selected a pair of bootcut jeans, long socks, and a light blue sweatshirt she had gotten from participat-

ing in a horse camp. She headed off to the bathroom where she quickly showered and dressed. Then she headed for the kitchen to get a bowl of cereal. In the kitchen, Mr. Wilson was making coffee and Mrs. Wilson was pouring herself a bowl of cereal. "Morning," Savannah said opening the cereal cupboard and selecting a box of Cheerios. "Morning. You're up early," Mr. Wilson commented. On most mornings Savannah would have preferred to stay in bed until at least eight o'clock.

"Yeah! This morning I'm heading to Oakland Stables to see Dick Nelson's horse, the one I was telling you about at dinner last night."

"We better send you with a horse trailer," Mrs. Wilson joked. It was true, Savannah jumped at any opportunity to bring home a new horse.

Savannah laughed and took another bite of cereal. She looked around at her four other siblings who were also eating their breakfast. They were younger than Savannah and were used to her rushing off and spending her days with the horses or her best friend Adeline. Adeline was thirteen; two years younger than Savannah. Savannah and Adeline, who each had a love for horses, had become good friends two summers ago at a horse camp.

"Well, I'll see you when I get back," Savannah said, getting up and setting her bowl in the sink. Then she hurried outside, grabbed her bike, and began peddling toward Oakland Stables which was about a mile up the dirt road that the Wilsons lived on. When Savannah arrived, she parked her bike outside the barn and walked into a dimly lit area. Up ahead she saw stalls with horses poking their heads out. She walked along looking for someone who could tell her where she could find Dick Nelson. Finally, she spotted a middle-aged woman filling a large hay net.

"Excuse me, I'm Savannah Wilson. I was looking for a boarder by the name of Dick Nelson. Do you know where I could find him?"

"His horse is stabled in that barn. You can try looking there," the woman said pointing towards a large barn off in the distance.

"Thanks," Savannah said before hurrying off. As Savannah walked along, she admired the large, beautiful barns and rolling pastures of Oakland Stables. Horses peacefully grazed in the pastures, their manes and tails glistening in the morning sunshine.

When she entered the barn, she spotted a tall, dark-haired man standing in front of one of the stalls. He was staring hard at something, his hands on his hips.

"Hi, are you Dick Nelson?" Savannah asked as she approached. The man turned abruptly as if startled to see her.

"Oh, you must be Savannah Wilson," he greeted her, a smile lighting up his face.

"That's me," Savannah said, turning to look into the stall he was standing in front of. Inside was a coal black gelding who was eyeing his visitors suspiciously. There was a gleam of mischief in his eye. Savannah couldn't help but smile at him.

"Well, this is Thunder, the horse I was telling you about. Let me warn you, he's a handful, and he likes to bite," Dick grumbled, frowning.

Savannah reached out cautiously; Thunder took a step forward stretching his muzzle out to reach her hand. Suddenly he opened his mouth, bared his teeth, and tried to bite Savannah's arm. With a swift movement she yanked her arm away. She placed her other hand on his cheek where he couldn't reach her and firmly pushed his face away. Obviously, Thunder thought of himself as the boss.

"See what I mean?" Dick bristled.

"I see what you mean, but I think Thunder just needs someone who's firm and patient. He's trying to be the boss and he doesn't see me or you as his leader yet. He has to learn and accept that people are his leaders, and that people will take care of him. I get the feeling that before you bought Thunder, people didn't spend a lot of time with him. Now he doesn't completely trust people," Savannah explained.

"Well, do you want to try and train him?" Dick asked. He didn't seem to care about what was wrong with Thunder. He seemed as if he wanted to get rid of Thunder as fast as possible.

"Yes, I do, under one condition. I get to bring Thunder to my family's farm," Savannah said, waiting for Dick's response. She knew she would accomplish more training if Thunder was stabled at the Wilson's.

"Deal, you can pick him up tomorrow," Dick turned to leave and then stopped. "By

the way, I'll give you two months to straighten him out. I want Thunder to be calmer, more behaved, and able to be ridden. If I see no improvement, I'm selling him," With that, he turned and strode down the aisle.

The next morning Savannah picked up the phone to call Dick. Her parents had agreed to letting Thunder stay at the farm and Savannah was eager to pick him up. She called Dick, arranged a time to pick Thunder up, and then rushed to get the trailer and a stall ready. Half an hour later Savannah and Mr. Wilson pulled into Oakland Stables lot. Dick was standing next to the barn. Thunder, who seemed to be behaving well, was standing next to Dick. Thunder was haltered and Dick was holding loosely onto the lead line. Savannah unlatched the trailer door and slowly lowered the ramp; she had a large hay net already attached to a hook up in the trailer. Mr. Wilson was talking to Dick as Savannah walked over.

"Here he is," Dick said, pressing the lead line into Savannah's hand. She reached out to stroke Thunders dark face. He stood perfectly still and allowed her to rub him. "Guess he's in a good mood today," Dick said with a chuckle. Mr. Wilson smiled.

"Better load him up so we can get him settled back at home. My daughter will take good care of Thunder for you," Mr. Wilson said, studying Thunder.

Savannah slowly led Thunder up to the trailer; she talked soothingly and urged Thunder to step onto the ramp. Obediently, Thunder began to walk up the ramp.

"Good boy!" Savannah praised. After a few more steps they were into the trailer. Savannah quickly connected the lead rope onto a hook in the wall of the trailer. She praised Thunder and patted him as she walked out. Mr. Wilson lifted the ramp and secured it behind Thunder who was contentedly munching hay. Dick placed Thunder's saddle, bridle, and grooming items in the truck. With a quick goodbye to Dick, Savannah and Mr. Wilson drove away.

When they reached the farm, Savannah unloaded Thunder and settled him into his stall. Thunder was curious about his new home, but he didn't act up as Savannah settled him and ran a dandy brush over his sleek coat. Savannah watched Thunder, who was looking around curiously at his stable mates. With a final pat, Savannah latched the stall door and headed back to the house. Savannah wondered if what Dick had said about Thunder was really true; she supposed she would find out when she started training him.

The next day dawned clear, sunny, and warm. Savannah decided to start Thunder's training by seeing how he walked on a lead. She could take him down the driveway and onto the dirt road that paralleled the Wilson's pastures. Savannah stepped into the barn and saw Thunder poking his head out the stall door.

"Hey Thunder, want to go for a walk?" Savannah smiled. She was sure Dick had been wrong about Thunder. She unlatched the stall door and snapped a lead line onto his halter. Thunder obediently followed Savannah out of the barn and into the sunshine. They easily walked along. The grass swayed and birds chirped in the trees. Thunder flared his nostrils taking in all the new smells. Suddenly Thunder planted his feet and threw up his head letting out a shrill whinny to his stable mates.

"Easy, Thunder," Savannah said calmly as she stroked his neck. When Savannah began walking again, Thunder broke into a trot and tried to cut Savannah off. Savannah firmly grabbed the lead rope and made him back up until he was once again standing at her shoulder. The next time he thought about cutting her off, she waved the end of the lead line in front of him. For the next hour, Savannah walked Thunder away from the barn, toward the barn, and in large circles. By the end, Thunder was walking calmly in all directions. Savannah brought Thunder back to his stall and began to brush him down. As she brushed, her mind began to wander. She knew Thunder still had a lot of training left and she only had two months until Dick was coming. She mentally listed the things she would need to accomplish before Dick came. Thunder needed to be able to walk on a lead, lunge, tie, accept a rider, and so much more. Savannah sighed; she realized she had just taken on one of the biggest projects of her life.

Over the next week Savannah walked Thunder and began to do basic groundwork exercises with him. Occasionally, Adeline came over to watch her work Thunder or go on walks with them. Thunder was improving daily. Gradually, their walks grew longer and each day they went farther from the farm. By the end of the week Savannah was walking Thunder one mile a day. He also smoothly walked or backed on command. Savannah was happy with the improvement, but she felt as though Thunder was being rushed. Savannah knew she hadn't formed a bond with him yet, one of the most important steps in training. She needed to put him in a round pen and get him to join up with her. Savannah had seen many trainers teaching horses to join up, but she had never done it herself. Tomorrow Savannah would try a join up.

The next day was overcast and breezy. Savannah put on a lightweight jacket before heading out to work Thunder. When she got to his stall, she carefully slipped on a halter. Just as she clipped on the lead line, Thunder tried to nip her.

"No!" She scolded. Thunder immediately forgot the idea as Savannah made him back up. Although Thunder occasionally tried to nip, he was getting much better about it. Savannah led Thunder to the round pen and detached the lead line.

Thunder, like most horses, walked off to investigate his new surroundings in the small pen. Savannah picked up a lunge whip and strode to the middle of the pen. She lightly cracked the whip on the ground, asking Thunder to move out at a walk like he would on a lunge line. Thunder jerked his head up and began trotting around the perimeter of the round pen. After a few laps, Savannah asked him to change directions, which he did obediently. After two more laps Savannah dropped the whip, turned away from Thunder, and began walking in the opposite direction. If a horse was ready to join up, they would begin to follow the person. Thunder hesitated, and then cautiously began to follow Savannah until he caught up with her. Savannah stopped; her heart was pounding. Thunder had joined up with her. She felt like clapping and shouting! Instead, she turned to praise Thunder.

"Good boy, Thunder!" she said, scrubbing his neck. Thunder blew out a long, contented breath. Now they were getting somewhere.

Three weeks later, Savannah and Adeline walked down the neatly swept aisle at the Wilson's farm. Thunder was doing well in training and the two girls had been taking Thunder and Twix, who was an experienced trail horse, for trail rides around the property. A week ago, Savannah had started riding Thunder, and he had been doing very well. As Savannah approached Thunder's stall, he stuck his head over the door.

"I'll meet you in front of Twix's stall in ten minutes," Savannah called to Adeline who continued down the aisle toward Twix's stall.

"Okay," Adeline called over her shoulder.

Soon the two girls had set out along a grassy lane that led to open rolling fields. Twix led the way with Thunder following. The girls chatted easily about the upcoming school year. Soon they had reached the open field. Thunder tossed his head up in excitement.

"Should we trot them?" Adeline ventured. She was already gathering her reins.

"Let's canter," Savannah called. She knew it was a daring move, but she had been dying to canter Thunder in the field.

"Okay," Adeline murmured. She sounded unsure; however, she quickly urged Twix into a canter. Savannah urged Thunder into a canter too. Thunder took a few strides in a canter and then lowered his head. Savannah caught her breath. Thunder was going to buck! She tried desperately to pull Thunder's head up. She was too late; Thunder gave two tremendous bucks. The first buck unseated Savannah; she felt herself being thrown forward onto Thunder's neck. She tried to grab a hunk of mane to steady herself. Before she could get a good hold, Thunder bucked again. This time she felt herself being hurled through the air. She hit the ground with a thud, and everything went black.

When Savannah finally awoke, she was in a white room surrounded by medical equipment. She felt a sharp pain in her right arm and winced. Then it all came flooding back:

the trail ride, the cantering, and the fall. She shuddered at the thought.

"Hi honey, you're in the hospital. You took quite a spill on Thunder. I'm afraid you've sprained your wrist," her mother talked softly and pushed a strand of hair out of Savannah's eyes. Savannah blinked back tears. This could only mean one thing: she wouldn't be able to ride for weeks. She wondered how she could train Thunder with a sprained arm.

"No," was all Savannah could whisper. With that she flopped back onto the pillow and fell into a restless sleep. She dreamed about Dick selling Thunder to an awful home where no one fed or cared for him. When she awoke, the hospital room was dark; her cheeks were tear stained from crying in her sleep. Savannah couldn't help but feel that she had gotten herself into a big mess.

A few days later Savannah and Adeline were brainstorming how to finish Thunder's training. Savannah had a small brace on her arm, and the doctor had made it clear she was not to ride for three weeks. Unfortunately, Dick was coming in two weeks. Savannah couldn't ride Thunder and that was the main thing he needed to work on. Suddenly Savannah gasped.

"I know! Adeline, you could finish his training! I can coach you." Savannah looked expectantly at Adeline.

"I don't know if I could handle him, Savannah. I don't have nearly as much training experience as you do," Adeline looked reluctant.

"Please, Adeline, just try it. Thunder just needs practice in the arena at a walk and trot. You have to trust me, Adeline. I promise I won't let anything happen. If you don't, Dick will sell Thunder and all of our hard work will be wasted," Savannah pleaded.

"Okay, but you have to coach me every step of the way. And I don't want to do any cantering," Adeline said looking doubtful.

"I will, I promise. You won't have to canter. Dick said he would be happy if Thunder was safe at a walk and trot. Besides, I obviously don't know how to properly train a horse to canter," Savannah said referring to the accident.

Over the next two weeks, the girls worked hard. Adeline rode Thunder most days and if she didn't ride, she did other things like groundwork. Gradually, Thunder grew to like Adeline. Finally, it was two days until Dick was supposed to come visit Thunder. The girls stood outside Thunder's stall. Savannah toyed with the brace on her wrist wondering how Thunder would behave when Dick came. Most days Thunder behaved wonderfully, but occasionally he had an off day. Savannah hoped Thunder would be on his best behavior when Dick came.

"Should we practice everything we are going to show Dick?" Adeline asked abruptly.

"That's what I was thinking. Thunder likes routine. If we practice it, he'll be more familiar with it and likely will behave better," Savannah said.

For the next two hours the girls rehearsed. First, they would show Dick how Thunder walked on a lead at both a walk and a trot. Next, they would show basic groundwork skills as well as how Thunder worked on the lunge line. Finally, Adeline would ride him. The girls decided that Adeline would walk him around the ring, trot him around the ring, and lastly show Dick the barrel pattern they had taught Thunder.

On Saturday, Dick pulled into the drive at nine o'clock in the morning. The girls had Thunder ready to go. So far Thunder seemed to be on his best behavior. Mr. and Mrs. Wilson were standing talking to Dick.

"Ready to see your horse?" Savannah asked. "I think you'll be surprised at his transformation." Adeline looked tense. She was stroking Thunder's neck. Savannah flashed Adeline a thumbs up. Adeline managed a small grin. Adeline walked Thunder around within good view of Dick. After doing a large circle, she asked Thunder to trot and began to run next to him. Thunder trotted easily, his muscles rippling under his gleaming coat. Next Adeline worked Thunder on the lunge, he switched directions and gaits on command. Then she did a few basic groundwork exercises. Savannah caught her breath; this was the final test. Thunder already had a saddle on, and Adeline easily swung into the saddle. She began to walk around the arena. Suddenly, Thunder stopped and flared his nostrils. Savannah gasped; Thunder couldn't

misbehave now. Adeline talked soothingly to him before urging him forward again. Thunder moved forward. In a few minutes, Adeline had him trotting around the ring. Finally, she trotted him through a barrel pattern. He behaved well and when they were finished, Adeline walked Thunder over. Savannah held her breath, wondering what Dick had thought of Thunder. He looked deep in thought. Finally, he spoke.

"Wow, you've done a wonderful job!" he exclaimed.

"Would you like to try working him?" Savannah asked hesitantly. She hoped Dick didn't want to sell Thunder.

"I would if I thought I was going to keep him, but I'm not going to keep him," Dick stated. Savannah's heart plummeted. Dick still wanted to sell Thunder. "You're going to keep him," Dick announced excitedly. Savannah gasped.

"I...I...can't," Savannah stuttered.

"Yes, you can, and you will. I have no right to own this horse. He obviously loves his new home, and he obviously loves you and your friend!" Dick exclaimed. Savannah gasped and threw her arms around Thunder! Then she turned and hugged Adeline.

"Thank you so much!" she cried. "But I couldn't have done it without Adeline," Savannah felt on top of the world. She had a horse of her own that she had trained! The whole time Savannah had been training Thunder, she knew she wanted him but she had never dreamed he would one day be hers.

While Mr. and Mrs. Wilson worked out the details with Dick, Savannah and Adeline talked excitedly about all the things they could do together now that Savannah had her own horse. Savannah thought this was the best day of her life, she hoped it was the best day of Thunder's life too!

Analise VerBerkmoes is an eighth grader at Copper Country Christian School. Analise enjoys many horse-related activities, snowboarding, basketball, reading, and writing. Currently she is training her own nine-year-old horse, Crimson.

The Birthday Party

by Skye Isaacson

◆❖◆

"Summer, look what I found in my mailbox! We should *totally* go!"

Summer looked up as her cousin and best friend, Riley, burst through the door, waving a pamphlet around in the air.

She's always worked up about something, Summer thought with a smile, then asked, "What is it?"

Riley was bouncing with excitement as she spoke.

"It's a sleepaway camp that's next weekend, out near Blackroot Forest! You get to stay at these old cabins out in the woods and have fires and cook marshmallows. My mom said all of us could go as a birthday present for me."

"Where are we going?" Chloe inquired as she, Grace, Stella, and Olivia came traipsing in the side door. The six girls had been friends for years. The group had started out with just Chloe, Summer, and Riley when they were barely walking. Riley and Summer were cousins and Chloe lived right next door to Summer. Then came Stella when she moved from Kansas in second grade. Next was Grace, a quiet, mousy girl. The most recent addition to the group was Olivia, who came in sixth grade. Now, Summer, Stella, Chloe, and Grace were freshmen in high school while Riley and Olivia were a year younger in eighth grade. As the girls sat in the kitchen eating cookies, they listened with growing excitement as Riley told them about the sleepaway camp.

"That sounds fun!" Stella exclaimed.

Grace, who was afraid of anything scary, stated nervously, "It's on the weekend of Halloween. I heard there's supposed to be a full moon."

"It's also Riley's birthday, and she wants to do something fun. It'll be fine, Grace," Olivia reassured her. "Nothing will happen."

"Yeah," the other girls chimed in. "We'll have fun. It's just for the weekend." Grace nodded in agreement after a minute of thought.

"Okay."

•••

A week later, Summer was finishing up packing her bags after dinner when the phone rang.

"Summer, it's for you!" her mom called up the stairs. "Got it!"

As Summer picked up the upstairs extension, she could hear Riley's impatient voice through the other end.

"Finally! Are you ready yet?"

Summer laughed, then replied, "I just finished packing. What about you?" "Of course I'm ready! I was ready days ago!"

"I figured you were. What about the other girls? Have you talked to them?" Summer asked.

"Yeah, it seems like they're pretty much on the same page. Stella's super excited, but Grace is still a little bit nervous. I'm sure she'll be fine once we get there, though."

"Yeah, me too," Summer said, stifling a yawn. "It'll be fun."

"I should probably go, you sound tired. Plus, I have to triple-check my list to make sure I didn't forget anything. See you tomorrow, bright and early!"

"Yup, good night," Summer replied, then hung up the phone.

•••

As Summer was eating breakfast the next morning, she heard a car honk outside. "Mom, my ride's here," she hollered as she threw her dishes in the sink. "I gotta go!"

"Wait, come give me a hug first!" her mom exclaimed, hurrying down the stairs and pulling her daughter into an embrace. The horn honked again.

"Come on, Summer! It's time to go!" Riley yelled through the front door as she invited herself in before spotting Summer and her mom. "Oh, hi Aunt Sarah! Sorry, but I have to steal Summer now. We're going to be late."

Summer waved at her mom as she allowed Riley to pull her outside.

"Bye!" she called as she threw her bags in the back of her uncle's minivan and hopped in with all the other girls. The car zipped out of the driveway and the girls chatted excitedly amongst themselves.

When they got to the bus stop that was taking them to camp, the girls gave their bags to the people loading up the luggage and settled in the back, watching as other campers filed inside and sat down, eager to get going.

"I heard this place is haunted," one boy whispered excitedly to a nearby friend.

"Yeah, right," Stella, who had overheard, proclaimed. "By what?"

"It is," the boy insisted, "My older sister went there and said so herself. She said that it's been haunted for almost 100 years!"

Jeers of disbelief and laughter rose up among the other kids, but they all pressed in to hear the story.

"Way back in 1918," the boy began, "there was a girl named Emily. She grew up in what's now Blackroot Forest, in a castle that used to belong to her great-great-grandfather. Her mom died when she was little, so it was just Emily and her dad. Although she lived far away from other people, she went to town every day to attend school, where she was very popular and everyone liked her.

"Emily's best friend was named Beth, and they were inseparable. Every day, they would walk to school and sit at the same desk, then they'd walk home together afterward and played at each other's houses.

"One day, Beth became sick. It turned out that she had the Spanish flu and although Emily was forbidden to see Beth to prevent her from getting sick too, she snuck over every night to see her. Soon, Beth became too weak to eat and move. She knew she wouldn't make it to her fourteenth birthday and made Emily promise to celebrate for both girls when her own birthday came. Emily did, and Beth's prediction came true, with her passing away just days before she turned fourteen.

"Unfortunately," the boy continued, finishing up the story and bringing everybody out of their thoughts. "Emily caught the flu, too, and ended up dying about a week later. She never fulfilled her promise, and to this day, she haunts the woods and camp, looking for someone's soul to take over and turn fourteen in."

"Riley turns fourteen tomorrow!" Grace exclaimed, worried.

Riley smiled, dismissing the thought while adjusting the friendship bracelet that had been on her wrist since she and Summer had made them years ago.

"Uh-oh!" someone yelled, "She better watch her back!"

"Well, I don't believe it," Stella declared as the bus pulled into camp and everyone trooped out. "It was a good story though."

"Hello, campers!" a woman greeted them as they stepped out into the fresh, pine-smelling air. "I'm Ava, the head counselor, and this is Emory, my assistant," she said, gesturing to a tall woman beside her, who had been on the bus ride there as a supervisor.

"Oh, uh, hi," the older woman stammered, shaking her head as if clearing her thoughts. "As you know, we're here if you guys need anything or have any questions, so don't be afraid to ask." Emory vaguely continued, then looked away, silent again. Her dull green eyes held a vacant look, Chloe noticed, and she seemed distracted by something. Emory's curly hair was pulled into a messy bun on top of her head, and she looked flustered.

That's strange, Chloe thought, I thought she'd be more put-together. That's not what she seemed like when I read about her in the pamphlet. Oh well, she shrugged, some things just aren't as they seem.

•••

Later that evening, after everyone had settled into their cabins, the girls sat outside on their little porch, watching the bright orange hue of the sunset fade into darkness.

"Hey, look over there!" Oliva pointed towards the edge of the trees, as a flash of whitish-blue disappeared into the forest.

"It's a ghost!" Grace breathed, a chill running down her spine.

"No, that story was just something someone made up to scare other people," Chloe stated defiantly. "Don't worry, Grace, it'll be fine. Let's just go inside and go to bed."

The other girls nodded in agreement, but Grace still couldn't shake the feeling that they were being watched.

•••

Summer awoke suddenly in the middle of the night. *Something feels off,* she thought, wracking through her brain for possibilities. When she couldn't think of any reason, she rolled over, trying to ignore it, but she couldn't get rid of the feeling. Thinking of a way to distract herself, Summer climbed down from the top bunk to get a drink. When she got to the bottom rung, she glanced at Riley's bed, then did a double take. What she saw made her blood run cold.

Riley's bed was empty!

"Chloe, Chloe! Wake up!" Summer whispered, shaking her friend's arm. "Riley's gone!" Chloe shot upright, suddenly awake. "What?!" she exclaimed. "What do you mean?" "She's gone! I looked all over the cabin, but she's not there! Come on, let's wake up the others."

The two went around the cabin, waking up the rest of their friends in hushed whispers to prevent waking up the other girls in the cabin next to them.

"What do we do?" Grace asked.

"Let's go look for her," Stella declared.

"But what if she comes back?" Olivia inquired.

"Someone can stay behind if they want," Stella suggested, but all the girls shook their heads in unison, not wanting to be left alone. Soon, they were racing around the cabin grabbing jackets, shoes, and flashlights. When they were ready, they trooped outside and headed down the hill leading towards the main building.

"Wait," Summer called, spotting something on the ground near the edge of the woods. "What's that?"

They all ran over to the item laying on the ground, and when Summer picked it up, she saw it was a bracelet that matched the one on her wrist.

"Her bracelet," Olivia breathed. "She never takes that off. She must've gone this way!"

The girls tore down the path leading deeper into the woods until they came to a fork in the trail.

"Which way?" Chloe asked.

"Look, right there!" Stella exclaimed, pointing to a set of footprints that traveled unevenly down the muddy lane. "She must've gone this way."

"Good eyes!" Olivia congratulated. "Let's go."

A few minutes later, they appeared at a clearing in the middle of the forest. Ahead of them was the outline of a huge building. The girls looked at each other fearfully, then crept slowly up the hillside leading to it. When they got to the top, they saw that the enormous shape looming just ahead of them was an old aging castle with high towers rising up into the light of the full moon. Grace pointed silently to a light flickering out of a tower window and the girls shut off their flashlights to avoid being seen.

"Get down!" Stella suddenly hissed urgently, pulling the others down with her to the ground. "Someone's coming!"

The girls held their breaths as a dark form hurried by, and Chloe spotted a few curly wisps of hair sticking out from the hood over the person's head.

"I think that's Emory!" she exclaimed after the person disappeared into the castle.

"What is she doing here?" Oliva questioned, just as bewildered as the others.

They decided to follow her quietly, but as soon as they entered the large doorway in the front, Emory appeared out of nowhere as if she was waiting for them. The girls stifled their screams as Emory demanded, "What are you doing here?"

"We thought Riley might be here. She disappeared and we followed some tracks we saw on the trail. What are you doing here?" Stella, the boldest one, answered.

Emory hesitated before answering. "I knew Emily would be out tonight. I heard you on the bus earlier and figured she somehow knew, too."

The girls looked at her with confused expressions. "So, she is real?" Chloe inquired.

Emory nodded. "Yes, but you can't see her unless she shows herself to you. Spirits can do that, and for some reason, I'm the only one I've known of who can see her. I've worked here for many years now, and she's always watching and listening. At first, I would ask others if they saw her too, but they thought I was a kooky old lady, so I left the subject alone. For years, she's been waiting for someone to arrive, someone who'd celebrate their birthday here, so she can take over their soul and finally celebrate the birthdays like she promised."

"Is that why you looked so unkempt when we first saw you?" Grace asked. "Because you knew she was coming, and you were worried?"

Emory nodded.

"But why is that so bad?" Olivia inquired. "Can't she just give Riley's soul back after she turns fourteen?"

"If only," Emory shook her head sadly. "No, once Emily takes over Riley's body, she can't give it back, unless you reverse the spell, but that's nearly impossible."

Stella headed for the steps. "Well, come on, let's go," she called impatiently. "I don't want to leave Riley alone any longer. We have to help her. Who knows, maybe we can stop Emily." The other girls followed, determined to save their friend. As they traveled up the winding stairs, the soft glow of the light above grew brighter and brighter. When they reached the top, they found a hallway that led to a room at the end, where the yellow light faded into an icy blue hue that vibrated down the walls as they approached. When they peeked around the corner of the doorway, the girls saw a long table set with plates and silverware, as if someone was preparing to have guests over for dinner. A cake sat in the center of the table, with fourteen candle flames dancing merrily. Riley was seated in a chair at the head of the table, transfixed and staring straight ahead, her eyes glassy. Oliva gasped quietly and looked at Emory for an explanation.

"She's under a spell," the woman stated bluntly.

In the corner of the room, the girls saw a pale blue mist floating near an old wooden desk.

When they looked closer, they realized it was a girl about their age, sitting primly on top of the desk. Her neatly-braided hair was flowing down her back and she was reading a book.

That must be Emily, Chloe thought as she stared at her. As if sensing the girls' eyes,

Emily looked up. She smiled upon seeing the girls, then stated, "At last! You must be here for the party! I'll finally turn fourteen today. Come, sit at my table with me." The girls obliged, and they each took a seat at the opposite end of the table, as far away from Emily as possible.

"Let's sing," Emily suggested, but Emory shook her head.

"Don't do it, girls," she cried, "it will finalize the spell and you'll never get Riley back!"

"Happy birthday to me, Happy birthday to me..." Emily began, urging the others to sing along.

"Why are you doing this?" Stella asked. "Can't you let Riley go?"

"I made a promise to Beth, and I must keep it."

"There must be some other way," Chloe insisted. "Please?"

"I must keep my promise.

"Happy birthday dear Emily..." she continued.

Grace jumped up and ran over to the book Emily had been reading. It was a book of spells, and she frantically flipped through the pages, looking for something to stop Emily. She landed on a page and began to read in a loud, clear voice:

"Today's the day; It's my birthday,
And I'm going to have a party, With cake and hats,
And fun placemats,
We'll all be at the party!"

"Happy birthday..." Emily kept on, while the others urged Grace to read faster.

"Except for one, We'll all have fun;
she can't be at the party, She doesn't belong,
She should be gone,
Miles away from my party."

"Tooooo..."

"So, stones and stew, And witches brew,
We'll banish her from the party,
To never return, Maybe she'll learn,

It's not her birthday party!"

"Meee-" Emily tried to finish as Grace ended the poem, but she disappeared in a puff of smoke before she could. As she vanished, Riley snapped out of her trance and all her friends surrounded her, relieved.

"What happened?" she asked, puzzled as to why she was sitting at a table in the middle of the night. As the girls explained, Riley realized how true her friends were.

"Well, that's rude," she stated with a smile when they finished. "What is?" everyone asked.

"She didn't even blow out her candles before she left!"

Skye Isaacson is a ninth grader at Houghton High School. She enjoys playing volleyball, going outside, and spending time with her friends and family.

Silberkaskade am Oberen See

Historical · engravings chapel canoe piro

Starved

by Miina Chopp

◆❖◆

Wednesday, September 13th, 2019, River Birch Post - Obituaries

Mallory Amelia Hayes, age 17, was sadly pronounced dead on Saturday, September 9th following her disappearance four years earlier. Mallory, also known as Rory, lived in the town of River Birch all her life. She is survived by her parents Terrance and Naomi, her older brother Percy, and her closest friend Erin, who she considered family. Mallory was a beloved member of the community and was always ready to help those in need. With ample kindness and empathy, she befriended everyone she met and was a truly wonderful person to be around. She volunteered at the local animal shelter and had dreams of being a veterinarian after finishing school. To honor Mallory's memory, the Hayes family will be holding a funeral service this Tuesday at 4:45p.m. and extend an invitation to all who would like to attend.

•••

Erin thought that the service had been nice, if not a little crowded. People who had known Rory, people who'd helped with the search, even people Erin had never seen before came to pay their respects. Rory's family gave a speech, saying how much they missed her, how they hoped she was in a better place. Erin gave a speech too, but it didn't sound as warm and appreciative as she'd meant it to be. Everyone around her was silent and respectful, watching her with sad eyes filled with pity. Rory had been her best friend. Erin watched as people slowly filed out of the cemetery, offering their condolences as they passed her. She let her curly black hair hide her face. She didn't like the way people looked at her, as if she might shatter any minute.

The funeral offered some closure, but not as much as it should have. Rory had gone missing years ago with no warning. They never found any trace of her aside from a few footprints. She'd been planning to hike a new trail in the woods, one that led to a large river cave. The best anyone could guess was that she went too far into the cave and fell into the water with no one to help her escape the current. Erin had always felt guilty for not offering to join her on the hike. Maybe she could have. Erin stopped herself before she could feel worse than she already did. Rory wouldn't have wanted her to be so hung up on something she couldn't fix, events she couldn't change. Erin smiled. Rory had always been nicer than anyone deserved. She was hopeful that she was happy wherever she was now.

Erin walked out of the cemetery with her family, Rory's family close behind. The car ride home was quiet and melancholy, no one attempted conversation. When Erin arrived home, she was looking forward to going straight to her own room. She'd made it halfway to the front door before she heard her mom yell for her.

"Erin!" her mother called, "Could you please grab the mail before you go in? Thank you."

Erin nodded, trying not to show her exasperation. The mailbox wasn't very full, and only contained a copy of the local paper and an unmarked letter. Erin grabbed the paper and letter and brought them inside. She tossed aside the paper and studied the letter more closely. It had no address, no stamp, and not even the name of who it was for. Out of curiosity, Erin opened the letter and found a singular sheet of paper with scratchy handwriting scrawled across it. The paper had suffered from water damage, but Erin could still make out the handwriting that belonged to someone she thought she would never see again. The letter said:

Erin, I know you will be able to tell who sent this to you from the second you open it. You always said I had horrible handwriting, even though I never thought it was that bad. Come to our spot in the park by the river birch tree. Maybe you'll find something there.

-Rory

Erin stood as still as a statue as she read the paper. It couldn't be true, it couldn't. Yet here it was, a letter written in Rory's own hand. A letter that shouldn't exist. Erin clutched the crumpled paper tightly; she

didn't want to let it go. Erin ran to her room and changed from her black funeral clothes into a navy-blue T-shirt and old leggings. She hurtled down the stairs, trying to find her sneakers and hoodie.

"I'm going to the park!" Erin shouted as she sprinted out the door. She didn't wait for an answer.

When Erin arrived at the park, her heart beat faster than it ever had before. She knew she shouldn't place so much hope in a small piece of paper that had mysteriously shown up at her house, but she couldn't help it. She longed to see her best friend again. If there was a chance that a miracle might happen, she was going to make sure she was there for it.

Erin ran to the tallest hill in the park, where a river birch tree slowly swayed in the wind. This had been where Erin and Rory had played every day after school. But for the past few years, it had not been a happy place. When Erin reached the tree, she looked around desperately. She couldn't see Rory, or anyone else for that matter. The park was deserted.

"Hey Erin," a voice whispered.

Erin whipped around to face the voice and nearly screamed when she realized who it belonged to.

"RORY!" Erin yelled at the top of her lungs as she lunged to embrace her long lost friend. "I missed you so much! What happened? Are you okay? They thought you had drowned, and we looked for you for years! We need to go back *right now*; everyone will be so happy!"

Erin pulled out of the hug to look at her friend. When she had first seen Rory, it had seemed like nothing about her appearance had changed aside from her being a little taller and older. However, upon closer inspection, she could see that Rory's clothes were fraying and that she was barefoot in the grass. Rory had always been pretty thin, but now she looked sickly and emaciated. Her eyes were dark and sunken.

"What happened?" Erin asked, her voice heavy with concern.

"Nothing," Rory replied, "I'm fine." She grabbed Erin's hand. "Let's not hang around here. Why don't we go for a walk and catch up before we go anywhere else. There's so much you need to tell me about."

"But don't you want to see your family? We could get something to eat, you look absolutely starved. When was the last time you-"

"I'm fine," Rory insisted rather harshly.

Erin didn't resist as Rory pulled her toward a forest trail that connected to the park. She was too scared to let go of Rory's hand, even if she was acting strangely. She had always trusted Rory more than anyone else. The two walked down the rough trail and enjoyed the scenery that surrounded them. The trail was bordered by luscious greenery and wildflowers that grew wherever there was room. The leaves on the trees had already turned, causing them to cast orange and yellow light on their surroundings.

Rory asked so many questions about things that had happened in her absence that Erin had trouble answering them all. The conversation was so distracting that before she knew it, Erin found herself at the end of the trail and facing a river that flowed into a gaping cave entrance. It was *the* river cave.

"We shouldn't be here," Erin said, glancing worriedly at Rory.

"Why not? It's just a cave; it's not like I drowned in there!" Rory laughed and her thin frame shook violently as she chuckled. She didn't seem concerned in the least.

Before Erin could object further, Rory pulled her into the cave's mouth and led her down the long and winding passage. Erin pulled out her phone for light and saw that the cave now split into multiple paths that seemed to go on indefinitely. With a laugh, Rory ran down the nearest opening and disappeared into the darkness. Erin scrambled after her, wondering how she could run so fast in that condition.

"Rory, slow down! We need to go back!" Erin's voice echoed through the long passageway. It was met with distant laughs and beckoning from Rory.

"Come on! Let's see where it leads!" Rory called back.

Erin continued to run, ignoring her foot catching on stones and cracks in the cave floor. Suddenly the narrow pathway opened up into a larger passage with the river running through the middle. The water was deep and fast. Erin took a step back from the river. The current was strong enough to pull her away if she wasn't careful. Erin followed the river further into the cave, occasionally gazing into the dark water. Maybe it was paranoia, but she had a feeling that something bad was going to happen when she was this close to it.

After what felt like an eternity of wandering through the cave, Erin finally stopped to take a break. She sat down on a boulder and rested her feet on a smaller nearby rock. Erin leaned back against the jagged wall; she was exhausted. Every time she turned a corner, she would see a flash of Rory's ragged clothes, but she could never catch up. Whenever she felt like turning back and waiting for Rory to leave on her own, she would hear Rory yell for her to keep going. But Rory was never there when she continued. Erin sighed, she was not going to leave without her best friend, no matter how odd and reckless she was acting. She hoped this was all just a game, a joke.

As Erin rose, she tilted her phone flashlight to the wall behind her and something caught her eye. Words covered the cave wall from top to bottom, all in different handwriting styles and even languages. Phrases overlapped and wound around each other, creating an unintelligible mural of warnings and last-minute cautions. Erin searched the wall for things she could understand and immediately wished she hadn't looked.

She led me here.

You can't leave once you enter. Don't follow the river.

It was a trick, they're already gone.

Erin tried to rip her eyes off the wall, panic building inside of her. She shouldn't be here. Erin turned to the middle of the wall and saw a nearly untouched piece of writing. It was written larger than the other phrases and sent a chill down her spine when she read it.

It's starving.

"Erin!" Rory called from deeper in the tunnel. "Come on!"

Erin flinched at the sound and as she opened her mouth to yell back, she heard a shrill scream from Rory's direction. The sound echoed through the cave, filling the space with the sound of shrieks.

"Rory?" Erin yelled. She was met with silence. "Rory?!" This time it was a scream. The echo of Erin's own voice faded and all that was left was the sound of the river.

Erin ran faster than she ever had before. She ignored the tiredness in her legs and pushed herself to keep going. She was not going to lose Rory again. As she ran, the size of the passageway slowly increased until it opened into a cavernous room with no way forward. Erin stopped, suddenly tense.

The cavern was so dark it was almost impossible for Erin to see any of her surroundings, but she could make out a few things with her flashlight. One of the few things she could see was that the river that flowed beside her emptied into a large lake in the center of the cave. The inky water swirled slowly and patiently, as if waiting for someone to fall in.

Don't follow the river.

The second thing Erin noticed was that Rory was nowhere to be seen. She began to feel her trust in Rory slip away as her eyes searched the darkness warily. There were no other pathways besides the one she had come from, so she had to have ended up here. Unless Rory could walk through walls, she was in this room.

It was a trick, they're already gone. She led me here.

The third and most terrifying thing Erin realized was that she wasn't alone in the cavern.

She watched in horror as a great shadowed mass rose slowly out of the water, causing small ripples to glide across the surface of the lake. The looming figure rose to its full height in the water and looked down on her with three dark and sunken eyes. The creature was as dark as its own shadow and the edges of its body blurred in and out of focus. It was so gaunt that Erin could count each of its ribs through its thin skin.

It's starving.

Erin couldn't scream, she couldn't even move. She stared into the starving creature's eyes and watched as it curled back its lip, revealing thousands of white teeth that shone in comparison to the monster's darkness. Erin found courage and began backing away towards the previous passage. However, when she turned to run, she found her path was being blocked by a similarly skeletal body. Rory stood in the way, face blank.

You can't leave once you enter.

Erin felt her heart sink. She had placed so much hope in that letter, so much trust in her best friend. Now she realized there was no hope, no need for trust. She turned back to the creature and saw it lean toward her expectantly, salivating at the thought of a new meal. There had never been any hope.

•••

Thursday, November 23rd, 2023, River Birch Post - Obituaries

Erin Marie Alexander, age 21, was sadly pronounced dead on Monday, November 20th following her disappearance four years earlier. Erin lived in the town of River Birch for most of her life. She is survived by her parents Keith and Emmi, and her younger sisters Anna and Charlie. Erin was an upbeat and valued member of the community and will be thoroughly missed. Even after her best friend's disappearance, Erin always looked on the bright side of things and brought happiness wherever she went. She was a smart student and dreamed of becoming a costume and set designer after she graduated. To honor Erin's memory, the Alexander family will be holding a funeral service this Friday at 5:00 p.m. and extend an invitation to all who would like to attend.

Miina Chopp is a freshman at Houghton High School. In addition to writing stories, she enjoys reading, drawing, playing video games, and hanging out with friends.

There are No Happy Endings

by Leah Johnson

The music at the Qui Plume La Lune Café is too bland for my taste. However, Delphine argues that the warm, chocolate croissants make up for it. Although, I must admit that the sweet scent of cinnamon that fills the air along with the plentiful amount of lit candles along the window sills are attractive features. I'm sitting at a small metal table near the street view window. The café is quite full today, with only two out of the ten tables being empty.

I peer out the window at the gray sky of Bordeaux. Today is the perfect day for a warm cup of hazelnut tea. I glance towards the door to see Delphine eagerly strutting towards my table with a troubled look on her face, her deep orange ringlets bouncing with each eager step. She plops down onto the wine-red metal chair.

"Navier, I need your help." I can sense the shakiness behind her voice.

"Let me guess, you lost Bijou again?" I raise one eyebrow as I tuck a piece of my strawberry blond hair behind my ear.

"Yes…" She tilts her head down slightly, an embarrassed expression spreading across her face, aware that this is the third time this month that she's lost her orange tabby cat. "Please help me out; you can find anything, no matter where it may be!"

As I'm about to respond, a small, clearly stressed waitress approaches our table with two glasses of the ever so lovely hazelnut tea and two freshly baked, chocolate-filled croissants,

Delphine's favorite. I slide the food to Delphine and thank the waitress before continuing our conversation.

"I wouldn't say anything…"

"Well just about anything then! Please Navier, I beg you!" She pleads as she takes a large bite of her croissant.

"Of course, anything for my dearest friend," I say, with a small sigh in my voice, making it known to Delphine that I'm only doing this because I care about her.

"Thank you! I'll be sure to repay you!"

I take a long sip of my tea. Everything about this magnificent tea reminds me of the first seven years of my life. It was perfect, I was able to live without a care in the world. I was safe. I was happy. Oh, how I long for life to go back to how it was. If it weren't for the disgusting sight of both my parents, slaughtered by a sickly rich man and hung from our kitchen ceiling, my longings might've never existed. I snap back to the present and look up from my tea. Delphine is waving her hand in my face in an attempt to regain my attention from my fantasyland.

"Hm?"

"You were zoning out there," Delphine says with a chuckle, "I've been meaning to ask you, have you caught any leads on Pierre Dupont?"

"One; it's extremely small, but we might be able to use it against him." I sigh, taking another sip of my tea.

"Really?! Well, go on, tell me!"

"His daughter."

"His daughter?"

"Yes, Amandine Dupont."

"Navier, what exactly are you suggesting?" Delphine asks, her nerves showing in her voice.

"It's simple, my dearest Delphine, we kidnap Amandine and kill her if her father still refuses to show himself. I've been keeping track of her routine for the past year along with the names of everyone she has been associated with."

"Navier! Have you lost your mind? Truly, you cannot fathom doing such a thing to her!" Delphine is tearing up at this point. Perhaps choosing such a softie to be my accomplice wasn't such a great idea.

I had grown up with Delphine. Despite us not being related by blood, she was more or less my sister. Her parents were killed in a house fire when she was no older than five. My family took her in from the orphanage as my mother's heart shattered after hearing her tragic backstory. She has been by my side ever since, and I couldn't be more grateful for everything she's done for me.

"Don't stress about it too much, Delphine. I won't hurt her unless Pierre refuses to cooperate."

"I don't know about this one, Navier..."

"Let's change the topic. I don't feel like discussing this matter in public."

"Ok, then, what shall we discuss?"

"Nothing. I'll be leaving now. Thank you for coming. Oh, and don't worry about the bill. It's already paid."

Delphine stays seated, her gaze following me as I leave the dreary atmosphere of the café. I step outside into the slightly busy streets of Bordeaux. As I begin my stroll towards the market, I see something from the corner of my eye. I turn my head to see Amandine Dupont sitting on a washed-out oak bench conversing with a young man who appears to be around her age. I must admit, Amandine is a strikingly beautiful young woman. The only flaw she possesses is a large, coffee-colored birthmark on her left cheek, and even then, most would consider it an

addition to her beauty rather than a flaw. In a way, I envy her. Not because of her beauty, but because she still has a family to run home to; for now, at least.

My gaze shifts from Amandine to the young man sitting next to her. His hazel eyes are locked on her, a love interest I suppose. I study his face, making note of how he can be of some use in the future. I turn back to my original path, but I don't make it more than two blocks before I overhear a conversation between a police officer and a seemingly troubled young woman.

I've never seen her before in my life, but just from seeing her blank expression, I can make a fair guess at what has just happened. I watch her fall to her knees, a steady stream of tears flowing from her empty eyes. I know her emotion too well as it was the same way I reacted when struggling to explain to the police what had happened to my parents. I pity her. I truly do. However, I must not focus on her emotions too much; otherwise, I fear they'll consume me.

I kept my head down for the rest of my stroll, deciding to pass on the market as I only had enough francs for half a loaf of bread. I'm sure whatever may be in my pantry will suffice for a fair enough dinner. The rest of my walk home is quiet, except for the occasional sound of the train passing through the mountainous countryside.

When I step inside, I throw my small beige handbag onto the small kitchen table and make my way over to my two-seater cream-colored sofa. I throw my head back as I sit down with only one thing on my mind. I need to act fast on Pierre if I'm going to avenge my parents. I raise my head back to its regular position and pull out the notebook from under my left sofa cushion. It contains Amandine's daily schedule, hobbies, and connections built up from the past three months. I flip through the first few pages, which contain her usual morning routine. As long as she keeps to this routine, sweeping her up off the street should be no problem.

I'm about to go eat my bread and jam when the telephone begins to ring. I slowly walk over to the telephone. This is the third time anyone has ever called me. Cautiously, I answer.

"Hello?" I ask curiously.

"I know what you're doing," answers a stern voice from the other side. It sounds like a male, no older than twenty-two.

"I beg your pardon?"

"I know who you are and what you plan to do to Amandine." I try to respond, but the mysterious man's voice cuts me off.

"Don't even bother. It's my job, and I intend to fulfill it without you getting in my way," he says, ending with a brief chuckle of amusement.

"I'm sorry, but I believe you have the wrong number. I know of no Amandine and certainly nothing about this kidnapping you speak of." I'm about to hang up the phone when I hear his voice come from the other side.

"Who said anything about a kidnapping, Miss Monet?"

Damn it; I just screwed this all up. But how does he know my name? Who even is he? "My apologies sir, I'm not Ms. Monet." A sudden shakiness begins to form within my voice.

"My, Miss Monet, you can make up these lies all day if you must, but it's no use."

"And what makes you so sure?"

"Look out your window."

My window? Who is this guy? A stalker? I set down the phone as I make my way over to the small window that's placed in the center of my wall. I carefully peel back the dark gray curtain to an unsettling sight. Outside, a man is standing inside a phone booth near the streetlamp. He's wearing an olive-green suit under a long, black trench coat. He looks out from the booth, and I see his face, but not for the first time. I recognize him immediately as the man sitting with Amandine earlier this evening. We make eye contact as he presents a large smile across his smug face. I quickly shut the curtain and hurried back over to the phone. "What do you want from me?" I demand in a fit of rage.

"It's simple. Just leave Amandine alone and I'll take care of it." He states this like I'm a five-year-old crying over a toy I can't have.

"Who are you?" I'm surprised I haven't asked this question sooner considering that I've never spoken to this person before.

"I'm afraid that's none of your concern. My sincerest apologies."

"Hey. You know who I am; why can't I know who you are?"

"Good day, Miss Monet."

"Hey, you can't just-".

He hangs up the phone. I don't think that I've ever wanted to strangle someone more than him in my life. Well, besides Pierre Dupont. I quickly run back towards the window in an attempt to spot the man, but he was already gone. I fight the urge to throw my lamp to the floor. I angrily throw my body onto the couch and drift off to sleep.

I awake the next morning sprawled across the floor. I cannot recall my dream, but based on how much I moved, I can imagine that it wasn't pleasant. I slowly stand up, holding onto the sofa for support. I sit back down and throw my head back. It feels heavy, maybe it's because there are so many thoughts running around inside. I fight the urge to go back to sleep and instead head over to the telephone. I need to call Delphine and inform her about the mysterious man from last night, along with his intentions. The phone rings, but to no avail, she doesn't answer.

This is strange for Delphine, maybe she had gone for breakfast? I decide to shrug it off. I quickly dress myself and head out the door to the eerie streets.

I begin to saunter towards the Qui Plume La Lune café to search for Delphine. I walk no more than two blocks before I'm suddenly dragged into an alley between two abandoned shops. I feel a rag, laced with Rohypnol, pressed over my mouth. I can't move. My thought-heavy mind begins to feel as if an anvil has just been dropped upon it. My eyes begin to feel the same and slowly fall shut. I collapse to the floor, limp and lifeless. Despite my body's dysfunction, I can still hear faint conversations every now and then.

I hear the voices of two men; I assume they are the ones who jumped me.

"So, what do we do with her now?" one says with a sense of regret in his voice.

"He said that we are to bring her back to the old Château de Charmante," the other replied.

The Château de Charmante is an abandoned winery about 260 miles south of Bordeaux. It was only abandoned due to an accident that resulted in more than thirty casualties. The police refused to give details of the incident to the public; however, the incident was more than twenty years ago, so it simply slipped the minds of many.

"How do we get her to the car? Do we drag her? Carry her?"

"I'll pull the car around the other side. You drag her over and throw her in the trunk," the first man whispers in an almost threatening voice. "Be quick; he's getting tired of the first girl."

I feel him tightly grip my ankles as he drags my limp body the long thirty feet to the other side of the alley. They aren't gentle when they thrust me into the trunk of their car. I lie there, limp and useless, for the majority of the long ride. After what felt like two hours, I can feel my eyes begin to open and feeling come back to my body. I regain my mobility and begin to panic. While I'm quite smart on the topic of logical matters, defending myself is another story.

My arms are comparable to twigs and I'm not skilled at fighting others. I'm done for. I lie in the damp trunk for the remainder of the drive, tears are fighting to form in my dry eyes.

It feels like hours have passed by the time we arrive. I remain in the trunk for roughly twenty minutes before I can hear the two men from earlier standing outside of it. Their voices grow louder as one of the men pops open the trunk. The look on his face tells me that I shouldn't be awake right now. Without hesitation, he takes his left fist to my face. The taste of metallic and salt as blood fills my mouth. I barely have time to comprehend what's happening before he strikes again. This time, an aggressive left hook, straight to the nose. I can feel it begin to crack and crumble, like a stale piece of cornbread. This isn't good. I take one final swing from him and then, just like before, my eyes grow heavy.

•••

I wake up again. This time, I'm tied to a chair with a gag stuffed into my mouth.

However, I see the silhouette of a girl tied onto a chair. I assume she has a gag too as her cries are muffled and hard to understand. Suddenly, a bright light turns on above us. The girl sitting before me, all tied up, is none other than Delphine. Her eyes are red and swollen from crying. I don't know how to feel. All Delphine was in this mission was an alibi if I ever needed one. I never meant to drag her into this part of my risky endeavors.

Before I can do anything, I hear footsteps approaching from behind me. I look at Delphine, her eyes are as big as baseballs. I wait for the figures behind me to make themselves known as I cannot turn around to see them myself.

"What a foolish girl. I thought you were supposed to be smart?" laughs a deep, strangely familiar voice. I recognize the man behind me within seconds. If my memory is serving me right, I believe it's none other than Pierre. I feel my chest tighten.

"Did you really think that you'd be able to touch my dearest Amandine?" he says with great force. He walks in front of me and gives me a clear view of the man who murdered my parents. My memory did serve me right. In front of me stands the one and only, absolutely disgusting, Pierre Dupont. His bald head would look great mounted on a wall.

"Oh, how I understand your pain." He slowly lowers and shakes his head. "However, you are in no place to act upon my family in such a manner."

What does he mean I'm in no place? Out of everyone in this whole cruel world, I deserve this the most. I deserve a man's severed head at my feet while his daughter sits there in horror.

Then maybe she'll know how I felt. How it feels to be alone, lost, scared.

"Don't be so upset my dear, as I still have one more lovely little surprise for you." He begins to laugh. He walks over to the wall and flips on another light switch. And to my surprise, the mysterious man is tied to a chair, just as I am. His head was hung low with a look of defeat on his face. He lifts his head slightly, just enough so I can see his recognizable hazel eyes, then proceeds to shut them as he lowers his head.

"All three of you children are in the wrong. Therefore, you must pay. It only hurts for a second; and you'll be free to roam in hell together as soon as I'm finished with you all." A sinister smile grows across his disgusting face. He raises his shotgun, and the light glints off of it, shining right into my eyes.

If I'm faced with an eternal wall of darkness, I won't know how to feel. How should I feel? I'm a failure. I failed at everything: keeping Delphine out of this gruesome situation, avenging my parents, and mounting Pierre's head to a wall. It's truly a shame that things ended up this way. I guess there are no happy endings after all.

I raise my eyes to meet the barrel of the gun. The last thing I hear are three quick gunshots, each one striking one of us three hostages.

Bang. Bang. Bang.

Leah Johnson is a freshman at Houghton High School. Some of her hobbies include: reading, writing, dancing, and playing the baritone saxophone. While writing is something she hopes to pursue as a hobby in the future, she hopes to become either a nurse or a physiologist.

Historical · Loggers in the woods

Author Bios

John Adamcik is from Michigan, lives in North Carolina, and married into the U.P. over thirty years ago. Although he has at times lived vicariously through his wife Jeaneen's "official" Sisu (from her parents – both native Yoopers), John's love of family and the U.P. shows up in his travels and writing. His poems have been published in UPPAA's *U.P. Reader* and the Michigan Society of Poets' *Peninsula Poets*.

Nancy Besonen is a retired newspaper reporter for the *L'Anse Sentinel* and former U.S.P.S. rural mail carrier. She enjoys writing, fishing and running a small herd of grandchildren at and near her and her husband's home in Watton, MI. Besonen's collection of humorous newspaper columns titled *Off the Hook* was published in 2023 by Modern History Press.

Tom Conlan lives, writes, and tends his grapevines on a small farm in Northern Michigan. He previously sailed a Coast Guard cutter around the world's lakes and oceans. Tom now enjoys writing and searching for elusive brook trout in backwater streams. Tom's prose and poetry has appeared in *Walloon Writers Review* and *Michigan Trout Magazine*. His memoir *My Journey Begins Where the Road Ends...* was released in June 2017. His novel *Gentle Spirits* was released in May 2023. Visit Tom at www.thomasfordconlan.com

Nina Craig is Ojibwe/Odawa and enrolled with the Sault Ste. Marie Tribe of Chippewa Indians with Scottish and Swedish heritage. Nina has deep roots in the Upper Peninsula where she was raised. Nina currently resides in Kalamazoo near her children and grandchildren, where she writes poetry, short stories, memoir. Nina has poems published on the Poetry of Michigan website; *Among the Happy Poets: Theodore Roethke's Influence in a Time of Disruption* Anthology, and in, UPPAA's *U.P. Reader Vol. 7.* Nina is a board member of the Eastern Shore Writers Association.

Art Curtis was writing ad copy when he turned to poetry in 1991 after reading Jim Harrison's *"Letters to Yesenin,"* during a major personal crisis. His work has appeared in *Peninsula Poets, U.P. Reader, Walloon Writers Review, Dunes Review* and *TADL: Poets' Night Out.* He lives near Bellaire with his cat, Mr. Strider, and finds Petoskey stones in his sandy garden nearly 400 feet above Lake Michigan.

Julie Dickerson, a retired teacher, grew up in Flushing, MI. Trips to Northern Michigan and the Upper Peninsula captivated her as a child and served as inspiration for her to learn more about the Great Lakes. She divides her year between a hobby farm with her family in Lower Michigan where she enjoys gardening, reading, writing, traveling, and hiking; and the U.P. where the splendor of the Great Lakes region is an idyll for all who visit there.

Adam Dompierre is the author of *Wild Bolts Electric.* He holds a bachelor's degree in psychology from the University of Michigan and a master's degree in education from Augustana University and has worked as an English teacher since 2010. Adam lives in northern Michigan with his girlfriend Riley, their dog Pilot, and their cat Max. In his free time, he enjoys playing guitar and tennis, though not simultaneously.

Rosemary Gegare, after receiving her Master of Arts in poetry from UW-Milwaukee, was awarded a three-year Fellowship to Northern Michigan University's Master of Fine Arts Degree program in 2001. She and her husband built their new home on the shores of Lake Superior, hence calling herself the "Poet from Wisconsin". Part of her Fellowship included teaching Introduction to Composition each year, which she loved. She has two poems published, "Halves on the Beach" and "A Meal of Manners".

J. L. Hagen, writer, musician, poet, and former non-profit executive, is the author of *Sea Stacks*, a short story anthology that references the fictional U.P. community of Loyale, Michigan. In 2022, his story "Runtley Goes Rogue" received a gold medal from the Royal Palm Literary Awards. A graduate of University of Michigan and University of Chicago, he grew up in St. Ignace. He and his wife Joy commute between Lake Michigan and Tampa Bay.

Mack Hassler's poems in this set are all in sonnet form. He has found that wrestling with form helps the mourning process. Though he sold their cabin on Vermilac in Baraga after his wife's passing, his ties to the U.P. are still strong.

Richard Hill has lived in Michigan's Eastern U.P. most of his life. He enjoys the contrasting four seasons up north and would never survive the heat further south. His published books include: *Lake Effect: A Deckhand's Journey on the Great Lakes Freighters; Hitchhiking After Dark: Offbeat Stories from a Small Town; Lost in the Woods: Building A Life Up North,* and *West of the River, North of the Bridge: Stories From Michigan's U.P.* Contact: moosician59@gmail.com

Kathleen Carlton Johnson is both a visual artist and poet. She has been published in the Origami Poems Project, has twelve chapbooks published, and has published work in *MacGuffin*, *Rattle,* and the *William and Mary Review*, to mention a few venues. Her poems have been heard on Public Radio 90: Voices from the Past. She was a presenter at the UPPAA Conference in 2022.

Larry Jorgenson first became fascinated with Michigan's Upper Peninsula while writing and reporting for television news in Green Bay. In high school, he worked for the weekly newspaper in Eagle River. Later he was employed by a newspaper in Milwaukee and moved on to radio and television news in Texas and Louisiana. During those years, he looked forward to return visits to the Keweenaw Peninsula. His book *Shipwrecked and Rescued* was a U.P. Notable selection in 2023.

Rick Kent feels blessed to live, with his wife, on the banks of one of Iron County's five blue-ribbon trout rivers. His roots go back deep into the U.P. with his grandfather settling there in the early 1870s. He is a retired public-school superintendent of a large downstate district. He is a former commissioned officer in the U.S. Army, serving in Vietnam in 1967-68.

Tamara Lauder is a professional artist in the Northwoods of Wisconsin who enjoys combining her passion for writing with her artwork. She is published in a variety of genres, and is the author and illustrator of an inspirational pictorial book. Inspired by the beauty of the Keweenaw Peninsula, her writing was selected for the *Houghton Selected Short Story Contest* performed at the Rozsa Center at Michigan Tech University.

Ellen Lord is a Michigan native. Her writing has appeared in *Bear River Review*, *Dunes Review*, *Walloon Writers Review*, Haiku Society of America/Frogpond, and elsewhere. She is a two-time recipient of the Landmark Books Haiku Contest, is a member of Michigan Writers, UPPAA, Freshwater Poets in Traverse City, and Charlevoices Writers' Group in Charlevoix. Ellen is a behavioral health therapist specializing in addiction and trauma. She resides in Charlevoix and Trout Creek, Michigan. Ellen's chapbook, *Relative Sanity* is available at: ellenlordauthor.com.

Raymond Luczak, a proud Yooper who grew up in Ironwood and Houghton, is the author and editor of over 30 books, including the U.P.-centric poetry collections *Animals Out-There W-I-l-d, Far from Atlantis, Chlorophyll,* and *once upon a twin*. Most recently, he has edited *Yooper Poetry: On Experiencing Michigan's Upper Peninsula* for Modern History Press. An inaugural Zoeglossia Poetry Fellow, he resides in Minneapolis, Minnesota. [raymondluczak.com]

Gregory M. Lusk, a native Yooper, lives in Hancock, Michigan with his wife Sandra. In 1969, he received a BS in Forest Management from Michigan Tech. He enlisted in the Army and served in Vietnam as a platoon leader; was a resource protection manager for the Michigan DNR, retiring in 1997. He was also a real estate broker and a gas pipeline construction inspector. His first book is *The Great Seney Fire, A History of the Walsh Ditch Fire of 1976* was selected as a U.P. Notable book for 2024.

Beverly Matherne, U.P. Poet Laureate, author of seven bilingual books of poetry, is professor emerita at Northern Michigan University, where she served in the Department of English as director of the Master of Fine Arts program in creative writing. She has received seven first-place prizes, including the Hackney Literary Award for Poetry, and four Pushcart nominations. Her latest title—*Love Poems, Teas, Incantations*—is a collection of ekphrastic poems and short short fiction.

Maria Vezzetti Matson enjoys sharing stories, whether they are about nature or her relatives. Matson's three independently published books depict her Michigan family's experience as Italian American immigrants, aviators, and entrepreneurs. She writes to engage and inform readers.

Becky Ross Michael gains writing inspiration from her memories of growing up by Lake Huron and later living near Lake Superior. She loves local folklore and is open to seeing friendly ghosts. Currently residing in North Texas, Becky works as a freelance editor, and her personal writing pieces appear in print and online. Visit Becky at platformnumber4.com

R. H. Miller is a retired professor of English and Humanities. At the University of Louisville, he served as chair of both programs for fourteen years and taught courses in both for over thirty-six years. He is author of scholarly books and articles, fiction, and poetry. His recent widely-acclaimed memoir is *Deaf Hearing Boy* (Washington DC: Gallaudet UP, 2004). He lives in Louisville with his wife Diane and his Llewellin setter Molly, who has retired from hunting.

Hilton Moore is an award-winning short story writer living in his cabin in the wilderness of the U.P. He's held numerous jobs including a stint as a pipe-welder in the oil fields of West Texas. Currently he is restoring an old sailboat that he hopes to sail on Lake Superior and continuing his writing. He likes to fish with worms.

Mark Nelson is a professor emeritus from the University of Wisconsin-Madison. His first trip to the UP was in 1962. His mother and grandmother were totally tied to the UP, and he has continued to stay off and on.

Alex Noel was raised in Northern Michigan and recently found her way back, this time landing even farther north in the U.P. She has spent her life exploring the world and pursuing her many interests, accumulating a rollercoaster ride of memories and fostering a unique global perspective along the way. While she enjoys spending most of her time being active in nature, she can always be found online at www.theshakingvoice.com

M. Kelly Peach lives in the beautiful Upper Peninsula of Michigan. He hikes, reads, collects books, and bakes. His author's website is mkellypeach.com; Twitter is @michaelpeach. He has work forthcoming in *Suicid(al)iens*, *42 Stories*, and *Calliope*.

Jodi Perras is a writer, amateur historian, and genealogist who grew up in the 1970s near Nadeau, Michigan. Father Sperlein would have baptized her grandmother in 1911 and presided over the 1919 funeral Mass for her great-grandmother, Minnie Gamache Perras. A former Associated Press journalist and environmental activist in Indianapolis, Jodi now blogs about the history of Menominee County and her family at: leavesofmenominee.com.

Jane Piirto was born and raised in Ishpeming, and her B.A. is from NMU. She is the author of twenty-five single-authored literary and scholarly books and chapbooks. She spent twenty-six full years in the U.P. and every summer until 2022. She is a retired trustees' professor from Ashland University and lives near Columbus, OH. Her website is janepiirto.com.

t. kilgore splake ("The Cliffs Dancer") lives in an old mining row house in Calumet. He has become a legend in small literary circles. Street Corner Press in Sister Bay, Wisconsin recently published two books about Splake by Robert Zoschke that trace Splake's path from backwoods poet to international literary acclaim. Splake's most recent book, *A Poet of the Wild*, was edited by Walt McLaughlin.

Bill Sproule is a Professor Emeritus, Department of Civil, Environmental, and Geospatial Engineering, Michigan Technological University, Houghton, Michigan, where he taught and conducted research in transportation engineering and hockey history. He is a member of the Society for International Hockey Research and the Houghton County Historical Society, and is the author of several hockey history articles and books.

David Swindell is an author and poet, with a deep passion for the Upper Peninsula of Michigan. He is a bus driver for his local school district and loves interaction with his kids. David likes history, reading, railroading, and car shows, plus has a close circle of friends from church and civic organizations.

Ninie Gaspariani Syarikin was born and grew up in Indonesia, an archipelago of more than 17,000 islands. Because of that, although she has lived in the US for over thirty years, seafood remains her first choice of meal. She enjoys gardening in the short summer of Michigan's Upper Peninsula, where she plants vegetables from which she can also harvest the leaves, such as tomato, zucchini, pumpkin, chili, cucumber, and beans.

Brandy Thomas is a professional editor who lives and works in Marquette, Michigan. In addition to editing the written word, she is also an audiobook narrator and audio engineer. She is the voice of the *U.P. Reader* and several other series. Brandy currently serves on the UPPAA and Revolve CC(Creative Collaboration Conference) boards of directors. When she is not refining other's words, she writes poetry and short fiction, quilts, and is a musician. www.ThomasEditing.com.

Tyler R. Tichelaar is a seventh-generation Marquette resident and award-winning au-

thor. He has spent his life capturing the people and history of Marquette in both fiction and nonfiction works, including *The Marquette Trilogy*, *The Best Place*, *Haunted Marquette*, and his latest novel *Odin's Eye: A Marquette, Time Travel Novel* was named a U.P. Notable book for 2024. Tyler is also a professional editor and the owner of Superior Book Productions. Visit him at www.MarquetteFiction.com.

Edd Tury is a backwoods-north country guy: exploring the wilds of Michigan's forests and waters on foot, bike, or kayak. He likes to hunt, fish, forage and make maple syrup. He is renowned for his sourdough bread and various Hungarian delights. Edd's writing has appeared in *Dunes Review*, *Walloon Writers Review*, *Michigan Out of Doors*, and elsewhere. He is currently working on a dystopian novel. A Michigan native, he lives in Charlevoix County with an old cat and another crazy poet.

Victor R. Volkman is the president of the Upper Peninsula Publishers & Authors Association (UPPAA) since 2019 and has been on the Board since 2009. He is the Senior Editor at Modern History Press (Ann Arbor, MI) which is the publisher-of-record and indexer for the entire *U.P. Reader* series. He is a graduate of Michigan Technological University (class of '86). He can be reached by email at victor@LHPress.com.

Historical · Shipwreck Lake Superior trade card Clark's

Help Sell The U.P. Reader!

◆❖◆

The popularity of the *U.P. Reader* is growing, but we need it to grow more.

Help us sell the *U.P. Reader* by selling the *Reader* alongside your other books. The *U.P. Reader* at its wholesale discount allows those who wish to carry it to make a nice profit on the sales. Bookstores and individuals can all benefit from helping the U.P. Reader grow.

If you have writing that has been published in the *U.P. Reader*, you should be selling copies of the Reader alongside your other work. This not only helps get exposure for your writing but for all the others that were accepted alongside yours. Part of the mission of the *U.P. Reader* is to get the many voices of the writers of the UPPAA in a single publication so that readers would have a place to find and sample the incredible talent that makes up the authors and poets of the Upper Peninsula.

Taking a few *Readers* to an event can make the difference in selling. Those who have been selling the *U.P. Reader* have seen good sales and considerable interest in the publication from readers and customers. Many customers ask the seller if they have a piece in the book to sign it. As the *U.P. Reader* is helping you as a writer, you can be helping the *U.P. Reader*.

Do you have local booksellers in your area? Encourage them to stock the *U.P. Reader*. Bookstores that are selling the Reader are seeing brisk sales. Many of the bookstores have restocked their issues several times and are saying how much they enjoy them. They are profitable and returnable. The *U.P. Reader* is a win-win situation for bookstores.

Take a copy of the *U.P. Reader* to your child's English or Language Arts teacher. The Dandelion Cottage Award is open to all children in U.P. schools and homeschool. There is never a fee to participate!

Back issues of the *U.P. Reader* are also still available. They can still be ordered right alongside the new issue and can be combined to sell as a set. There are many who still haven't discovered the *U.P. Reader* yet, and a package set is a nice way to introduce them to the joys of reading a *Reader*. These can still be purchased wholesale just like the current issue.

There are hardcover versions of the *U.P. Reader* as well. These are beautiful bound versions of the *U.P. Reader* that are a wonderful keepsake for the real *U.P. Reader* fan. Again, these can be ordered wholesale and sold right alongside the paperback versions.

To order, go to UPReader.org/publications on the web and put in your order. Contributing authors will be emailed a discount code and their orders will be discounted to the wholesale price (50% Off!).

Please help us, help you make the *U.P. Reader* a success!

Come join UPPAA Online!

The UPPAA maintains an online presence on several websites and social media areas. To get the most out of your UPPAA membership, be sure to visit, "like," and share these destinations and posts whenever possible!

Web Sites

- **www.UPPAA.org**: learn about meetings, publicity opportunities, publicize your own author events, add your book to the catalog page, read newsletter archive.
- **www.UPReader.org**: complete details about deadlines, submission guidelines, how to place a print advertisement, where to buy U.P. Reader locally, and more.
- **www.UPNotable.com:** all the information about the U.P. Notable Book Club meetings
- **www.UPBookReview.com**: publishing 36 reviews of books by U.P. writers or about the U.P. every year!
- **www.DandelionCottage.org**: complete information for Young Writers interested in participating in the short story contest

Facebook Pages

- **UPPAA**: www.facebook.com/UPSISU/ —OR—type in **@UPSISU** into the Facebook "search" bar
- **UP Reader**: www.facebook.com/upreaders/ —OR— type in **@UPreader** into the Facebook "search" bar

Twitter

Twitter

- Message to **@UP_Authors** or visit https://twitter.com/UP_Authors

Comprehensive Index of U.P. Reader Volumes 1 through 8

Adamcik, John
"Faultfinder's Quarry, The", v8, pp. 98-102
"Michigamme Grades", v7, p. 61
"Negatives at a Funeral", v8, p. 97
"Onward, Inward, Upward, Home", v7, p. 62
"Softer Echoes of a Frozen Roar", v7, p. 63

Agbozo, Edzordzi
"Final Welcome", v1, p. 54
"Rewinding", v1, p. 54

Ambuehl, Kaitlin
"Free", v3, pp. 67-69

Argeropoulos, John
"Tales from the Busy Bee Café", v2, pp. 5-8

Arten, Lee
"Iced", v1, p. 40

Askwith, Leslie
"Geology Geek Finds God, A", v2, pp. 9-11

Bartel, Barbara
"Your Obit", v5, pp. 4-6

Bellfy, Phil
"Nimishoome: Chronicle of A Life Untold – Questions for Curt, the Uncle I Never Knew", v6, pp. 131-135

Ben Bohnsack, Ben
"Dead Tree Standing", v6, p. 130
"Massive", v6, p. 129

Bertineau, T. Marie
"Kalamazoo, The", v4, pp. 98-100
"Memoir as a Healing Tool", v5, pp. 112-120
"Snow Child", v6, pp. 129-130

Besch, Binnie
"Little Magic, A", v5, pp. 7-9

Besonen, Nancy
"All Customers Great and Small", v8, pp. 71-74

Billie, Miah
"Shadows of the Mind", v7, pp. 144-150

Bissonette, Aimée
"Katydids", v1, p. 44

Bodey, Don
"Deal Me Out", v5, pp. 10-14
"How to Hunt Fox Squirrels", v5, pp. 15-19
"Kid", v6, pp. 123-128

Bohnsack, Ben
" Massive", v7, p. 129

Brockman, Craig
"Fairy in a Berry Can, The", v5, pp. 20-24
"I Watched Someone Drown", v4, pp. 103-104
"Shirley's Cabins", v4, pp. 105-108

Brule, Stephanie
"Walk, The", v5, pp. 25-26

Brunner, Sharon Marie
"Active Dreams", v1, pp. 56-59
"Pasty Smuggling Ring, The", v6, pp. 118-122

Buege, Larry
"A.S.S. for State Slug", v5, pp. 27-29
"Amorous Spotted Slug, The", v3, pp. 6-7
"Party Animals", v4, pp. 101-102
"Purloined Pasty, The", v3, pp. 4-5
"Silent Night", v2, pp. 14-17
"Song of Minehaha, The", v1, pp. 5-11
"Troubled Waters", v6, pp. 115-117

Carr, Tricia
"Clark Kent Says It All", v4, p. 40
"Domestic Violence", v4, pp. 41-46

"Final Irony", v7, pp. 77-78
"I'm So Sorry Margaret", v6, p. 114
"Matter of Time, A.", v5, pp. 30-32
"Silent Witness", v6, pp. 112-113

Chopp, Miina
"Starved", v8, pp. 162-165

Classen, Mikel B.
"About the Cover - Grand Sable Falls", v6, p. 4
"About the Cover: "Painesdale Rock Shaft House #4"", v7, p. 4
"Au Train Rising", v2, p. 18
"Grand Island for a Grand Time", v3, pp. 8-11
"House on Blakely Hill, The", v1, pp. 37-39
"Introduction", v1, p. 4
"Introduction", v2, p. 4
"Light Keeper Hero of Passage Island Lighthouse", v4, pp. 94-97

Conlan, Tom
"Places Few Have Seen", v8, pp. 35-39
"Yellow Eyes", v8, p. 40

Craig, Nina
"Rootedness", v8, p. 132
"The Frost Line", v7, p. 109
"When Ice Cracks Open", v8, p. 133

Curtis, Art
"Letters to Harrison #11 "Trout" (4/25/21)", v7, pp. 110-111
"Letters to Harrison #32 (11/10/21) "The Fitz"", v7, pp. 111-113
"Letters to Harrison #37 (12/11/21) "Birthday", v7, pp. 113-115
"Letters to Harrison #8 (03/26/21) Untitled", v8, pp. 127-128
"Wrapped: An Elegy for My Father", v8, p. 129

Dallman, Ann
"Awareness", v4, p. 93
"Bear Woman", v2, pp. 21-22
"Menominee County/
MyHometown Abandoned", v1,
p. 42
"Wolf Woman", v1, p. 42

Dankert, Annabell
"Dagger of the Eagle's Eye,
The", v5, pp. 124-130

Dennis, Walter
"Ash", v5, pp. 140-143

Dickerson, Julie
"A Call in The Night", v7, pp.
58-59
"Walk Along Lake Michigan, A",
v8, p. 20
"Walk in the Woods, A", v8, p.
21

Dionne, Karen
"Karen Dionne Interview – The
Wicked Sister", v5, pp. 101-
111
"What I Learned from Writing
my Breakout Book", v4, pp.
110-114

Dompierre, Adam
"Hotel Bantam, The", v8, pp.
24-29

Elderkin, Giles
"Minié Ball", v2, pp. 32-34

Farwell, Frank
"Source", v1, pp. 45-49

Frontiera, Deborah K.
"#2 Pencils", v3, pp. 12-16
"Fragile Blossoms", v1, p. 12
"Lunch Kit, The", v5, pp. 30-32
"Spring Haiku Trio", v7, p. 17
"Stone's Story, A.", v4, pp. 88-
92
"Stubborn Snowblower, The",
v6, pp. 109-111
"Superior Sailing", v2, pp. 23-
29
"The Giant Flower", v7, pp. 14-
16

Fust, Elizabeth
"Abandoned Dream, An", v1,
pp. 27-28
"Alphabet Soup", v5, p. 37
"Astronautical: A Yooper
Translates the Song of the
Space Whales", v7, pp. 80-83
"Finders & Keepers", v6, pp.
106-108
"Great Divide, The", v4, p. 87
"Paper Tracks", v4, pp. 84-86
"Typewriter, The", v2, pp. 30-
31

Gast, Lilli
"Azalea Tea and Other
Poisons", v7, pp. 142-143

Gegare, Rosemary
"Afterglow", v8, p. 23
"I Want to Say", v8, p. 23

Gischia, Brad
"The Sideroad Kids (Review)",
v6, pp. 141-142

Goodney, Siena
"Letters Under the Flooboards,
The", v6, pp. 150-152

Grede, Robert
"Rescue of the L.C. Waldo,
The", v5, pp. 38-43

Griffin, Paige
"Olive Branch", v6, pp. 161-166

Haeussler, John
"Joe Linder: Hockey Legend
from Hancock, Michigan", v6,
pp. 31-35

Hagen, J. L.
"The Most Remarkable Thing
Starring Norwegious Ida G",
v6, pp. 98-105
"Two Bells", v7, pp. 101-108
"When Christmas Changed to
Easter", v8, pp. 111-117

Hand, Charles
"Night to Remember, A", v5, pp.
44-46

Harriman, Betty
"Mushroom", v7, pp. 156-160

Hassler, Mack
"Dog Park", v8, p. 75
"Innovations on History", v6,
p. 88
"On the Death of Two Finn
Patriarchs", v7, p. 88
"Our Silent Spring, Read for
Friends", v8, p. 75
"Three Poems Linking
Emerson, Besonen, and
Custer", v6, pp. 96-97

Helppi, Heidi
"Blood of My Love", v6, pp.
153-160

Hill, Rich
"Bait Pile, The", v4, pp. 76-80
"Bestseller", v7, pp. 45-48
"Chiblow Lake", v8, pp. 76-79
"Iroquois Island", v6, pp. 87-89
"Maxwell", v6, pp. 90-95
"The Robin's Nest", v7, pp. 49-50
"White Knuckles/Black
Wheels", v7, pp. 51-54
"Whiteout", v4, pp. 81-83

Holmgren, Kyra
"Treasured Flower, The", v5,
pp. 131-136

Hoover, Douglas
"Document, The", v6, pp. 82-86
"Extinct", v6, pp. 76-81

Isaacson, Skye
"Birthday Party, The", v8, pp.
157-161

Jackson, James M.
"Winning Ticket", v1, pp. 13-16

Johnson, Kathleen Carlton
"April in the U.P.", v7, p. 120
"Art Fair Summer", v7, p. 120
"Coffee in the Morning", v6, p.
61
"Dying in Rural Rockland", v8,
pp. 40-41
"Feeling Important", v5, pp.
47-48
"Hunting Season", v6, p. 61
"When It Comes: A Poem for
Voices", v8, pp. 42-43

Johnson, Leah
"There are No Happy Endings",
v8, pp. 166-170

Jorgensen, Larry
"Memories of the Copper
Country Limited", v8, pp. 94-
96

Jukkala, Jaclyn
"The Window", v7, pp. 138-141

Kellis, Jan Stafford
"Addiction", v4, pp. 71-72
"Please Pass the Wisdom", v2,
pp. 35-37
"Ratbag Family, The", v4, pp.
73-75
"Rolls K'Nardly, The", v3, pp.
17-18
"U.P. Road Trips", v1, pp. 20-21

Kennedy, Sharon M.
"Blew: Incarnation", v5, pp.
49-50
"Cut Me", v3, pp. 33-36
"Day at Marlene's Beauty
Parlor, A", v6, pp. 72-75
"Demise of Christian Vicar,
The", v3, pp. 37-38
"Janet", v7, pp. 5-7
"Katie: Purity", v4, pp. 62-65
"Lemon Cookies", v6, pp. 69-71
"One Shot Alice", v2, p. 38
"Quale and Agnes", v7, pp.
8-11
"Quiet Times", v4, pp. 66-70
"Saturday Mornings on
Chestnut Street", v2, pp. 39-42
"Thomas: Fortitude", v5, pp.
51-54
"Tribute to Dad, A", v1, pp.
50-51
"We Are Three Widows", v1, pp.
18-19

Kent, Chris
"Christmas Eve at the Dead
Wolf Bar", v6, pp. 62-68
"Death So Close", v5, pp. 57-60
"Keepsakes", v7, pp. 121-128
"Muses from a Deer Shack
Morning", v4, p. 61
"Spearing Shack, The", v5, pp.
55-56

Kent, Rick
"Two Rivers", v8, pp. 88-93

Klco, Amy
"Death Comes to Visit", v2, pp.
46-47

"Lovers, the Dreamers, and Me, The", v3, pp. 21-25
"Seeds of Change", v3, pp. 19-20
"Story-Seer, The", v1, pp. 22-23
"True Confessions of an Introverted, Highly-Sensitive Middle School Teacher", v2, pp. 43-45

Koski, Allan
"The Gift", v7, p. 134

Lammi, Jennifer
"On Turning Forty", v2, p. 48

Lancour, Emilie
"Worth Fighting For", v7, pp. 42-43

Lauder, Tamara
"Captive Spirit", v7, pp. 25-31
"Dementia Is:", v8, p. 59
"Expanding Horizons – Seeking Harmony", v7, pp. 33-34
"Novel", v6, p. 60
"Right Judgment", v5, pp. 61-62
"Saying Goodbye", v6, p. 60
"That Morning", v5, p. 63
"U.P. Summers Are For the Bugs", v4, p. 60
"Wonder of Snow, The", v7, p. 32
"Writing Is on the Wall, The", v8, pp. 58-59

Lehto, David
"Best Trout I Never Ate, The", v3, pp. 26-27
"Coyote Pups", v4, p. 54
"Pirates, Gypsies and Lumberjacks", v3, pp. 28-32
"Shepherd, The", v4, pp. 55-59

Locknane, Emma
"Trouble with Terrans", v3, pp. 54-60
"Welcome to the New Age", v2, pp. 85-94

Locknane, Teresa
"My Scrap Bag", v5, p. 64

Lord, Ellen
"Another COVID Dream", v5, p. 65
"Dorothy's Apple Pie", v8, p. 62
"Guillotine Dream", v5, p. 65
"Interlude", v6, p. 59
"Memory Trails", v7, p. 12
"North Country Connection", v8, p. 63
"Sorrow's Lament (A Found Poem)", v6, p. 58
"Traveler", v8, p. 63
"Two Riders", v7, p. 13

Luczak, Raymond
"A. Lanfear Norrie School (1917–2016)", v8, p. 54
"Bricks across West Oak Street", v7, p. 98
"Colonial Skateland", v7, p. 99
"Gogebic County Fairgrounds", v6, p. 100

"How Copper Came to the Keweenaw Peninsula", v2, pp. 52-54
"Independence Day", v4, pp. 47-53
"Jacquart's", v8, p. 54
"North Country Sun, The", v8, p. 53
"Solivagant", v6, p. 57
"Truck, The", v4, p. 47
"Woodpecker", v6, p. 56
"Yoopers", v2, pp. 49-51

Lusk, Gregory M.
"Taking Care of the Dog", v8, pp. 30-31

Mack, Bobby
"Warmth", v3, pp. 37-38

Martin, Terri
"Rants of a Luddite", v2, pp. 55-57
"Yooper Loop, The", v2, pp. 58-61

Matherne, Beverly
"Epistolary Poem", v8, p. 118
"Haiku for Roger Magnuson", v8, p. 119
"Paranormal or Normal? That is the Question", v8, pp. 118-119

Matson, Maria Vezzetti
"Good Evening, The", v8, pp. 60-61
"Michigan's Dogman", v7, pp. 23-24

Maurer, Sarah
"Visitors, The", v1, p. 55

McEachern, Katie
"Attack, The", v2, pp. 80-84

McEvilla, Robert
"Doe Season", v6, pp. 53-55

McGrath, Roslyn Elena
"Hoffentot Magic", v1, p. 41
"Mail Order Ministry", v7, p. 55
"Recipe", v7, p. 55
"Stop Clocks", v2, p. 63
"Winded", v2, p. 62

Michael, Becky Ross
"Dinner for Two", v6, pp. 51-52
"Lonely Road", v1, pp. 24-26
"Much Different Animal", v4, pp. 31-32
"Shelf Life", v7, pp. 56-57
"Slip of the Lip", v2, pp. 64-66
"Sumac Summer", v5, p. 66
"Waters of Change", v8, pp. 55-57
"Welcome to Texas, Heikki Lunta!", v3, pp. 43-45

Miller, R.H.
"Homage to the Pilgrm", v8, pp. 51-52

Mills, Charli
"Called to the Edge of Gichigami", v4, pp. 36-39

Mills, Leigh
"Vicarious Vacationer", v7, pp. 95-97

Mitchell, Nikki
"Astrid the Lighthouse Keeper", v6, pp. 46-50

Moore, Hilton
"Dog Named Bunny, A.", v5, pp. 75-82
"Hole in the Bucket, A", v8, pp. 6-10
"Requiem for Ernie", v5, pp. 70-74

Mueller, Cora
"Thief of Hearts", v4, pp. 129-137

Nelson, Mark
"Baraga County Redemption", v8, pp. 130-131

Noble, Eve
"Despondent", v8, pp. 138-142

Noel, Alex
"Mozambique", v8, pp. 80-86
"Soak", v8, p. 87
"Spring", v8, p. 87

Oommen, Serah
"Overcoming Hardships in Life", v7, pp. 154-155

Painter, Nicholas
"Imposter Among Us, The", v5, pp. 137-139

Peach, M. Kelly
"Dying Autumn White", v7, p. 44
"In Echoless Regions", v7, p. 44
"Old Friends Having Lunch", v8, pp. 18-19

Perkins, Cyndi
"Dry Foot", v4, pp. 33-35
"Seeds Well Planted: Healing Balm from a Keweenaw Garden", v6, pp. 41-45
"Superiority Complex", v6, pp. 38-40

Perras, Jodi
"One Last Chance", v8, pp. 64-70

Peterson, Isla
"Echo", v8, pp. 143-150

Pfister, Shawn
"Legend, The", v2, p. 67

Piirto, Jane
"Three Selections from The Seasons, the Years, the Decades", v8, pp. 103-109

Preston, Gretchen
"Old Book", v5, p. 83

Ramme, Lauryn
"Birdie", v6, pp. 144-149

Rastall, Janeen Pergrin
"Stocking Up", v1, p. 17

Saari, Christine
"Abandoned Dreams", v6, p. 37
"At Camp", v1, p. 43
"At Camp: When the Cat Is Out of the House", v2, p. 71
"Beaver, The", v6, p. 37
"Habitat", v2, p. 72
"Nonetheless", v1, p. 43

Sanders, Terry
"Aiding and Abetting", v3, pp. 46-50
"Inception Through a Shared Fantasy", v2, pp. 73-75
"Jacqui, Marilyn, & Shelly", v1, pp. 29-31
"Jacqui, Marilyn, & Shelly", v1, pp. 29-31
"Mi Casa en El Paso", v4, pp. 25-29

Saxby, Gregory
"Last Tear, The", v2, p. 76
"On the Circuit", v2, p. 76

Schneller, Ar
"Champ", v1, p. 52
"Her skin", v1, p. 52
"Nightcrawlers", v1, p. 52
"Twinkle Twinkle Imaginary Star", v2, p. 77

Scott, Joni
"Woundwort, The", v4, pp. 19-22

Searight, Frank
"Calamity at Devil's Washtub", v5, pp. 84-91
"Three Roads", v3, pp. 51-52

Shapton, May Amelia
"Crucify and Burn", v4, pp. 126-128

Simons, Donna Searight
"Calamity at Devil's Washtub", v5, pp. 84-91
"Cousin Jack Foster", v4, pp. 23-24
"Ghosts in the Calumet Theatre", v7, pp. 89-94
"Three Roads", v3, pp. 51-52

Splake, T. Kilgore
"Another Morning", v2, p. 95
"becoming zen", v3, p. 71
"Brautigan Creek Magic", v2, p. 95
"Cliffs magic", v6, p. 36
"coming home", v8, p. 17
"god's country", v4, p. 18
"good life", v3, p. 71
"holy holy holy", v5, p. 92
"opening day", v8, p. 17
"Poet's dream odyssey", v6, p. 36
"soft forest symphony", v7, p. 79
"those who stayed", v7, p. 79
"untitled symphony", v4, p. 18
"upper peninsula peace", v5, pp. 82-92

"we love it", v7, p. 79
"yooper haiku", v8, p. 16

Sproule, Bill
"Charles Uksila: From Calumet to a Career in Hockey and Figure Skating", v7, pp. 18-22
"Doc Gibson and Professional Hockey in the U.P.", v8, pp. 10-15
"Joe Linder: Hockey Legend from Hancock, Michigan", v6, pp. 31-35
"Joe Linder: Hockey Legend from Hancock, Michigan", v6, pp. 31-35

Sundquist, Aric
"Bottom Feeder", v2, pp. 96-100
"Catching Flies", v3, pp. 72-75

Sutherland, Megan
"Confliction", v4, pp. 118-125

Swindell, David
"Animals Sing Their Songs to You, The", v6, pp. 28-30
"Death of Old 289, The", v8, pp. 32-34
"My Surprising Encounter With a Baby Raccoon", v6, p. 28

Syarikin, Ninie G.
"Catching the Butterflies", v4, p. 29
"Copper Country Crochet", v6, pp. 25-27
"First Time, The", v6, p. 24
"Last Blooms, The", v8, p. 110
"Love Is...", v4, p. 30
"Luxury by the Michigamme River, A", v5, p. 93
"Morning Moon above Norway", v5, p. 94
"Snake Charmer, The", v3, p. 78
"You Are Beautiful", v3, pp. 76-77

Tavernini, Rebecca
"Heartwood", v1, p. 53

Taylor, Jon
"How to Tell", v4, p. 17
"River of the Dead, The", v4, p. 17
"Song Cover, A", v2, p. 101

Thomas, Brandy
"Autumn Jewel Box", v6, p. 23
"Meat", v8, p. 126
"Opportunity of a Lifetime, The", v8, pp. 120-125
"Ospreys, The", v6, p. 23
"Service Alert", v4, pp. 14-16
"Waves", v5, p. 98
"Way Leads on to Way: A Choose Your Own Adventure Story", v7, pp. 116-119

Tichelaar, Tyler
"Blueberry Trail, The", v2, pp. 102-106
"Firekeeper's Daughter (Review)", v6, pp. 137-138

"How Ya Gonna Keep 'Em Down on the Farm after They've Seen Marquette?", v8, pp. 44-50
"Lucy and Maud", v6, pp. 18-22
"Many Lives of Pierre LeBlanc, The", v4, pp. 7-13
"Marquette Medium", v1, pp. 32-35
"Poetic Grief Diary in Memory of My Brother Daniel Lee Tichelaar, A", v5, pp. 95-97
"Summer of the Yellow Jackets", v3, pp. 79-86
"Tin Camp Road (Review)", v6, pp. 139-140
"Victorian Nightmare", v7, pp. 35-41

Tolonen, Fenwood
"Attention", v4, pp. 137-138

Tury, Edd
"In Camp", v7, pp. 131-133
"River Gypsy", v8, p. 134
"Up in Michigan", v6, pp. 13-17

VerBerkmoes, Analise
"Time Deprivation", v8, pp. 151-156

Volkman, Victor R.
"Pictured Rock is Worth 1000 Words, A", v8, pp. 4-5
"The Freshman", v6, pp. 8-12

Wakkuri, Halle
"Karate Club, The", v7, pp. 151-153

Welsh, Cheynne
"Rain Falls from The Sky as the Stars Bleed Away Their Dreams", v6, p. 7

Whitney, August
"Bottom of the Cider Barrel, The", v7, pp. 64-69
"Free in the Harbor", v7, pp. 70-76

Winters, Donna
"Cedena's Surprise", v2, pp. 107-114
"Moving Up", v4, pp. 4-6
"My First Kayak Trip", v5, p. 99
"Problems We Can Solve", v6, pp. 5-6

Wisniewski, Jan ("Jon")
"Final Catch, The", v2, pp. 115-118

Woods, Lucy
"Stellae", v3, pp. 61-66

www.ingramcontent.com/pod-product-compliance
Lightning Source LLC
Chambersburg PA
CBHW080916020726
47502CB00008B/2464